HOOKED ON DRUG COURT

to my friend

Leslie

with love

LYNN DURYEE

pal Lynn

2010

ISBN: 1452809984
ISBN-13: 9781452809984

NONFICTION BY LYNN DURYEE

With All Due Respect … Reflections on the Judging Life

Trial & Error … Further Reflections on the Judging Life

DEDICATION

To my amazing and accomplished daughters
Katie and Sarah Moran
For filling my life with joy
And to my devoted and beloved mother
Mary Duryee
For teaching me the healing powers of
home baking – and everything else.

DECEMBER

ANDY

1. THE HALL

Of all the places to wake up, Juvie is the worst.
I got my bony white butt thrown in here
for the weekend so I could "think about my
life," which is the lamest thing ever. There's
no way you can *think* when you're locked in
a cell with pink-streaked floors, puke-green
walls, and the nonstop roar of TV sports.
Even if you could stomach the stench of
industrial-strength disinfectants, you'd never
have a clear thought wearing these baggy-ass
orange sweats, which, trust me, rob you of
your last shred of dignity. No, the only thing
to do here in Juvenile Hall is sleep.

Okay – how hard can that be? I could use
some sleep. I've been partying every night this

week, slipping out my window and racing to Pixie Park where my friends and I have been hanging all winter break. But oops, last night I messed up. I didn't make it home in time for Dad to yank me out of bed and pack me off to school. When you're a juvenile delinquent, you get shoved into school over winter break, which is the biggest joke in the world, three hours of flatlining it with a disturbingly cheerful sub. I don't know what happened last night, we were just kicking it in our camp, smoking a little and drinking some of Syd's special brew, which tasted like cherry-flavored gasoline with a dash of NyQuil stirred in for sex appeal. I must've nodded off because when I woke up, my head was exploding, everyone had disappeared, and Deputy Big Butt – do I have to even tell you what she looks like? – was shoving a combat boot into my ribs.

"Andy, Andy, Earth to Andy!" Deputy B. Butt said in a not-too-cruel voice.

"Eff off," I mumbled, through dirt-caked lips. Ecckh.

The Butt busted a gut on that. "Oh, joy! Praise the day! The world is still graced with your delightful presence."

She's always nice to me in her gold-badged way. Why is that? I don't deserve it – I'm nothing but rude to her. Maybe having a huge butt like that makes you extra nice, although that can't be true, because the judge who threw mine in here had a mammoth one too. She might think she's hiding it in that black muu-muu of hers, but I can tell, she's been accumulating hippage for decades. She wasn't at all nice when she ordered me to *think* about my life – no fakey smile, no motherly nod of sympathy. Most likely she just wanted me processed and packaged so she could dive back into her super-sized sack of Pepperidge Farm cookies.

So, fine, I can sleep through the weekend – no biggie. I won't have to worry about Dad coming home pissed off about some screw-up at work or my stepmom going all nuclear because – omigod! – dishes are in the sink! There's been a breadcrumb sighting on the counter! And is it asking so much to help with the twins? Blah, blah, blah. I can catch up on some sleep, skip an episode of domestic drama, and when Monday morning rolls around, I'll be rested and repentant. When I see Judge Pudge again, I'll feed her that stuff they love – you know: I'm so sorry; really, *thank you* for the timeout; I did nothing but *think* about my life all weekend; finally, I've learned my lesson! And I'll be back with the pack at the park by dark.

Sweet! I can so do this.

❖ ❖ ❖

When I wake up to velvet darkness, I know I've had the dream – I don't remember the images, just the familiar, crappy feel of it. For a moment I panic: where am I? Just as a scream is about to escape, I hear a commercial for Bud Lite and the deep laugh of night-duty guards. Yeah, I hate the Hall, but what a relief I'm not passed out in a ditch or wandering some sketchy street in search of a ride. I'm just stuck here for the weekend, dumbass that I am. Now go back to sleep for a day or two and serve your sentence to society for violating Penal Code Section 647f, Public Intoxication.

Except – I don't want to have that dream again, and if I go back to sleep, I will. Wouldn't the judge love this? She sticks me in the Hall for the weekend, which is a completely cinchy gig, but I end up punishing myself. This is what my eighth-grade English teacher would call "ironic." Crap, I never knew what he meant back then.

At least I have the cell to myself. That is a piece of luck. Last time The Butt snapped her dominatrix handcuffs on me – I was curled up in the closet of my so-called best friend's house while on the run – I landed in the Hall with a coked-out *loca*. Not crazy in a zany-fun way, but crazy in a creeped-out way. Healey was her name. Rich girl named after her dad's favorite car. Hello? I can imagine naming a car after your daughter, but doing it in reverse? That's pretty weird. Healey was with me here in the Hall, coming off a fat bender. The crazy girl screamed and growled all night in the speediest word barf ever. You couldn't track what she was saying/growling, except that she was going to bust out of jail, fill her Juicy bag with Euros, and jet over to Amsterdam where she could live her life the way God intended. Hours and hours of crazy mumble about Jimmy Choo shoes, all-night clubs and legal pot. I begged her to shut up, and when that didn't work, threatened to report her to the psych ward. The funny thing is, when Daddy came to visit the next morning, she was this meek little thing, the kind of girl you'd see in a plaid school uniform, not in scuzzy Hall sweats.

I hated her nonstop brag about boyfriends and benders, but maybe it wouldn't be so horrible having her here now. At least she could take over the noise in my head. Wouldn't it be wild if she got hauled in tonight? She could tell me if she made it to Europe, modeled lingerie in shop windows, became queen of the party scene – her career ambitions, I believe.

Then I remember – Healey's days at the Hall are o-v-e-r. Her dad was about to ship her off to residential treatment in a locked-down Christian academy in Missouri or Montana when Healey went out for a quick spin in a killer Porsche. The car belonged to her mother's newest boyfriend. Most likely, Healey shook down the BF's pockets while he was soaking in the hot tub with Mommy Dearest. She must've figured she'd struck gold when the key was right there for the taking. Along with the BF's embarrassed quote on the front page of the paper, there were two pictures of Healey. One was a super-cute school portrait from seventh grade. The other showed the Porsche wrapped around a big-ass tree.

I sit up and turn on the light. Crap! I can't be filling my head with pictures of dead girls. What I wouldn't do now for a Tylenol PM – or ten. A shower wouldn't hurt either – I'm sweating like a pig and smelling worse than Wilbur and the rest of his barnyard buds. I'm not the only one around here having a rough night either. Through the cinderblock wall, I hear the girl in the next cell crying for her mama.

Mama. Mama. Waaaaaaa.

Crap. I'm never gonna sleep. I hate the fucking Hall.

BRYAN

2. JUVENILE COURT

Bryan has given up counting the number of times he's been to court at Juvenile Hall, but let's just say he's spent more time with his daughter in court than he's spent with his wife at a half-decent restaurant. Which is just the kind of thing Monica reminds him of when that soul-killing call comes at 2 a.m. from Juvenile Services. Not that he can blame his wife for complaining. She didn't exactly sign on for an out-of-control teenager when she married him, but that is sure what she got.

The windowless waiting room is as depressing as ever, molded plastic chairs scraped against the wall and thumbed-through magazines scattered across the scuffed-up floor. A vending machine buzzes in the corner, offering ranch-flavored chips and sour gummy worms. Someone has taped a hand-lettered OUT OF ORDER sign on it, but the machine is still wolfing electricity, obviously, with its bright lights and old-refrigerator hum. Bryan thinks he could fix up this room in a day or two just by hauling out the vending machine, rolling on a fresh coat or two of bright paint, tossing out the germ-heap of dead toys, and laying down some carpet squares. Instead, he's stuck sitting in a hard chair staring at last year's TIME magazines and brochures offering low-cost parenting classes.

Monica was not a happy camper when he broke the news this morning about coming to court to bail out Andrea. Well, it's not like this is the first time. She's sick of her stepdaughter ruining her day, especially get-away day. "You can't go to court today!" Monica pleaded. "We're going to Tahoe! You promised! You have two sons, remember them?" Yeah, of course he remembers them – he planned the whole damn trip to the snow around them. He wanted to be on the road this morning at seven, which is a little unrealistic with 3-year-olds, but he likes to beat the traffic when he can. Plus, he promised the boys they'd hit the slopes if conditions were right and there was still some light out. Now Andrea has managed to throw a wrench into their Christmas vacation, and she's the one who loves to snowboard. At least she used to love it. To be honest, Bryan would have to say he doesn't know what his daughter loves anymore, other than trouble.

There aren't many other parents in the waiting room this morning, and no wild children are here, thank God. Sometimes the younger siblings are so out of control, treating the room like an outdoor playground, that Bryan is tempted to say to their mothers, "Just a couple more years before they're next door in court, like your older one." But he only thinks rude stuff like that, never says it. One of the unwritten rules of the waiting room is, don't embarrass another parent by talking to them. Who wants to talk about why you're here? It doesn't reflect well on you as a parent. He always worries he's going to run into one of his customers. That couldn't be good for business, even if they're here for the same reason he is. There's a lot of shame having your kid in the Hall. So the unspoken agreement is, Mind your own damn business.

"Mr. Bretano, Andrea's case is next," Faro, the nice court hostess, announces, entering the room soundlessly in old-lady shoes. "Let's go into court."

Faro is about a hundred years old. She volunteers, out of the goodness of her heart, to work at Juvenile Hall. She likes being around young people, she says. Bryan wishes he'd brought her a latte and a scone. Not that she'd eat in court, but still, who'd volunteer to work in this rat hole, especially the week after Christmas?

"In re Andrea B.," the clerk announces as Bryan enters the small courtroom.

It's embarrassing how familiar everything is. As is often the case, he's the only man present. Commissioner Boswell, the gray-haired, heard-it-all judge who has presided over juvenile court since he grew up in this county; her staff, consisting of the clerk, court reporter, and bailiff; the young district attorney, who takes the position that every juvenile is a menace to society and should be punished accordingly; Andrea's public defender, a tired champion of the underdog; Andrea's probation officer, a burned-out social worker who wears her silver hair in long braids; and his daughter, Andrea.

She's so beautiful! Even though she looks like hell. Jesus Christ, it's horrible to see your child in jail clothes. He doesn't see any bruises or signs of injuries – not like last time. She looks thin and tired, and – wow! pissed off! – but otherwise okay. His girl looks up as he enters the courtroom and smiles. Her beautiful smile! She reminds him of her mother, who once was quite a looker. But that was before her crazy personality got in the way.

His heart lurches for a moment, as he sees the girl who was his angel, his doll, his darling; his smart, sweet, devoted daughter. His little girl who showered him with her love, who was always thrilled to see him. What happened to that girl? He sits down next to her and she grabs his hand. He squeezes back. She smells awful – a bitter mix of sweat, stress, and street drugs.

"Morning," Commissioner Boswell says, glancing up from the stack of files before her and peering at his daughter through reading glasses. "Andrea, I'm not pleased to see you, though I am not surprised. You were arrested again in the park on December 28 for public intoxication. You were on home restriction, yet you snuck out of your home. You were to abstain from the use of alcohol and illegal drugs, and your UA shows evidence of both. You were ordered to stay away from Justin P., Benito R., Syd S., and Gina N., and apparently you were with them that night. You've been non-compliant with probation and have picked up another law violation. What is happening?"

Andrea has been gripping his hand throughout the judge's speech. "I'm really sorry, Your Honor," she begins.

Commissioner Boswell shakes her head. "Save it," she says. "I don't want to hear from you yet. Let me talk to your probation officer."

Bryan feels a flash of annoyance that his daughter was cut off. He thinks Andrea was off to a solid start by offering an apology. He swallows his anger because it's not his turn to talk. But he pats his daughter's hand, hoping to tell her that he's proud of her for trying.

The probation officer reports on his daughter's performance on probation, and, jeez, it's a sorry story. A lot of the details of the last year he'd forgotten, and it's sickening to have them aired here in court. Open container. Petty theft. Public intoxication. Minor in possession. Resisting arrest.

"Has the minor been assessed for Drug Court eligibility?" the judge asks.

"Not yet," her probation officer answers. "It was initially thought that she would respond better to probation. We did not think she would require the structure of Drug Court to improve. But at this point, it's an option worth considering."

This happens a lot in court; the regulars have lengthy conversations that they find fascinating. But to an outsider, even though you know most of the words they're using, you don't really catch what they're saying.

"Andrea, are you familiar with our Juvenile Drug Court?" the judge asks.

His daughter shakes her head no. He finds himself doing the same thing. They must look like bobbleheads to the judge. Father and daughter bobbleheads.

"It's a therapeutic, long-term program for teens with law violations associated with drug and alcohol use," the judge explains. "If you want to change your life, this is your chance. Drug Court offers treatment, therapy, and family counseling. Participants attend self-help meetings, appear regularly in court, take UA tests, and meet with their probation officer. If you finish it successfully, the charges are dismissed. And if you graduate, which most kids do, you will have turned your messed-up life into something worthwhile. What do you think?"

"Uh…okay," Andrea mumbles.

"What do you think, Mr. Bretano?" the judge asks. "I warn you: It's as much work for the parents as the participants."

If there's one thing he's not afraid of, it's work. "I'll do anything to help my daughter," he says. Which is true, and he has the legal bills and high blood pressure to prove it. "But does it work? This is all new to me."

Andrea's public defender speaks for the first time. "Your Honor, if I could answer the dad's question. Yes, Drug Court works. It can be amazing. But it requires a tremendous amount of effort. Andrea has to *want* to change. She might find it easier to do the Hall time. She's already served a weekend and her only new charge is for public intoxication."

"With plenty of prior petitions and probation violations," the judge adds.

Somewhere in this talk of Drug Court, Andrea has withdrawn her hand from his and is scribbling a note to her lawyer, who then asks the judge if she can speak privately with her client for a minute. The judge agrees, and the three huddle.

"What the *fuck*?" Andy whispers. "Just tell them whatever they want to hear. I have to get out of this shit hole!"

"Shhh! Andrea!" the public defender cautions. "The judge wants you to join Drug Court. You're not ready for it. And your new charges aren't that serious."

"What do you mean, 'ready?'" Bryan whispers. "Does she have to go out and get in more trouble before she's 'ready?'" The thought of how his daughter might find new ways to get into trouble makes him shudder.

The public defender nods. "Maybe. Drug Court requires a major effort. Andrea is only 15. She might not be ready to change. In my experience, Drug Court is easier and more effective for older teens, who grow tired of spending time in the Hall while their friends move on to college and careers."

Bryan's cell phone vibrates in his pocket. He doesn't need to answer it to know that it's his wife wondering where he is and when he'll be home.

"Well, I'm ready for Andrea to change," Bryan says. "Our family is about to leave for Tahoe. Could we talk about it when we get back? Would you be willing to do that, honey?"

His daughter shrugs. "I just want to get the fuck out of here."

"Your Honor," the public defender announces. "My client and her father are interested in Drug Court, but they ask that Andy be released today. Her family has a pre-planned vacation, and they're leaving today. We request that she be released to her father's custody."

"That won't work," the probation officer argues. "I need Andrea here for a few days to do an assessment."

His cell phone vibrates again in his pocket. Suddenly, he pictures a way this day could turn around for him. He could be out of court and on the road with Monica and the boys in 25 minutes, off to the mountains for a few restful days, while his wild one cools her heels in Juvenile Hall. Why not? She's kept him up all night with worry. The family could use a little breather from her.

"I think it's a good idea, Your Honor," Bryan says. "Drug Court sounds like something Andrea could use, and I wouldn't mind it if she had a safe place to stay on New Year's Eve."

Andrea looks at her father, angry spots of pink dotting her cheek. "You can't do that! I'll go to Mom's!"

The judge ignores the minor's outburst and orders her to spend the next four days – including New Year's Eve and New Year's Day – in the Hall. The probation department is ordered to conduct a Drug Court assessment. The judge signs the papers and they're shown the door, just like that.

"Asshole! Mom's going to kill you when she finds out!" Andrea hisses, as the guard secures his daughter's wrists to her waist-chain.

Bryan surprises himself – and no doubt, his daughter – by snapping back, "It's my custodial weekend, honey. Your mother has no say in what I do when you're with me."

He feels bad slamming his girl like that. Well, at least his wife will be thrilled with this turn of events. But his daughter is exactly right on this point. Bryan will have hell to pay when he returns. If there's one thing he can count on his ex-wife for, it's combat. Costly, killer combat.

HON. STRATHMORE REED, JR.

3. IN CHAMBERS

A few miles away, in Sequoia County's main courthouse, Strathmore Reed, Jr. removes his judicial robe and is pleasantly surprised to find himself looking forward to a quiet morning in chambers. His lovely courtroom clerk, Miss Bettina, is brewing a single perfect cup of decaf cappuccino for him, and he plans to catch up on his stock portfolio's performance in the quiet solitude of his office. Lunch is still several hours away, but he is pleased to think upon his standing weekly lunch date at the Witness Chair with Hank Hellman, his oldest and dearest friend, recently retired from the Sequoia County Superior Court. Yes, now that his tiresome morning calendar is completed, the young and ill-behaved lawyers chastised, chastened, and chased along their merry ways, he finds himself quite looking forward to the day.

For what must be the fourth or fifth time that morning, he consults his embossed leather day planner, a gift from his beloved late wife, Dory, to ensure he has not overlooked any obligations – no bothersome committee meetings, no contentious bar association gatherings, no intrusive medical appointments – and notes his six o'clock obligation with Mother and her investment advisors in the City. He'll have to go home first to change into something dressier – Mother certainly would not abide his lavender dress shirt: "More suitable for an Easter egg than a man of your stature," she might observe. Strathmore shakes his head in a familiar, resigned fashion. Mother, after all, is no spring chicken, and without her largesse, he would not enjoy many of the creature comforts otherwise unavailable on the lean salary of a state court judge.

Judge Reed straightens his arms, pulls the cuffs of his shirt over his wrists, centers his monogrammed cuff links in their bindings, and opens the window on his computer to view the status of his stocks. He is now ready to devote his full attention to his investments. But first, a few relaxing rounds of solitaire.

"Knock, knock!" comes a cheery voice at his chambers door, accompanied by the crack of knuckle on wood. "May I come in?"

Immediately, Strathmore's good mood evaporates. It is his overbearing colleague, Judge Marion Berkeley. There is no one he would less prefer to see than she. Loud, opinionated, and overly tall, she is the very personification of the qualities he most despises in female professionals. Unfortunately, however, she also serves as the court's presiding judge, so he has little choice but to permit her entry.

Strathmore sighs heavily and eliminates the card game from his computer screen. "Come in," he instructs, in a strained and inhospitable tone. Why *should* he welcome her, after all? She must want something from him, else would not be at his door. Whatever it is, the answer is "no." He has enough already on his docket, and she can well and jolly find some other lackey to do her bidding. He himself was the first car in the judges' parking lot this morning at seven, as he is most mornings, except the third Thursday of the month, when he breakfasts with the good (if slightly dull) Reverend Proctor. No one can say that he doesn't do his fair share. And why, after all, should he be pressed to do *more* than his fair share? Let the young turks pull their weight; they need the experience, whereas he surely does not.

"Good morning, Strathmore!" Judge Berkeley greets him in her annoyingly upbeat manner. Though twenty years his junior, Marion and he were appointed the same year to their judicial offices – well, to be painfully precise, she was sworn in seven months before he was, giving her seniority over him. Strathmore could never understand how the astute governor who appointed him could also have selected her. The two judges could not be more dissimilar in politics, interests, manners, or social circles. Undoubtedly political pressures of the day forced the otherwise right-thinking governor to fill a certain number of positions with overbearing, outspoken women.

Marion is garbed in one of her gypsy getups, as Strathmore has come to think of them. Today it is a magenta blouse, a gaudy turquoise-and-coral skirt, and loopy gold jewelry – obviously of the drugstore variety. Makes one glad at least that the law requires all judges to preside in court wearing solemn black robes, though Strathmore can't help but wonder whether a garish outfit such as Marion's might somehow emit an eerie glow, judicial attire notwithstanding. Instantaneously, Strathmore feels himself choke, as he realizes he is envisioning his insufferable colleague underneath her robes.

"Marion," he mutters by way of response. He knows better than to ask how she is or what he can do for her. It is all he can do to speak her name civilly and to look upon her in only a mildly irritated fashion.

The presiding judge sits down in the cardamom leather chair directly across from him. She draws the chair a few inches closer to the desk, which causes Strathmore to squeeze his sphincter muscles reflexively.

"I have something difficult to discuss with you," she begins. "Last June, when we made judicial assignments, your friend Henry was assigned Juvenile Drug Court beginning January 1. But then he surprised us by retiring, and now we are short one judge until the governor fills the position. The last opening took a year to fill, as you remember. So, I've decided that, beginning next week, I will assume Henry's caseload, with the exception of Juvenile Drug Court, which I would like you to handle."

Strathmore has the sensation of being held underwater in the deep end of the pool. Her words are blurred, and he cannot quite understand her point. He notices his heart pounding in his chest, his fingertips tingling. Is he perhaps having a heart attack? He feels quite ill. Maybe it isn't a heart attack he is experiencing. Maybe it's that dreaded winter flu coming on, although that wouldn't be quite fair, since he submitted to his annual flu shot a month or so earlier.

Marion is sitting back in her chair and appears to be waiting for a response. At that moment, his clerk taps on the door and pokes her head in. "Your honor?" she says. "Here's your coffee!"

Not trusting himself to speak, Strathmore nods, and the lovely, lithe, long-haired Miss Bettina sets the steaming cup in front of him. Just as quietly, she exits the room and secures the door behind her.

"N-N-No," Strathmore manages to sputter.

Marion recoils slightly. "No?"

"No, I will not do it," he repeats, this time firmly and confidently. "I have said yes to each and every assignment sent my way. I volunteered to serve in that appalling family law assignment when no judge would touch it with a ten-foot pole. I believe in saying yes for the good of the order. But this time, I put my foot down. Find someone else to handle it. Why not you, for example?"

"I would love to take it," Marion replies unfazed. "But I don't see how I could, with the 600 cases that I'm adding to my workload."

"Well, then, why not Commissioner Boswell? She's already out in juvenile court. She could do Drug Court."

Marion shakes her head. "She is overbooked as it is with her current caseload in juvenile and probate."

He clears his throat a few times and fixes his gaze just over the crown of her head so he doesn't have to look at her. "Marion. I did not become a judge to babysit some incorrigible delinquents who smoke, spit, and grunt until they're old enough to be sentenced to jail. Therapeutic courts and their warm-and-fuzzy approach to the law are a waste of my expertise and our court's resources. Find a judge who voted for it. I didn't."

Marion crosses a leg and leans forward in her chair. "I'm sorry you are making this difficult. Strathmore, I've given this a lot of thought, and I'm afraid you are the only answer."

Strathmore feels his face redden. His upbringing tells him it would be the better part of valor to defer his response to a time when he might express himself more judiciously, but this unacceptable breach of conduct from a colleague is entirely objectionable. "That's it, then? You're just going to shove it down my throat? You're not even going to discuss it with the rest of the bench?" It is absolutely unacceptable that the presiding judge would announce a unilateral decision, as if she were his boss or something equally distasteful.

"Look, we have to do something," Marion says. "It's December 28. We need a judge in Juvenile Drug Court beginning January 1. Your friend Henry left us in a difficult spot. Had we known he was going to retire, we might have been able to plan otherwise. Unfortunately, we have few options. I need and expect you to serve in this assignment."

"This is disgraceful!" Strathmore cries. "Hank would never have permitted something like this to happen when he ran the court."

Marion smiles without warmth. "I'm sure that is completely true. But as I'm the presiding judge and not Henry, it is my job to make sure a judge is serving in every department. I'm sorry you're unhappy with this decision." Marion stands and walks to the door. Before closing it behind her, she adds, "Anyway, it's only until the governor makes the appointment. Then you can go back to checking your stocks and playing solitaire, instead of presiding in court."

"Bih…bih…bihhh!" Strathmore struggles to restrain himself before uttering the only noun that ever comes to mind when he speaks with the presiding judge. He slams his fist on his desk, causing his untouched coffee to stain the sleeve of his shirt and smear the ink on the open page of his date book. Blasted, blithering balderdash! The b-b-beast has ruined his day.

ANDY

4. NEW YEAR'S EVE, NO MOM

Anybody home? I'm all alone in the effing universe. All the people who supposedly love me are out celebrating New Year's and have left me behind.

Not a single friend has called. My own father blew me off in court – that backstabber! Plus – he's so obvious, it's insulting. There he was, playing Mr. Concerned Dad for the judge, patting me on the hand, cooing like he's on my side, ready to do whatever it takes to set his troubled teen on track. What a fake! As soon as his stupid cell phone rang, he was sucked back to his new life, the problem-free one with the matching sons and picture-perfect wife. He dropped me so fast – he should be nailed for speeding *and* illegal u-turn. Now he's on vacation in Tahoe, leaving me stuck in this Hall-hole. I hate him.

And where is my mother? My devoted mother? She is just as bad, if not worse. Oh, she says she's *always* thinking about me, says her heart *grieves* when I'm staying at Dad's house, says any time I want to come back to her, I don't have to call or explain, I can just show up and she'll be "pleased as punch" to have me back where I belong. "Call me any time, honey, any time, day or night. I'm your mother, your one and only mother, always here for you." God, she's like a country-western song except with a Lexus instead of a pickup truck.

So I decide to give her a chance to make good on the big promises. But first, I had to sweet-talk a guard into letting me call Mom on his cell phone. It was going to be worth the beg, though, because Mom would so bail me out of this joint. She has a way with the people at Juvenile Services. At any moment, she can launch into a rant over "special needs child," "carefully calibrated medication," and "imminent psychological trauma," with juicy dashes of lawsuits thrown in here and there to keep the people at Juvenile Services worried. Yeah, Mom was my ticket out of here. I had it all worked out how I'd rat out Dad, how he'd sold me out for one little snowboarding trip, how I was now ready to move in with her for good.

The softy guard gave me two minutes to use his phone, but that was all I needed. Mom has her cell surgically attached to her ear, and one word about where I am and what an asshole her ex is, and BOOM! she is off and running. I call. Her phone rings. And rings. And rings. My call goes through to voicemail. No problem, I'm thinking, maybe even better – I can leave a desperate message and she can listen to it again and again and get herself really worked up in a frenzy over my mistreatment. But then – eeeeeeeeeek!! The computer voicemail comes on and tells me that her message box is full, to please call back later, and that my call will now be disconnected. Blown off by a voicemail operator!

I hate her!

I hate everyone!

I hate them, I hate them, I hate them.

I'm all alone in the world, stuck in this butt-ugly room, abandoned by my family and friends. Maybe I'm going crazy too, because I start to scream. Loud!

Aaagh! Aaaaagh! Aaaaaaaaaaaaaaaaaaaaaa aaaaaaaaaaaagh!

My cell door opens mid-scream. A guard pokes her head inside. "Someone having a cow in here?"

It's such a dopey expression, so the kind of thing my granny would say, that I laugh, kind of a tortured, snorty laugh, in spite of my pathetic self.

"Yeah," I cry. "Me. I'm having a big, freakin', ugly cow."

The guard utters code into the radio attached to her shoulder, something like, "37 secure J-25 over." She slides into my room, closing the door behind her.

"Mind if I mosey in?" she asks, in a friendly enough way.

She's a little on the old side, with pokey gray hair, old-lady skin, and wire-rim bifocals, but unlike any grandmother I know, she has a compact, muscled body. She's wearing a uniform with a metal nametag that says, "A. Lyon." She makes me think of a lion, too – like Nala from "The Lion King." My all-time favorite dress-up for Halloween. Nala might look sweet and here-kitty-kitty cute, but you know she's all muscle and pounce when circumstances require.

So, okay. I'm not stupid. A. Lyon could flatten me with a swat of her veiny hand, to say nothing of what she could do with that big-ass stick in her belt. I tell her it looks to me like she's already in.

"Deputy Lyon," she says with a slightly comical bow of the head. "At your service."

"Andy," I say, using my orange sweatshirt sleeve to wipe the dumb tears from my eyes and the snot from everywhere else. "But – you probably know that."

"Affirmative," she answers. "Now that we've dispensed with the introductions, may I be so bold as to inquire: What's the beef?"

"You can ask," I say, "but I won't answer 'til you stop it with the lame cow jokes."

"Deal," she says agreeably. "I guess I was milking that one for all its worth."

I roll my eyes. She giggles.

I examine her sun-spotted face, her droopy eyes and goofy smile. For some reason, even though she's wearing a uniform and a pointy gold badge, I kind of like her.

"My life sucks," I offer.

"It sucks," she repeats, sitting up straight and stroking her chin like a philosophy professor. "Sucks like a mosquito, a tic, a leech, a bedbug, or what?"

"Yeah," I answer, though I'm not totally clear on what a bedbug is, whether it's a real thing or a thing from nursery rhymes. I tell her about court, how my dad blew me off, how my mom wasn't there for my call, how I'm all alone in the universe, blah blah blah.

When I finish dishing up my tale of woe, A. Lyon says nothing. She doesn't nod, sympathize, advise, interrupt, question, argue, mm-hmm, or any of the other things grown-ups do. She just looks at me, with, I don't know, with all her attention, I guess. When the silence lasts too long, I fill it with a few wrap-up words.

"So, I'm pissed. I'm spending New Year's Eve in the Hall. I think I'm entitled to scream my head off."

"Or," she adds, "to bawl like a bovine. While creating coronary concern for your friendly deputy sheriff."

She says it with good enough humor, but suddenly I can't stand it anymore. My head is pounding, my skin is clammy, I feel empty and gross. I squeeze my eyes tight and wish for a way to wake up from this nightmare.

But when I open them, I'm still in orange sweats, stuck on a metal bed, miles from home. The sounds of this torture chamber seep through the walls; the TV, of course, the unfamiliar adult voices shouting orders, the pound of footsteps, and something else – something soft and moaning. I tilt my head to listen better. What is it?

The crying next door.

"Hear that?" A. Lyon asks.

"Yeah."

"That girl just came back from a week-long speed run. Walked in the front door and found her mama sprawled on the couch with a needle in her arm. Dead as a doornail," she says.

"Ecck." You always hear stories like that, but you never think it happens to real people. "Where's her dad?"

"Excellent question," A. Lyon says. "She doesn't know. I'm not sure if she ever knew him. Oh, that's my radio. Excuse me." She leans her ear into her shoulder and speaks into it. "37 10-4 to commons. Over."

"Gotta go, huh?" I ask.

"Duty calls," A. Lyon says. "I've enjoyed our talk. No bull."

She backs out the door. "Call me if you want to talk. I'm at your service."

I nod. Like I'd ever call a sheriff's deputy to "talk."

"Okay, you're not going to friend me," she says. "So, listen up: One, for a girl who enjoys her freedom, you spend a lot of time in lock-up. Two, all suffering comes from the inability to accept things as they are."

Speaking of bull, what's that supposed to mean? "Are you telling me my problem is not that I'm *imprisoned* at Juvenile Hall, but that I can't *accept* it?"

She winks and says, "You'll figure it out. Happy New Year, doll."

Her words hang in the thick, sticky air of my cell.

I'm 15 years old and spending New Year's Eve in Juvenile Hall. So far, this is shaping up as the worst year ever in my short, pathetic life.

BRYAN

5. NEW YEAR'S EVE WITH THE MOTHER OF MY CHILDREN

"Monica," Bryan whispers, "This has been the best night of my life."

It's true, too. Monica went all out for him tonight, and he is in love with her all over again. She got the boys to bed early, fixed him a manly meal of grilled steak and red wine, didn't mention the kids once during dinner; not a word about money, the boys, Andy or his ex. No, she kept it nice and light, just the way he likes it.

When dinner was over, she told him to get ready for dessert, said it might take a while to fix, that he should sip a little wine and relax. She surprised the hell out of him and lit a joint, like they were kids again. It was all giggles and gropes, like the old days. They made out like teenagers, and then she told him she'd be right back with his surprise.

He kicked off his shoes, stretched out on the couch, and enjoyed the moment. She returned all dolled up in a sexy see-through Victoria's Secret thing, and boy, she looked great. She carried a bottle of champagne and two glasses, told him he'd have to wait for the bubbly.

"Bryan," she said, her eyes full of softness, "After dessert, I want to talk to you about a New Year's resolution."

Of course, he was ready to give her whatever she asked for. As soon as he had dessert.

And his wife, who was blowing his mind, did something he never thought she'd do. She explored the Southern Hemisphere, down the Eastern Seaboard, around Punta del Fuego, and up the western coast. He went nuts. His eyeballs crossed, the pleasure was so intense. Fireworks! Bliss!

Afterwards, she poured a few drops of champagne on his chest, licked it off, asked if he was ready for more. That's when he tells her it's the best night of his life.

She puts on thick socks and wraps herself in a blanket. He pours champagne into glasses and pulls on his T-shirt.

"I think we can do more of that this year," she says. "I want our next year to be the best one ever."

"Fantastic!" he says, unable to believe how good this night is. Thinks, what a lucky guy I am!

"So, here's my idea," she whispers. "I want you all year long. Not just tonight. And not just Saturday nights. You know what I'm asking, don't you?"

"Yeah, I think so," he says, handing her a glass of bubbly. "And I'm the guy for the job."

"Great," she says. "I want you to put me first. No more fighting with your ex. No more lawyers. No more legal expenses. Your sons don't come first, your daughter doesn't come first, your job doesn't come first. You put your goddess first, and we will have a whole year of fun."

He signs on for the program without hesitation. Before nodding off, he thinks: Finally! I'm going to have a good year – a good, good year.

All he has to do is keep his crazy ex-wife from taking him back to court.

The only tiny glitch is, he hasn't been able to do that since he divorced the bitch, ten years ago.

HON. STRATHMORE REED, JR.

6. MOTHER REED ON NEW YEAR'S EVE

Strathmore Reed, Jr. stifles a yawn and consults his Rolex for perhaps the fifth time in as many minutes. Good God, will this evening never end?

The Reed dynasty, at least what's left of it, is gathered at an ornately appointed table in the private room of Mother Reed's country club, located high in the wooded hills of Sequoia County. Mother is, of course, enthroned at the head of the table, a slim, sharp-witted matriarch of 83, attired tonight in one of her many full-length glitter gowns from her glory years. To her right sits daughter Clara, Strathmore's younger sister, best known locally as the club's reigning female golf champ. Next to Clara is her dull, dull Dick – little wonder Clara plays so much golf – and around the table are their three adult children along with spouses and their six offspring of various irritating ages. An au pair is also in attendance, although of course not seated with the family. Strathmore is positioned across from Mother at the opposite end of the table. On his left is his only child, the plain, dour Elizabeth who, at age 33, is now closing in on her third post-graduate degree. Bitsy, as he has always called her, has never married. Over the years, Strathmore has entreated her to bring at least a date if not a fiancé to the function, to bolster their presence at a table his sister's family threatens to overrun. Although Bitsy has made various vague promises, she has never had a single escort to Mother's New Year's Eve gathering.

As Reed finishes the last of his too-rich tiramisu, he notes his cummerbund is snuggled uncomfortably close across his middle. He cannot fathom how he could have gained weight this last year – it doesn't seem as though he has eaten more than three or four decent meals since he lost his beloved Dory to cancer two years ago.

How could she have predeceased him? Damn it all! It still doesn't seem right. She was six years his junior and fit as a fiddle. Her absence is notable at all times, but especially during the holidays, although, in truth, he supposes that Dory might rather be dead than here tonight at Mother's Annual Evening of Giving, where one must be present to win.

He and Dory had some of their most regrettable rows because of this very dinner. It started the year Bitsy was born. Dory refused to attend with a 6-week-old baby, though her husband warned her it was a command performance. His wife said some terribly unkind things about his priorities and the unreasonable demands of his family. Strathmore declared in no uncertain terms that he simply could not and would not inform Mother of her stubborn refusal to attend. In the end, Dory called Mother herself and explained that while her husband would happily join the Reed family for its annual gathering, she was simply too tired to go out, even for an event as delightful as Mother's, and was equally unwilling to leave her newborn at home with a sitter. Mother said she quite understood, and the Strathmore Reed Juniors thought that was that. Strathmore was amazed (and secretly impressed) that his wife had actually said no to his sometimes-domineering mother, and mildly surprised that the earth did not stop rotating on its axis.

Or so Reed had thought. At the conclusion of that dinner thirty-three years ago, Mother presented each guest with a thick vellum envelope. It was, and remains, the tradition of the family to open the envelope well after saying one's goodbyes. So it wasn't until he returned home that night that Reed discovered how costly his wife's decision had been. Mother had given Strathmore a check for $50,000, but had failed to issue the anticipated checks for his wife and daughter in like amounts.

Strathmore grunts involuntarily at the stabbing memory. They lost $100,000 that evening. Invested wisely over thirty-three years with a reasonably competent investment adviser, that money would be worth close to a million now. Even better, had that amount been put into skyrocketing Sequoia Valley real estate, it would represent real money in today's dollars.

"Something wrong, Father?" his daughter asks. It's the first time she's spoken to him since sitting down to eat.

"Nothing at all, Bitsy," he answers.

"Father. My name is Elizabeth," she corrects him. "Please."

"Very well, then, 'Elizabeth,'" Strathmore says, weary of the reminder. It doesn't seem quite fair for one's daughter to change her name after so many years, and Strathmore simply cannot adapt to her new preference. Perhaps he will take to calling her "Dear" and be done with it.

Mother taps her teaspoon against her water glass. Instantaneously, the crowd falls silent, except for the au pair, who, everyone now notices, is crouched in the corner speaking in Spanish on her cell phone. Clara's oldest daughter manages that embarrassing distraction in a heartbeat.

"Let us move to the next item on the agenda, shall we?" Mother asks.

Strathmore groans inwardly. He could script the next part of the evening down to the word. Before Mother parts with her money, the family must endure the Reed ritual of reciting one's goals, wishes, or resolutions for the New Year. As Mother puts it, "She who pays the piper calls the tune."

The ritual had been Father's idea originally. Strathmore was but a boy some fifty years earlier when the game was launched at the end of a loud and talky party overridden by show-offy lawyers from Father's elite law firm. Father kicked off the game by announcing his goal of procuring a dozen high-profile clients by name. His partners bragged of income figures they planned to achieve or cases they hoped to win. Strathmore's older brother, Thurston II, said he wished to play professional baseball, and everyone laughed indulgently. Strathmore – stunned to have so many grownups waiting for him to speak – idiotically said he'd like to sail to Timbuktu. Expecting applause, young Strathmore was quite stung when Father dryly remarked that Timbuktu was unfortunately more accessible than Harvard for his younger son. The game, for Strathmore, had not improved over time.

Mother finishes describing her plan of setting up a charitable trust for the performing arts, and Clara chirps dutifully about her goal of winning a golf tournament; this year it's the Dinah Shore. Just as dreadfully dull Dick is about to unleash his annual unachievable pipe dream, an attractive hostess from the club enters the room, whispers to Mother, and approaches Strathmore with a folded note.

It is a message from the Sheriff's Office requesting an Emergency Protective Order. Never has Strathmore been more pleased to serve as the night-duty judge. He excuses himself from the table and follows the hostess.

From behind, she reminds him a bit of Dory –
fit, trim and attractively packaged – although
years younger and with chic silvery-blond hair.
Dory's hair was an ordinary brown, much like
Bitsy's, and it never changed in style or color
from their wedding day forward.

Strathmore clears his throat several times.
"Thank you, Miss. I appreciate an excuse to
stretch my legs."

"You are quite welcome, Your Honor," she
says with a pretty pink-lipstick smile.

"Permit me to introduce myself," he says.
"I'm Judge Reed."

"Yes, of course. I'm Saundra." She has
tastefully made-up blue eyes and modest
diamond studs in her ears. "A pleasure to
meet you."

"Thank you, Shaunna," Strathmore says,
somehow managing a stammer before he
enunciates her name.

The hostess smiles politely. "Well, have
a nice evening, sir," she says, signaling the
men's private lounge.

Strathmore wishes her the same before
initiating his call. He remains on the line
with the communications center as long as
possible. New Year's Eve is a busy night at
the jail. Excessive alcohol consumption leads
to a night full of bar fights, car crashes and

domestic disturbances. Midnight is still two hours away and already the jail is packed. When the judge at last returns to the family party, he is pleased to see that his timing is perfect. Mother has just started her march around the room, delivering envelopes and dry kisses to each guest.

"Happy New Year, Strathmore," Mother says, handing him his envelope. In a low voice, she adds, "You may call me tomorrow with your goal for the new year. Be sure to ask Bitsy what hers was. I think you'll be pleased."

Within minutes, the guests round up cranky children, bundle into winter coats, and say their overly enthusiastic goodbyes. Strathmore escorts Mother to the entry hall, where he is delighted to see the attractive hostess – what was her name? – stationed by the front door, delivering gift bags to departing guests. Sheila? Sharon? Suzanna?

Strathmore sucks in his belly and stands a bit taller. He searches his mind for something witty to say on his way out the door. If only he could impress her by addressing her personally!

"Happy New Year, Mrs. Reed," she says to Mother Reed, handing her a gift bag with a split of French champagne.

Strathmore readies himself for the charming *bon mot*, but the hostess beats him to it.

"And Happy New Year to you, Your Honor," she says. "What a lovely family the two of you have. You must be very proud parents!"

Proud *parents?* How dreadful! Strathmore's words are strangled in his throat.

"Oh for pity's sake, Strathmore," Mother says, tugging his elbow. "Stop standing there with your mouth open. It's late. Take me to my car at once."

Good God, Judge Reed thinks, what a nightmare! I must get out more this year.

ANDY

7. PHASE ONE, WEEK ONE

I have never been so terrified in my entire life. "Scared shitless" is more like it, and I'm including the time the cops surrounded me with guns, searchlights, dogs and patrol cars while I was half-naked on the front lawn of my middle school at three in the morning. That was bad. *This* is worse.

Boom-BOOM, boom-BOOM! My heart is hammering so fast and so loud, I can't hear anything else. Please, please, please! Let the floor open up and swallow me. Earthquake, tidal wave, monsoon – I'll take any natural disaster; just make it now!

I hate it here, I hate it here. I want to run away and never come back.

I'm in Drug Court.

Not just in it, but right smack dab on display in the front row, with two others from the Hall. Behind us are twelve or fifteen Drug Court kids, dressed in normal clothes, probably whispering about the freaks in orange sweats with hands chained to their waists. We're in a huge courtroom at the main courthouse, not the usual kidlet court at Juvenile Hall. This one is packed with bailiffs, probation officers, parents, and evil-looking suits, possibly lawyers but they could be paid assassins.

I'm dying! If I could just dematerialize, email myself to Kuala Lumpur, time travel to another century, disappear from the face of the earth! Something, anything. I can't stand this feeling.

Scared to death. I get what that means now.

I want to be released from the Hall today, and up until this moment, I thought I had it wired. Oh, I really want to go home to my own room! I want my own bed and my own clothes. I'll do anything. I'll be good. I'll go to school, do as I'm told, wipe the crumbs off the kitchen counter with my tongue. I want my Dad. I'll be nice to Monica, even if she is a bitch to me (which she always is). I'll follow the rules, pick my clothes off the floor, turn the volume down on my speakers. Yes, yes, yes, I will! I mean it! I want my own pillow, a shower with hot water, herbal shampoo. I want to put two kinds of conditioner in my hair, crawl into my own bed and sleep. Sleep for weeks.

What was I supposed to say to the judge? I went over it again and again, but sitting in this hair-prickling place, I can't remember a word. I'm afraid I won't be able to say the right stuff, which means I'll rot in Hall. I have to get out!

My new probation officer, Deputy Karla Washington, is in front of me at the table where lawyers sit during trials. Actually she looks like a lawyer today, and not the G.I. Jill look she sported when I met her. Today she's got the Land's End look happening – navy blue pants suit, white collared shirt, low-heeled shoes. Short black hair, flawless café-au-lait complexion; no jewelry, scarves, or accessories. She interviewed me at the Hall yesterday, along with a bunch of other hell raisers, and told us what we needed to say to the judge to get into Drug Court. Said the judge was new to juvenile court, wasn't sure what he might do with us today. Karla is one tough chick – the exact words she uses to describe herself. She served in the army, fought in Iraq, played college lacrosse, and is now training for an Ironman. Her biceps all but scream, Go ahead, mess with me before I crush you like a can of Coke.

Karla told us not to bother with Drug Court if we're wusses, said a little Hall time and some cushy probation are wa-a-ay easier than what it takes to graduate Drug Court. But if we've got the *cajones*, she says Drug Court can save us a buttload of trouble and put us back on the right path.

Maybe she didn't say "buttload," but that was the idea.

The PO was baiting us, really. Hinting we were too wimpy to do it was nothing but a dare. That got under my skin. So what interested me wasn't the tough talk. No, what hooked me was her promise that if we do what she asks, we will be off probation in nine months – as opposed to the three centuries of probation I'm already on – and we won't ever, ever, ever spend another night in the Hall. So sign me up! I wanna go home! And never come back.

Until this moment, I thought I had it nailed. But suddenly I'm weak in the knees and dead in the head.

"All rise and come to order!" shouts a weasely-looking bailiff with a massive gun belt.

The judge enters the courtroom with kingly fanfare, and everyone jumps to their feet. My balance is messed up, because I'm wrapped up in chains and shaking so bad that my knees might buckle out from under me. HON. STRATHMORE REED JR., announces the name plaque at the bench. The judge is old and scary-looking. Has a sharp, beaky nose and mean, squinty eyes. Perched over us on his raised bench, he looks like a hawk, and not a happy one either.

He calls the first name, Sahari H., and I practically faint with relief that he doesn't call mine. A short girl with beautiful, long hair comes forward and sits at the table next to PO Karla. I recognize her from my first stay in the Hall. She's gotten chubbier since then, but her skin isn't all red and rashy anymore and her blue-black hair is shiny and spectacular. She answers the judge's questions in a voice too soft to hear. When Karla reports to the judge that Sahari has 90 days of sobriety, everyone in the courtroom applauds. The judge seems as stunned as I am by the audience participation, and he kind of pitches forward in his enormous swivel chair. You can see that Sahari is embarrassed by the attention. She is ordered to return with four AA meetings in two weeks.

"Andrea Bretano." Aiiieeeeeeeyyyyyyy! I know I'm supposed to stand up, but I'm stuck. My legs will not move. The judge stares out at the crowd blankly, waiting.

"Bretano!" Karla whispers sharply, glaring at me. "Move it!"

I nod. Rise. Pitch myself forward. Fall in the chair next to her. Behind me I hear footsteps. It's my father! He can save me! I smile gratefully, only to have my momentary elation replaced by sickening dread. Monica is with him, her hair clipped back in a neat up-do, and, oh my God, just when you think things couldn't get any worse: my *mother* is here too. And boy, she looks *pissed*.

"Your Honor," my probation officer begins, "this is Andrea B.; she goes by the name Andy. She is 15 years old, here today for the first time with parents and stepmother. The team recommends her admission into Drug Court. I met with her in the Hall. Andy agrees to come to court every week during Phase One. She will attend two self-help meetings per week and meet regularly with her probation officer."

I can barely hear my PO's voice over the pounding in my ears. My stress level is Code Red and rising. It is way past weird for me to be seated between my parents. Although they spend a lot of time talking *about* each other, they never spend any time *with* each other. They can barely tolerate living in the same city, but here they are, sitting six feet apart, and I am between them.

PO Karla is still talking about my new obligations. "She will be required to give UA tests as directed. She understands the program will last a minimum of nine months. She agrees to obey curfew, attend school, and stay away from alcohol and illegal drugs. Andy, her father and stepmother are ready to commit to Drug Court. I haven't had a chance to speak with the mother yet."

Judge Reed clears his throat before speaking. "Do you understand that?" he asks me. "What you will be required to do if admitted to Drug Court?"

My heart is pounding in my throat. I can't believe my mother is here! How will she mess this up for me and Dad? They haven't agreed on anything in the last decade except a divorce. If they start fighting in court here – and let's face it, they've fought in front of everyone from teachers, coaches, and friends all the way down to complete strangers – I won't have to worry about Drug Court because I will die right now.

"Young lady? Ms. B-Bretano?" The judge asks again. "Do you understand what will be required of you in Drug Court?"

"S-s-sorry!" I manage in a tiny, choked voice. I'm shaking everywhere, inside and out.

The judge looks at me disapprovingly. He clears his throat.

"Her mother and I divorced eleven years ago –" Dad offers.

"Ten!" Mom corrects. She's dyed her hair some weird red-purple since I saw her last. She's wearing the black suit she bought for Grandpa's funeral, only now the shoulder pads look ridiculous and the pants look too tight. I'm guessing she put lipstick on while driving, because it's applied at a whacky-ass angle.

Dad nods. "Ten years, then. The separation has been rough on Andy."

"It hasn't exactly been a walk in the park for me either," Mom says. Next to correcting my father, Mom likes nothing more than to explain every single world event by its effect on her. For example, you wouldn't necessarily think that buying an embarrassed 12-year-old girl her first bra would be an event starring a middle-aged mother, and yet it was.

"Right," Dad says, closing his eyes to gather his thoughts. "We think Drug Court is a good idea for our daughter, and we will do whatever it takes for her to succeed."

"He does not speak for me!" Mom charges. "I was out of town for New Year's weekend only to return and find out my daughter is in Juvenile Hall for yet another law violation committed while in her father's custody. She never gets into trouble when she is at my house. I also discover that her father, without bothering to consult with me, has signed her up for some program I've never heard of. I need time to investigate it before I can commit to it. This is simply not his decision to make."

I open my mouth to speak, but no words come out. Could she humiliate me more?

The judge looks horrified. He glances at the clock on the wall. Three minutes, and already my case is off to a bad start.

Of all people, *Monica* comes to the rescue. The strangeness of it all is dizzying. My stepmother takes an audible breath and stands. "Your Honor, my name is Monica Bretano. I'm Andy's stepmother. Andy has twin brothers at home. They are 3 years old, and they miss their big sister terribly. Andy has been in the Hall for a week. We would like her to come home with us on the condition that she obey the rules outlined by her probation officer, Ms. Washington. We will enforce them in our home."

My mom is not going to mess this one up. She would love nothing more than to take on Monica, especially in a courtroom with fifty witnesses. My stepmom would be KO'd quicker than the judge could stutter a call for order.

"Your Honor," I say. "Please let me join. My PO says it's the right program for me. I know my mother is mad. I don't blame her. But she should be mad at me, not my dad. I'm the one who f-f-f, uh, messed up. I want to do Drug Court. I promise I'll do my best. I learned my lesson in the Hall. I just want to go…" Before I can say "home," my voice breaks like a 4-year-old's, and I suffer the further humiliation of tears sliding down my face in public.

My mother starts to object, but the judge holds up his hand, and, amazingly, she shuts up.

"Very well, young lady," the judge rules. "You are placed on an indefinite period of probation, and you are to lead a law-abiding life." He then reads from a form, which my probation officer places in front of me so I can follow along. When he gets to the part where it says I will be released from the Hall today, I exhale hugely. It must've been louder than I thought, because my PO nails me with an elbow in the side and hisses at me to keep a lid on it.

When the judge finishes with my case, Karla whispers a reminder about being on home restriction. I nod. Before stepping back to my seat, she tugs on my sweatshirt and issues one final command: Stay away from your mother's house until further order.

Honestly, I have no idea how I'm going to do any of the stuff the judge just told me to do. But this last order from my PO? Not a problem. I wish it could last forever.

Because "forever" is more or less how long my mom's gonna be pissed off about today.

BRYAN

8. BRETANO'S

You want an iced latte in most parts of the world, you think Starbucks. But if you want one in Sequoia Valley, you think Bretano's. Bryan has eight strategically located shops in the county, and customers line up for their daily jolt of java beginning at 5 a.m. and continuing more or less nonstop until the post-yoga-class chai crowd closes the shops at 9 p.m. In addition to your lattes, cappuccinos, mocchiatas, mochas, beans, teas and Italian ices, Bretano's also offers the county's best selection of cakes, cookies, tea breads, scones, and pastries available anywhere outside of your grandma's kitchen. You simply cannot buy desserts like theirs anywhere else, not at your fancy-schmancy "green" grocers, not at your favorite foodie restaurant, not at your donut and birthday cake shop. Back in the beginning, they baked everything in their own kitchen, so they could honestly say their goods were homemade. But once they expanded beyond their flagship shop, Bryan had to outsource it. After a string of disastrous baking contracts involving an assortment of potheads, college kids, and soccer moms, he found a great group of local gals who worship organic butter, farm eggs, pure vanilla, lemon zest, ground almonds and unbleached flour. His bakers are not stuck in some blueberry scone/bran muffin/chocolate-chip cookie rut. No way. Every day, it's some new selection of enticing, buttery treats – today, for example, he has cinnamon sticky buns, cranberry-pecan tea bread, and oatmeal-walnut cookies with flax. The baked goods keep customers coming back just as much as the beans.

Bryan is the first to admit that he's not the smartest guy in the world. But he did have one brilliant idea in his life, and that was to open his first shop in upscale Sequoia Valley moments before the coffee craze hit. He likes to call it brilliant, but truly it was more like dumb luck. If only he'd been smart enough to keep Mr. Happy in his holster, he'd be a fairly successful man today. But like he says, he's not that smart.

Sixteen years ago, he was delivering newspapers before the sun came up and driving an airport shuttle until well after it set. There wasn't a lot of money in that line of work, so he signed on for extra shifts, often working seven days a week. His life was a continuous loop of asphalt, brake lights, and road rage, with no promise of improvement. College was not an option – he barely squeaked out of high school. One of his regular airport runs was a leasing agent who was looking to fill some space in a high-end Tuscan-style mall under construction at the central Sequoia highway exit. He had a small space and needed a food-and-beverage tenant, something along the lines of a croissant-sandwich or a fro-yo shop. Said he could make someone a very sweet deal on the rent. At the time, Bryan had an on-again, off-again dating relationship with a beautiful babe who was as good in bed as she was in the kitchen and who was plenty of fun when she wasn't bonkers. She baked the lightest lemon scones ever, killer peanut butter cookies, and a spice cake that made you moan. Her mother happened to be pretty well-off, and she was interested in investing some dough, especially if it would get her grown-up daughter out of the nest. So, Bryan started talking to them about this lease opportunity. What about forming a business venture? Mom would front the money. Connie would do the baking. Bryan would run the shop.

He was folding newspapers one morning and happened to read one of those little filler articles that nobody ever reads. He was probably the only guy in the universe who didn't already know this, but this article said that fast-food restaurants, which at the time were multiplying like bunnies, made their money not on the burgers they advertised for 39 cents but on the soft drinks they sold for $1.59. That's because the burgers cost money; the soft drinks cost nothing. That little bit of information blew his mind.

Well, what are you going to sell with lemon scones? Not soft drinks. Milk goes pretty well with desserts, but how much money are you going to make on that? Coffee was the answer. Connie's mother had just come back from Italy and – to give credit where credit is due – she had the idea of buying one of those beautiful Italian espresso machines. It's hard to remember this far back in time, but at that moment, when people thought cappuccino, they were more likely to picture Taster's

Choice with Coffee-Mate than espresso with steamed milk.

True to his word, the leasing agent made Bryan a very sweet deal. The leasing guy later spent a little time at Club Fed for some shady pyramid scheme, but that was long after he'd given Bryan a year of free rent on a five-year lease with several below-market options to renew. After multiple delays, the copper espresso machine arrived from Milan, and Bretano's opened in the mall. Connie baked desserts from morning 'til night, but most of them went to the St. Vincent de Paul soup kitchen. Nine days after they opened, TIME magazine ran a piece about Starbucks, how people in Seattle were lining up to pay two bucks for a fancy coffee. Two bucks! It was unheard of. But so was a latte. Pretty soon, locals wanted to find out what it was. Bryan had the espresso machine. Bretano's was in business.

That was his one brilliant idea.

Now for the long list of his really stupid ideas: The top three colossally stupid ones are (1) Believing crazy Connie when she swore up and down she was on the Pill; (2) Marrying her when she got pregnant; and (3) Keeping her on as a limited partner after they divorced.

In his defense, it didn't seem like such an idiotic idea to allow her to remain as a limited partner when they divorced, even though his lawyer railed against it. The way Bryan saw it was, his ex and her mother helped start the business, and it was only fair that they should remain on as limited partners. He could still run the business on a day-to-day basis, and all he'd have to do is share the profits with them. It would keep his alimony payments down. Plus, letting them stay on as limited partners saved him from having to pay several hundred thousand dollars he didn't have in the divorce.

Well, that's what he thought, and it just goes to prove what a moron he is. Most people could figure out that owning a business with your crazy ex-spouse would turn your life into a living hell. And yet he, Mr. Successful Businessman, negotiated a deal that allows his ex-spouse to stick her nose in his dish whenever she damn well pleases, and she has the partnership agreement to back her up.

Take today, for example. He's got a few things on my mind. A jumpy teenage daughter at home who refuses to come out of her room for fear she'll do something stupid again and wind up back in Juvenile Hall. A wife who overspent on holiday gifts and is putting pressure on him to bring home more money this month. An employee at the Bayview shop who's been slipping twenties in his apron every time he takes a smoke break. So you could say the last thing he needs today is a process server showing up at his place of business with new legal papers from his ex.

ORDER TO SHOW CAUSE RE MODIFICATION OF CHILD CUSTODY screams the title on the front page. Poor Andy! This is going to kill her! And just when she's struggling so hard to get her shit together. Her mother is asking that primary custody be changed from Bryan to her. What a nightmare! They have been to court over and over again on every detail of Andy's child-rearing. He's had to get court approval for everything and anything in this girl's life: summer vacations, after-school activities, pediatricians, braces and even – no shit – her haircuts. He hates having to go to court for the hundredth time to argue over his daughter. It's humiliating to take up court time for stupid domestic squabbles, to have your business thrown out in public for all the world to see. Connie does all her own legal work, so it never costs her a penny. But he's not that quick with words, so each time she drops one of her little bombs, Bryan runs up several thousand in legal fees and something more in grief. And how in the hell will he break the news to his wife? He can't afford to fight, but he can't *not* fight. He owes it to his daughter to do what's best for her. Because in the end, it's Andy who suffers, and he won't stand for that. He's her father. And if he can't protect her, what the hell?

But here's the worst part of it: Even if he wins, his ex will have her next legal motion queued up and ready to go. There's never an end to this hell. She'll file her bi-annual ORDER TO SHOW CAUSE RE PARTNERSHIP ACCOUNTING. Under the partnership agreement, Connie has the right to demand an accounting every other year. All she has to do is ask, and he has to turn his life upside down with tax returns, invoices, profit and loss statements, lawyers and accountants. His ex will examine every single slip of paper with the precision of an IRS auditor. In the end, she may find that the profits have not been correctly reported to her.

Well, he paid every cent he could pay. He couldn't pay her anymore than he did, and still can't. His overhead is outrageous, especially with all of Andy's therapy, tutoring, and legal problems, the expenses of the twins, plus keeping his wife happy.

Oh, and get this! His ex doesn't even want to win! She doesn't actually want to be the primary parent, although that's what she says in the legal papers. No, he knows her, unfortunately. What she wants more than anything else is revenge. She wants him to suffer as she suffers. And she will not stop until she has accomplished that.

How the hell will he break the news to Monica? She'll go nuts when she hears that the crazy ex is dragging his ass back to court. Monica expects him to focus on her and the boys. She wants him to end it with the ex.

Whoever said nice guys finish last was some kind of genius. Because when Monica hears the news, his ex will be the only woman screwing him.

HON. STRATHMORE REED, JR.

9. THE HELLMAN HOME

What was I thinking? Strathmore Reed, Jr. asks himself as he smoothes the collar of his navy blazer. Somehow he let his retired buddy, Hank Hellman, talk him into a blind date – a foursome consisting of cocktails and appetizers at the Hellman home in Oakdale. Although the two judges worked together for 10 years on the Sequoia County Superior Court – met every morning at eight o'clock for coffee in the cafeteria, lunched together twice weekly with their retired colleagues, sat side-by-side at every judges' meeting – Strathmore has never before visited his friend's home. Little wonder. Hank's castle is more dismal than imagined – a cookie-cutter ranch sandwiched between a speedboat and RV on the one side and garden gnomes illuminated by flashing lights on the other. Why hadn't he insisted on a rendezvous in neutral territory? Because, were he to answer his own question truthfully, Hon. Henry H. Hellman (Ret.) would never go along with an arrangement if it weren't his idea. So Strathmore is stuck for the evening in a three-bedroom, 2½ -bath tract home, with a tray of Costco egg rolls and an apprehensive blind date waiting for him inside. The whole dreadful setup makes his teeth ache.

Strathmore checks his watch and sighs. Still several minutes early. For once he wishes traffic or road conditions had hampered his arrival. Although it has been several decades since he has been on a date – and how preposterous is it for a man of his age to be using that term again? – he refuses to present himself before the appointed hour. He went to college, after all, and remembers how people made merciless fun of early arrivals. Show up five or ten minutes early, as he once did in a fit of youthful enthusiasm, and you might as well wear a sign announcing, "Hello, I'm lonely, desperate, and overanxious." Which, now that he thinks about it, is how he feels now, shivering in his late-model Mercedes outside of Hank's home: Anxious, extremely anxious, overanxious. Worse, he can think of several valid reasons to justify his anxiety. What right-thinking, semi-attractive woman would want to date him? How could he be anything but a disappointment? He's not particularly brilliant, witty, or charming. No one would call him dashing, dapper, or debonair. Nor could he be described as tall, dark, or handsome. As far as first impressions go, an accurate description by an objective observer is closer to ho-hum and tedium.

Still, he consoles himself, he does have a little money, and, thanks to his famous father, he can boast of name recognition the likes of which any politician would envy. And he has his position with the court. While not exactly a "babe magnet" (as the bailiffs like to say) of the same force as, say, firefighter, heart surgeon or rock star, the job of judge rarely fails to impress.

Not that his job has been anything to write home about lately. In addition to the usual assortment of quarrelsome lawyers and their dreary parade of lawsuits over car crashes, property lines and unpaid credit cards, he has the added headache of Juvenile Drug Court. Never has he felt more out of place than there. It is almost as if he has been dropped in a foreign land with alien customs, costumes, and culture. The language, for starters, is unfathomable. Not the comfortable, Latinate legal terms he has mastered over the course of his career – litigate, mitigate, castigate, adjudicate – but unfamiliar acronyms and codes. The Drug Court team – consisting of a probation officer, deputy district attorney, public defender, and treatment professional – meets with him before court and deluges him with their talk of UA's, AA's, NA's; searches, sponsors, sanctions; home visits, home restriction, home detention. What in God's name are they talking about? And these adolescents! What a sorry band of misfits! Little wonder they're using drugs – who else would have them, other than the most marginal members of society? The boys shuffle into court attired in baggy pants and billowing T-shirts, accessorized with tattoos and eyebrow rings. As predicted, they smoke, spit, and grunt. The girls are done up in skimpy attire, distracting tongue rings, and plenty of black eyeliner. Sometimes he can scarcely tell mother from daughter – both appear to dress from the same slatternly closet. Oh, the apple does not fall far from the tree, that much is clear. One father came into court reeking of alcohol. Another set of divorced parents launched into a custody battle right before their horrified daughter's eyes. Whatever is he to do with these losers? Babysit them until another judicial appointment is made, that's what.

Six o'clock on the nose. Strathmore sighs, wishing one last time he were at home wearing his comfy slippers, listening to music, sipping a glass of port. Pull yourself together! He chides himself. It's just cocktails with Hank and his wife. If all else fails, he and Hank can always talk shop while the women catch up on girl-talk in the kitchen. These are decent people. In fact, they have put this evening together for his benefit. He can certainly grin and bear it, pretend to have a nice time, and say a polite goodbye at 7:30 at the latest.

Strathmore removes the key from the ignition as a sleek silver BMW pulls up behind him. It's that limited-issue model he saw advertised recently in the Wall Street Journal, boasting a sticker price of twice what he paid for his first home. Behind the wheel is, well, an angel – at least that's how she appears in his rearview mirror, illuminated by an overhead cabin light. She's beautiful, with creamy skin and short silvery hair. Heavens! This couldn't be his date, could it?

He will find out.

Strathmore steps from his sedan, pulls back his shoulders, and stands tall. She's going to be so disappointed when she sees him! Nevertheless, he clears his throat decisively, and strides to the car behind him. Almost immediately, the BMW door opens and the angel emerges, smiling, petite, dressed in an elegant gray skirt suit, carrying an enormous bouquet of beribboned and fragrant lilies.

"There's my judge!" she exclaims, her face lit up as if she is in the presence of sexy spy-film star and not the widowed charity-case of friends.

"Skylar?" he asks, smiling shyly. "I'm Strathmore."

"I know who you are," she sings, slipping an arm through his as if they were old chums. "Brrr! It's cold out here, isn't it? Yes, you're my judge! I served on a jury of yours!"

"You d-did?" Strathmore asks. The knot in his stomach releases and a sense of relief washes over him. Why hadn't Hank given him this valuable bit of information? It would've changed Strathmore's view of the entire evening. She's already met him, in a way; seen him – admittedly, in his most favorable light – and agreed to the blind date anyway. She must've stared at him for days on end, noticed his thinning hair, observed his sometimes-irritable demeanor, his stuttering concern. And still she said yes to tonight! All

Hank had told him was that Skylar was an attractive gal – which, Strathmore observes, is the understatement of the year – who was perhaps ten years his junior. She'd lost her husband and was a successful self-employed financial advisor.

"I was Juror Number Seven, the first seat in the front row of the jury box, closest to you," Skylar says. "Before coming to your court, I didn't want to serve on the jury at all – I know! I'm sorry! But my work keeps me so busy. You gave me quite a lecture about my civil obligation to serve."

"Yes," Strathmore nods, registering a small shiver of embarrassment. Though he himself has never served on a jury – has in fact ordered the court's CEO to strike his name from the juror rolls so that he will never be bothered with a jury summons – he firmly believes in the obligation of others to discharge their duty of citizenship. "It's a talk I regularly deliver. I hope it wasn't too—" Too what? Strathmore wonders. Predictable? Tiresome? Humorless?

Graciously, Skylar fills in for him. "No! Not at all. You weren't too anything, except right. You made me think about jury service in a different way. I had only seen it as a burden meant for others to fulfill – something for retirees, trust-fund children, unemployed executives. But you made me realize that if – knock on wood! – I were ever involved in litigation, I would want a cross-section of willing citizens to serve on my jury, not just people with a lot of time on their hands. So, the first break we took, I called my office and instructed my secretary to cancel everything, told her that I was going to serve if you would have me."

"Excellent!" Strathmore comments. He searches his mind but has no memory of ever meeting this beautiful lady with the lively gray eyes and perfect complexion. Undoubtedly he had been more focused on the evidence and the dark suits vying for his attention. "What an unexpected pleasure to meet you again."

"Thank you. Just for the record, you did scare me a bit." She laughs lightly. "That black robe is intimidating."

This much Strathmore knows. Unlike some of his colleagues – the colorful Presiding Judge Marion Berkeley, for example, who rarely identifies herself as a judge and who sheds her robe as soon as she is out of the courtroom door – Strathmore thinks of his judicial robe as a management tool. He is perfectly aware that most citizens would rather endure a colorectal exam than jury service. The judicial robe, together with the raised bench and a certain reproachful gaze, is particularly effective when urging individuals to do the right thing when summoned to serve. "You must remind me of which case you had," he says.

From seemingly another world, a house door opens and his friend Hank shouts out, "Hello? The party's inside!"

Strathmore all but jumps out of his wingtips when he realizes he has been standing outside on a cold, starry January night, with the arm of a lovely woman tucked into his.

"Right-o, Hank!" he calls back.

Hank's wife joins him at the front door and waves. "The drinks are getting warm and the food is getting cold!" she cries.

"Wouldn't it be perfect if we could stay out here by ourselves?" Skylar whispers, giving his arm an intimate squeeze.

Strathmore registers a conspiratorial thrill. "Shall we gulp a drink and say some quick goodbyes? We could meet at Tre Sorelli at eight."

"Is that an order?" Skylar asks, with a flirtatious smile followed by a most welcome and generous nod of assent.

ANDY

10. DRUG COURT HOMEWORK

A Cage with a View

When I was little and my parents were still together, Mom came home from the flea market all wide-eyed and excited, her cheeks as red as her rain coat. She had a surprise; she loved surprises and couldn't wait to show us! But first, first! We had to guess what it was. Twenty questions, yes-or-no only, come on, guess! Dad was terrible at these games. He could never get the difference between a regular question and a yes-or-no-question, so he asked semi-sarcastic things like, "Well, how much did you overpay for it?" and "Why don't you just tell us what it is?" While I, clever child and mother expert, asked permissible but not very useful things like, "Is it pink?" "Does it taste yummy?" "Can I have it?" Dad gave up after a couple questions, dropped his broom and picked up a beer, while I played along. When I lost, she made me close my eyes, and I waited for her to surprise me with something that was green but didn't go in a salad.

"Ta-da!" she exclaimed, pulling a sheet off her package to reveal a green-orange-turquoise parrot. "His name is Pepita! Isn't he gorgeous?"

"Shit!" Dad scowled. "I hate birds. They make a mess, they're noisy, and these damn things, they live for-fucking-ever. Take it back. We're not getting a bird."

"You're right, honey," Mom said. "We're not 'getting' a bird. We 'got' one."

This kind of thing made Dad insane. Mom had a way of taking his words and using them against him. He could never understand how she did it, and then he would try to choose his words carefully, but that would get him all tangled up, and in the end, he shut up altogether. But this time, before surrendering, he tried one last ploy: me.

"Your cute little bird here? He's got jaws of steel. He can crack open a little girl's finger like a peanut. He can peck out a little girl's eyes like kernels on a corncob. If that vicious shit so much as touches my daughter, I'm taking the cage outside, opening his little door, and telling him to take a flying leap."

Mom won, of course, and Pepita was hung in his cage in the living room, well above my reach, in front of a window. Mom was his only friend. I *was afraid of him because of what Dad said and because he made this blood-curdling scream every time you walked near.*

Mom made me teach him how to talk. "Hi, my name is Pepita!" I'd recite over and over. He'd tilt his little green head, and I wondered if he was listening or picturing how my fingers tasted like peanuts. "Try singing!" Mom would say. So I'd sing, "Hola Chiquita! Me llamo Pepita!"

Pepita did not sing. He screeched.

Dad yelled at him to shut up. Mom yelled at Dad to do the same.

Then things got worse.

Why was Pepita shedding? It was summer, the days were warm, so it made sense, sort of, that we found smelly fluffs of grayish puffballs under his cage. Dad would sweep them up, and the next day, there would be more. This went on for a while, until Mom noticed that Pepita had bald patches. Pepita wasn't shedding at all. He was using those jaws of steel to yank out his own feathers.

And then one day, like someone flipped a switch, Pepita started talking. But instead of singing in my cute little voice, "Hola Chiquita! Me llamo Pepita!" he spoke in the voices of my mother and father, angry voices with dead-on impersonations. Pepita would repeat snatches of their arguments, usually when we were eating dinner.

"Bryan! You dumbshit!" Pepita would screech in my mother's voice, just as Dad was washing up. "What did you call me?" Dad would say. "Shut up!" Pepita would shout in Dad's voice. "I didn't say anything!" Mom would argue, throwing down a plate of spaghetti and running off to her room.

It was horrible. I hated hearing my parents argue the first time around, but usually there was a cease-fire during dinner. Pepita picked the one quiet time of the day to replay their fights.

Finally, one night as we were sitting down to eat, Pepita let loose with a vile exchange. "That's it!" Dad grumbled, pushing back his chair. He stomped into the living room, unhooked the bird cage, and took it outside. He opened the cage door and started yelling, "Go on, you little fuck! You're free! Fly away! Go!"

But Pepita did not go. His door was wide open. The night was warm. There were trees on every side of our house – oaks, bays, manzanita, redwood. He could have had any kind of home he wanted. But he stayed in his cage, yanking his feathers, repeating horrible fights in my parents' voices, until he died a few days later, huddled at the bottom of his cage, a bald lump of scarred flesh.

It was a relief.

850 words.

My probation officer, Karla (or, as I call her, "Killer"), is keeping me out of school for a while, making me work at home where I'm not exposed to the "people, places and things" associated with old friends and using. She gives me homework every couple of days, like this 850-word essay. She's got a million shitty ideas of things to write about. Like today's topic, a happy memory from my childhood. I don't know why I thought it was happy, but it's 850 words, and I'm not about to write it again.

I bet she drops by today. The Killer never tells me when she'll bust in, wants to keep me "scared straight," as she says, by surprise visits. I'm on house arrest now, thanks to Monica. The bitch felt it was her moral obligation to rat me out for ONE FUCKING 12-OUNCE CAN OF BEER that wasn't even hers but Dad's. I didn't even get drunk and I got placed on house arrest again, which basically means I'm a prisoner in my room. The Killer says I have to detox, start thinking again like normal (whatever that's supposed to mean), before I'm allowed to rejoin the human race. Other than the fact that I feel mostly dead, I don't mind that much. I still have nightmares about how horrible the Hall was. It's like being sick – when you don't feel great, your bed is pretty much where you want to be.

Wanna know what your PO does when she drops in for a visit? She sniffs through your underwear drawer – not an exaggeration. She searches your pockets, peaks under your mattress, reads your diary from when you were 11. Finds empty wine bottles and makes you talk about the night you drank it and the fuckface you drank it with. She tells you your room is like an x-ray of your brain, that whatever is going on inside your brain she sees on the outside, and what she sees in my room is a spoiled child with too much free time. You'd like to tell her to stick it, but you're pretty sure she carries a lethal weapon. You never know when she'll pop in, but I bet she comes today: I've got 30 days clean and sober. The Killer will express surprise. She will question me closely, look for ways to find out whether I'm lying. In the end, she'll give me a pep talk and a squeeze of the shoulder. I know she expects me to feel happy! Joyous! Free!

Instead I feel like shit.

I hate my life. It's dull. Bleak. Boring.

Outside it's raining. I used to love the rain, the sound of it on the roof and the way it made you feel so cozy inside. I used to love putting on winter clothes, rubber boots, mittens, a funny hat crocheted by Granny, and skipping outdoors with an umbrella. I remember racing down the street, putting my nose up to the sky, feeling so happy to be in the rain. Why was that fun? Now I don't see the point of it.

My room feels cramped and stale, but I can't stand to leave. If I venture so far as the hallway, I get in a fight with Monica or one of my innocent little brothers. No one is safe from me. I'm mad and mean and nasty. And the worst thing is, everyone is super-nice to me. I say something shitty like, "Turn the TV down!" and they say, "Sure, dear!" I'm the ogre living under the bridge. The people feed me and speak softly to me, act like I'm a person and not an evil ogre. They hope, hope, hope that if they're nice enough, I will stay under the bridge where I won't attack them.

Other than my weekly court appearances, I haven't seen or talked to a person my age in a month. It's weird. Not one of my friends has called. It's like I never existed. I had friends – I know I did. We did stuff together. We laughed until our stomachs hurt. We shared lunches. We hated our parents together. Did they forget about me already? It's so freakin' lonely in here. But then, there's nothing I can do with them anyway. The Killer has made it very clear that if I so much as think about slipping out of my room, running over to the park and taking a puff, she will personally deliver my ass to a cinderblock cell, dress me in orange sweats, and leave me there for a long time. As The Killer says, "If you can't hack a few weeks in your own room, you don't have what it takes to stay in the Hall."

The only freedom left is freedom of thought. And so, yeah, I do think about getting high, but only every minute of the day and most of the night too.

But here's the thing about house arrest. It keeps me locked in my room. It stops me from living my life. But it also keeps the world out. Like my friends, who would get me into trouble, and my mother, who is killing me. Shit! She is *still* pissed at Dad for signing me up for Drug Court. So she did what she does best: filed new legal papers to make me live with her. Dad hasn't broken the news to me yet, but I found her latest rant on the kitchen table. Page after page about what a horrible father he is, how my sucky performance in school and in life are his fault. Lucky for me, I have an order from Judge Reed confining me to the home, and as long his order is in effect, my mother can't touch me.

So this must be why Pepita stayed in his cage. The cage might've kept the bird in, but it also kept the world out.

BRYAN

11. LAW OFFICES OF R. SEAMUS SHIELD

Bryan arrives at his lawyer's office a few minutes shy of the appointed hour. The lawyer is still yakking with a client, so Bryan shoots the breeze with his flirty receptionist, Misty. She's one of those great gals with the big hair and the wide eyes who hangs on to every word you say, so that you feel bigger and sexier when you're with her. It doesn't hurt, either, that she's endowed with a breathtaking bustline and wears the ruffly blouses to showcase her stuff. She also happens to be his lawyer's third wife, and, just like the bad cliché goes, she looks a lot like the first two, if a bit younger and blonder.

"Finally!" she says, removing her headset and smiling broadly when he enters. "It's my favorite guy in all clientdom!"

"Aw, you just say that because I bring you food," Bryan responds, handing her a box of today's pastries, knowing of her fondness for them.

"I can think of no greater basis for a deep and meaningful relationship," she murmurs with mock seriousness. Misty opens the box and buries her nose in the croissants. "Ohhhhhnnnn," she moans. "I'm in love."

"That is such bad luck for me, doll," he answers. "I'm already married with three kids plus I've got a crazy ex on my back."

"That *is* bad luck." She drops the box to her lap and sighs. "I guess I'll have to settle for this chocolate almond croissant." She closes her eyes, takes a bite of the croissant, and chews it slowly. She moans a little, licks her lips seductively, then opens her eyes. It's a damn good show for a law office receptionist.

"I feel used," Bryan winks and hands over the coffee. "Nonfat mocha, no whip, extra shot."

"You are my hero," she whispers, taking the cup. "I'll make sure all your legal bills are cut in half."

"He'll still find a way to get in my wallet," he says, rolling his eyes toward the lawyer's closed door. "I swear, I get billed when he dreams about my case."

She shushes me with her long, pink fingernail. How she types with those nails is anyone's guess. "He's coming! Pull up your zipper and look respectable!"

He backs into a chair just as the inner door opens. A lithe woman emerges, early thirties with drop-dead-gorgeous hair: waist-length, wavy, and red. Wow! Honestly, it's the exact kind of hair they show in advertisements for high-end salon products. She's wearing yoga clothes, a skimpy top that shows off a fit midriff, and form-fitting pants that reveal a firm derriere. She's toting a designer handbag that retails for a small fortune. In it is one of those yippy dogs that are all the rage these days for rich women. He hates it when those pocket pooches show up in the shop – creates all kinds of problems with the health department and annoys the hell out of the cat lovers. It looks like she's been crying, but he drops his gaze so she won't think he's staring, which, obviously, he is.

As if they were in a funeral parlor, the lawyer escorts her through the waiting room. He's decked out in his Tony Soprano courtroom uniform – dark pinstripe suit, starched black shirt, silver tie. He still looks like a linebacker, broad across the shoulders, long torso, short legs. Bryan is fairly sure he colors his big head of bushy hair so that it's still the shiny black of his prime, but in spite of the many things they've shared, that's the kind of info he'll never disclose. But who is Bryan kidding? He'll be the first guy to rub in a little shoe polish when the temples go silver. The lawyer shakes the hand of Lady Godiva, mutters some soothing advice, and quietly closes the door behind her.

"Oh. My. God," he exhales slowly, backing against the door as if blocking intruders. His dark eyes are round and shiny, and his mouth is twitching at the corners. "Quick! Into my office! You won't fucking believe this one!"

The lawyer, R. Seamus Shields, and Bryan go way back. So far back that Bryan knows that the "R" stands for Rocco, and that's what he calls him, even if the rest of the world refers to him as "Seamus," "Mr. Shields," "Counselor," "My ex," or a not-so-choice name that references his owing money for high-risk sport betting. Rocco and Bryan played football together in high school – or, more accurately, Bryan sat on the bench while Rocco intercepted the ball and the girls. They messed around a lot the way dumb kids do. After almost flunking out of junior college – they smoked a lot of pot back in the day – Rocco made it into San Francisco State and then night school at Golden Gate. It took him a couple stabs to pass the bar exam, but he made it to the finish line, and holy crapoli, did they party like there was no tomorrow. The day Rocco was licensed, he set up shop in their hometown, and he's represented Bryan ever since. He's still pissed off at Bryan for running off and marrying Connie while he was in college, says it's the biggest fucking mistake of Bryan's life, even if it has kept him in business over the years and catapulted him into the "matrimonial specialist" that he is. The lawyer actually made his client swear that he would never marry again without getting his approval first. Luckily Rocco gave his blessing to the union with Monica. No surprise, since Bryan is pretty sure his lawyer tried to hit on her once or twice himself, the swine.

"Who was that?" Bryan asks. "She looks familiar."

"Wait'll you hear this!" Rocco says gleefully. "This is the best one yet. But! Business first." He opens his top drawer, removes a check, and waves it in front of Misty.

She drops her jaw and snatches it from him. "Ten thousand clams! That makes me hot. I'll hammer this one *tout de suite*!"

Rocco hangs up his suit jacket, drops into his big swivel chair, and folds his hands on his desk. "Ladies and gentlemen of the jury," he enunciates solemnly. "I preface my remarks with this simple observation: You cannot make up the shit you see in this job! I swear to God!"

Misty laughs appreciatively, as if she has not heard him say this a hundred times. Bryan knows he has, and he's not even married to the fucker. Rocco does tell juicy stories about the stuff he hears from his clients, but it always makes Bryan nervous. Even though they are friends, it doesn't seem right. For starters, Bryan doesn't think his lawyer would talk shit about him when he walks out, but still. That's another of those things they never talk about.

"Members of the jury, I trust you are familiar with the raw food, vegetarian restaurant on Fourth Street?" Rocco says in his Boston Legal best.

"Jessica's!" Bryan claps his hands in recognition. "That's where I've seen her. She's the owner, right? She's Jessica."

"I've always wanted to eat there," Misty says, twirling a stray wisp of blond hair and frowning slightly. "But then I end up stopping at the corner deli and ordering a hot pastrami and swiss."

Rocco shakes his head sadly. "I'm sorry, baby, but your raw food option has expired. Last Saturday night, Jessica served up her final alfalfa sprout."

"Really?" Misty leans forward, giving her husband a great shot of the goods. "Did something happen?"

"Yes, you could say that," Rocco answers. "Jessica's husband is a jillionaire, made a fortune in investment banking. He was underwriting the whole restaurant operation to support the raw-food passion of his babe-a-licious bride. Last Saturday, he popped into the restaurant for a little carrot-gingko pick-me-up while he was thought to be at a birthday party with the kids. Surprise! He discovers the head chef, a dude he hand-picked for the position, doing the nasty with his beloved bride on the bread board. The bread board!"

Misty and Bryan gasp. Rocco is doubled over in laughter, and maybe it is kind of funny, but jeez, if you're the husband walking in on that hubbub, wouldn't that sort of kill you? Shit.

"Husband grabs a paring knife but apparently thinks better of it, which is too damn bad because it really would've maximized my client's settlement if he'd gone a little postal on her. Oh, if we had him on D.V. charges, his buckets of ducats would've been ours to plunder. Alas, it was not to be. Husband, cool as a cucumber – an organic cucumber, no doubt – waltzes into the dining room and announces to the assembled, 'Bon appétit! Dinner's on me! Thank you for your patronage.' Then he scoops up the boys from the birthday party, flies off to their winter home in Sun Valley, and leaves a text message telling Jilted Jessica to get herself a lawyer by Wednesday, so that his people can finalize the terms of the divorce, on better terms than the pre-nup permits."

"Amazing," Misty says. "I'm wondering, honey, would it be a conflict of interest for you to give me his phone number? I mean, he's free now, and probably kind of sad and lonely, and, gosh, he's sitting on all that money…"

Rocco looks at Bryan and rolls his eyes. "Can you believe my wife? A looker and a wit, all in one package!"

Bryan is still trying to get the picture of Jessica, the chef and the bread board out of his mind. He doesn't understand how it could have happened that way. He knows that if one of his baristas shows up with something as simple as a hangover on a Sunday morning, it backs up the lines. But horizontal folk dancing in a restaurant kitchen on a Saturday night? That had to slow the dinner orders to a screeching halt.

"It's like I always say," Rocco laughs in advance at his own hilarity. "I hope the fucking you got is worth the fucking you're gonna get."

"On that note," Misty announces, standing and rearranging her ruffles. "I'll let you men talk business. Bryan's file is on your credenza." She points to the banker's box with "Bretano" hand-lettered on the side. It is overflowing with file folders, legal pads, tax returns, bank statements, cancelled checks, deposition transcripts and other expensive memorabilia you collect after years of murderous litigation with your crazy ex-wife.

"Speaking of 'the fucking you're gonna get,'" Rocco says. "Get ready to bend over the fence post on this motion. This is gonna hurt."

"So, what else is new?" Bryan snorts.

"She's asking for sole legal custody of Andrea, as usual, but this time she's got a new angle. She's blaming Andrea's drug problem on you. She wants you to cough up ten grand for some genetic testing that will prove you have the DNA responsible for Andrea's marijuana jones."

He lets that sink in before handing his client a big stack of papers. It's an amended declaration Connie filed with the court, and he's circled the bad part for Bryan to read. It says:

"I was out of state over the New Year's holiday and Andrea was in her father's custody. I am informed and believe and thereon allege that Andrea was permitted to sneak out the window of her father's home one night. She used intoxicants and was subsequently arrested for public intoxication. Her father enrolled her in Juvenile Drug Court without my consent, even though we currently share joint custody of our daughter.

"I have serious concerns about the suitability of this program for my daughter. The participants in the program appear to be defiant, deficient and drug-addicted criminals with histories of street-gang affiliations or prostitution charges. I do not believe it is in the best interests of our daughter to associate with these deeply disturbed adolescents.

"I do not believe it is in Andrea's best interests to remain in her father's home. Father drinks alcoholically. He is a recreational marijuana user. He was once arrested for possession of marijuana. His current spouse was and may still be a soft porn model. Some of her photos are available on the Internet. [See Exhibit C to this declaration]

"Andrea does not consume intoxicants in my home. She does not leave the house without permission. I do not use illegal drugs or drink alcoholic beverages.

"Andrea's grades have plummeted since she started high school, and this bears a direct relation to the increase in time she has had in her father's home.

"It is detrimental for Andrea to remain in her father's home. The conflict generated by his unilateral parenting decisions is deleterious to the health and safety of Andrea. I therefore request that sole legal and physical custody be awarded to me, with the right of limited visitation reserved to Father."

His hands are shaking by the time he gets to the last page. All the anger and grief she has caused him for the last ten years is roiling through him, and he wants to scream. When will it end?

"How can she tell these lies to the court? This is all a bunch of made-up crap! How can she get away with this? Can we file papers and say she's a blood-sucking vampire? I mean, why not? What are the rules here?"

"Calm down, Bryan," Rocco says soothingly. "Don't get your damn panties in a knot. This is the usual shit she throws at you, just dressed up in a new package. None of it ever sticks. You know the drill."

"It's so outrageous!" he shouts, refusing to be calmed. "She just makes up this crap, and it all costs me thousands of dollars! Why can't she be punished for saying this stuff? Monica a soft porn model? This is pure, unadulterated horseshit! Monica modeled lingerie once for a catalog when she was in college fifteen years ago. My arrest for smoking pot? I was 16!"

"Stop," the lawyer orders, all the jokiness drained from his voice. "Bryan, I was *there*. I know. We've been through this before, and we'll go through it again. It's going to work out. None of her stuff ever flies. The court mediation people will talk to Andrea. She'll tell them she wants to stay with you. Or she won't. She's a teenager now – it's not like anyone can make her stay anywhere she doesn't want to stay."

The thought of losing Andrea to her mother kills him. Kills him! He has always promised to protect his daughter, take care of her, fight for her. They both know her mother is nuts, that she feels safer with her father. "I've told Andy I will do whatever it takes, and I will. I'm not going to roll over on this."

"Nor should you. But it's going to be a ball-buster," the lawyer says. "This Drug Court thing might create more problems than it solves."

"What's that supposed to mean?" Bryan shouts. Come on! Is he saying he can lose his daughter because he put her in a court program? What kind of a messed-up fire drill is this?

"Well, it's gonna get personal. Connie's come up with a clever angle on this addiction thing, claiming Andy's problem with drugs is related to your fooling around with drugs. There could be some Fifth Amendment issues here. We're going to have to be careful. We might need to bring in a criminal lawyer. And it's going to cost you some dough."

Bryan buries his head in his hands. "What are we talking about?"

"Probably 10-15 thousand dollars. I'm going to need a retainer. Anyone else I'd charge them ten. For you, I'll make it five."

Five thousand dollars. Bryan moans. "I can't. It's Monica. She's had it with the fighting. She won't let me spend more money on lawyers. Says it's costing us tens of thousands of dollars a year, money we don't have. She's sick of going to court, says I need to get out of this relationship with my ex."

Rocco is dismissive. "Monica will understand. She's a good girl. And if you choose to keep this a secret from her, well, no one but no one tells their spouse everything. Cut me a check from the business account. I'll apply it to one of your corporate bills. Monica doesn't need to know about this. Why don't I have Misty put in a discreet call to your bookkeeper?"

Bryan nods. Even in his stunned state, he knows he is making a mistake, but what choice is there? He simply can't let his only daughter hang out to dry.

Rocco puts his arm around Bryan. "Hang in there, man. We'll get through this."

Suddenly Bryan can't wait to get out of his office. The whole thing is making him sick. His ex is like this gigantic monster that can't be destroyed and is sucking him dry. "Okay," he says, jumping up. "Do what you have to do. Prepare whatever papers need to be filed with the court. Put it off for as long as you can. Hopefully I can get Monica to change her mind on this lawsuit thing."

"Deal." Then Rocco says what he always says. "You asshole, you should have talked to me before you married the bitch."

If there ever were a time Bryan thought that was funny, it was long, long ago.

HON. STRATHMORE REED, JR.

12. BLACK & WHITE

Strathmore Reed, Jr. was utterly unprepared to enjoy himself so thoroughly at the annual Sequoia Valley Symphony Dinner-Dance. Historically, it is an evening of forced small talk, cold hors d'oeuvres, and long speeches. But tonight, with Skylar on his arm (outfitted in an understated black cashmere dress and looking like royalty), the conversations flow like wine, the guests look elegant in their black-and-white attire, and the food is surprisingly presentable. So when Skylar squeezes his arm an hour into the cocktail party and asks if he is having a good time, no one is more stunned than he when a smile breaks across his face and he responds affirmatively.

"But I don't understand it at all," he confesses. "It is entirely irregular. I can only conclude that it is your doing."

She looks up at him adoringly, her gray eyes judiciously made up, her ears graced with substantial emerald-cut diamonds. She draws his arm a bit closer to her, so that he inhales her intoxicating French perfume. "I plead guilty, Your Honor," she whispers playfully. "I only ask that you show me some mercy."

"'The quality of mercy is not strain'd, It droppeth as the gentle rain from heaven, Upon the place beneath,'" Reed recites. When he was a history major at Dartmouth, he didn't read much Shakespeare, but back in the day he enjoyed a photographic memory and developed a modest reputation for his ability to read and recite anything from econ theory to complex mathematical functions. During keggers, frat brothers would challenge him to memorize various materials, mostly dry but sometimes risqué, and one of these dares involved Portia's famous speech. Although Reed has long since forgotten the tedious textbook selections, the poetry passages have not only stayed with him but have proven surprisingly useful over the years.

Skylar shakes her head in awe. "You're brilliant. Is there anything you don't know?"

Strathmore blushes with pleasure. "Let me think, my dear. Yes, there is one thing: I don't know why we aren't at the bar refilling our glasses."

The silver-haired couple strolls across the room, arm in arm. The new Sequoia Valley Sports Complex has been magnificently transformed for the night's festivities. The large hall is filled with round tables covered in white linen tablecloths and expertly adorned with artistic floral centerpieces, formal dinnerware, and hundreds of flickering candles, reflected brilliantly in strategically placed mirrors. The hardwood floors are gleaming, and the ceiling is decorated with flowing black and white banners. The string quartet on stage is playing a lovely piece by, if Strathmore is not mistaken, Vivaldi. Large black-and-white photographs of the symphony are displayed on the walls. The youthful and energetic wait staff, attired in crisp tuxedos, greet guests, offer hors d'oeuvres and serve champagne in fluted crystal. All in all, the room has the feel of a bustling San Francisco ballroom, blemished only occasionally when a lost swimmer from the outdoor pool wanders in barefoot in search of the locker room.

As they work their way to the bar, several vaguely familiar lawyers greet Reed respectfully. In each instance, Skylar introduces herself and shakes the lawyer's hand, a gesture Reed appreciates enormously – not just because her social ease and self-assuredness impress him, but also because he honestly can't tell one lawyer from the next. He knows he should recognize the regulars by now, but the fact is, he has no clue. They are all dark-suited, quick-witted and younger than he, and any superficial differences he might observe fade away when they start talking volubly and interminably.

Following one set of introductions, a fortyish lawyer tells his wife about a recent case he tried before Judge Reed. His wife listens, clearly bored but making an effort to be polite. Strathmore feels much the same. After a long week in the courthouse, the last thing he wants to hear about on a Saturday night is another legal case. But it seems to be an occupational hazard that judges are doomed to endure: listening to lawyers wax poetic about their legal victories, any time of the day or night, with or without a courtroom.

"And then during jury selection," the lawyer continues, now in full swing, "Judge Reed tells me to take the first twelve in the box and get on with it! So when the first twelve are seated, I accept the panel, and it's the best jury I've ever 'selected'!"

"Isn't he brilliant?" Skylar interjects. "That is just so interesting! And if you would forgive my wicked lapse of modesty, I believe I have an even better story about jury selection."

"Better than *that*?" the lawyer's wife asks, her tone dripping with sarcasm. "Oh, do tell!"

"I met my date when I was summoned for jury duty!" Skylar gushes.

This little bit is sufficiently enticing for the lawyer to drop his braggadocio and beg to hear more. Before answering, Skylar looks up at Reed and smiles tentatively, as if asking permission.

"When I was called for jury duty, I had a pre-planned business trip out of the country scheduled for later in the week. After spending the morning in Judge Reed's courtroom, I was so taken with the judge's commanding presence, legal brilliance, sharp wit, and, well, unmistakable charm, I practically pleaded with the lawyers to select me to serve on the jury. As soon as the first break came, I called my assistant and told her to cancel my business trip."

The crowd reacts appreciatively, and no one more so than Reed, who, for the life of him, still cannot believe he had an attractive female juror paying more attention to him than the evidence. How could he have missed that? He must've been taking copious notes during that trial.

"He doesn't even know this part yet," Skylar says to the lawyer and his wife, with a shy glance toward Reed. "As soon as the case was over, I phoned everyone I knew in legal circles to see if they could make a social introduction of me to this judge. Finally I found someone who would fix me up with him. We hit it off immediately, and here we are!"

"Wonderful!" the lawyer says, enthusiastically. "That *is* the best jury selection story I've ever heard! I've heard of jurors dating after a trial, never about a judge and juror striking up a relationship. It should be in the legal journals!"

Reed smiles broadly as Skylar steers him away from the knot of lawyers and toward the bar. Not only did Skylar's conversational gambit rescue him from a lawyer's endless self-promotion speech, but she recounted this entertaining gem and cast him in the starring role!

"That was quite a remarkable story," he says to her privately.

"Thank you, Judge" she whispers. "I hope to have more of them."

At the bar, he places their order for one chardonnay and one pinot noir. Because the night is going so splendidly, he slips an uncharacteristically large bill in the bartender's tip jar.

"Ratty, old man! Is it you?" comes a booming voice from behind.

Strathmore Reed groans inwardly as he feels a sloppy arm thrown across his shoulders. Only one person in all of Sequoia Valley refers to him as Ratty, and it's Maxwell Lloyd Taylor, his former law partner from Father's firm. Over the last 20 years, Reed has informed him on multiple occasions that he does not appreciate being addressed as such, but Max is unstoppable. He is an arrogant son-of-a-bitch who married into one of the wealthiest families in town, making him filthy rich on top of his other annoying qualities. Although he must be 50 or 55 years old by now, Max somehow has managed to retain his boyish good looks. He is lean, which helps, and still has a full head of hair. If it's a rug, it's a damn good one. He doesn't look a day over 40, with the perennial tan of a sailor. Tonight he is wearing an all-white tuxedo, and instead of looking like a horse's ass, which any man would, he looks rather dapper.

"Good evening, Max," Reed manages. "Skylar, let me introduce you to my former law partner, Max Taylor."

"Max Taylor," Skylar says with a charming smile. "How nice to meet you."

"I saw that old Mercedes of yours in the parking lot and wondered if you could still be driving it," Max says with his typical hail-fellow-well-met humor. "How the hell are you?"

The crowd has thickened and somehow Reed finds himself squeezed into a tight spot, with no easy way to escape. Good Lord, stuck in a crowded corner with the most insufferable fathead in the room. Well, he consoles himself, dinner will be served shortly and the crowd will be seated; Skylar is at his side, which makes an event like this much more bearable; and, with a conversationalist like Max, there's no need to say a thing, since Max has a limitless ability to talk about himself. This time, Max launches into a lavish tale involving stupendous dollar figures and a new home on Molokai, pointing out how vastly superior it is to "those crappy condos in Kauai. Oh, that's right, Ratty, didn't you buy one of those?"

Reed winces. Skylar excuses herself for a moment, handing her wine to Reed, who is tempted to drink it along with his own. He doesn't, of course, ever mindful of the legal limit for drinking and driving as well as his lot in life to be, as well as appear, "sober as a judge." But a blowhard like this could drive even a devout teetotaler to drink. Where are all the other lawyers in this crowd, and why don't they break in on this dreadful conversation? Max describes his new Ferrari, golf club membership, and sailboat. It's as though he is opening his toy box and showing off every shiny new toy in it. "How you could give up the partnership draw to live on a state court salary is beyond me," Max adds between toys.

When Skylar rejoins them, she is smiling radiantly. Reed greets her and hands her the glass of wine. "I'm just hearing about Max's delightful new sailboat."

"So what's new with the courts, Ratty? Didn't I just read something about you in the Daily Journal?" Before Reed can answer, Max answers his own question. "I know what it is! It's your new position with Juvenile Drug Court!"

"Yes, that's right," the judge says. "Therapeutic courts are very big right now. I'm still finding my way with these young people. It's quite a different approach from the 'crime and punishment' model of our law school days. The focus is on long-term rehabilitation, and the research shows that drug courts work. Improve lives. Reduce recidivism. Save taxpayers money."

Max chuckles. "You've come a long way, baby. You started your career with the biggest law firm in the U.S. doing complex business litigation, moved on to Fortune 500 mergers and acquisitions, appeared once or twice before the Supreme Court to shape new law of the land. And now here you are, at the pinnacle of your career, hearing about 15- year-old punks smoking pot and joyriding! Bet you're sorry now you didn't hold out for an appointment to the federal bench!"

Reed has had enough of this clown. He's just about to excuse himself when Skylar breaks in.

"Ah, but you might want to learn more about drug courts," she says. "It would have been perfect for Max, Jr., don't you think?"

"Excuse me?" Max glares at Skylar, like she's a little dog who just bit his ankle.

"If we'd had Drug Court when your son was in prep school, you could have addressed his addiction issues early, so he wouldn't have had to suffer through all those awful consequences – flunking out of Providence College in his first year, serving time in jail, crashing your wife's Lexus," she explains sweetly. Where did she get this information? It's too good, and the appalled look on Max's face is worth twice the price of admission.

Skylar continues, "I surely hope his rehab works out for him this time. That's where he is now, right? I understand there's no better place than Sobriety Meadows for his particular problem. His disease must be especially difficult for you, sharing a name with him as you do, when all of his financial problems show up on your credit report. Good luck, really. Judge Reed and I hope for nothing but the best."

At that moment, the wait staff begins to usher guests to their tables, and the crowd finally breaks up. Max races off, just as if the gun sounded at the regatta.

"I hope you'll be sitting with us at our table," Skylar calls out to Max's back. "I'd love to continue the conversation!"

Reed stands still in utter amazement. The crowd around them swirls and jostles as guests rush to refill glasses, embrace old friends and jockey for good seats. He knows he's holding up the crowd by standing still, but he can't help but stop and stare at this amazing lady. For the first time, he takes her hand and looks at her face-to-face – a sweet, lovely smile on hers; a goofy new smile plastered across his.

"How did you do that?" he asks, holding his free hand across his heart. "It was better than the most polished closing argument from the most experienced lawyer! It was a calculated, articulate thing of beauty! And it was deft and unexpected to boot! I am in awe."

She giggles like a carefree girl. "Did you like that? I'm so pleased. No one is calling my judge 'Ratty.' My word, what an egotistical ass!"

Reed laughs. Not a chuckle, not a courtesy ha-ha, but a real, bottom-of-the-belly laugh, a laugh he hasn't felt in years and years and years. He had forgotten about the feeling of that laugh, the delicious, light wonderfulness of it all. "Do you know what my mother would say? 'The basis for any true friendship is not liking the same people, but hating the same people!'"

The string quartet starts playing a lively number, designed to motivate stragglers to take their seats. But Reed remains glued to the floor with his date.

"And where, if I might ask, did you get that juicy information?" Reed poses. "Is any of it true? Not that it matters!"

Skylar withdraws her cell phone from her evening bag. "We live in the information age, dear. Credit reports are my business. I did a quick search when I excused myself to go to the ladies' room, and it came up gold! Whether it's true or not, well, you saw the expression on his face. *You* be the judge."

Reed laughs again, at her resourcefulness as much as her wordplay, and this time his laugh is fuller and more delicious than before. People are going to think I'm drunk, he supposes. Yet oddly, he doesn't care.

Within moments, socialites from the planning committee spot Reed and his date and escort them to their chairs at the head table. As he takes his seat, he thinks of the hundreds of charity functions he has suffered through in his life, dull evenings spent checking his watch and waiting for the earliest opportunity to slip out the nearest exit. But he hopes this evening will never end. And in the same moment, he can scarcely wait for dinner to finish, so he can ask his delightful date to join him on the floor, where – dare he even hope? – they will dance the night away.

ANDY

13. WEEKEND UA

Monica and I fidget in opposite chairs in the living room while waiting for the weekly visit from my badass PO. Neither of us says a word, though we both fake-smile when our eyes accidentally collide. Deputy Killer laid down a new policy at our group meeting: All probationers must be awake, alert, and seated with a responsible adult when she comes a-calling. As she put it, "I'm done with pounding down doors at nine o'clock, eating your mom's cookies, and waiting for your sorry adolescent asses to roll out of bed!" One of the guys in Drug Court, Jess, who has epic acne from years of Ecstasy use, countered: "Maybe you could come after breakfast, say around three o'clock?" The Killer was not amused, especially when none of us could hold back on our smart-ass smirks.

The twins are in daycare so the house is unusually quiet, and Monica is coming off a cleaning bender, so the house is unusually orderly. She has set out a pot of tea and a plate of banana bread, sliced apples and a glob of fat-free cream cheese-like spread. She has taken extra care with her appearance today – her bouncy brown hair is secured by a neat headband, she's put on earrings and some pink lipstick, and is wearing one of her coordinated urban-mom get-ups – a little lime T-shirt paired with white yoga pants and hoodie, each with a matching lime stripe. By contrast, I look like the runaway kid on the back of the milk carton: straggly hair, slept-in shirt, ripped jeans, barefoot. It must make my stepmother's frosted nail polish curdle. She busies herself with a basket of the boys' clothes, fresh from the dryer, and folds them with factory-like precision.

"Is Dad coming?" I ask, hating my whiny voice and already knowing the answer, but hoping, always hoping, for something different.

She shakes her head and frowns. "I'm sorry, honey. He has a meeting."

I look down at my frayed homework assignment, some weak essay about the importance of telling the truth, which I cobbed off an Internet homework site. My fucking father. It's just not fair. When I joined this joke of a program two months ago, Dad promised the judge that he would participate in family meetings with the probation officer. I'm doing all the crap they ask of me, or most of it anyway, and so far, he's managed to skip out on every one of his obligations. Now that I think of it, only Monica has shown up every week. Of course she's not doing it for me – she's just covering for my dad.

The moment the doorbell rings, my stomach drops. Monica leaps from the chair, opens the door, and welcomes The Killer into our home with a cheerful hello. I fucking *hate* probation. Never ever agree to give up your rights under the Fourth Amendment. You have a constitutional right to be secure in your person, house, papers and effects! Until you're on probation, that is, and you can kiss your privacy rights *adiós*. Your probation officer has the right to search your home any time of the day or night, "with or without a warrant," as the court order says, "with or without probable cause." Translated into plain English, this means: your life sucks.

"Good morning, Monica! And look who's up and at 'em, Little Miss Sunshine!" The Killer flashes her ultra-white teeth. She's in full commando mode, wearing a trench coat with the collar flipped up, stiff khaki pants with a crease down the front, and shit-kicking lace-up boots. She has a large leather bag strapped across her chest, filled, no doubt, with search warrants, handcuffs, instant UA tests, billy clubs, and other tools of her trade.

"Care for some tea?" Monica offers, gesturing toward her snack setup.

Karla winces. "Any chance I could get some coffee? I left home at 5 A.M. to get in a run before work and didn't have time for coffee."

Monica giggles in her annoying girly way. "Are you kidding? You're in the Bretanos' house. I've got five kinds of beans, several grinders and an espresso machine. What would you like? Cappuccino? Latte? Soy? Nonfat? Regular? Decaf?"

"You are about to make my day," The Killer smiles, draping her coat carefully over the back of a chair. "When parents complain that their kid can't stop smoking pot, I say: Try giving up coffee. You'll feel sick for a few days, then dull and depressed for ages. Every time you pass a coffee shop, you'll want to go in for one little cup of hot, fresh java. Giving up pot is like that, only harder. Because, according to my sources who are experts on the subject, pot makes you feel a lot better than coffee. Right, Andrea?"

I shake my head, unwilling to join this stupid coffee klatch convo.

"Fortunately, my drug is legal," La Killer says. "Yes, Monica, I would love a latte. Two shots. Nonfat milk. A little sugar."

Monica races off to fulfill her barista duties, and The Killer nods at me with a cruel expression, all humor instantly evaporated.

"What?" I ask. It hasn't been two seconds and already she's ripping into me.

"Come on," she says. "Don't waste my time. You missed your weekend UA."

Bitch! Not, "Hi, how are you, how was your week?" Not, "You poor doll, this must be so stressful for you, going to court every week, jumping every time your PO calls!" Not, "Good job, you're dressed and ready to meet me with homework in hand." Just: "Guilty. You can't even meet the low expectations set for you."

"There's nothing to tell," I say, feeling the knot in my stomach tighten. "I overslept. Sorry."

"Overslept?" she repeats, her voice reeking with skepticism.

I shrug my shoulders. "Yeah. It happens. Happened."

"Pffffft," she replies. "Liar."

I drop my jaw. I can't believe she just said that to me! Why isn't Monica here to protect me? But then she'd never say such a thing in front of her. Monica carries on about how professional Karla is, how "experienced" and "professional." And isn't it so typical of grownups to be one way when parents are around and another when they're not? "Thanks for the vote of confidence," I practically spit. "Glad you're on my team."

"Oh, please, Andrea. Lose the fake indignity or learn to sell the line. You're not telling the truth, and you know it."

Now I'm really pissed. "Give me a break, will you? I stayed up late on Saturday night, watching a G-rated movie with my family. You've had me on home restriction for a hundred years. I'm stuck at home, bored to tears, doing loser family activities. I overslept on Sunday. You can ask Monica."

"I could," La Killer replies, as heartless as can be. "But she's not on probation. You are."

"Well my dad was supposed to wake me up and he didn't. I overslept. I wasn't perfect. Excuse me." It's true, too. You have to call Juvenile Services between eight and ten o'clock to find out if your UA number is up, and if it is, you have to be at their office by

11 A.M. and give a pee sample. I didn't even wake up until 11:30.

"How old are you?"

I snort. "Fifteen."

"Oh, phew. For a minute I thought you might be 7. At 15, you are old enough to use these inventions called alarm clocks. They work well. You can use the alarm clock to wake yourself up in the morning. In that way, you don't need to depend on your daddy."

Somewhere in this humiliating conversation, Monica delivers The Killer's coffee and slips out of the room, leaving me to fend for myself.

"Fine," I snap. "I didn't realize that oversleeping was the crime of the century."

The Killer sips her latte and backs off a bit. "So. Did you use this week?"

"No."

"Why do we require weekend UA's?"

"So you can tell if we used."

"Exactly," she says. "Sometimes teenagers aren't completely honest about their activities on weekends. But the UA never lies. Sometimes tests come back dirty when a kid swears up and down that she hasn't used. Your test helps me trust you when you say you're clean."

"Yeah," I say. "I know." I hate being treated like a child.

"Ready for your test?"

"Of course," I answer. I get up and walk toward the bathroom, like it's no big deal for me to pee in front of her, which maybe it shouldn't be, but somehow I find completely degrading.

"Anything you need to tell me about this sample you're about to give?" she asks.

I love talking about my pee. "Nope."

"Here," she says, handing me a plastic cup. "Let me do a quick search before we get down to business."

I raise my arms over my head, and she pats down my body, pockets and waistband. Her fingers are so strong I have the impression she could crumple me like a piece of trash. Considering how much I hate her, it's creepy having her fingers all over me. I hang my head and pretend this isn't happening. One of the boys in Drug Court was just caught with a vial of pee tucked into his coin pocket. He had talked his baby brother into giving it to him. The Killer found it during her search, and now he's spending spring quarter in the Hall. Ninety days. I would die.

"Fine," she says. "You know the drill: Go in the bathroom, leave the door ajar, pee in the cup. Hold the cup with one hand and place the other hand on the wall where I can see it. No running water from the faucet. I won't look at you, just at the hand on the wall. As soon as you're done, put the cup on the counter." She does a final search of the bathroom to make sure there are no signs of cheating.

It's every bit as demeaning as it sounds.

"By the way," she says as I'm in the bathroom posed in the most vulnerable position imaginable, "if you smoked on Saturday night, it'll show in this sample. Unlike alcohol, which dissipates within hours of use, pot stays in your system for days and days. I don't care how much water you drank, how many vitamins you chewed, or how many grapefruits you ate. The test won't lie."

I put the cup on the counter. She reaches in, removes it and closes the door.

If there were a window in the bathroom, I would crawl out of it and run away. But I'm stuck in a tiny, under-the-stairs, half-bath shit hole, and the only way out is through the door I came in. I look at my reflection in the mirror. I'm not fooling anyone. Fuck my life.

Back in the living room, The Killer checks my AA card for attendance and is looking over last week's homework assignment with an expression of undisguised disgust.

"Okay," I sigh, all but feeling the noose around my neck. "You're right."

"Finally," she says, nodding in agreement.

"Please don't send me to the Hall." I could kick myself for sounding like such a crybaby, but truly I'll die if I have to go back. And I was clean for a long time, the longest time in years. And Saturday night, I actually *was* watching a lame-ass movie with my family. It was the most depressing night. So when I found that joint in an old spot, it was like I'd won the lottery. But since everyone was home, where was I going to smoke without getting busted? I finally figured out that I could smoke it in the shower, which I did, and probably not get caught, which I didn't. The stinking truth is, it wasn't even fun. I mean, smoking pot alone in the bathroom? In the fucking shower? Not many people brag about spending a Saturday night like that. And now my PO is gonna break my ass.

"Good," she finally says. "Now we're getting somewhere."

We are? Wherever we are, I hate it here. Hate it.

BRYAN

14. SECRET THAI

Bryan wants to follow his lawyer's slick advice about keeping the ex's new legal attack a secret from Monica, but in the end he just can't get it to sit right in his mind. How could he keep something like that to himself? It's not just the lawyer's fees – it's the endless phone calls, legal papers, meetings, and stress. Jesus, he thinks, it'd be easier to keep a love affair a secret than a motion to change child custody. Every day he promises himself he'll break the news to his wife, and every night he drifts off to sleep cursing himself for letting another day slip away. Finally, after driving to work this morning, he sucks it up and calls home. He's sure he'll get voicemail, but figures he can at least dance around the general subject to get the ball rolling. Monica, though, shocks the hell out of him by answering the damn phone.

Since he hasn't figured out how to pitch it, he sputters out an invitation for dinner. Just the two of us, what do you say, honey? How bad is it when even he can tell what a disappointing dickwad he is? Monica sounds suspicious, but agrees to dinner if she can find a babysitter. God, Bryan thinks, she's a good person.

But by the time he's back home after work, the part of him that wants to get it over with is losing out to the part of him that wants to let it go another day. It's chaos on the home front. The boys have trashed the living room by building one of their multi-level forts, and the noise they make climbing under tables and over chairs is the soundtrack for a headache commercial. Monica and Andy have just gotten back from Drug Court, and Monica is charged up, beaming out enough nervous energy to power a neighborhood. Please, Lord, he prays: tell me she hasn't found a babysitter. But wouldn't you know it, for the first time since the twins were born, Monica can't wait to bust out of Dodge, and Andy, for probably the first time in her life, says she's happy to take care of the boys; tells her dad and stepmom to stay out as long as they want. Something about her probation requires her to work a certain number of hours in the house every week, and babysitting counts. So Bryan is a goner.

In the car, Monica is still so wound up it sounds like a wasp nest in the passenger seat. She's looking out the window so he can't see her face, but it sounds like she's losing the argument with herself. Jeez, if she's this upset now, tonight will not be pretty. Bryan decides to break the ice with a little small talk.

"I tried to make a reservation at Jessica's, that new raw food restaurant," he says, "but it closed down already."

Monica snaps her head toward him. "You? Vegetarian? That's ridiculous. You're like the founding father of Sir Loin and Chop. The only raw food you've ever eaten is carpaccio. You won't even eat a carrot unless it's cooked within an inch of its life."

"Come on, honey," he pleads, reaching over to stroke her hand. "Play along with me, okay? You're supposed to say, 'Really, dear? It closed? Why?'"

She rolls her eyes and shakes her head a couple quick times, as if trying to dislodge water from her ear or a sticky, mean thought. "Okay, hon. Let's hear it. Why *did* it close?"

So he relates the story of Rocco's new divorce client with just a little embellishment here and there, telling her about the husband popping in on a Saturday night and finding his wife with the chef on the breadboard, yukking it up in all the places Rocco did. And, holy moley, he doesn't know if it's his timing, delivery, or what, but she doesn't give him so much as a courtesy chuckle.

"Your lawyer is a creep," she says, shivering for emphasis. "How can you stand him?"

"Aw, he's not that bad," he says, at the same time wondering, Why am I defending him when I have the exact thought ten times a day?

"And anyway, why do people marry and have children if they can't stay together?" she rants. "I don't understand! It's so unfair to the poor kids. Their whole future, their whole happiness, depends on having a mom and a dad! How can people do that to their own kids?"

They're going to eat at the Secret Thai, a back-alley restaurant with good food but impossible parking. Amazingly, there's a guy leaving a spot right out in front, so Bryan activates the turn indicator and brake. "It's not that simple," he says. "Divorce is the worst experience you can have. No one signs up for it because they really want it, like a raffle or a vacation or something. It's just the lesser of evils. And, you know, it might be easier for a kid to have her parents divorce than for her to suffer the constant fighting in her home."

"That's just how people rationalize it," Monica shoots back. "Couples should be able to work things out. They shouldn't be fighting all the time. They should be able to solve their problems."

The assbite in his parking spot has apparently chosen this moment to read his owner's manual cover to cover. Or reprogram his radio so that it will pick up Canadian stations. What in the hell does he think this is, his own private piece of acreage? Bryan lays into the horn and waves. The assbite gives him the finger and honks back, but starts his car. Jerk!

"Yeah," Bryan says, maneuvering into the spot at last. "Couples should. But in real life, what if you're married to someone crazy? Because all bets are off with a crazy person. You can't reason with 'em. I tried. Jesus Christ, I tried."

Monica unbuckles her seatbelt and throws a pretty floral silk scarf over her shoulders. She is such a babe. Here she's had this long day taking care of the boys, going to Drug Court with Andy, and still she manages to look great. Her light brown hair is loose at the shoulders and she's wearing a little makeup, pink lipstick, and flowery perfume. She's wearing a short, feminine dress. It's her best color, an orangey-pink, and it flatters her golden complexion. On her ears are some sparkly earrings that match her dress. Lots of cute women go to hell after their kids are born. But his wife, in a certain light, still looks like a school girl. And a damn sexy one at that.

"True," she says. "Connie is difficult. But you know what, Bryan? You should have figured that out before you had a child with her. It's just not fair to the kid."

She steps out of the car and Bryan takes a moment to swallow his rage. Holy shit! Could someone cut him some slack for one minute? His wife might be right, but number one, she is forgetting that horny young men don't spend a lot of time *thinking* about sex before *having* it, and number two, if he'd followed her perfect-world advice, Andy would never have been born, and she's the light of his life. Next to his wife, of course, and their sons.

He joins Monica on the torn-up sidewalk. The Secret Thai is right under the freeway between the Golden Venus massage and the all-night donut shop. Bryan would never open a Bretano's in this location, but then the donut place must brew a little coffee, and it has operated out of this location since dirt was invented. Who eats donuts anymore? Maybe they're selling crack out the back door. The Secret Thai looks a little seedy next to it, but it's nice enough inside, and, more importantly, his wife loves the place, says it serves the best Thai food in the county.

"Couple of Thai beers," he says to the young waiter once they're seated.

"None for me," Monica says, holding up her hand. "Just tea, please."

Tea? That's not what he had in mind at all. He was hoping to loosen her up a little, and a couple of cold ones usually does the job. Nothing goes better with spicy curries than cold beer, she always says. Monica orders the food, thank God. Bryan can never remember which dishes they like, and if he had to pick from 177 choices, well, they'd be there 'til breakfast.

"No beer?" he asks after the waiter leaves. "Honey, is something wrong?"

"I don't know," she sighs, settling into her chair and turning down her tension control a notch or two. "I think it was Drug Court today. You should come. It's interesting. Heartbreaking. Horrible."

He nods like he agrees, but honestly he'd rather dig a ditch than sit through another session of court. He hopes that beer arrives in a hurry – he can hardly stay inside his own skin.

"These kids are told they can't drink or use drugs," she continues. "Meanwhile, their parents are getting plastered every night. Does that seem right? To ask kids to do something their own parents can't do?"

Personally, he doesn't have a problem with the concept, but he's guessing that's not the answer she wants. So he shrugs noncommittally, like he does with the customers who want him to share their outrage about the daily bee in their bonnet.

"One girl, Anya, told a hideous story of buying drugs for her father. It was his birthday and he wanted to celebrate, so he sent out his 16-year-old Anya to score a bag of meth for him. When she came back with the goods, he accused her of sampling the stuff herself, which, she confessed to the judge, she had. The girl was thrown in the Hall for relapsing, while Dad is free as a bird, probably home getting loaded and watching reruns of *Family Guy*."

"It's better that you go to court," he says, feeling his face heat to a burn. "I'd want to beat the living crap out of a loser like that." What kind of father would do that to his daughter?

The waiter sets the beer in front of him. He drains half of it in one swallow. Kind of bad timing on his part, but he's hot and thirsty. And maybe a little nervous, too. "You want a sip?"

She shakes her head and frowns, wipes pretend crumbs from the table. "Let's get it over with, honey. I know there's something you need or we wouldn't be here. What's up?"

Christ! Are all wives so much smarter than their husbands? Or is it just his? How do they figure out this stuff? If my wife asked me out to dinner, he thinks, I'd figure she wants to share a meal with me. He'd never make a guess that good, and never will, not in a million years. Not for the first time, he thinks: A dumbshit like me doesn't stand a fighting chance in marriage.

"It's bad," he says, trying to warm up to the topic. "You're not going to like it."

She doesn't say anything. Just gazes at him and sips her tea.

"You're going to be mad at me," he warns. She nods. Waits.

"I don't want you to be mad," he begs. "I hate it more than anything. And I can't say I'd blame you."

"Honey," she says after a moment. "This is twice as much foreplay as we have before sex. Get to the point. I'm not going to say it for you."

"It's Connie," he says.

She frowns.

"She filed more legal papers."

Nod.

"I have to defend it. I know you said no more attorneys' fees, and no more fighting with the ex, but I can't roll over on this. She wants to take Andy away from me. This time, she's saying Andy's problems are all my fault."

"How so?"

This is so hard for him to answer. He hates this. His wife is going to think he's a failure. But he's not! He loves her so much, would do anything in the world for her and the kids. Work as hard as he can, and it's all for his family. "I can't explain it."

"Bryan!" she uses her scolding voice, like she uses when the boys are throwing food or running around the pool. "You're a successful businessman! Use your words."

Monica's tea is gone. She takes a sip of water. He signals the waiter to bring more drinks. He can't down that second beer soon enough.

"Basically, she makes this whole Drug Court thing seem bad – not only that I put Andy in it without her permission, but that

Andy's drug use is my fault. Says I'm a big pot smoker and have been since I was a teenager, that I was arrested for possession of marijuana, and that she takes after me. She's asking for a DNA sample to prove I passed on the dope gene to her."

"Wow," Monica says. "That is a new tactic. What else?"

He can't bear to repeat the stupid slander stuff about soft porn, so he tells her that's basically it.

When the second round of drinks arrive, he reminds himself to take it easy, drink this one a little slower. But he's still nervous, and that makes it hard to pace himself.

"I don't see how this can be all your fault," Monica says thoughtfully. "I like to have fun as much as you, and I bet Connie indulged too, at least when you were younger. Andy has done a good job of finding her own way to trouble. I'm sure we all have played a role. It's not fair to pin it all on you. I don't know if Connie can force you to give a DNA sample, but it seems like if she's asking that of you, she'd have to give a sample too."

He smiles in spite of his misery. I swear to God, he thinks, the best part about married life is having someone on your side. See how she is? She's already thought of an argument his gold-plated lawyer never mentioned. Plus she has this gift of being able to see a situation from the other guy's point of view. She says it comes from having kids, that once your kid is born, you lose your own viewpoint and see the world through theirs.

Dinner arrives. The waiter puts down each dish, naming them as he does. "Panang salmon. Garlic eggplant. Pad Thai. Rice." The food smells fragrant and inviting, and Bryan realizes he is starving.

As Monica spoons rice onto plates, she asks about his day, tells a cute story about the boys racing their Power Wheels in the park. They chat about taking their bikes out of cobwebs and going for a family ride on one of Sequoia Valley's new bike paths. They talk about how nice it's been having Andy on home restriction, how she hasn't been so cooperative in ages, how she is growing up and won't be with them much longer.

When the plates are cleared, Monica excuses herself and goes to the ladies' room. Bryan passes on the offer of fried bananas but jumps on the opportunity for a beer. It feels good to relax a little. Monica returns with her hair combed and with fresh lipstick.

"You look beautiful, honey," he tells her. "We should do this more often. Just the two of us, you know."

She nods. "Mind if I tell you a little about Drug Court today?"

"Sure!" He answers, like a good husband. He can think of a hundred things he'd rather talk about, starting with a little pushin' on the cushion. But he is not in the driver's seat tonight. "Whatever you want! It's nice to have you all to myself."

"There are a lot of damaged kids in Drug Court," she starts.

That's not news to him. The girls look like sluts, excuse his French, and those boys with their big T-shirts and tattoos are all but advertising "damaged."

"You made a good decision enrolling Andy in this program. It's perfect for her. She's starting to settle in, talk with some of the other girls, find her way. She still looks terrified when she talks to the judge, but who wouldn't be? He's very intimidating."

Reminds him of the joke Rocco told, that a good judge needs only three things: gray hair, to look experienced; glasses, to look wise; and hemorrhoids, to look concerned. The Drug Court judge seems to have all three of those going for him.

"I've been going to court with Andy almost every week for two months now," she continues. "And it's like a reality show. I know all the kids. Some of them will never make it. But others, I find myself thinking of them during the week, hoping they're doing what they said they'd do, praying that they're not getting into trouble. Yes, it's a lot like a reality show, except sadder and sweeter."

Only his wife could find an entertainment value in something as awful as court. But then, she does enjoy a little daytime TV.

"Also, we're lucky that Andy is doing so well on probation," Monica says. "A lot of kids got in trouble this week – they were using, lying, late for school, missing meetings, missing their UA's. Andy was one of only two kids who did everything right. You need to let her know how proud you are."

"Okay," he says. "I will."

"When we get home," she adds emphatically.

"OK." Jeez, what is the big deal here?

"Bryan, none of these kids has parents telling them what's right and what's wrong. That's why you need to tell your daughter how proud you are of her effort. I'm looking at these kids today, listening to them whine, lie, make excuses. And then it hits me: Every single one of them is from a divorced home. Every single one of them, Bryan!"

"Huh," he says. The third beer is kicking in, and even though he's not tracking Monica's lecture 100 percent, it feels better having the problem on the table instead of holding it all in. Back in the day, he could never have had this conversation with his ex in public. She'd start screaming at him – it wouldn't matter if they were out at a nice restaurant. She'd screech, rip him to shreds, tell him what a worthless piece of shit he is. What a horrible memory.

"Doesn't that seem strange to you?" Monica continues. "*Every* kid? If the divorce rate is around 50 percent and you have a population of teens where the divorce rate is 100 percent, you have to wonder whether their parents' divorce has anything to do with their drug use."

He is groaning inwardly now, and his chances of being able to change the subject are slim and none – and like the cowboys say, Slim just walked out the door. He gazes over her shoulder in the crazy hope that the Secret Thai has installed a widescreen TV that maybe is showing the UConn-UCLA game, but no such luck – just the usual gold portrait of a multi-armed goddess and a deer.

"Think about Andy. You and Connie had a horrible, drawn-out divorce. You think that didn't affect the only child of your marriage?"

He guesses it did. It must have. He just hasn't given it a lot of thought. Mostly he has noticed how miserable Connie has made his life.

"I don't want that to happen to our boys," she says fiercely.

"Of course not, honey," he says. "It won't happen." Jeez. They're not going to get a divorce. Why's she talking like this?

"No, I mean, it really will *not* happen," she says. "We're going to stay married and face our problems, even if it kills us."

"Okay," he says, "'til death do us part."

"We have to do better as a family. We have to help Andy – for her sake and for ours. We have to try something new, be better people," she says. "If that means therapy, classes, coaching, religion – I don't care. We need to do whatever it takes."

"Okay."

"So here's a start," she announces. "You go ahead and give your lawyer his rip-off retainer. But whatever amount he's asking for, give him half."

The weight of the world falls from his shoulders. What a lucky guy! Why had he doubted her? He finishes off the beer and manages to bury a burp in his napkin.

"Tell him to do as little as possible. We don't want to fight but we don't want to roll over either. Meantime, we're going to work on setting a better example for our kids," she says. "No more pot in the house. Your ex has a point – it's not good for the kids to have that around. We're too old for that stuff anyway, and it's too risky."

He is practically wagging his tail like a puppy. He has his wife back! She's not mad at him! And she's going to help him. Thank you, Jesus! "Sure, that's fair," he says. And then he whispers: "But New Year's Eve sure was fun." Just the best, most intensely pleasurable night of his life, pot or no pot. He smiles at the memory. She doesn't smile back.

"Good," she says. "And maybe we should do away with the booze too – at least at the house."

"What?" It's like a slap across the face. That came out of nowhere. She can't be serious. "In my own home? You aren't telling me I can't have a beer in my own home! That's – that's – that's ridiculous!"

She glances at his third beer and slowly shakes her head. "Don't you see? It's the only way. Otherwise, how are our boys not going to have Andy's problem? How can we ask them not to drink like their father? Who knows, maybe there is a genetic component? Connie could be *helping* us this time, honey. Maybe she's right. We've got a problem – the same one every parent has in Drug Court. Our problem is, we need to be better parents."

"Honey!" He is shocked. "I'm a good parent already. I've been fighting for Andy for ten years! And I do not have a drinking problem!"

"If you don't have a drinking problem, it'll be no big deal for you to quit." She squeezes his knee under the table. "I'm going to miss it too. I love a beer as much as you do. But we have to do better for our kids. We can't tell them marijuana is evil and then smoke it before sex. We can't expect them not to drink if there's a twelve-pack in the fridge."

"This is stupid!" He argues. "We're not underage kids! We're parents! We get to have a life too. There are some things that grown-ups get to do that kids do not get to do!"

She strokes the inside of his thigh. "Yes," she says. "Like this. I'm well aware. Listen, I'm not excited about spending another two grand on legal fees, okay? But we're a team, and we're going to face our problems together. We'll have a good time being intimate. I know how much you would miss that. So lose the booze, darling. We're in this together."

She slips her purse on her shoulder and stands. She's telling him that they're going to have relations tonight. He knows she's trying to make him feel better, but instead he feels like he's been run over by a goddamn moving truck.

Which, by the way, does not feel so good.

HON. STRATHMORE REED, JR.

15. WHEN SHE'S GONE

The personal injury trial of *Barnum v. Bishop* is in its third predictable day, with three equally predictable ones to follow. The jurors file in, exhausted already at 9:30 A.M., carrying their coffees, cough drops, water bottles, notebooks and neck pillows to assist them in the discharge of their civic duty. The matter they will be deciding is known by insiders as a "LIST," an industry acronym for Low Impact, Soft Tissue. LIST cases are mostly minor rear-enders with minimal injuries to the drivers and not much more than a scratch to the cars. To jurors, it's a "fender-bender," and to Judge Reed it's as routine as it gets. He has heard hundreds, if not thousands, of them. Most settle before trial for modest amounts of money because Sequoia Valley jurors are notoriously unsympathetic to an injured party's claim for pain and suffering. A victim might still recover a substantial sum if hurt by a reckless red-light runner or a drunk driver; otherwise, unless his car shows major collision damage, his case is likely to go nowhere with a jury. As Judge Reed hears the plaintiffs' lawyers say to their disappointed clients out in the halls, "No crash, no cash."

Today's case is typical in all aspects. Mrs. Barnum had just dropped her boys off at softball practice and was on her way to Whole Foods to pick up dinner. She was driving her Subaru Outback and wearing a seatbelt. She came to a complete stop at the busy red light one block before the market and was reaching for her purse on the passenger side floor when she was rear-ended. The force of the impact caused her to bang her head on the front console. Since then, she told the jury, her life has been a living hell of headaches, back pain, diagnostic tests, and frustrating medical appointments. She is in constant neck and back pain, and no amount of analgesics, anti-inflammatories, chiropractic adjustment, physical therapy, yoga or massage can return her to her pre-accident condition. Although she tried to resume her part-time position as a sales clerk at Macy's, she could no longer tolerate prolonged periods of standing. She has gained thirty-five pounds, feels tired all the time, and suffers from depression. Her children miss their high-energy, helpful mom; her husband misses his once healthy, attentive wife; and the strain on the family is reaching its breaking point. Mrs. Barnum wants her old life back and is angry at the person who plowed into her. "She was talking on her stupid cell phone, not paying any attention to road conditions, and she rammed into me. I didn't do anything wrong, but I'm the one suffering!" Mrs. Barnum testified earlier. "*She's* forgotten all about this day, and I'm stuck with it forever. It's not fair."

For Judge Reed, it's strictly business as usual. He could script the rest of the testimony, down to the jury's verdict (well, within five percent anyway). But he doesn't mind the repetitive nature of his work; in fact he rather appreciates it. Years ago, when he was new to the bench, he had a fleeting concern that hearing the same half-dozen or so cases over and over might grow old. When he confessed this to his wife, Dory threw back her head and laughed. "You'll be fine, dear," she reassured him. "You thrive on routine." He hadn't known this about himself, but as it turned out, she was exactly right. What troubles him now, in fact, is not the routine case, where he enjoys a sense of mastery, but the innovative, cutting-edge stuff, where he is most at risk of becoming rattled. Juvenile Drug Court comes to mind, with its gum-cracking, fast-talking band of hooligans and their unpredictable behavior. He can barely understand their uncouth and slangy vocabulary, much less their attraction to illegal activities. All he can do is watch them until another judge is assigned to deal with them. Today's matter, a car accident with competent lawyers on each side, is almost restful for him; he need only look interested, and when the occasional objection arises, simply select "overruled" or "sustained" from the ruling menu.

"We call Dr. Barnaby Chase as our next witness," plaintiff's lawyer announces.

Dr. Chase is the go-to expert for injured plaintiffs. For $500 an hour, he will find something wrong with any patient, and will make the injury sound serious, if not downright life-threatening. Never does a word like "whiplash" wend its way into his vocabulary. Instead, he diagnoses microscopic tears of the myofascial tissues, post-traumatic arthritis onsets, fibrocytis, and somatic disorders secondary to psychological sequelae. For $2,500 a half-day, he will find time in his busy schedule to come to court and describe his findings in convincing detail, with models and anatomical charts to illustrate and explain his findings to the jury.

"Good morning, Judge Reed," the doctor says after he's been sworn. Dr. Chase is apparently so busy that he has come to court today attired in his white lab coat, stethoscope trailing out of the waist pocket and all. That device must have wreaked havoc on the court's perimeter screening device. "Nice to see you again, Judge."

It's a sleazy expert witness ploy, and Reed recognizes it immediately: to greet the judge as if he's an old friend, telegraphing to the jury before the first question that this expert is called upon to come to court so frequently that he's friendly with the judge. Reed will have none of it.

"You may proceed with your direct examination," Judge Reed directs plaintiff's lawyer, without dignifying the doctor's greeting with a response.

Dr. Chase is quizzed about his educational background and degrees, his professional experience and affiliations, the articles he has published, the lectures he has presented, and the number of times he has been retained as an expert witness. He discusses the examination of Mrs. Barnum, the review of her medical records, diagnosis of her condition, course of treatment and prognosis.

But Reed cannot keep his mind on the testimony. He simply does not feel like himself. Whatever is the matter with him?

In truth, Reed knows exactly what it is, but he does not care to acknowledge it.

It's Skylar. Or, more precisely, the absence of her.

They had their night, that glorious night at the Symphony Dinner-Dance. Their dinner conversation was intimate and easy – once they sat down, the tables were so large and the centerpieces so imposing, that guests quickly realized they could only speak easily to the person sitting on either side of them. Skylar and Reed began dinner by conversing politely with the person sitting on their other side, but as soon as the two of them fell into conversation, they were inseparable. When the dessert dishes were removed, they found themselves on the dance floor, swaying and swirling to the lovely music. Skylar was a dreamy dance partner – graceful and adaptive. Reed silently thanked his mother for making him attend Cotillion those many years ago and mastering basic dance steps. Dancing permitted the two of them to connect more intimately, rhythmically responding to one another with the flow of music rather than the distraction of words. When at last the evening ended, Reed drove Skylar home, and even in the car, they continued to talk – about what was it? Oh, Reed couldn't remember, it was all so wonderful. And when he escorted her to the door, beginning only then to feel awkward, Skylar, the compliant dancer, the one who so smoothly let him lead her on the dance floor, slid both arms through his and pressed her petite body against him. "Darling," she whispered, almost as if she were about to cry. "I'm quite overcome. You must kiss me. Please." Oh, that kiss, that warm embrace, he can still feel the tingling of it deep within him.

They parted quickly, agreeing to talk the following day. He called her house at the earliest decent hour, but she didn't answer. She must still be sleeping, he concluded. A few hours later, he tried her again, this time on her cell phone. No luck. He passed the day fitfully, considered driving to her house, even got in his car and started the engine, but then thought better of it and retreated to his study. The following day, an email from her appeared, full of apology, explaining she was called out of the country on a last-minute business emergency, that she expected to be gone for three weeks, that she would call him as soon as she knew more, and hoped they would get together the very minute her feet were back on the ground. "Please do not forget our kiss," is how she ended her note. It was not until he read her last line that he realized he'd been holding his breath.

"Objection, Your Honor. Hearsay!" the defense lawyer thunders.

Reed looks up from his blank notebook. He hasn't written a word since yesterday and has no idea what the question was, much less whether it was objectionable. All twelve jurors stare at him expectantly.

"Counsel, please rephrase the question," he responds sternly.

"Very well, Your Honor," the plaintiff's attorney replies, looking somewhat perplexed.

At the morning recess fifteen minutes later, Reed locks the door to his chambers, washes his face with cold water, and orders himself to pull himself together. He simply cannot permit his mind to wander like that at work. He checks his calendar and notes that he has the monthly judges' meeting at lunch. It's not an event he ordinarily enjoys, but today it calms him, somehow, to have something secure in place, a regular and unsurprising commitment to fill the time between his morning and afternoon sessions.

She won't be back for at least a week. Because the two of them are not only on different schedules but in different time zones, they have spoken just twice and then only for only a few frustrating minutes – both distant, choppy conversations with distracting, intermittent cell phone reception. His only consolation is that she sounded as unhappy as he. He is certain she wishes to see him again. So, good Lord, man! Put your feet on the ground and get back to living your normal life!

The problem is normal life feels utterly empty without her. His work at the court seems dull and tedious. His social life feels rote and tiresome. Last weekend he was obliged to attend a charity auction for the hospital board. The contrast between the hospital auction and the symphony dinner could not have been starker. What is happening?

"'I wandered lonely as a cloud, that floats on high o'er vales and hills,'" Reed recites wistfully to his empty chambers.

Immediately, he hears at rap at the door. "Your Honor?" asks his sweet courtroom clerk. "Is everything all right? The jurors are ready. We're a few minutes late!"

"Thank you, Miss Bettina!" he answers, opening the door quickly to her concerned and lovely face. "Everything is fine. I just lost track of the time. I'll be right out."

Back in the courtroom, Reed squares his shoulders, opens his notebook, and rolls his swivel chair closer to the witness stand, determined to focus on the next round of evidence. Plaintiff calls as her next witness her husband. Mr. Barnum is about 40 years old, round-shouldered, balding, soft around the middle. He is a CPA, obviously ill at ease in the courtroom, and strings his words together with distracting "uhs." Even a simple question like, "What is your name, sir?" earns two verbal tics: "I'm, uh, Barry uh Barnum." He has the charm and vivacity of a banana slug. Reed anticipates the "before and after" testimony he is about to hear, how active and able the wife was two years ago, how tired and incapacitated she is now. Well, bring it on, Reed thinks: this is your day in court.

In his trial notebook, Reed writes:
Pre-accid:
PTA since first grade.
Active kids' school.
Snack chair for baseball team x 3 yrs.

Never missed boys' sporting event.

Enjoys baking. Turtle brownies=her specialty.

Does own housework. Uh

15 hrs/wk Macy's – boy's dep't. uh…uh

Hobbies: uh, knitting, uh, gardening, uhhhhh.

The plaintiff's attorney directs Mr. Barnum's attention to the day of the accident, and Reed understands the jury will hear a rehash of the details, this time from husband's point of view. Reed glances up at his computer screen, and notices the flashing icon for a new email message. Idly, he clicks on it.

"Darling Judge: I'm home early! Lunch? Tre Sorelli 12:30. Your Sky"

She's home! Yip-yip-yipee! He's rescued from his empty life. Reed replies immediately: YES! He then composes a quick email to his courtroom clerk: PLEASE INFORM PJ CANT ATTEND J'S MEETING. JT ISSUES. His emails read like telegrams: all caps and not a wasted word. His clerk nods at him, then slips out of the courtroom to call the presiding judge and inform her of Judge Reed's inability to attend today's judges' meeting because of issues that arose in his jury trial. While attendance at the monthly meeting is considered mandatory, the business of jury trials always takes precedence. Reed checks the clock: 11:05. He will be out the door in under an hour, on his way to meet his sensational Skylar!

When Reed tunes back in to the testimony, Mr. Barnum has moved on to his wife's current condition. Reed uncaps his fountain pen and writes:

Post-accid:

Tired

Complaining

No energy

Headaches

Chiro 3x/wk

Moody

DN help w/homework

Uh takeout food

No uh uh sex

Reed groans inwardly. It embarrasses him – and jurors as well – to hear the sordid details of litigants' private relations. Better to barely hint at the subject than to blunder into the unwelcome and overly personal facts.

"How frequently were you and your wife having sexual relations before the accident?" the plaintiff's lawyer asks.

Reed sizes up the poor witness, embarrassed for him already. Without a doubt, Reed concludes, Barnum is a twice-monthly "let's do the deed and be done with it" man.

"Five uh or six uh times a week," Barnum answers, his face reddening noticeably.

Could it be true? Five or six times *a week?*

"WONDERFUL!" Skylar replies on-screen. "Come without your robe!"

Judge Reed's involuntary snort occurs at a very bad time in the trial. He tries to mask it with a throat-clearing cough, but the witness is staring at him in horror, and all twelve jurors are trying to suppress giggles.

"Pardon me," Reed says, with as much dignity as he can muster. What a lapse of judicial decorum! Really, he absolutely must put his feet back on the ground. Just as soon as he returns from his upcoming lunch with his angel Skylar, he intends to do so.

Thirty-nine more minutes! He can barely sit still in his big swivel chair.

ANDY

16. DRUG COURT HOMEWORK: THE FIRST TIME

I was 12 years old and kind of a nerd – the last person in the world who'd try drugs. Although – duh – obviously not. Kept to myself mostly, but had a best friend, Brittany. I couldn't understand what she saw in me. I was shy and scared. She was smart and confident. Most everyone liked her, but if they didn't, she wasn't bothered a bit. That kind of bravery was unheard of in middle school. Not only was she an Honors Student with a plan to go to Stanford, Britt was a natural-born leader who didn't gossip. And I was her best friend.

It was that time of your life where you start to feel like you might actually grow up – you're getting taller, showing the tiniest signs of developing, hearing little bits and pieces from the wild world of exotic teenagers. They flirted! They smoked! They French-kissed! It was still a ways away, and it was scary and slightly unbelievable, but if you squinted your eyes and held your breath, you could almost see yourself in that magical universe. And boy, we wanted to be there NOW. We'd had it with tights and tennis shoes and were panting for bare legs and high heels.

Britt was the leader of the pack, about to turn 13. Even though no one considered 13 as, you know, a real teenager, Britt liked to say that, "13 is the new 16." She wanted to start a movement of big bashes to usher in official teendom. Preparations began months in advance. Who would come? Boys were out of the question – too messy and unpredictable – and girls would suffer shame or superiority depending on who was included. What would the invitations look like? The current fad favored expensive invitations with hand-lettering and a baby picture. What activities would we do? Beading and pottery painting seemed babyish but limo rides and dance clubs were out of our league. There was so much to talk about! Dares, games, snacks, movies. Oh, and decorations!

In the end, Britt invited every girl in the class to a pizza-and-movie overnighter. You had to come dressed as a movie star, but the plan was to change into sweats as soon as the pictures were taken. Everyone knew about the party – all the boys in our class, of course, who threatened to throw rocks at the window, scare us with loud noises in the middle of the night, annoy us with crank calls. But we knew them too well – all talk and no jock. Even the teachers were in on the details, and by the time the party weekend arrived, they didn't dare assign homework.

I made Britt her birthday present and was so proud of it. It sounds stupid now, but at the time, Mexican peasant blouses were all the rage, due to the popularity of that girl band, La Chica Boom-Boom. I made one for Britt and couldn't wait to give it to her. I'd found this beautiful white cotton fabric that was just a little bit see-through – light enough to be racy, but not so much that your mom wouldn't let you out of the house. It came out cuter than anything you could buy. With tiny bright stitches, I embroidered a design around the neckline and sleeves. Turquoise, orange, and yellow, her favorite colors. The design was one I made up myself: 13131313131313, tons of little 13's. They looked like flowers – you had to look really closely to see the numbers. I knew she wouldn't notice it on her own – I would have to show her, and she would love it, like a private joke. I even made the wrapping paper for the present. I got a big sheet of black paper and covered it with silver and gold glittered "13's."

When the day of the party arrived, Britt and I talked a dozen times about last- minute details. She wanted me next to her when we ate the pizza, wanted me next to her when she opened her gifts, wanted me to record who had given her what. She even bought a special feather pen for the occasion.

Finally night came! I was all packed up and ready to go, my seatbelt fastened, overnight bag stowed in Mom's Lexus, Britt's gift protectively in my arms.

"Where are you going, Mom?" I shouted when she turned left instead of right at the light. "Britt's house is the other way!"

"I know, honey," Mom said. "But I have to take you to your father's. I'm not allowed to drive you to the party. It's his weekend. I wish I could take you there. But under the court order, I have to deliver you to his house."

I sighed hugely. This was annoyingly familiar territory for me. I hated court orders. I didn't understand how some judge who'd never met me could tell me where I was supposed to be and when. But this was a big night, and I didn't have the energy to get into that. So I just said, "Okay, well hurry up. Britt is waiting for me."

When we got to Dad's, I grabbed my stuff and ran. She and Dad never spoke – the court order said she was to drop me off at "curbside." Mom sped off and I didn't notice all the cars in the driveway. As soon as I opened the front door, I knew something was wrong.

Fat, pregnant Monica stood at the entry, dolled up in a huge dress with a phony smile. She held a healthy glass of tomato juice and was surrounded by pretty moms in short skirts. A tower of fancy-wrapped gifts grew in the middle of the living room.

"There's our Andrea," Monica announced. "Welcome to my baby shower, honey. Oh, you brought me a gift! How sweet!"

As she reached for Britt's box, I yanked it out of her hands, bumping her glass and spilling the smelly tomato mess all over her dress. "Where's my dad?" I demanded. I knew I sounded like a brat, but I had to act quickly.

Monica kept her smile plastered on, as her friends circled around to mop up the mess. "Well, gosh, honey, I'm not sure. Maybe he's by the barbecue in the back yard."

I dropped my overnight bag at the door, but before I could escape her zone of domination, Monica said in her careful step-mother voice: "Honey? Let's not have anymore accidents. Please. Put your bag in your room. I can't have guests tripping on it." I felt, rather than noticed, the quiet, sympathetic clucks from her friends and the exchanged, knowing looks.

ARRGGGHHHHH!!! I picked up my bag, took the stairs two at a time, dropped the bag and gift on my bed, and flew down the stairs in search of Dad.

There were so many people in the house! All the women were in the kitchen and living room, talking babies, childbirth, and twins. They tried to pat me on the head and ask stupid questions, but I would have none of it.

The men were on the patio, drinking beer and yelling at a baseball game on the big-screen TV. But where's my dad? Where is he?

He wasn't at the TV, he wasn't at the barbecue, he wasn't at the ice chest. I raced through the house again, kitchen, living room, bedroom, growing crazier by the second. Where could he be? I needed to get to Britt's! How can he not know this!

Finally I found him in the garage, pulling a case of beer from the refrigerator.

"Dad!" I shouted.

"Oh, hi, honey!" He smiled. "Can you hand me that case of Diet Coke?"

"Dad! I have to go! I'm going to a party tonight at Britt's! You have to drive me! Now!"

He stood up and closed the refrigerator door. His smile evaporated. "What are you talking about?"

So I told him, again, about the party, the preparations, the best friend, everything. How can my parents be so stupid about my life? "Come on! I'm late!"

At that moment, wicked Monica walked in, looking bitchier than ever. She was wearing a different outfit, even less flattering than the tomato juice dress. "There you are, Bryan. Everyone's asking about you. I need you in the house."

Dad nodded. "Be right there, hon."

She turned her icy gaze on me. "Andrea? That was quite an entrance you made. I'm waiting for your apology."

"Sorry!" I screamed.

She widened her eyes dramatically and retreated into the house.

I yanked on Dad's sleeve and tried to pull him to the car. "It will only take 15 minutes. I asked Mom to drive and she said she couldn't, that it was your weekend."

He closed his eyes and clenched his jaw. "Yes. It is my weekend. Not hers. She can't keep doing this to me. Our court order says neither parent can schedule an activity during the other parent's weekend."

I felt desperate. I couldn't believe this was happening. I'd been looking forward to this night for months, and now my parents' fighting was ruining everything.

"Please, Dad, just take me there. I'll be here the rest of the week. I have to go now."

"I'm sorry, honey," he said. "I can't. Monica needs me."

I burst into tears. I needed him too.

But it didn't matter. He left me alone in the garage and rejoined the party.

I stormed to my room, locked myself in, and howled. I was so angry. I called Britt, hoping for some magical solution, but she had the whole class over, the party was in full swing, and she couldn't talk. I was tearful, outraged, frustrated. I hated my parents, hated my helplessness. I wanted to be grown up and powerful, able to go where I wanted to go, not blown about by the arguments of my messed-up parents.

By the time I cried all the tears I could cry, the party had died down. I was empty and exhausted and starving. I crept out of my room and went downstairs in search of food.

The place was trashed. I'm not sure what led me to the cooler outside. Was it all the empty beer bottles in the house? Did I hope to find my dad at the big screen TV? Was I thinking a fairy godmother could appear and rescue me from my life? Most likely I didn't think at all. But when I got to the cooler, I plucked out a bottle of Dos XX and popped the top off, just as I imagined a sophisticated 17-year-old might do. And right there on the patio table was what I knew with certainty to be– though I had never seen one before – a joint. I snatched that, loaded a paper plate with sandwiches and pretzels, and ran back to my room.

I locked my door, opened my window, and sat down on the floor. I had no idea what to expect. I took a sip of beer. It was disgusting. But I made myself take another and another, until I felt a little spinny. "Well, here goes!" I said to myself and lit the joint, burning my hair. I inhaled deeply, wanting to take it all in. It was weird. The wet paper tasted gross. Little flecks of stuff felt gritty in my mouth. I smoked slowly, looking at the stars, letting the future happen. When the room started to float, I slowed down a little, ate the sandwiches, sipped beer, went along for the ride.

Then it happened. I felt delicious! Giddy! Free and light. Grown up and brave. Things were going to be okay. It was amazing, really. One moment things were awful and sad, and with this little trick, I could make things better, all by myself!

When I started to nod off, I crawled around the floor, not trusting myself to stand. Britt's glittery gift was on my pillow, and I felt a wave of sadness wash through me. I pushed it off the bed and fell asleep.

That was the first time.

But by the time I gave Britt her present, I felt bad about everything. I felt bad about drinking, smoking, missing the party, making a dumb present. Why hadn't I just bought a real present at Target, like a normal girl? Britt was polite when she opened it, said all the right things, admired the colorful stitching, thought the 13's were B's, for Brittany. I could tell that she'd never wear it, and that's when I knew I wasn't her best friend anymore. Was she mad at me for missing her big party? Was she, like me, anxious to separate herself from my parents' fighting? Or did she see, once all the other girls were assembled, how easy it was to upgrade from me?

I didn't smoke or drink for a long time after that. I was not the kind of girl who drank beer or smoked pot. I wanted my old life back. Britt and I drifted apart. I never knew if she had changed or I had. I kept the memory of that wonderful floaty feeling carefully stored away, like an emergency response plan. If life ever dealt me another awful blow, I would be ready.

My probation officer is a super-slow reader. Our meetings are at school now. She pulls me out of class to check in on me, give me a pee test, and collect the homework she assigned. I don't mind meeting with her at school – my school is for drop-outs; everyone is on probation, and class is not exactly riveting – but I do mind sitting next to someone who is reading the pathetic story of your life. Especially your life in middle school, right? I mean, that's got to be the most humiliating time of your life. The Killer's face reveals nothing as she plods through my essay.

Finally, she reaches the last word, sighs, and places the pages face-down on the table.

"That was a sad night," she says. "I wish your parents hadn't done that."

I snort. "I wish I hadn't cared so much about a middle-school birthday party."

"You know you're an addict, right?" Karla says.

"That's what everyone keeps telling me," I answer.

"Yeah, well they're right," she says, sliding my homework into an official-looking file with my name on it. "Addicts think about the first time they used with the fondness of a love affair."

That's pretty embarrassing, so I say nothing.

"You know what I hate so much about drugs?" Karla asks. "That they work so well. Too well."

That's what I like about them, I think.

"You've done a nice job," Karla says. "Thank you. I'm going to read it again. I like your writing."

I smile. Can't quite manage the word "thanks," so I shrug my shoulders.

She pierces me with her hard, dark eyes. "I get what you're saying about holding that first use as a memory. I know if I searched your room now, I'd find something somewhere." She holds up her hand to stop my protest. "Don't bother to argue. You know I hate lies. You have some emergency stash in the house. Get rid of it. Okay? Answer me. Okay?"

"Okay," I say. I can't *believe* she got me to cop to that!

"You can thank me later," she says. "I could find it right now taped to the underside of your dresser, and you'd be back in the Hall."

Life lesson: Never mistake your PO for your friend.

Now I have to find a new hiding spot.

BRYAN

17. LOADED GUN

Bryan is relieved to see his daughter waiting outside of her run-down continuation school as he drives up, but as soon as she notices him, she scowls.

"Da-aad!" she snarls, opening the car door and heaving her backpack inside with a thud. "What are *you* doing here?"

If there is a more insulting way to greet someone – especially someone doing you a favor – well, what the hell is it? Here he is, interrupting his whole damn day to take her to court, and she's giving him grief. Jeez, if Bryan ever said anything like that to his father – and he's pretty sure he never did – he would've been cuffed twice in the ear. Once for being a snot-nosed jerk and the second time to make damn sure he never did it again. But then, his father was sort of an asshole.

"Hi, honey," Bryan says between gritted teeth. Sometimes, being a parent takes everything you've got. Today is one of those days. This morning Monica interrupted a meeting with his tax people to tell him that the boys needed to see the pediatrician for their croupy cough. The only appointment was at 3:00, the exact time of Andy's Drug Court. Which would he prefer, pediatrician or court? She may as well ask, Dear, would you like your hand slammed in a door or your 'nads squeezed in a vice?

"C'mon, Andy, I brought you food."

"You did?" His daughter's face brightens considerably. "God, I'm starving! What'd you bring me?"

The snack was Monica's idea. She warned him that Andy would be cranky, said it never hurts to show up with a little something to eat. So he stopped at the Italian deli and picked up a sandwich, apple, and one of those pink vitamin waters so popular with kids. He also grabbed a couple of ginger-molasses cookies from the shop, and – just for insurance – a classic chocolate chip cookie. How can you stay mad at someone who gives you a great cookie?

Andy attacks the sandwich. "Pepper jack with avocado! Sprouts, lettuce, tomatoes, cucumber and Dijon mustard!" she exclaims with a mouthful of food. "Dad! It's my favorite! Thanks!"

You have to hand it to teens. They might be moody, but a little thing like a sandwich can turn things around for them. Jeez, if only a deli sandwich were all it took to snap him out of his funk. He's been miserable – it's like he became an old man overnight. Complaining all the time and a generalized feeling of crappiness. Going to court today does not help his outlook. The building alone freaks him out, as loaded as it is with bad memories. But the real reason for the rotten mood? He hasn't had a drink in almost a month. Who knew it could be so rough?

Drinking is all he thinks about anymore. Never in his life has he been a daytime drinker, except maybe on vacation. Now he's calculating how he could sneak in a drink or two during the day and no one would be the wiser for it. At lunch, he finds himself staring at all the happy guys downing an ice-cold beer with their burgers, fantasizing about how good it would taste and how that could satisfy his thirst. When he comes home at night, he heads for the fridge out of habit, and is immediately annoyed when Diet Coke and juice boxes are his only options. Recently, he woke up at 2:20 A.M., remembering the six-pack of Bud in the garage refrigerator. Hallelujah! Right there in his own home, in the middle of the night when no one would know! He jumped out of bed and padded barefoot to the garage, only to discover that Monica must have remembered the six-pack first. Gone. He about cried.

Here's another thing: What red-blooded all-American male likes being told what to do by his wife? It's ridiculous that a man can't enjoy a little liquid comfort in his own home. A man's home is his castle, and whoever heard of a castle that didn't serve beer?

He keeps telling Monica he doesn't have a drinking problem, that he should be able to have a beer or two from time to time, and, really, where does she get off setting the rules in the house? But holy crapoli, if he doesn't have a problem, why in the hell is it so hard to lay off the stuff?

How bad is it for him right now? It's so bad that even the old in-and-out isn't helping. Monica has been trying to ease the pain by offering up the goods every other damn night, and, jeez, he doesn't know what's happening, but he doesn't even want to have sex anymore, especially not a mercy poke. He's having to fake-snore just to get her off his back. It's so weird – he's usually Mr. Ever-Ready, Slow-n-Steady. Now who is he? Mr. Boozehound, more like.

So to snap him out of his funk, he would need a six of Bud from the cold case along with that deli sandwich.

"I hate going to court," Andy says softly, wrapping up the scraps of her sandwich in the paper.

He pulls into a beautiful parking space, a two-hour zone right near the entry, and cuts the engine. "Yeah?" He says. "Well I hate it more than you, so there."

"You can't hate it more than me," she says. "This is only your second time. I've been coming every week since January 1. I hate it the most. I've been here more."

"Yeah, I could," he counters. "I'm older than you and have been going to court a lot longer."

"Good one, Dad," she smiles. "But I'm younger, more sensitive, and feel things more profoundly. So I can hate it more than you, and I do."

She has her mother's devilish debate gene, that's for damn sure. He pities the poor fucker who marries her some day. That poor guy better start practicing "Yes, Dear" right now. "Okay, you win," he says, opening the car door. "Come on. Let's just get this over with."

After they shuffle through security screening – for once Bryan left his Swiss Army knife at home so he doesn't sacrifice yet another one to the cause – Andy joins the other kids in the jury box and hugs the girl sitting next to her. Bryan hangs back, close to the door. The familiar dread creeps into his gut, and he senses a major headache coming on. He digs around his pockets and finds a small tin of aspirin. The courtroom door is locked because hearings for kids are closed to the public, so he gulps the aspirin without water. The bitterness stings his throat, but he manages to swallow it without gagging.

Once things get under way, it's not near as bad as the first time. The judge seems slightly less pinched; the probation officer puts a positive spin on each kid's case – even when a few of the boys are thrown in the Hall for missing UA's cutting school, the PO mentions a thing or two they're doing right, like abiding by curfew or attending their therapy appointments. But the biggest difference is Andy. When her case is called, the PO gives a glowing report. Bryan has never heard a probation officer speak well of his child! It makes him proud! She talks about Andy's "excellent effort" on Drug Court essays, her perfect compliance with working around the house, her thirty-five days of sobriety. The judge glances up from his stack of files and smiles at Andy. He looks almost like a human being with a smile on his face, not a cardboard cutout of a mean judge.

"That's an impressive accomplishment, Ms. Bretano," he says to her. "To what do you attribute your success?"

The question must catch her off guard, because she rocks in her chair a few times before answering. "I never want to go back to the Hall," she explains. "So I do what my PO tells me to do. I've been on home restriction since my last relapse, so I haven't had much freedom."

The judge congratulates her, tells her to keep up the good work, and releases her from home restriction. Andy thanks him, and the next case is called. Holy shit! For the first time ever, a judge has said something positive to his daughter. She is not in trouble. She is not going to the Hall. The aspirin is kicking in. Maybe it wasn't such a bad decision to enroll her in this program after all! Maybe her mother will see the light and appreciate his decision to start Andy in Drug Court! Damn, all that worrying for nothing.

He's glad Andy is off home restriction. It'll be good for her to venture out of the house, act more like a normal teenager – just as long as she doesn't go back to her wild ways. Not that he'd ever say this to Andy, but it's been tough on Monica having a teenager underfoot all the time. And it's been making his crazy ex even crazier *not* having a teenager underfoot. If Andy resumes her regular visits with her mother, Connie might relax the reins on her legal battle against him. That would be sweet.

The cases move along at a fast clip. One girl, who looks vaguely familiar – he wonders if she's a friend of Andy's from the bad old days? – is given a Drug Court graduation date in two weeks. She is beaming! The PO says she was a daily pot smoker before joining Drug Court. You'd never know it from looking at her shiny black hair and her clear eyes. They're on track to be out the door at 3:30, when suddenly a fight breaks out between the judge and a mother.

"With all due respect, Ma'am," the judge says sternly. "Please don't tell us you're doing everything you can for your son. As I understand the situation, you are consuming alcohol every night. That does not help your son. That hurts him."

"How dare you! You can't tell me what to do in my home!" the mother yells. She's in some sorry shape, uncombed hair, splotchy face, rumpled clothes. Plus she can't be thinking very clearly either – yelling at a judge? How does that help your case? "My *son* has the problem, not *me*! I'm an adult! I am allowed to have a drink in my own home!"

That gives Bryan the creeps, because this out-of-control mom is saying pretty much the very thing he's been thinking all week – and she sounds like a total whack job.

"Quite right," the judge says in a measured voice. "I cannot order you to abstain from the use of alcohol. But I can remind you of its consequences."

"Excuse me, Your Honor," the probation officer says, standing up. "May I ask Miguel's mom a question?" The judge nods, and the PO turns to the crackpot mother. "If Miguel were suicidal, would you keep a loaded gun on the kitchen table?"

"Of course not!" she snaps. "What an outrageous question! I don't want him to kill himself. I love him!"

"Exactly," the probation officer says. "You love your son. But keeping alcohol in the home of an alcoholic is like having a loaded gun on the kitchen table – tempting and dangerous. If you have it, he will drink it. There is not a teen here who could resist his drug of choice if it's in the kitchen."

Is she saying a can of beer is the same as a loaded gun? A little twelve-ounce Bud is a deadly weapon? Bryan wonders how Monica can stand listening to this stuff every week. No wonder she gets so wound up.

The PO eyes the group of teens in the jury box and asks, "If you could get a beer tonight from your own refrigerator, or a pipeful of whatever you smoke from the cookie jar, and you knew you wouldn't get in trouble for it, is there anyone here who might be tempted? Raise your hand." The teens laugh a little, exchange a few playful words, and every single one of them raises a hand, including his daughter.

The dumpy mom launches into a rant, but Bryan doesn't hear a damn thing after that. Too many new thoughts are colliding in his head and exploding like grenades. How is he different from Miguel's mom? He's a guy whose wife asked him to lay off the booze, yet would happily grab one from the fridge if one were there. Why didn't he ever realize that the parents' drinking is related to the kid's? Honestly, in all the times he has been to Juvie, he never thought his daughter had a drug problem. He thought it was a stage, that she was just acting out, experimenting, going through a wild phase the way that normal teens do.

When court is adjourned, Andy and Bryan race down the stairs, as fast as if someone shouted FIRE. In the car, Andy seems relieved and lighthearted, but her father feels crappier than ever. He somehow remembers to tell Andy how proud of her he is, how well she's doing in Drug Court. That was another thing Monica drilled into him, and it's a good thing, too, because Andy is actually starting to look like she might be happy again someday.

"There's an extra cookie in here if you want one," she says, rummaging through the lunch bag. "What'd you think of court, Dad?"

He nods, stalls for time; tries to think of something true. He can't get the picture of the loaded gun on the kitchen table out of his head. "That last mom seemed kind of nutty."

"Yeah, she's got a major drinking problem. Miguel says she passes out every night. She promises him she's going to stop drinking, but she can't do it."

"It's hard," he says. God, it is so fucking hard.

"Tell me about it!" Andy says.

Jeez, what if it's as hard for his daughter to stop using as it's been for him? He has never talked to her about that. They drive on the highway in silence. He can't think anymore.

"Dad, there's something I want to tell you, but I don't want you to get mad at me."

What has he done to his girl? She should be mad at him, not the other way around. He's feeling like the lowest level of pond scum – all wrapped up in his having a beer without once thinking it could hurt his kid.

"Oh, honey," he says, "I won't get mad at you. I promise." That's a lie, of course. Anything could set him off now, and he isn't sure he really wants to hear what she has to say.

"Do you remember that night, three-and-a-half years ago, when Monica had that baby shower? I was invited to a party at my best friend's house? And you couldn't take me?"

He searches his memory for details: big shindig in the home; gals inside talking babies, guys outside drinking beer and watching ball; the house trashed the next day; a huge paper and cardboard recycling project afterward. He has a vague memory of Andy sassing Monica, but that could just as easily have been some other time. "I'm sorry, honey, but I don't remember much. What happened?"

"I was so pissed off at you! You were supposed to take me to a sleepover at Britt's, but you couldn't leave Monica. You and Mom had some mix-up around whose responsibility it was to drive me, and I got stuck without a ride. How could you do that to me?"

There's a question. But that Connie! She was always lining up stuff he didn't know about during his time with Andy.

"That was the first night I used. There was a bunch of beer in the patio. I found a joint. I took it to my room and got high for the first time."

As a parent, you're supposed to be relieved when your kid is willing to talk to you about drugs; at all those parent education classes, they tell you to welcome the conversation. But Bryan is about to explode. WHAT? WHEN YOU WERE 12 YEARS OLD? YOU TOLD ME YOU DIDN'T START EXPERIMENTING UNTIL YOU WERE 14! HOW COULD YOU SMOKE POT IN MY HOUSE? HOW DID I NOT KNOW THIS WAS GOING ON? WHAT ELSE IS THERE I DON'T KNOW? Bryan wants to shout. He just keeps his eyes glued to the road, but imagines they must be bugging out of his head.

"I wish I could undo that night," she continues in a little-girl voice. "That's when it all started. When I used, my problems disappeared. It was like magic. Except a part of me always felt guilty and ashamed. I knew it was wrong."

What kind of a father am I? He thinks. Raising a daughter with beer and pot left out from a party? He thought they were more careful than that. Jesus, talk about your loaded gun. Right there on the kitchen table for an angry 12-year-old. If Connie found out about this, her case would be proven beyond a reasonable doubt. He'd be ruined.

"I wish I had never started using," she says. "Then I would never have had to stop. My life would be so much easier."

Oh, fuck a duck! What if all those things his ex has been saying about him are true? That he is the shittiest dad in the world? He always figured the ex said that stuff just to yank his chain. Maybe she was trying to protect her daughter – from him.

"I'm sorry honey," Bryan says, reaching over for her hand. "I let you down. I should've been more careful. I wasn't being a very good dad."

"It's not your fault," she says quickly. "I knew better. I'm not blaming you. I would have found drugs on my own eventually. It's not hard to find pot, you know."

He makes the last turn to their street. There's a lump in his throat the size of a baseball.

"Thanks for coming to court with me today, Dad. It means a lot to me."

And, damn, his headache is back with a vengeance. It's been a long day, and he wishes like hell he could throw back a couple of beers when he walks in the door. But his daughter is back, and he cannot fail her. He doesn't deserve her, and he wishes he knew what to say. But he feels stupid with words, so he just squeezes her hand.

Thank you, Lord, for giving me another chance, he prays: I'll try not to mess it up this time. He just wishes he had the tiniest clue about what he should do, because he is lost in the middle of the fucking woods with not so much as a single match to light his way.

HON. STRATHMORE REED, JR.

18. GRADUATION

Judge Reed is only seventeen minutes into the morning session of his trial and already is calculating how much longer until he can call a break: 57 minutes until the morning recess; 3 hours and 43 minutes until lunch. An eternity. At least Drug Court will meet that afternoon, it being Thursday, so he can adjourn this whinefest at noon. He peels his eyes from the sluggish courtroom clock and makes himself focus on the witness on the stand. She is your basic train wreck – a sad sack, perennial victim; the kind of person his father would have dubbed "one of life's losers."

According to the legal pleadings, today's matter is styled as a quiet title action. However, Reed thinks of it as a "Mom always loved you best" case. It is a fight between siblings over ownership of their childhood home. The mother died ten years earlier, leaving her modest home in equal shares to her two adult children. The daughter, who is now on the witness stand, moved into the home shortly before the mother's death and has lived there ever since. She appears to be in her early fifties, and in spite of her obvious intelligence and impressive collection of post-graduate degrees, has never held a steady job. Her life has been an endless stream of relationship and financial disasters. At the moment, her head is in her hands and she is weeping, as she recounts the final days of her mother's life.

On the other side of the courtroom sits the brother who filed this action against her, taking careful notes on a yellow legal pad. He could not be more different from his sister. He is a few years older than she, married for twenty-six years with two achieving children, and recently retired from a career in the insurance industry. After graduating high school, he attended Villanova University and has lived in Pennsylvania ever since.

During his direct examination the previous day, Brother described the many times over the years he bailed out his sister financially, to the point of causing occasional discord with his wife because of his fraternal generosity. He placed into evidence (Exhibits 3-19) a sheaf of handwritten notes and letters from his sister, desperate ones begging for money and heartfelt ones thanking him for it. He produced a stack of canceled checks and receipts demonstrating how, over the years, he paid most, if not all, of the taxes, insurance, and maintenance on the home, (Exhibits 20-38), never once asking his sister to reimburse him or to pay him rent for living there. "What would be the point? I knew she couldn't afford it," he testified. "She didn't have anywhere else to live, and I figured it would be a good investment for both of us."

A few years ago, his sister begged him for yet another loan – "as much as you can send!" – and whether it was the audacity of the request or the accumulated weight of his wife's disapproval, Brother this time suggested they sell the house and split the proceeds. "The market in California was hot; we stood to make a killing. My sister would be able to pay off her credit card bills and put a tidy sum in the bank. My son at the time was starting college, and the extra cash would've helped."

The proposal proved fatal to their relationship, as Reed could have predicted. People don't change – why is that such a difficult concept to understand and accept? Liars don't become truth-tellers, deadbeats don't become achievers, and losers don't become winners. The sister, cast forever in the role of impoverished victim, was dumbfounded by the proposal. Sell *her* home because she couldn't afford to live there? Unthinkable! She accused her brother of being greedy and evil; reminded him that *he* had a beautiful home that *Ma* helped finance; and, just before hanging up on him, vowed that he would have to sue her if he ever hoped to see a penny out of the home – which, incidentally, she considered 100% hers as did their mother. Brother and sister have not spoken a word since then.

Miss Bettina, his experienced courtroom clerk, had the foresight to place an extra box of tissues on the witness stand. Reed can hardly bear listening to this woman's tale of woe. The gist of her defense is that her brother has a lot of money and she has none; he has a spouse whereas she is all alone; he has a home and she deserves one too; and Ma would be devastated if she knew her children were in court battling over her humble estate.

In short, she has no legal defense whatsoever. Reed wanted to rule for the brother after opening statements, but the law requires that process be observed and both sides be given their day in court. Such a colossal waste of time and money, to say nothing of public resources. Given the many details this witness has provided about her relationship with her mother and brother, she would have been better off investing what little capital she had on psychotherapy and some fast-acting pharmaceuticals, not spending it on a lawsuit, for heaven's sake.

As the witness drones on and on about one childhood slight after another, Reed struggles to maintain his judicial demeanor. If only he might receive one of Skylar's witty e-mails! But there's no chance of that today. She left town early last Saturday to meet four dear friends from college for their annual spa week at Rancho La Puerta. No phones, faxes, or computers allowed; those are the rules. "Just a week of girly giggles," she explained. "Our annual pilgrimage to get buffed, puffed, and fluffed!" Happily, Skylar made dinner reservations for the two of them this upcoming Saturday at his favorite San Francisco steak house. "After subsisting for seven days on cottage cheese and celery,

I want to come home to a rare filet mignon, a stiff martini, and you!" That was the last he'd heard from her; now he was just counting the days until her return. He can picture her now, sipping coffee by a pool, perhaps telling her friends about her new boyfriend. The thought makes him smile despite his miserable circumstances. Could life really be so full and unpredictable as to permit him, at his age, to be a lovely lady's "new boyfriend?" Apparently so, and Reed can scarcely believe his good fortune.

"Ma thought I should have the house after she was gone because my brother already had a big house in Pennsylvania," the witness says, sounding like a petulant child. "Plus, she always felt bad about the way Dad treated me growing up."

Reed stifles a groan. Has the opposing lawyer never heard of the hearsay objection? Get on your feet, man! Moreover, what is the possible relevance of this testimony? The witness launches into her teenage years, recounting the abuse she suffered at the hands of her drunken father. Judging by the pained expression on his face, the brother shares Reed's discomfort with this line of questioning.

Families. There are a lot of lawsuits in the courthouse, but the worst ones by far are not the dim-witted felonies of the criminal department but the vicious fights between family members or neighbors filed in the civil department.

"I was cheated out of my inheritance!"

"His pool is on my side of the fence!"

"He was off having sex with his girlfriend while I was in the hospital giving birth to our third child!"

Reed has heard them all, and they are ugly battles to referee – so emotional and uncivilized. He used to come home from work and say to Dory, "I'd better be really nice to you, because I'm not going to get a divorce and have you tell a judge the kind of thing I hear! And if we ever get in a fight with our neighbors, we're moving!"

The official break time is still 30 minutes away. The witness is describing "possibly the most traumatic event" of her life, the night when she was 16 and her intoxicated father woke her up "ranting" about his depressing, sexless marriage, and how wrong she, his daughter, was to always side with the mother. The witness is sobbing, and everyone in the courtroom looks worn down and dejected. Reed declares a recess. As he steps off the bench, he experiences a confusing wave of emotion – relief at escaping the weeping witness's airspace, and dread that the hearing will take even ten minutes more than necessary.

The afternoon session, by contrast, is upbeat and engaging. Reed, who prides himself on his meticulous preparation of each and every legal proceeding, finds himself utterly unprepared for his first Juvenile Drug Court graduation.

The capable probation officer, Ms. Karla Washington, explains to him in advance of the ceremony that he need only present the graduate with her diploma, shake her hand, and declare on the record that she has successfully completed Drug Court, that probation is terminated, and that her case is dismissed. With these catchphrases duly noted in his trial journal, he sits back and observes the novel events as they unfold in his courtroom. Imagine, after 30 years in the law, witnessing something utterly unprecedented!

His ragtag crew of juvenile delinquents assembles in the jury box. The goofy 15-year-old boys sit together in the back row, all wearing knee-length T-shirts, trying with all their might to convince the world of their super-stud toughness, while behaving like unruly fourth-graders infected with a bad case of spring fever. The provocative girls sit in front of them, no doubt robbing the boys of any shred of concentration they might have brought to the proceeding. Bleached hair, thick eyeliner, swelling curves – the girls seem ages older than the boys, except for their tell-tale giggling, note-writing, and penchant for pink bubble gum. Unattached to either clique are Reed's two top performers. The serious and scared Andrea B., daughter of the Bretano's coffee shop owners, and the quiet but driven Jacob S., a curly-haired senior who, in recent weeks, has come to understand that he is about to be launched into adulthood, and will need a diploma, driver's license, and clean criminal record if he's to make anything of himself. Week after week, Reed is heartened to hear of their small accomplishments as they successfully move through the tasks assigned to them.

But the star of today's show is the graduate, Sahari H., seated separately from the others with her probation officer at counsel table. This young lady, with her eye-catching, lustrous, blue-black hair, is beaming. Her grandfather, mother, and younger brother sit behind her in the front row, sporting the exact same hair and smile.

Reed realizes that broad smiles in courtrooms are few and far between. It is a rather welcome change of pace.

"Welcome to the graduation of Sahari Hamid from Juvenile Drug Court," the probation officer announces. "This young lady is living proof of how far a person can go in a year. When she started Drug Court last year, Sahari was a daily pot smoker. She had a hard time getting to school every day, and when she went, she had a hard time paying attention. As a result, she was flunking out of school. She didn't think she had a problem with pot and had zero interest in stopping. She fought constantly with her mother, and had been running away from home for several years, disappearing for weeks at a time. But there was always a little part of her that knew if she ever wanted to have the life she dreamed of, she needed to stop getting into trouble, graduate high school, and attend college. So she reluctantly agreed to join Drug Court – not that she had much choice. She also swore up and down that she would smoke a joint the night she graduated from Drug Court."

Reed notices the dark-skinned Sahari blush profoundly at her brash indiscretions from just a year ago. But the audience – mostly parents and Drug Court graduates – laughs appreciatively.

"Sahari got off to a rough start with our program. It turns out, it wasn't quite as easy for her to stop smoking as she thought. She had lots of dirty UA's, lots of time in the Hall, and one frightening instance of disappearing for six weeks. When we finally found her, she was quite sick. In addition to her physical illness, she was also sick of living on the streets, sick of telling lies, sick of – believe it or not! – having nothing to do: no school, no job. She begged to be readmitted to Drug Court, and, with some trepidation and after a long stint in the Hall, we let her return."

As the probation officer describes Sahari's slips and successes in Drug Court, Reed looks at the 17-year-old in wonder. This smiling, sweet-faced girl was a daily drug user? This clean and clear-skinned child was living on the streets? Where were her parents? Well, Reed knows the answer to that, having read the probation report in the file: Her father left shortly after her birth, never to be heard from again. Her mother raised the child herself, subsisting at or below poverty level.

Around the time the mother gave birth to a second child twelve years later, Sahari started defying her mother, running with the older kids, and picking up law violations. And yet, here she is, almost safely to the other side of her dangerous teenage years, about to graduate Drug Court. Quite a miraculous transformation!

"Sahari has now been sober for five months," the probation officer says, to much applause. "She will graduate from high school in June. In August, she starts nursing school at City College. Congratulations, Sahari! I am as proud of you as if you were my own daughter. You have come a long, long way. But because I'm still your probation officer for five more minutes, I have one more order for you."

Reed leans forward in his seat, as does the graduate. The only noise in the courtroom is the hum of fluorescent lights.

"Promise me that you will not, under any circumstances, celebrate your graduation by smoking pot tonight!"

In truth, Reed does not see what is quite so funny about the probation officer's remark, but he is apparently alone in that, as giddy applause and hoots of approval erupt across the courtroom.

"I promise," Sahari answers in a small voice.

Such a sweet young girl! Reed can't help but think of his daughter, Bitsy, when she was this age. Painfully shy, not many friends, kept everything inside. Good heavens, it's been months since he's seen her. Reed makes a note to call her after court. If she doesn't already have a degree in psychology, she's getting one now, and, he thinks, maybe these juvenile court proceedings might be of interest to her. It would be nice if the two of them could talk about something other than the weather.

Sahari's grandfather is summoned to the podium. He doesn't walk so much as shuffle to it. He is not a native English speaker, and his eyes are filled with tears. "Thank you, nice people," he says, looking directly at his beloved Sahari. "Is happy day for Hamid family. You give us back our precious jewel, we thought was lost, our beautiful girl. She granddaughter, daughter, sister, is our Sahari. Thank you."

The graduate speaks last. She has a soft voice, and it is difficult for Reed to hear her. Her manner is slow and gentle, perfect for a nurse, thinks Reed. She thanks her probation officer, the Drug Court team, and her family for their support of her. Especially she thanks her younger brother for inspiring her to want to be a better big sister. "But if I ever catch you doing any of the things I did, I'm going to kill you myself," she tells him. Finally, she turns to the teens and addresses her final comments to them.

"Good luck to you all," she says. "I hope you get through this. It's not that hard to do but you have to want to do it. No one can do it for you. For myself, I'm happy not to be lying to my family and feeling guilty all the time. I lived on the streets for a long time, and every single user I met wished they could have their teenage years back. I feel like I magically got mine back, just in time to go to the prom and walk with my class. If I can do this, you can, too. Thank you."

The probation officer hugs Sahari, and they turn to the judge to conclude the proceeding. Their faces shine with hope, happiness and – my goodness! But what else could it be? – love.

For the second time that day, Reed is grateful for the foresight of his courtroom clerk. He yanks a tissue from the box, wipes his eyes, rechecks his notes and clears his throat prodigiously before conferring the diploma. He stumbles his way through his short speech, altogether stunned by his watering eyes and his thumping heart.

ANDY

19. WHO AM I?

Who am I?

I've been staring at this question for 27 minutes...28...29...

When The Killer gave this assignment, I thought – Wow! For once, she cut me some slack. I got an E-Z topic, a break from the soul-searching stuff she usually lays on me. "Who am I?" Gosh, any dope could knock out a couple quick pages on that topic in ten minutes, fifteen max – What a picnic, a day at the beach, a piece of cake.

35...36...37

My fingers are on the keyboard, I'm ready to attack the topic, spill my thoughts across the screen. Here I am! (I want to shout) See how fun and loveable I am! So I type a few wimpy, weasely words, read them, shake my head, clear the page, think some more, and...nothing. Oh, maybe it's true what The

Killer warns us: Drinking and smoking wipes out our brains, hijacks our thinking, corrupts our hard drive, and now I am nothing.

Stop it, that negative all-or-nothing thinking. That's how an addict thinks. We must be positive, The Killer tells us! We must not feel sorry for ourselves! The negative thinking leads to negative behavior! I know I'm not nothing. But who am I?

I'm someone who is trying to fill this page.

I'm someone who is trying to believe she couldn't be so clueless as to not know who her own self is.

Shouldn't I be able to say: I am a 16-year-old girl – yes! I'm 16, even if I'm not sweet! – who has lots of friends, enjoys school, has many interests! I have a favorite food, lucky number, special talent, book that changed my life, song I sing when I wake up in the morning.

Or: You see that group of muscle girls over there – the ones with the huge triceps? Those are the crew girls. They get up every morning at 4:30 so they can be on the water in their boat, all eight of them rowing together at 5:30, putting in two hours of exercise before their first class. They shower together, drink out of each other's Nalgene bottles, wear each other's spandex. I'm one of them.

Or: See that group of frizzy-haireds over there? They are the math girls. You didn't even know there was such a thing as math girls, did you? These frizzy-haireds spend lunch with the math teacher every single day. Those aren't sleek cell phones they hold – those are calculators! They think math is *interesting*. They think the super-geek math teacher is *cute*. I'm one of those.

Or: Oooh, what about that group, way at the end of the campus, the ones in short skirts, slipping into someone's car? Everyone knows who they are. They've been around for years – only the hair styles and makeup change. They steal cigarettes and eyeliner from the drug store, cut class, swap boyfriends, text each other at two in the morning. I'm one of those.

Except I'm not. I'm not any of them. I'm between groups right now. Which is fine, sort of. I can't go back to the friends I used to have – either they won't take me or I can't take them. I'm going to have friends again, as soon as I get things figured out. In the mean time, it's awkward. I picked a very tricky time to be groupless – well, obviously; this is high school. Even the weirdos, misfits, and loners have their own group. Once you have your group, ding! ding! ding! You know who you are – all you have to do is look at your people.

45…46…I'm dying here. I did a report once on Madagascar. Maybe The Killer would let me run with that topic instead. She could learn that it's the fourth-largest island in the world, that it has 10,000 species of plants, and that 90% of them aren't found anywhere else in the world. I could talk about the varieties of lemurs and orchids…why doesn't she give me Madagascar?

When I was a little girl, we had a big earthquake. This is California, and Sequoia Valley sits right on top of the San Andreas fault. When people come from out of state, they say: Yeah, you guys have great weather, beautiful trails, nice beaches. But how can you stand living on a fault line? When you live here, you don't think about it until an earthquake happens, and then you're like: That is *not* a big truck making the ground shake. That is an earthquake. When it's over, you turn on the TV, check the computer. Was that the big one?

I was home with Mom when the earthquake took us on a wild-ass ride, and she yelled for me to come, grabbed my shoulders and pulled me outside to the front yard. She wrapped her arms around me, screamed she would take care of me, swore she'd never let me get hurt. When the ground stopped shaking, she was sobbing and squeezing and telling me how much she loved me. I had to pry her arms off me, squirm out of her iron embrace, and explain to her that it was over, the shaking had stopped and we were okay. Later, on TV, we watched the footage of the ruins: the collapsed freeways, the fallen buildings, the fires and lost dogs. We walked around on tiptoes for weeks, not trusting the ground beneath our feet. We looked at overpasses with suspicion, worried they would collapse on us. We noticed cracks along the foundation of our house that we'd never seen before. The world, after 17 seconds of rocking and rolling, had become a scary stranger to us; the things we thought we could count on were suddenly alien and unreliable.

The feeling after an earthquake is: Everything I thought I knew is wrong.

That's how I feel about myself right now.

I know who I *used* to be. I was a good little girl – so smart and funny! My dad said so all the time. He told me I'd be running Bretano's by the time I was 20, and once I'd turned that little startup into a Fortune 500 competitor, I could do anything I damn well pleased. He called me his lawyer. When he got home from work and had some bad news to break to Mom, he'd slip into my room and ask me how to pitch it to her. Mom does not like surprises and she doesn't like feeling left out – it's so obvious, I don't know why he could never get this about her – so I'd show him a strategy where he could set it up so his solution would come from her. He loved having me explain this stuff to him! "You're a genius, honey!" he used to say, so full of pride. "I don't know how a dumbshit like me could be your dad."

Yeah, unlike other dads, my dad swore around me, and it tickled me to pieces. It made me feel grown up. Like I was his friend. His smart and funny girl.

He stopped talking that way about me right around the time I left my good little girl phase and moved on to became a party girl. I liked being a party girl! It was so different, and it happened so fast. One year I was this quiet little reader and the next year I was skipping school, meeting the older kids, and doing some wild stuff.

It was the freedom that I liked so much about being a party girl. The freedom to go to the beach instead of school, stay out late – honestly, the world is a whole different place after 11 P.M.! – and meet new people. The freedom to laugh as loud as you want, be as stupid as you want, do things your mother would never let you do – and realizing, there is nothing she can do to stop you.

It was quite an eye-opening experience! Yet for all that excitement, being a wild girl gets old too. Just putting aside the trouble with your parents, school, and the law; the horrible, long days you spend in Juvenile Hall; and the constant, nagging feeling that you have something to hide. What gets old is the build-up of all the stupid things you did when you wanted to use. If you're even a semi-cute girl, you never have a problem getting drugs. It's that simple. So you end up doing some things you'd rather not think about, and the only way to not think about it is to use some more. As soon as you're using some more, you're doing those stupid things again, training yourself to turn off your brain so you don't have to know what you're doing.

The Killer says, you're only as sick as your secrets. I'm not sure what it means, but I have a feeling it's not good news for me. I have some secrets I keep even from myself.

Yes, I used to be a party girl. But then my partying landed me in a pit of trouble, so I'm not one anymore. I lost my good girl friends. I lost my party girl friends.

So that's pretty much where I am: lost. I lost my way, lost my sense of who I am and what I like. I am lost.

But The Killer tells me: I must be positive, that our thoughts are powerful things, and if you tell yourself you are going to have a lousy day, that's the way it'll pan out. If I tell her I'm lost, she'll bark at me to get off my "pity pot," another expression of hers I don't completely understand.

66...67...68...Wait...Here's something I can say that's true. It's not as definitive as I would like, but it's not negative either, and it's all I know for sure right now.

Here's who I am:

Searching. I am searching.

BRYAN

20. SWEARING UNDER OATH

SUPERIOR COURT OF CALIFORNIA
COUNTY OF SEQUOIA

In re the Marriage of
BRYAN BRETANO,
    Petitioner
vs.
CONSTANCE BRETANO,
    Respondent

_____/

DEPOSITION OF BRYAN BRETANO

BE IT REMEMBERED that on this 29th
day of April in Sequoia Valley, California,
at 1:30 p.m., before me, Justine Rider, CSR,
there appeared Petitioner Bryan Bretano for

his deposition under oath pursuant to Code of Civil Procedure Section 2025.

Appearances:

Constance Bretano, Respondent in propria persona

R. Seamus Shields, Esq., Attorney for petitioner

Bryan Bretano, Petitioner

(Oath administered by court reporter at 1:31 p.m. Direct Examination commences)

MS. BRETANO: Please state your full name and spell your last name for the record.

MR. BRETANO: Aw, come on, Connie. Don't bust my chops. You know my name. I don't have time for this crap. You've got 30 minutes. Just ask the damn questions and be done with this.

MS. BRETANO: That is not a lawful objection under the Code of Civil Procedure. I repeat: State your name and spell it for the record.

MR. BRETANO: I'm the chump named as the petitioner in this never-ending, goddamn divorce. My last name is spelled just like yours. My first name? You used to write it in whipping cream across my naked chest. I still spell it that way.

MS. BRETANO: Madam Court Reporter, please certify the question. The witness is refusing to answer.

MR. SHIELDS: We stipulate that the deponent's name is Bryan Bretano. B-R-E-T-A-N-0. Next question.

MS. BRETANO: I would like to have marked as an exhibit to this deposition Respondent's Order to Show Cause to modify child custody.

(Whereupon the document was marked as Respondent's Exhibit Number 1)

Showing you what has been marked Respondent's Exhibit Number 1, do you oppose this motion to change custody from joint physical and legal custody to sole custody of the minor child to respondent?

MR. BRETANO: Yes. Absolutely. With every fiber of my being.

MS. BRETANO: Do you object to giving a DNA swab for the purpose of determining your predilection for drug and alcohol addiction?

MR. BRETANO: Hell yes. Look, you've already taken me for everything I have. You're not robbing me of my DNA. And what about you? Are you going to have the lab examine your DNA? Because I'll tell you what that shows. If there's a gene for crazy, you'll have it in spades.

MR. SHIELDS: Bryan. Just answer the question.

MS. BRETANO: Do you contest the facts asserted in support of respondent's motion to modify custody?

MR. BRETANO: That pack of lies you call your declaration under penalty of perjury? Yes. It's horseshit and you know it.

MR. SHIELDS: Excuse me, Connie. I think this might go a little easier if I talk to my client for a minute. Off the record.

MS. BRETANO: No, we will not go off the record! Everything here is on the record. I object! Counsel, you have no right to talk to your client during my examination. You are coaching the witness. I am entitled to his testimony, not his lawyer's dressed-up version of the facts. This is totally unacceptable. This is highly irregular. I object. I object. I strongly object.

(Whereupon Mr. Shields and Mr. Bretano confer inaudibly)

MR. SHIELDS: Next question.

MS. BRETANO: Do you admit that you enrolled the minor child of the above-captioned marriage, hereinafter known as

Andrea, in the Sequoia County Juvenile Drug Court?

MR. BRETANO: Yes, I admit it. Is that a felony?

MS. BRETANO: And do you further admit that you did not obtain respondent's consent prior to enrolling Andrea in Juvenile Drug Court?

MR. BRETANO: Guilty as charged. I believe you were in New York at the time, on a shopping spree financed no doubt by the alimony collected from yours truly. You know what kills me? I've paid you all this money and you don't even know how to spell my name.

MR. SHIELDS: Excuse me again, Connie.

(Whereupon Mr. Shields and Mr. Bretano confer inaudibly)

MS. BRETANO: Did you at the time believe that enrolling Andrea in Juvenile Drug Court was in the best interests of the child?

MR. BRETANO: Yes.

MS. BRETANO: Had she been in your physical custody the days immediately preceding her enrollment in Drug Court?

MR. BRETANO: Yes.

MS. BRETANO: On or about December 27-28 of last year, did she leave your home to consume alcohol and marijuana in a public place, resulting in her arrest?

MR. BRETANO: Yes.

MS. BRETANO: Did you give her permission to leave the house?

MR. BRETANO: No. No. Of course not.

MS. BRETANO: Did you supply her with alcohol and/or drugs that night?

MR. BRETANO: Oh for Christ's sake, Connie, give me a break, would you? What kind of father do you think I am? No, never mind, don't answer that. No I did not supply our daughter with drugs and-slash-or booze.

MS. BRETANO: Did you hear her leave the house that evening?

MR. BRETANO: Jesus Christ, Connie. I'm here for 15 more minutes. If you want to waste your time with stupid goddamn questions, go right ahead. But I'm leaving at 2:00. This is the fifth fucking time I've sat for my deposition. You don't get to hold me hostage forever. There's a limit. No, I didn't hear Andy leave the house. If I had, I would have thrown my body against the door and stopped her from going out.

MS. BRETANO: When did you first discover she had gone out that night?

MR. BRETANO: At 8:00 the next morning, when I went to her room to wake her up. Ice ran in my goddamn blood when I figured out she'd slipped out of the house again. I called the cops right away. They found her passed out in the park, surrounded by empty bottles of cheap booze. Our precious daughter! Drinking and smoking her life away! We're lucky she didn't die of alcohol poisoning. I didn't know whether to feel relieved or furious.

MR. SHIELDS: Bryan, all you were asked is when you first discovered your daughter had gone out. You don't need to get into the color commentary. Just answer the question.

MR. BRETANO: Sorry.

MS. BRETANO: Was it your idea to enroll Andrea in Drug Court?

MR. BRETANO: My idea? I wouldn't say that exactly. The judge brought it up. The public defender told us that it was a good program, but hard. It all happened pretty fast.

MS. BRETANO: Well were you even paying attention? Or were you zoning out and letting other people do all the heavy lifting, as per usual?

MR. SHIELDS: Objection. Argumentative. Instruct the witness not to answer.

MR. BRETANO: Sorry, Connie. I'd like to answer that question, but my lawyer told me not to.

MS. BRETANO: What factors did you consider in reaching the decision to enroll our daughter in Drug Court?

MR. BRETANO: What factors? Jesus. Okay. Factor one: she'd just been booked for drunk in public. Factor two: it wasn't her first, second, or even third arrest. Factor three: she is on probation and isn't supposed to be getting into trouble. Factor four: her friends are dopers. Factor five: the judge seemed to think it was a good idea. Factor six: all the other good reasons I'll be able to remember when you aren't staring at me.

MS. BRETANO: In deciding to enroll her in Juvenile Drug Court, did you think Andrea had a drug problem?

MR. BRETANO: Yeah. I guess so. Pot isn't helping her any, that's for sure.

MS. BRETANO: Where do you think that problem came from?

MR. BRETANO: I don't know. Do you know? Bad friends. Peer pressure. Drugs are everywhere. Her age.

MS. BRETANO: Are you aware that there is a strong hereditary correlation between alcoholic/addict parents and their offspring?

MR. BRETANO: What? Repeat the question? Was that a question? I don't understand.

MS. BRETANO: Well, you used to smoke pot when you were a kid, right?

MR. SHIELDS: Objection. Irrelevant. Instruct the witness not to answer.

MS. BRETANO: Isn't it a fact that you were arrested for possession of marijuana when you were 16 years old?

MR. SHIELDS. Same objection. Don't answer.

MS. BRETANO: When was the last time you smoked marijuana?

MR. SHIELDS: Irrelevant. Don't answer.

MS. BRETANO: Are you instructing your client not to answer? Because it is relevant. It's totally relevant. If Mr. Bretano is smoking marijuana, Andrea is not safe in that house or in that environment. She must be getting the idea from someone. It sure isn't me.

MR. BRETANO: I take the Fifth.

MS. BRETANO: You're kidding. You take the Fifth? Do you mean that you refuse to answer the question because the answer might incriminate you? So you're still smoking marijuana? Did you know it's illegal?

MR. SHIELDS: Objection. Calls for a legal conclusion. Don't answer.

MS. BRETANO: Do you deny the fact that you smoke marijuana?

MR. SHIELDS: Objection. Don't –

MR. BRETANO: I do deny it.

MR. SHIELDS: – answer the question. Never mind. There it is. He denies it.

MS. BRETANO: May I remind you that you have taken an oath to tell the truth, the whole truth, and nothing but the truth?

MR. BRETANO: I don't know if you may or may not. Is there another option where I can ask you to shut the fuck up?

MR. SHIELDS: Bryan.

MR. BRETANO: Sorry. I'm done. You said this would take no more than 20 minutes. This is a complete waste of time. I am leaving.

MS. BRETANO: You can't leave. I haven't finished this deposition. I have lots more questions to ask. Bryan, sit down! You can't leave! I'm going to court!

MR. BRETANO: What else is new? I'm out of here. God damn it, I am so out of here. Get your hands off me. I'm leaving.

MS. BRETANO: May the record reflect that the witness has left the room.

MR. SHIELDS: Gosh, I'm sorry about that, Connie. Maybe we could resume at a more convenient time. I'm sure my client will be more accommodating next time. We don't need to go to court. I'll give you some future dates. Just tell me what works for you.

MS. BRETANO: Don't you patronize me. I'm letting the judge know he walked out of this deposition. I'm going to get sanctions against you and your client. He will pay for this. I'm going to move for contempt. He's going to jail for this, for violating my lawful right to discovery. You better bone up on criminal law, counselor. Your client is going to jail.

(WHEREUPON PROCEEDINGS WERE CONCLUDED AT 2:00 P.M.)

HON. STRATHMORE REED, JR.

21. THE WITNESS CHAIR

Ah, Friday, glorious Friday! Reed's jury dutifully returns its verdict just before lunch. How they arrive at their award of $999.99 is anyone's guess, but the duly elected foreperson is conscientious, the decision is unanimous, and if the award sounds more like the product of an infomercial than of deliberation, it is nonetheless good enough for government work. All the law asks is that the jury's decision be supported by sufficient evidence; it does not require the judge to agree with it. In fact, jurors frequently ask Reed if he would have decided the case the same way they did. He has developed a hundred ways to duck the question, and has yet to let slip that he cannot fathom how any right-thinking person on God's green earth could have come up with such an unprincipled result. As litigators are fond of saying, trials are a crapshoot. For the most part, jurors can do what they damn well please. On any given case, ten different juries might arrive at ten different results, and as long as the evidence is there to support it, the verdict can be entered, and judge and jury may rest assured that both have discharged their respective duties.

Reed is now ready for the weekend. Skylar says she has big plans for him, starting with tonight. He does not have a precise idea of what is in store for him, only that her driver will pick him up at six o'clock and deliver him to the grand Fairmont Hotel on Nob Hill, where he will join her for the tail-end of a press-the-flesh industry cocktail party hosted by her firm. "If you come to my get-together, I will more than make it up to you," she promised, rather seductively as he now recalls with a slightly embarrassed grin. "None of my friends believe I have a real boyfriend," she continued. "They think I'm making you up. Please let me show you off, if only for a few minutes!" When she found out his only serious objection was having to drive to the City on a Friday night, she proposed her driver pick him up, and the deal was sealed. "Thank you, my darling," she whispered. "Next time you have a command-performance, rubber-chicken bar function, I am your gal."

She is his gal! Reed smiles broadly as he pulls into the parking place reserved for him at The Witness Chair, the nearby watering hole and restaurant where he and his old friend Hank Hellman have dined every Friday (excepting only vacations) for upwards of ten years. Not only do he and Hank eat together at the same restaurant every week, they also order the same meal year in and year out: pan-fried sole with French fries and iced tea; $12.00 each, including tax and tip; you just can't beat it. At least that's what Hank always says. Truthfully, Reed wouldn't mind switching it up every so often. The Witness Chair has seen better days; the Naugahyde upholstery is bursting with age; tables are scarred with countless initials; and its décor of dusty law books and faded photographs of long-forgotten legal luminaries is downright depressing. Strathmore and Skylar enjoyed a heavenly meal at Chez Panisse a few nights earlier, and while the cost of their dinner was ten times that of today's repast, they weren't staring at sad-sack fellows hunched over liquid lunches at the bar nor ordering any previously frozen pan-fried sole, either. But Hank wouldn't hear of trying a new restaurant and that's that.

Reed understands and accepts that Hank's lunches at The Witness Chair have become the highlight of his week. Now that Hank is retired from the court, he looks forward to mingling with lawyers and law enforcement friends from his judging days, slapping them on the back and asking how the hell they're getting along without him. Plus, it must be said, Hank is treated like royalty at The Witness Chair, and he eats it up. He has his own table, and the old-timers come over, seek his advice, and pay their respects. Hank goes to hear the news, opinions, old jokes and courtroom gossip, while promoting his new private-judging business, which Reed intuits, is not as wildly successful as Hank had hoped when he retired last year. Damn the food, Reed is only too pleased to join his oldest and dearest friend at the restaurant of his choosing. Reed goes for the camaraderie, if not for the ambience.

Once inside, Reed sees that Hank is already seated at their table and is surrounded by smiling, sycophantic lawyers. They all look vaguely familiar to Reed, but he couldn't come up with a single name if his life depended on it. Hank unfailingly covers for him. Still, Reed hopes that none of them are the lawyers from today's case. Number one, it would be embarrassing not to recognize them when he took the verdict just a few minutes earlier, and number two, the lawyers would be constitutionally unable to restrain themselves from blathering on about the case. These out-of-court conversations cause him no end of heartache. Judges are absolutely prohibited from discussing any pending or impending case, and the fact that a jury has rendered a verdict does not end the case, as many lawyers erroneously suppose. There are any number of post-trial motions and appeals that resourceful lawyers can file, and until the deadlines for such legal maneuverings have passed, the case is still "pending," and Reed can neither discuss it nor hear a word about it outside of the courtroom. This strict rule sometimes makes Reed feel as though the only conversational topic he can safely pursue with lawyers is the weather, but such is the life of a judge: elevated and isolated.

"It's the Right Honorable Judge Reed!" announces his friend Hank.

"Good afternoon, gentlemen," Reed says, shaking hands and assuming his seat at the table.

"Attorney Seamus Shields here is telling me about a particularly difficult family law case of his, where the parties divorced years ago but are still battling over finances and child custody. Shields here is making a fortune off of their bickering!"

So! That's who the thuggish lawyer with the black shirt-and-tie combination is! Reed now recognizes him from those difficult years spent in the family law assignment. What distasteful cases. After two months in that assignment, Reed began maintaining a running tally of the months, weeks, and days remaining in the rotation. When he told Dory, she observed drily, "Marking time? Hm. Sounds like prison." And that's how it felt to him, too.

"I'm trying to steer the parties into mediation," the slippery Shields says. To Reed, he looks like the kind of lawyer more likely to settle a case by arm-wrestling than by handshakes. "My client is tired of going to court. If we can just get the crazy pro per Mrs. to agree to it, we'll give a call and set something up. My client would love it."

"Here's my card," Hank says. "I'd like to help. I'm pretty sure I had a piece of this case when I was on the court."

"I'd be surprised if you didn't," the lawyer says. "It's been pending for almost ten years. We've had four or five different judges on the case. What a nightmare!"

Hank turns his attention to Reed. "Well, you must know this case too. A high-conflict family law matter called *Marriage of Bretano?* It's the couple who started the coffee business in town."

That name! Reed recognizes it from somewhere. Slightly panicked, Reed holds up his hand like a traffic cop. "Please don't talk about pending cases in front of me!" Ach, this is so awkward! Now that Hank is in private judging, he's constantly talking up lawyers about their cases and forgetting, apparently, that Reed cannot join these conversations because he is still bound by the ethical constraints on sitting judges.

"I beg your pardon, Your Honor," the lawyer says with an obsequious bow. "Please excuse us. We'll let you enjoy your lunch. Good to see you both! I'll call you about that mediation!" With that, the lawyers step away, just as their waitress, Darlene, delivers two iced teas and confirms their customary order.

The two friends fall into their standard conversational pattern. They start by reviewing the cases they handled that week;

the quality of the lawyering they observed (never very impressive); their moments of frustration (the usual suspects are late and unprepared lawyers, obstreperous litigants, overbearing colleagues); and anything odd or entertaining. They then move on to discuss vital statistics. It used to be graduations, marriages and births, but now it's likely to be retirements, diseases and death. Today, Hank fills him in on the upcoming birth of his first grandson in Reno. Hank asks how Reed's daughter, Bitsy, is doing – any marriage bites yet? Reed mumbles something about a research project of hers, then brings his friend current on courthouse gossip. Before moving to new matters, the two of them like to spend a few minutes grousing about the distressing changes to the judiciary; their current pet peeves are mandatory sexual harassment training and the number of inexperienced women being appointed to the bench.

"Any word when you'll be paroled from that silly Drug Court assignment?" Hank asks with derision. Reed of course is well aware that the deciding factor in Hank's retirement was the Presiding Judge's announced decision to send him to Juvenile Drug Court. Hank refused to preside over "touchie-feelie" court proceedings, as he considers them an insult to the integrity of the court. Back in the day, Hank successfully opposed virtually any change put forth for his court. His philosophy was, why fix it if it's not broken? For years, Hank and Reed had been a reliable and effective voting bloc, standing up for the traditions of court procedures and opposing the experimental, politically correct programs proposed by the newer judges. They successfully opposed the so-called therapeutic courts for years, arguing that their small court lacked the resources to assign a trial department to a handful of hopeless druggies. When their court finally bowed to the political pressures of the day, Hank knew it was time for him to retire.

"Ah, it's not so bad," Reed answers mildly, reluctant to reveal to his closest friend that Drug Court is quite different than they thought it would be. Much of what he witnesses continues to appall him, but he cannot help but feel heartened by the progress of some of the participants. Besides, Reed has something he'd much rather discuss with his dear friend: Skylar. He's just waiting for the right moment to bring up the subject, but knows there's no sense in trying to rush things with Hank.

Darlene delivers their entrées, together with catsup, Dijon mustard, and extra pickles, and the judges dive into their platters of food.

"Here's a coincidence for you," Hank says, smothering his fish with the special tartar sauce. "My wife tells me that she and Skylar Stone had lunch together last Friday when you and I were eating here. What do you make of that?"

Skylar! Finally Reed has an opening into the subject he is longing to discuss! He is first tempted to correct Hank, as he would a lawyer, that it couldn't have been *last* Friday because, he happened to know, Skylar was on vacation in Mexico with girlfriends; his wife must be mistaken about the day. But he forbears. If there's one thing Hank cannot abide, it's being corrected. Hank prides himself on getting the details right. It used to make lawyers crazy because while they were citing rules to persuade the judge, Judge Henry Hellman was citing exceptions back to them. So instead, Reed asks his friend if his wife sees Skylar often.

But before Hank can answer and Reed can hint at his big news – news that has the added bonus of reflecting well on Hank, since he introduced Skylar to Reed – the retired sheriff ambles over from the bar, invites himself to take a seat at their table, and starts reminiscing about old times. Every single regular at the restaurant knows at least one thing about Sheriff Bruno Barbagelata (Ret.): The more he drinks, the more he talks. Judging by his thick speech, he's going to have quite a lot to say today.

Reed tolerates the intrusion but at the same time is sorry he can't continue the conversation about Skylar. How he would love to talk to his friend about the huge thing – the only thing! – on his mind. Not that he could go into any detail of it at The Witness Chair, where eager ears are everywhere. Still. He wishes he could tell someone his glorious news; news he himself can scarcely believe.

He and Skylar enjoyed an evening of sexual congress!

Barbagelata launches into the one about the Italian tomato farmer playing his first round of golf, telling the tale in a convincing Italian accent. Reed cautions himself not to think about the thrill of last Saturday night, the heart-stopping joy of their first sexual encounter. But even as he chides himself, he feels a faint, almost painful, stirring emanating from under the table.

Oh, how beautiful she looked that night! She'd just come home from her week at the spa and was absolutely radiant: relaxed, tanned, fit, happy. Manicured, pedicured, not a hair out of place. How clever and resourceful she was to have planned it all! First, the breathy invitation over cocktails in her lovely, well-tended garden. Did his jaw drop? He was shocked enough. But she was masterful! Her invitation was accompanied by the audacious (and, it turns out, exceedingly effective) gift of the little blue pill. She administered it to him tenderly, with a lightly perfumed hand, a small glass of chilled orange juice, and a demure kiss. Could this really be happening to him? They sat outside in cushioned wicker chairs, enjoying the warm evening air, the intoxicating aroma of honeysuckle and night-blooming jasmine, the calming sound of a waterfall in her pond. And then, as it grew dark outside, she took his hand and ushered him inside to her private chamber, which was lit with dozens of flickering candles. The expensive bed linens were suggestively turned down. Soft music played. Skylar handed him a sumptuous hotel robe and suggested he change into it. She next appeared wearing exquisite lingerie and looking, honestly, like the incarnation of a Greek goddess. Gorgeous beyond belief! He was absolutely speechless. Oh, everything was perfect; every little thing, down to the smallest detail. He hadn't anticipated it at all, thought that they were going out for a steak dinner in the City! How brilliant she was to plan it this way; if he'd suspected they were going to be intimate, he'd have fretted and sweated. Instead, he showed up at her door, she seduced him, and he loved every achingly satisfying moment of it.

The sex! After such a long drought! It was unbelievable. He felt like a hero, delivering pleasure to her as he did, and delighting in his own pleasure. Best of all, their union felt completely natural, and perfect, and right. And, oh, how he adored her all the more when, after the deed was done and superlatives exchanged, she told him to go home and sleep in his own bed; that they didn't quite know each other well enough to wake up in the morning without feeling a bit awkward, that there was no reason to rush these things, that she hoped he would have her again.

Have her again! Good Lord, it's all he's thought about all week, and here it is Friday, and he's joining her at the most spectacular hotel in all of San Francisco. Yes, he's ready for the weekend in more ways than one. Because this time, he has his own prescription, and his doctor tells him it's good for 36 hours.

Somewhere during Sheriff Barbagelata's recounting the one about the rabbi, the priest, and the leprechaun, Darlene refills iced tea for the judges and a scotch for the humorist. What always impresses Reed is how kind his friend can be. As impatient and abrupt Hank was reputed to be as a judge, he is generous and sweet with the old guys. He lets the old sheriff chatter on until the check arrives and the sheriff takes his leave to "talk to a man about a horse."

"You were on the quiet side today," Hank says, withdrawing $12 from his wallet. "I'm sorry about the old man busting in on our lunch. But everything's okay? You good?"

"Ah, yes," Reed answers, placing his money on top of his friend's. "Everything is quite well. We can talk more next week."

"Right-o," Hank says, standing up and putting his jacket on. "To answer your question: It was the first time my wife met with Skylar for lunch. The invitation came as a surprise. When she got home, my wife told me she felt a little uncomfortable. Apparently, all Skylar wanted to talk about was you. My wife had the distinct impression she was being pumped for information."

"Is that right?" Reed asks, as bland as can be. But damn it! He cannot suppress the goofy smile. He wishes he could have shared the glorious news with his closest friend, but this week, it will have to wait. He has to cross the bridge to meet his destiny. This day keeps getting better and better.

San Francisco, here I come!

ANDY

22. AN OLD FRIEND

I didn't write in my Drug Court Journal last week because I was at my mom's, and even though she swears she has the same respect for privacy as a Swiss banker (her words exactly), I'm not so sure Swiss bankers consider everything stored in their safe deposit boxes as items available for their inspection. Back in the third grade, I kept a diary and even then I remember including stuff that I knew Mom would enjoy reading. Like if we got in a fight, I'd write about how sorry I was, even if I wasn't a bit sorry and thought the fight was totally her fault. Once I wrote that everyone's mom made waffles by popping a frozen Eggo in the toaster, but that mine made them by mixing buttermilk with whole wheat flour and eggs. After that, she mysteriously began serving waffles every morning and sometimes at dinner too. I finally stopped with the diary because it was too hard for me to think about what to write and how she'd react to it. So I'd be a dumbass to believe that things would be different now.

For starters, Mom hates Drug Court and is on the lookout for any evidence that would justify pulling me out of it. She doesn't believe I have a drug problem, she believes I have an idiot father and wicked stepmother problem. She runs them down every chance she gets, and has some choice things to say about Judge Reed as well. "Has the man never heard of antihistamines? He cannot stumble through a single sentence without clearing his phlegm three or four times!" Which, now that I think about it, is true. Mom was happy to see me, her version of happiness anyway, but it was still a hard week, and I'm relieved to be back home at my dad's.

Just to give you an idea of how crazy things are over there: I tell her I need to do ten hours of housework a week as part of my probation. I explain how my PO said I was a spoiled rich kid who never had to lift a finger and how I'm supposed to learn the value of work while on probation [Memo to self: Unless you feel like signing on for extra work, never say to your PO, "Dishes are for bitches."] But my mother says I will do nothing of the sort, that she pays Merry Maids a small fortune to clean, and that I have better things to do with my time than scrub toilets. So, what's a probationer to do? The last thing I want is a fight with her. The only good *thing about her mega messed-up relationship with my dad is that she directs 95% of her nastiness his way. You do not want to be on the receiving end of the remaining 5%. On the other hand, I know where non-compliance with court directives gets you: Hall time or other humiliation.*

Out of desperation, I clean out my closet at Mom's. Clean living – shit! – it's like I'm channeling my damn PO. On the job, I am ruthless and determined, filling one huge plastic bag after another with a lifetime collection of outgrown clothes, shoes, backpacks, stuffed animals, pencil boxes, books, games and puzzles. It's hard to stuff the pieces of your childhood in a bag, but I keep saying to myself, let someone else use it; what good is it doing in my closet? It feels good to be busy, instead of sitting around watching TV or listening to my mom complain about how overly critical her mother is or how the idiot at the speedy-lube put the wrong kind of oil in her Lexus. Just as I am nearing the end of my ten hours of court-ordered hard labor, I find in the far reaches of the closet an all-but-forgotten piece of my childhood: my sewing machine. My first thought is: old toy – recycle it. My second thought is: Rescued by a Singer!

Yes, the sewing machine is the perfect answer to my predicament. At her house, Mom wants to spend every minute on mother-daughter bondingness. "Let's watch a movie!" "Let's go shopping!" "Where should we go for dinner?" She has a million ideas, and they all involve me. Other than school, there's no escape from her (s)mothering. Sewing offers the perfect out. Only one person can sit at a sewing machine, and, if you position yourself strategically, your back will be turned to the person trying to talk to you. Plus, sewing throws my mom off her game. She says her perfectionist mother – my Granny, who is an amazingly accomplished needle artist – ruined her for sewing, so she became a fabulous baker instead. (And by the way, my grandmother sticks to a very strict diet, no white sugar, no white flour, and no more than a tablespoon of butter in a year).

I clear everything off my desk and set up the Singer, along with the ironing board. Just before disappearing into my party girl phase, I'd cut out dozens of little 2" squares, half red fabrics and half white, with the thought of making a tablecloth for Mother's Day. I take the abandoned project out of its box, press the wrinkles out, and start stitching. I sew the little squares together, alternating red to white, in a checkerboard pattern. I'm so focused on threading the bobbin, making sure I'm assembling the pieces in the right order, clipping the threads, pressing the seams, that I lose track of time. Maybe because I look like I'm concentrating, Mom leaves me alone, checks in with me every few hours to see if I'm hungry or to ask how I'm doing. Every day *for three days, when I return to her house from my boring-ass school for idiots and addicts, I actually feel excited to have a project waiting for me in the safety of my room. When at last all the little pieces are stitched together, I sew a lining on the back side, hem the raw edges, and give it a final pressing. Wow! I'm in awe!*

I find Mom in her study, working feverishly at the computer at whatever her cause of the moment is. "Look what I made!" I say, sounding, and feeling, like an 8-year-old. "It's for you! Happy Belated Mother's Day!"

Mom almost faints. She spends forever admiring it, oooh-ing over my ability to make something so intricate, aaaah-ing at my workmanship, studying the various fabrics. We put it on her kitchen table, and I feel proud. It is beautiful. I forgot how satisfying it is to make something by hand.

It is a good moment, and, it turns out, the highlight of my stay. After that, everything goes to shit.

Because it's her week for me, Mom takes me to Drug Court, and it's the harshest court session ever. Mae-ling lies to the judge about forging her AA card and is sent to the Hall. She puts on a screaming show while the bailiff handcuffs her, and it upsets everyone. Jordan is busted for using the wiz-o-master during his UA and is tossed out of the program; Miguel is on the run and doesn't show up; the judge looks pissed. None of it does a thing to increase Mom's confidence in the program. On the drive home, Mom is getting teary-eyed that my week with her is coming to an end, so she acts all mushy and starts working her claws back in me.

"Why don't we stop at the fabric store?" she suggests. "You can pick up some material for your next sewing project."

I feel sort of downhearted from all the screw-ups in court, and truthfully I just want to eat some dinner and go to sleep. But it's sweet to see my mom trying to be a good mother. And it's not like she enjoys shopping for sewing supplies. So I go along with her plan, and by the time we find a parking spot and walk into Rainbow Fabrics, I am almost as excited as she is. We've decided to buy a book on quiltmaking so I can make my first quilt. What could be more innocent?

Embarrassing as this is to admit, I LOVE fabric stores. I love studying all the beautiful colors, patterns, and collections, love grazing my fingertips on the different textures and weaves. I find the perfect book right away; it's called "Freddy's House," and has lots of gorgeous pictures to give you ideas. I wander around through the calicos and cottons, almost as if in a dream, pulling one bolt after another off the shelf for my future quilt. Just as I'm deciding between two black-and-white polka dots, a glint of gold catches my eye. I glance up and see my old friend Brittany with her waist-length golden hair in the next aisle. I'm pretty sure we see each other at the same time, and both of us, for our own reasons, turn and pretend we haven't seen the other. However, I am not fast enough to snag my mom.

"Brittany!" she shouts loud enough for everyone in the shop to stare. "Brittany Fox! How wonderful to see you! It's Connie! Bretano! Andrea's mom!"

I want to die.

"Hi, Mrs. Bretano," Brittany says softly, as if that would normalize my mother's volume. "How are you?"

Naturally, Mom calls me over, and Brittany and I are forced to exchange clumsy greetings. I don't know why it's so uncomfortable to see someone who used to be your best friend in the world and no longer is, but it is. Brittany looks beautiful, glossy long hair, clear complexion, easy smile.

"You are the last person I expected to see here," she says. "But I forgot, you are good at sewing! What are you making?"

Suddenly, my project and fabric seem impossibly dopey; I can't believe I was giddy about it just minutes ago. She is doing community service work at a Spanish-speaking school and is buying felt to make puppets with the kids. She wants to become fluent in Spanish so she'll qualify for her prep school's immersion program next year.

"Well, have fun with your house quilt!" she says, undoubtedly as anxious as I am to extract ourselves from this awkward meeting.

My mom goes in for the kill.

"Brittany, you must come by and visit Andrea!" she says, grabbing her by the arm as if she might hustle her into her car. She lowers her voice to a stage whisper. "We need a positive influence in our home! We just left teen Drug Court now, with its dreadful little drug dealers and sluts. Andrea needs to associate with a better class of people! It was these hoodlums who got her into so much trouble in the first place."

I would feel sorry for poor Brittany being saddled with my mom's craziness, but at the moment I am too busy feeling horrified on my own behalf.

"Okay, Mom!" I say with gritted teeth. "Time to pay for our stuff and go home. Bye, Britt! Good luck with your puppets!" I drag Mom to the cashier and make her pay for fabric and supplies I will never use.

On the drive back to her house, I sit in the back seat of the Lexus and text Dad and Monica. I beg them to pick me up a day early. When we get to her house, I shut myself in my room. Luckily I have an apple and an energy bar in my backpack so I don't starve. Mom comes to the door a couple times and asks me to come out and eat dinner. All I say is LEAVE ME ALONE. She calls me on my cell, and *when I don't respond to that, she sends me a text. I turn off the phone and sit in darkness.*

There's nothing to do in my room, and I am furious. Then it hits me, like the flash of a fairy godmother – I have some old stash, taped up on the underside of my desk top. I stuff a sweatshirt in the crack at the bottom of the door, open my window, and crawl under my desk to retrieve it.

Fuck! Why am I not surprised? It is gone, vanished, nowhere to be found – confiscated, no doubt, by the Swiss bank security people.

I hate my mother. Hate her.

When The Killer gets to my last sentence, she winces, as if I've elbowed her in the soft spot – if she has a soft spot. Because it's raining today, we're meeting in the nurse's office at school, a tiny room with sickly yellow walls and blotchy linoleum floors. She doesn't look at me for several minutes, just sits like a statue on the nurse's swivel chair and stares at a purplish splat on the floor. I'm stationed on the paper-covered patient couch, and though I try to sit still, I am squirming like crazy and my every squirm makes a loud, crispy snap. The walls are decorated with lame-ass posters from the clearance bin of the corny emporium: furry kittens and cuddly puppies captioned with feel-good messages like, "A friendly smile is always in style" and "It's your temper – keep it." It's enough to make you puke.

"Andy," she says at last. "Andy. Look at me."

My face gets hot, and I pull my gaze away from the nauseatingly cute kittens and into the hard, dark chocolate of her eyes.

"I'm proud of you for not using," The Killer says.

I snort. "Don't be. I would have used in a heartbeat if I could've. I would have thrown down my sixty-three days of sobriety without a thought just to get away from it."

The Killer nods. "But you made it."

"Yeah," I say, heart hammering again at the indignity of my mother's humiliation of me in front of my old friend.

"Would you feel better now if you had used?"

That might make me laugh under less stressful circumstances. We both know how bad this would be right if I'd given a dirty UA.

"How do you feel?" she asks.

"Pissed! I never want to see her again. She ruins everything. I hate her," I say.

Karla reaches across the streaky linoleum and squeezes my arm. "It must have been hard in the fabric store. I'm sorry."

"Yeah," I say, a thick lump forming in my throat. I can barely swallow. "Okay."

"We should have merit badges in Drug Court," she says, withdrawing her hand and sitting up straight. "You would have earned one this week."

I nod at the imaginary merit badge. Who can resist a gold star?

"What you're doing is building a muscle. The muscle is called tolerance. You are learning to tolerate feeling bad. You know that people use drugs to feel better. You also know that drugs only seem to work. In the end, they make things worse."

My only response is a squirmy crinkle of potato chips.

"So you have to learn to tolerate feeling bad, feeling mad, sad, bored, all those red-light feelings that you were able to run from when you smoked. You build a muscle, and you learn that the feeling won't kill you. It will go away. You will feel better again."

"I want to believe you," I say, unable to stand the pity she is feeling for me. "But right now I can't imagine getting better."

Karla smiles a tiny smile. "I guess you'll have to trust me. Now, can we talk about your mother?"

"No," I say. "We can't."

"It was a rhetorical question," The Killer says. "Listen, she's your mother. She will always be your mother. Like everyone else, she has her issues."

I choke. "Understatement!"

"Seriously, you are overlooking the positive side," she says. "One, you have a mother. Do you know how many kids on probation would give anything for that?"

I get that now is not the time to offer up mine. But still, she makes a point. A bunch of kids in Drug Court have lost their moms to divorce, drugs, even death.

"Two," The Killer continues. "She loves you. She worships the tablecloth you made because she loves you; she took you to Drug Court when she doesn't approve of it because she loves you; she drove you to the fabric store because she wants to please you. Not all parents feel the need to do nice things for their kids, you know."

This is a sticking point with me. This whole idea that because someone loves you, it erases the horrible things they do to you. "Yeah," I say. "And her love is killing me."

"Shhh," The Killer warns. "You're back on the pity pot again. Get off. Number three: You are holding the key to your freedom."

"I am?" She has my interest now. "Explain."

"Here it is. You cannot change your mother. She will always be the way she is. But you can change yourself. You are in charge of the way you feel when you're with her."

"I am?" I ask again, wondering how the humiliation I felt could be anything but her fault. "How do you do that?"

Karla's watch emits a series of beeps. She shuts down the alarm and shakes her head. "Well, we're going to figure that out. It starts with knowing yourself. That's a major merit badge."

"Yeah," I nod. That I could be free of her is a dizzying concept, something I've never even imagined. "Pretty much the mother of all merit badges."

BRYAN

23. PARAGRAPH 20.2

TO: GENERAL PARTNER, BRETANO'S LTD.
FROM: CONSTANCE BRETANO, LIMITED
PARTNER
RE: DEMAND BY LIMITED PARTNER FOR
PARTNERSHIP ACCOUNTING

Pursuant to Paragraph 20.2 of the STATEMENT OF LIMITED PARTNERSHIP OF BRETANO'S LTD., the Limited Partner, Constance Bretano, hereby asserts her right to require the General Partner, BRYAN BRETANO, to perform and deliver a full partnership accounting within the next forty-five (45) days.

The accounting must be conducted according to Generally Accepted Accounting Principles (hereinafter known as "GAAP"). The General Partner is to account for all monies received and expended; all property acquired and alienated; all profits; all losses; all monies allocated to salaries and/or draws of the General Partner; and any and all transactions which a reasonably prudent investor would deem material. Demand is also made that the General Partner provide appropriate backup documentation for each transaction described in the Partnership Accounting, such as receipts, bank statements, tax returns, profit & loss statements, loan documents, credit card statements, electronic evidence, according to GAAP.

The Partnership Accounting must include a statement under penalty of perjury as to whether the General Partner has or has not breached any of his fiduciary duties owing to the Limited Partner. A breach of fiduciary duty would include a material misrepresentation of the partnership finances, a failure to disclose and/or disgorge any of the partnership profits, a breach of the duty of loyalty and fair dealing to the limited partners, or any other fiduciary duty prescribed by law and owed by a general partner to a limited partner.

HON. STRATHMORE REED, JR.

24. REASONABLE DOUBT

"What a marvelous update, Mother," Reed says, barely able to stomach his mother's brisk prattle about her newest pet project, the establishment of a charitable foundation for underprivileged young musicians. He supposes he should be grateful that his mother has the energy, interest, and capital for these endless endeavors of hers, yet he has long grown weary of hearing about them. Not to be small-minded, but she never shows a fraction of the interest in her own offspring that she showers on her little *causes célèbres*. With an eye on his desk clock, he is well aware that only three minutes remain until the morning calendar commences. He listens anxiously for an opening in her monologue so he can jump to the point of his phone call.

He has been carrying as an action item on his to-do list "Intro Skylar to M" for far too long as it is and cannot put it off another day. In the end, he gives up and interrupts. "Now Mother, you really *must* pardon me, but –"

"—from Lyle Livingston," she continues, undeterred, "that he will in fact serve on my board." Access denied – again! She will not permit her son to run the show. Period. If she has more to say, she will say it. Reed closes his eyes, clenches his jaw, and waits – what choice does he have? – until leave to speak is granted. For him, it's a bit like having a nutty litigant in the courtroom: While the judge technically has the power to interrupt and terminate argument, he's usually better off if he just sits there and takes it. Then again, maybe it's more like "Mother May I" – the reality show. No, you may not!

"Strathmore, it's 9 A.M.! What in the world are you doing on the telephone?" the old biddy barks. "What do you have to say for yourself? Didn't you call me?"

"Yes!" Reed says, jarred by her abrupt transition from prospective board members to him.

"Well, get on with it, then!" she orders. "We both have busy schedules to maintain."

"I called to tell you," he says weakly, his carefully worded script having evaporated into nothingness. "I have a, uh, a date."

"When?" she answers impatiently. "What for?"

He senses her confusion before realizing the ambiguity of his statement. But how best to market Skylar to his opinion-laden mother? He can scarcely describe her as his "girlfriend." They're hardly teenagers, after all. "Lady friend" sounds a bit seamy, as if she were a commodity from the escort service. And "lover" would result in his immediate removal from her last will and testament. And yet, it's true: she is his lover, his sexy, gorgeous lover – would that he could just say so. Good Lord, it's ridiculous that he should feel panicky rumblings in his belly. He is a grown man, a once-formidable advocate, a respected and experienced Superior Court Judge!

"I'm seeing someone, Mother. I want you to meet her." Ach! What a sickening new mortification, that at this stage of his life he could yet be nervous telling his elderly mother about a new romantic interest. It's her unkind judgment, of course, as well as her adept control of the purse strings. It took the better part of a decade for Mother to warm up to Dory – much to his wife's frustration – and she had introduced the two of them. If Mother had an inkling of his glorious weekend spent between satin sheets in the breathtaking Fairmont Suite featuring his intoxicating Sky-high Skylar, her wardrobe of alluring gowns, room service, and the miracle of modern pharmaceuticals – well, she cannot hear of it; it's that simple.

"Good heavens, Strathmore, surely you can't be serious! This is the news I should be hearing about our Bitsy, not about you. Dating? At your age?"

"I'm completely serious, Mother," Reed forges ahead bravely. And even though he braced himself for this particular indignity, he still registers the sting. He almost wishes he *could* tell his mother of his beloved's exquisite tenderness. His Sky, his beloved! This time, they had the whole night together, and there was no awkwardness in the morning. Just affection, romance, and a tiny hangover easily killed with a few Excedrin. "I'm not too old for companionship."

"I suppose that's true," she says. "Do we need to be concerned that she may be a gold digger?"

How has he been able to bear his mother's cruel words all these years? And to think,

Skylar has been begging him to disclose their relationship to his mother since the inception. After their weekend of supreme intimacy, he could deny her nothing. If only he could protect his sweet Sky from Mother's sharp tongue!

"She's nothing of the sort! Quite the contrary, Mother," Reed answers firmly. "She's a woman of substantial and independent means. Her name is Skylar Stone. She's lovely. Has a home here in Sequoia Valley. Is the founder and CEO of Stone Financial." At the mere saying of her name, his heart races. Skylar! He feels like a boy again!

"Stone. Is it her birth name?" she asks in a strained, remote tone. "Or a name from a previous spouse?"

How had he failed to anticipate the question? And how could he continue to be so humiliatingly ignorant in her presence? Nothing has changed since he naively brought home Ana-Maria Gutierrez some 50 years ago. It mattered little that Ana-Maria was adorable and friendly, along with being the brightest student at Sequoia Elementary; no, what mattered, as he learned shortly after the two of them completed their science board, romped in the pool, and ate sandwiches in the redwood grove; after father's chauffeur drove her home and he got to sit with her in the expansive leather backseat of the Jaguar, and life seemed suddenly full of thrilling possibilities; what mattered, Mother explained, is so very difficult to put in words, but hear me out and you will understand. Your little friend lives in the projects, Son. In those *apartments*, you saw them, where fathers sit outside in undershirts and drink beer, where mothers hang laundry and pop out one baby after another, where yards are filled not with lawns and roses but with broken-down couches and cars, and where all manner of unsavory things occur. She has her people, Strathmore. She has lots of nice brothers and sisters, cousins and grandparents, I'm sure. But her people are not our people. You know that already, Strathmore. If you thought about it, you'd realize that you already know what I'm saying.

And he did know. Mother had done her best to deliver the blow softly, but even at his tender age, he understood, without her ever having to utter the exact words, that he was not to bring home sweet, smiling Ana-Maria ever again. Although that late-spring afternoon was easily the most memorable episode of his entire young life, he did not, in fact, have much of an opportunity to risk repeating it.

268

That fall, he was shipped off to an all-boys prep school, where his older brother was already safely and securely ensconced and where there was precious little opportunity to interact with any girl, much less one from the projects.

"Excellent question, Mother," Reed responds, embarrassed that he does not in fact know Skylar's maiden name. He is dimly aware that she was once married but knows next to nothing about that period of her life, save and except that she has two adult children from the union, both of whom live out of state. If he had thought through this conversation fully, he would've asked his beloved to provide him with a current credit report so he could correctly respond to any inquiries his mother might pose. "May I answer that when we next meet? I was hoping to introduce her to you and Bitsy when we gather at the Edwards' home for brunch on Sunday."

His mother readily agrees to the proposal, and as she seems equally eager to terminate the conversation, the two simultaneously bid goodbye. Reed slips into his black robe and throws his office door open, annoyed that he will be starting his calendar some seven minutes late. Since he is notorious for chiding lawyers for their tardiness, it pains him to be guilty of the same transgression.

"Your Honor," his lovely courtroom clerk intercepts him before entering the courtroom. She holds a thick stack of files, no doubt some last-minute, urgent matters that disorganized lawyers expect him to read, understand, and rule on in the next 30 seconds.

"Yes, Miss Bettina. What have you there?"

"Judge Berkeley is covering Juvenile Hall today – the commissioner is out – and we are the backup department for her cases. She only has these five matters. They're on for status. Would you like me to place them on the bench? Or would you like to review them first?"

"I'm late enough as it is," Reed answers. "Let me have them, and I'll deal with them after I finish calling my cases."

"Very well, Your Honor," she says. "All the lawyers have checked in, including those appearing telephonically."

Judge Reed enters the courtroom and the few lawyers present rise at the bailiff's command. Reed has twenty-three minutes to finish his calendar before resuming his trial, a god-awful unlawful detainer case where landlord claims tenant has not paid rent in five months, and tenant counterclaims she paid in trade; she says landlord agreed to accept sexual favors in exchange for rent and allegedly has the video footage to prove it. Who are these people anyway? Not his cup of tea at all.

Not so long ago, Reed could walk into a courtroom and tell by the number of bodies how long it would take him to process the morning cases. But these days, most lawyers appear telephonically, so he never knows how many lawyers might be waiting for his pearls of wisdom in the virtual courtroom of the telephone.

"Good morning, ladies and gentlemen," Reed begins. "I apologize for the delay. We were transferring the telephonic appearances from Judge Berkeley's courtroom into mine, and that took a bit of doing. I am advised that all counsel have now checked in, and I will commence the morning calendar. I will first call the cases assigned to my department, followed by those from Department Seven. *Sayed Shore v. Buy-Rite.* Counsel, please state your appearances."

The lawyers shout their names into the speakerphone. It is, as always, difficult for Reed to make out what they're saying. Digital technology notwithstanding, Reed can only understand about one word in three. The rules for telephonic appearance require that lawyers call via land lines, speak into hand-held receivers and eliminate ambient noise. However, those rules are honored more in the breach than in the practice. Cell phones are ubiquitous; multi-tasking lawyers routinely place office calls from speakerphones; and the background noise grows ever louder and more intrusive. Reed's problem is enforcement. With 20 or more lawyers on the line, it only takes one cell phone caller stuck in traffic to create reception difficulties for everyone, and because all callers are essentially anonymous, Reed can neither pinpoint nor punish the offending caller.

After ordering the parties in his first case to participate in mediation and return to court in 90 days for a trial date, Reed, as usual, grows irritated by the distracting din issuing from his speakerphone.

"Would the lawyer who has his car radio on please turn it off?" Reed commands sternly into cyberspace. The music stops, but is replaced by crackly static. Reed raps the box sharply with his pen. "Someone is eating potato chips! Stop it!"

Reed moves on to the next case. Mercifully, the plaintiff's lawyer is in court. Midway through this presentation, the unmistakable noise of traffic and sirens emanates from the squawk-box on the bench and fills the courtroom. Reed apologizes for the disturbance, asks that all lawyers in cars roll up their windows. He is determined to get through the damn calendar without losing his temper. After all, the matters are strictly procedural, as bland as can be. Besides, Reed will need his full complement of patience later in the morning to evaluate the brash young tenant's explanation of how her yoga lessons with her landlord led to "therapeutic massages" which led to an exchange of sexual favors.

Reed struggles through the noisy calendar and issues various orders for arbitration, mediation, and dismissals; he sets hearings for various procedural failures and sets a few cases for trial. As he is about to begin calling Judge Berkeley's cases, he suddenly hears barking over his speakerphone. Good God! What's next, the dog and pony show? This is beyond the pale! He imagines some lawyer billing for a "court appearance" while padding through the kitchen in his pj's to let the dogs out. Where, oh where, are the rules of decorum?

"I will now pause for thirty seconds so someone can remove their dogs from my courtroom!" Judge Reed growls, feeling as if he himself is straining against a choke chain on his neck.

He slides the stack of his colleague's files to the center of his desk surface. The dogs are still barking like mad, oblivious to his order. The top file is rubber-banded to the one beneath it, which usually signifies either a very old case or a particularly contentious one. Out of habit, he glances at the caption. *Quinn v. Stone.* Quinn! Stone! Reflexively, he claps his hand over his mouth to prevent himself from groaning aloud. His next-door neighbors, Norton and Natalie Quinn, have apparently filed a lawsuit against Skylar Stone and Stone Financial. His neighbors! His Skylar! The case number informs him that the matter was filed last year, and the label states the case classification: fraud. Fraud? But there must be some misunderstanding. He has known his neighbors for 30 years. They are quiet, reasonable, and very wealthy people. And they are suing his beloved Skylar?

Reed's heart is hammering as he opens the file and observes that both sides are represented by reputable San Francisco lawyers. Neither lawyer is in the courtroom, so both must be appearing telephonically. Before announcing the case, Reed takes a moment to organize his thoughts. This is not his case. All he is doing is covering for the assigned judge. He need only give the lawyers a trial date, which Judge Berkeley's clerk has written on the file. That doesn't require any argument or information about the case. But … if his name is on any piece of paper, even one merely assigning a trial date, Skylar will see it, and then she would know that he knows about this particular embarrassment. And what about his neighbors? They might mention it to him, and talking to them about a case against Skylar would be dreadful in so many ways.

No, he absolutely cannot in any way, shape, or form preside over this matter, even to perform the most ministerial of functions. Under the canon of ethics, judges have a duty to hear all cases assigned to them as well as a duty to recuse themselves in any case where they have a conflict of interest or where they cannot be (or appear to be) fair and impartial. Although Reed has never had the occasion to consider it before, there must be some kind of conflict of interest if the judge is enjoying wild sex with one of the parties. He's not about to make that declaration in public. But what to do? Under most circumstances, Reed would learn of a conflict when reviewing a file in chambers, not when presiding in open court with God knows how many people observing. What if one of the lawyers is aware of his relationship with Skylar and plans to bring it up when he calls the case? Reed curses himself for not accepting his clerk's offer of reviewing the files before taking the bench. A judge must at all times act with dignity and decorum, yet here he is discharging his duties like a dullard in a dunce cap! Why can't he think lucidly?

He clears his throat. "In the matter of Quinn and Stone, are counsel present? Mr. Li for the plaintiff and Ms. Wynne for the defendant?"

"Yes, Your Honor," both lawyers answer.

"The court will recuse itself in this case," Reed states. "Judge Berkeley will be back in session tomorrow. If it is convenient for counsel, I will recalendar for tomorrow at 9:00. Any objection? No? Good. That is the order."

Reed finishes the remaining cases in a blur, barely aware of what the lawyers argue or what he orders. He will not think about Skylar. He will not so much as open her file. He will never, ever mention the case to her and can only pray that she will not breathe a word of it to him. Because, now that he thinks of it, another ethical rule prohibits him from talking about any pending case, even one pending before another judge.

"Any other matters that I have not called?" Reed asks the speakerphone, his clerk, and the empty courtroom. "Hearing no response, the court will stand in recess. We will resume in nine minutes."

Reed all but runs to his chambers and quickly closes the door behind him. Skylar! Involved in a big piece of litigation in his courthouse! What if her case doesn't settle? What if she is required to appear for a protracted trial? What if his colleague, Judge Berkeley, says something about the case at a judges' meeting? What if either lawyer sees them together at a social gathering? That would set tongues wagging. And poor Skylar, what has she done to earn the ire of his otherwise reasonable neighbors? Of course, people can be sued for anything, and just because a suit has been filed does not mean she has done something wrong. In fact, he vaguely recalls Skylar mentioning how some of her clients unfairly fault her with the mortgage meltdown and subsequent stock market crash. Still, the mere fact that Skylar has a case in his courthouse indisputably creates some unfortunate complications. What if his neighbors see him with Skylar? Depending on the nature of their claims against her, that could disrupt their comfortable neighborly relationship.

A knock sounds at his door. This time, Reed does groan, and quite audibly too.

But it is just the lovely Miss Bettina, and she is smiling sweetly. "Good news, Your Honor," she announces, waving a piece of paper. "Our unlawful detainer case settled. Here's the dismissal. No screening of 'Sex in the City' for us today!"

"That is good news," he concedes. He was not looking forward to hearing the unsavory details, much less viewing them.

The settlement of the trial leaves his day wide open. He picks up the phone to tell Skylar of their Sunday brunch with Mother. She has been looking forward to meeting Mother Reed. He has no reason to share her optimism.

But before punching in her number, he replaces the receiver. He simply cannot talk to his beloved Skylar right now. He's liable to say something about the thing he must never speak of.

Their first problem. What a pity it involves a legal case. Of course, something was bound to arise sooner or later. The odd thing is, Skylar is still blissfully unaware. She's altogether innocent, busily planning a romantic getaway for the two of them at her favorite Relais et Chateau in Napa. He wishes they could be there now.

ANDY

25. MAGIC BEANS

I'm gonna use. I'm gonna use. I'm gonna use. I *really* WANT TO USE. And the supremely weird thing is, I'm on my way to an AA meeting.

I wanna go back home, lock myself in my room, and smoke my way to oblivion.

What a sucky week! I can't keep it together for one more minute. I hate everything, most of all how stupid I am. Idiotically I put off my AA obligation until the night before Drug Court, so it's too late to catch a meeting for young people. Which means I'm stuck going to the old-timers' speaker-discussion featuring life's biggest losers at the down-and-out Redwood Rec Center. Wreck Center is more like it, and I'll fit right in because I'm a wreck, a total wreck.

The front page of tonight's paper has a picture of a group of cute girls with long legs and big smiles – the varsity baseball team from my old high school. I used to play with two of the starters on our middle school CYO team. They're on a luxury bus now cruising to Sacramento to compete in a once-in-a-lifetime statewide championship, whereas I'm in my stepmother's beat-up Honda driving to a loser AA meeting. Someone is not living up to her potential.

Monica could see that I was crabby – not that it was any huge secret, I was knocking around the house, slamming doors and banging into furniture – and offered to cover for me tomorrow in court like other parents do for their kids.

"Alec had a temperature of 103! That's why he didn't have his UA test!"

"Kali wanted to go to her AA meeting, but my car broke down."

"We're sorry we missed the family therapy – my husband was called out of town suddenly."

Jesus! These parents are worse liars than their kids. But Monica offered to lie, had some half-ass story she said she could tell with a straight face. But, shit! I was feeling so disagreeable, I couldn't even say yes to that. So now I'm stuck going to this crappy meeting, which is a mirror of my crappy life.

All week I've been thinking about using – how much I just want to check out, go blank, stop caring, get some relief from the stress in my life.

Q: How much stress could you have when nothing is expected of you?

A: You have no idea.

Top Ten Stresses of Andy B.:

10. Probation – It's like being the suspect of a terrorist plot; your every move is watched and analyzed.

9. Drug Court – You have to go to court every week, feel like a criminal, and listen to one lame excuse after another.

8. No friends – You have no friends! You're not even someone's charity case!

7. School for addicts and losers – Your teachers expect nothing of you. Half the kids are high, and the other half skip school altogether.

6. SVHS baseball team – They're going to the state championships. They have something to be proud of. What do you have? 122 days of sobriety, like that's some big accomplishment – *not* doing what you should never have done in the first place... and –pathetically – STILL wishing you could do it again.

5. No fun – Nothing in your life is fun.

4. Parents' divorce – Why can't your parents get a normal divorce? They've been fighting for longer than they were together!

3. Your mother – She's nuts. She's making dad nuts. She keeps filing more papers and my dad is going insane.

2. Your maternal unit – You love her and want her to be happy but you can't stand to be with her.

1. Your mom – She'll never be happy. She makes you crazy.

"Are you sure you're going to be okay?" Monica asks, interrupting my internal whine-a-thon.

"Yeah," I lie as she pulls up to the curb to drop me off. "I'm fine."

Monica looks toward the building entrance, where some sorry burn-out in an army jacket is trudging. "You want me to come in with you?" she asks, and she's so obviously worried I might say yes, I almost want to laugh in spite of my lousy mood. But I relieve her of her misery right away. About the only thing that could make this night any worse is having my super strait-laced stepmother as a chaperone.

"No, that's okay. The twins will be way better company for you. But thanks. See you at 8:15."

The meeting is just getting under way as I slip into a metal folding chair in the back row of a stuffy multi-purpose room. About twenty people are here, all of them hugging a white Styrofoam cup of vile-smelling coffee – definitely not Bretano's. Yoga mats are shoved up against the walls on either side. The whiteboard in the front is covered with present-tense conjugations of *avoir, être,* and *aller.*

When I started high school, we had to pick a foreign language, and mine was French. Who wouldn't want to speak the language fluently, live in Paris, read *Madame Bovary,* maybe study art history or fashion design? Of course my parents had to have a big blow-up over it. Mom thought I should learn Spanish, that it was a lot more practical. Dad agreed that Spanish was fine, but the decision should be mine and not hers. Mom said they were my parents, not my friends, and this was the kind of decision a parent should make. I had to sit in study hall for two weeks while my parents went to court for an order telling me whether I could take the fucking language. Can you imagine the humiliation of having to deliver that piece of paper to the principal's office? Other kids are standing in line with notes from their dentists and doctors, and I turn over a fucking court order! Yeah, I got to take French, like I wanted, but the class was way ahead of me by the time I started, and I never got much past *avoir, être*, and *aller*. Once I got kicked out of regular high school, the study of a foreign language was no longer required. About the only thing that's required at my school is an oppositional, defiant disorder and/or a problem with drugs or alcohol.

The meeting secretary is a fat lady wearing a butt-ugly, hand-knitted purple hat. Her current project is in her lap, and she starts clicking her needles right after turning the meeting over to Al. He is an old geezer in need of a shave, and he stumbles his way through a reading of the Twelve Steps and the Twelve Traditions – higher power, moral inventory, character defects, blah, blah, blah. The gray heads in front of me nod in agreement with his tortured reading. I let my gaze wander from the French verbs to the walls, which are plastered with yellowing craft projects featuring painted pasta. I remove my meeting card from my jacket pocket as a reminder to get the purple-hat's initials at the end – proof of my attendance to give to The Killer tomorrow.

Who would take an art class in gluing painted pasta shells to posterboards?

286

On the other hand, wouldn't I rather be creating macaroni flowers than listening to this crap?

Old Al introduces the speaker. I stare at the clock: still an hour to go. Her name is JD, and there's no telling if that's her real name, or if she's just taking anonymity to a new level. Anyway. She's young, maybe 25. She looks Chinese – long black hair, willowy build, soft voice. She's wearing dangly earrings and has henna tattoos on her hands. My focus on the pasta art wavers when I hear her say she grew up here, and was in the county's first Juvenile Drug Court! Ha! – she might have been sitting exactly where I'm sitting ten years ago, staring at the same lame pictures of painted pasta. Her parents were both in medicine, and they believed that for every ailment, there was a pill. If she had a fever, they gave her Tylenol. If she couldn't sleep, they gave her Ambien. If she couldn't concentrate on homework, they gave her Adderall. Sounds like a nice setup, but I guess it didn't work out too well for her.

"You remember 'Jack and the Beanstalk'?" she asks, and we nod in response. "Jack is supposed to buy bread with his mother's last bit of money, but he spends it on magic beans instead. This guy, Jack, could be my relative. My family believes in the magic bean."

She goes on to talk about her search for the magic bean, the one that would make her feel happy, confident, and normal. Who wouldn't want that? When things started going to shit – her grades tanked, her relationship with her parents blew up, she got kicked out of several schools, she stole and crashed her parents' car – she says she never once thought that her problem was using. She thought that school, parents, and the law were the problem, and using was the solution.

"I went to my first AA meeting when I was 15 years old because the court ordered me to go. I remember thinking, 'These old farts! What a bunch of losers! I have *nothing* in common with them!'"

I laugh right along with the old farts, having had that exact thought forty-five minutes earlier.

She says she finally gave up her search for the magic bean and chose to live with the ups and downs of real life. "I finally learned that fear, sadness, sleeplessness, even my inability to concentrate on homework, are all experiences that normal people have, that I didn't have to take a pill for them." She makes it sound so simple.

Just as she's about to sit down, she starts to say something, pauses, and then shrugs her shoulders and continues. "The funny thing is, after I got sober, I found that, for me, there really is such a thing as a magic bean. It makes you feel happier and look better every time you use it. It's legal and costs nothing. You know what it is?"

Someone shouts out "Sex!" Another tries prayer. The burnt-out guy says, "Well, shit, crystal ain't legal so I have no fucking clue."

She smiles. "It's running! For me, running is just like going to a meeting – I always feel better after, even if I didn't really want to go in the first place. Back when I was using, I'd come home, hide in my room, and smoke pot. I thought that was living. Now I come home, put on my running shoes, and run around our hills for an hour or two. When I finish, I'm energized, happy, and alive. Just like I feel now from talking to you tonight. Thank you."

I'm the first person to applaud. I can't believe it. She sounds just like me. Except for the running, of course. I haven't done any exercise since eighth grade, and even then I wormed my way out of P.E. every chance I could.

After the corny handholding and prayer at the end, I make my way to the front of the room to get the purple-hat lady to sign my card. JD is sitting next to her.

"Hey," I say. "I liked your talk. I'm in Drug Court too." I nod my head toward my meeting card.

"That's great!" she says, smiling. "I hope you do better than I did. It took me a long time to get sober. My PO finally sent me to placement. I always say, my probation officer saved my life."

I laugh. "It's the opposite for me. I say mine is ruining my life. In fact I call her 'The Killer.'"

"I still remember something my PO told me about meetings. He said, 'Don't go looking for ways you're different. Go and look for ways you're similar.'"

I nod.

"Well, good luck. I'm here every Wednesday if you ever want to talk."

The secretary hands the meeting card back to me. "Oh!" she calls out to the departing crowd. "Any volunteers for a service commitment? Pablo needs to retire from coffee next month!"

Surprising myself, I turn to her and say, "Sure. I'll do it."

"Why, thank you, honey!" she says, dropping her knitting in a large bag. "What's your name?"

"Andy," I answer.

"Well, Andy, welcome." She writes my name on her clipboard. "We are glad to have you here. Why don't you come back next week? Pablo will explain the setup to you."

JD smiles at me. "We'll talk."

"Sure," I say, wishing we could start now but Monica is probably waiting and I don't want to seem too desperate for a friend, which obviously I am. "Is it okay if I bring some different coffee? This stuff sucks."

BRYAN

26. INBOX

To   : Dad <bryan@bretanos.com>
From: Andy <andy@bretanos.com>
Re   : Coffee

Hi Dad, Would Bretano's be willing to donate some coffee beans to a really good cause? My Wednesday Rec Center meeting needed a new coffee monitor, and I'm it. Must be in my genes. And could I have the day's leftover pastries? I know a toothless guy who'd feel like king of the world if he got something sweet with his free coffee. ☺

To   : Bryan <bryan@bretanos.com>
From: Monica <monica@bretanos.com>
Re   : Movie night in the park

Hi Honeybun, just a reminder that my Improving Families workshop starts tonight. The boys are SO excited about their daddy date! I'll drop them off with you at 5:45 so you'll have time for dinner. Love, Your Monica

---

To : Bryan Bretano <bryan@bretanos.com>
From: Seamus Shields <seamus@shieldslaw.com>
Re : $$

Reviewed Connie's motion re partnership accounting. We need an expert to assist with our defense. Talked to our man at White & Wong – he's an accounting wizard. The firm requires a $15,000 retainer. I'll be a good boy scout and keep my fees down, but you need to shoot me $10K. I'll request attorney's fees and expert costs in our opposition papers. Lord knows she can afford this and you can't.

Tell me again why you married the bitch? LOL!

THIS EMAIL IS INTENDED FOR THE ADDRESSEE ONLY AND IS PROTECTED

BY THE ATTORNEY-CLIENT PRIVILEGE. IF YOU HAVE RECEIVED THIS MESSAGE IN ERROR, PLEASE DESTROY IT IMMEDIATELY.

HON. STRATHMORE REED, JR.

27. NOTHING BUT THE TRUTH

He despises himself for what he is about to do. Spying on his lover! What good can come of it? It's still not too late to turn back; certainly he should consider doing so when he has such a strong suspicion that this will be his last moment of happiness. And yet: He must. With a shudder of resignation, he picks up his phone and inches toward the precipice.

"Yes, Your Honor?" Miss Bettina answers from her intercom in the courtroom.

"May I speak to you personally?" Reed asks. And then, to further commit to the dreaded plan, he adds, "I need you to retrieve a file from the clerk's office."

She promises to be there forthwith, just as soon as she delivers to the sheriff that bench warrant he issued yesterday for the wild young man in Drug Court. Reed remembers the youth, if not his name: the boy gave several UA's with sky-high THC metabolite levels and then failed to appear in court. It saddened the team because the youth had been doing relatively well: attending school, working at Safeway, abiding by curfew. Until he succumbed to the siren call of drugs. What a waste of a young life. Reed was prepared to terminate the young man from Drug Court. But Ms. Washington, the hard-headed probation officer, refused to give up on him. She thinks he may be hiding out in the basement of his grandmother's house and asked to have the sheriff serve the warrant there. Reed remembers the grandmother too. What a fraud! Her bursitis – together with a prescription from an Internet doctor – permits her to possess as well as cultivate small amounts of marijuana. The D.A. on the Drug Court team suspects she's cooking up some special herb brownies and using her grandson as the distribution system. Reed would like to revoke her status as grandmother and throw her in jail along with her offending grandson.

The judge writes out his file request in careful letters on a sheet of yellow legal paper, then folds it in half so he won't have to look at it. Moments later, Miss Bettina appears in his chambers with a tired but cheerful smile. What's different about her? For years she has delighted him, as well as every male bailiff on the court floor, with her perky good looks – long, bouncy hair; stylish makeup; stockings and heels; clingy sweaters and short-ish skirts, racy enough to be interesting but modest enough for courthouse attire. Today, though, her clothing is subdued. Her hair is secured in a neat clip. She's wearing a charcoal pantsuit with a loose blouse, and not, as is her custom, calling attention to her tiny waist. Is this a recent change or something that has been occurring for some time? Reed cannot say and curses himself for his chronic inattention to such matters.

"How may I help?" she asks.

He gives her the folded sheet. "Two weeks ago, I covered Judge Berkeley's calendar. You remember the day, I'm sure. I recused myself on a matter. I'd like to look at the file, if I could."

Miss Bettina reads his note. "*Quinn v. Stone*. This is the name of the case?"

"Yes," he answers. "I'm afraid it is."

"Afraid?" she asks, tilting her head to one side.

He gestures toward the showy bouquet of fragrant lilies on his credenza. "Those flowers?"

"Yes," she says, admiring them. "They're beautiful. I love the way they smell."

"Yes. Intoxicating aroma. They were sent to me by a Miss Stone."

"Oh. *Stone.*" His clerk nods. "I see. Yes, I'll pick up the file. It will be here for you when you return. Don't forget your three o'clock meeting outside the courthouse."

He can hardly forget his "meeting" – coffee with Skylar. The timing is unfortunate, as he could surely use some extended solitude to reflect on the disturbing news he recently learned about his beloved. But she is leaving town again, and they won't see one another for a week. She'd invited him to join her in London – "just a few days of business, I promise!" – but he felt he had to decline. However, he could hardly say no to her kind invitation for a quick cup of coffee before takeoff.

Reed swivels his chair to face the bouquet. He rereads the simple, lovely card that accompanied them: "To my favorite judge from your Sky-high lady." She can't be a fraud, can she? Yet that is the damning assessment by his mother and daughter.

Needless to say, brunch had not gone well. Both Mother and Bitsy despised Skylar from the moment they laid eyes on her. The colder Mother was, the harder Skylar tried to win her over. Bitsy seemed so distressed by the gathering that she manufactured the flimsiest of excuses and fled before the meal was served. His dear Skylar was not herself that day either – but who could be, under such circumstances? No, something was off: her smile was too big, her stories too long, her laughter too forced. Their poor hosts, Chester and Edwina Edwards, family friends for several generations as well as Bitsy's godparents, did everything humanly possible to put their guests at ease, but the tension between Mother and Skylar was unyielding. The most demoralizing part of it all was that Reed was helpless to stop the carnage. He could not protect his Skylar from the intractable force of Mother's judgment. And so, at the earliest possible moment, Reed began clearing his throat and making noises about leaving. Sweet old Chester, who must be 85 if he's a day, all but leapt from the table to accompany Reed and Skylar to the door.

"Here's your hat, what's your hurry?" the old man teased, knowing Reed would understand. In the car, Skylar claimed she had a migraine and begged off their planned excursion to the Japanese Gardens. By nightfall, Reed had developed a raging case of hemorrhoids, some painful flamers which have yet to subside.

Still, it would have been possible for Reed to overlook his mother's cruel judgment. She is practically famous for her viciousness, so her reaction to Skylar, while painful and regrettable, was not exactly shocking. On the other hand, the letter received the following day from old Chester was alarming.

"My dear Stratty," the old man wrote in his spidery hand. "It grieves me to be the bearer of unpleasant news. Nevertheless, I am duty-bound to inform you that, whilst you were otherwise engaged at brunch, Miss Stone tried to solicit my business. Enclosed are the promotional materials she left with me. I fear she does not have your best interests at heart. I have reported this episode to no one, not your dear Mother, not even to Edwina. Yours Affectionately, Chester."

It is an awful breach of etiquette, at best, but Skylar deserves the opportunity to defend herself. She is, after all, a respected and successful businesswoman. She must have something to say for herself, even if he cannot imagine what that might be. If there's one thing Reed has learned during his 10 years on the bench, it's that there are two sides to every story, and often more than that. He just hopes Skylar's is a good one. Wouldn't it be wonderful if, for once in his life, his mother were wrong? Tucking Chester's letter in his coat pocket, he grabs his keys and drives downtown to Bretano's.

Skylar is seated already at the corner table with iced decaf nonfat lattes and a plate of Italian dipping cookies. She is wearing a soft brown suit designed for air travel. A striking Hermès scarf is draped around her neck, and at her side is an expensive carry-on bag, outfitted with laptop, cell phone, magazines, water bottle, and other travel accessories. She looks lovelier than ever.

"Thank you for meeting me here in the middle of your busy day," she says softly.

Reed sits across from her at the small café table. He feels himself melt into the allure of her intelligent gray eyes, but knows he must be stern with her. "It is my pleasure," he answers, more formally than he would have wished. He reaches into his coat pocket, removes Chester's letter, and places it in the center of the table for her to examine.

She picks up the letter, retrieves reading glasses from her bag, and reads.

"Darling, I've let you down," she says. "I'm so sorry. I've embarrassed you, created tension between you and your mother, made a mess for you with your friends."

Her forthrightness takes him by surprise, but really why should it? Once again, she is doing the hard work for him. "This is all I know. I'm sure you have some defense."

"Defense? Absolutely not. It is quite indefensible," she says matter-of-factly. "I am appalled at myself, and you must feel ten times worse. I apologized to Mr. and Mrs. Edwards today. I do not expect, nor deserve, their forgiveness. Whatever came over me? I wish I could say."

Reed is speechless. In court, *everyone* has a story to tell. Rarely, if ever, has he heard an accused fall on his sword and take full responsibility for his actions. It is so refreshing to hear his beloved say so without any prompting from him!

"Regrettably, dear," she continues with a slow shake of her head, "I have little hope of ever changing your mother's view of me."

"She's a tough nut to crack," Reed agrees. "She didn't like me either for the first 50 years."

Skylar laughs. "Oh, Strathmore. How I'm going to miss you."

How delightful to hear her laugh! Reed smiles, his first in days. Here they are, together again. Why must he always think things are so bad? Why must he forever expect the worse? She has given him little cause to feel fear or distrust. And it is so pleasant to be in her company once again.

She reaches across the table and covers his knobby hand with her light, perfumed one. "Now, my dear, listen to me. We don't have much time, and there's something I must say."

Reed nods, hoping she'll tell him about a romantic getaway she's planned; perhaps a weekend in Carmel; or perhaps something even grander – a cruise to Hawaii or a summer in Provence. Whatever it is, his answer is YES! Enough of his obligations to his work; enough of his kowtowing to Mother. It is high time for him to say yes to life!

"I know you can't see me anymore. I accept that it's over between us. But you have given me a tremendous gift, nevertheless. You reawakened my passion. Before I met you, I was dead. I thought my work was enough to sustain me. I was wrong. Thank you for making me feel like a girl again. I will never forget you." She looks at her watch, frowns, and rises. "Now I really must go."

"What?" he answers, rising from his chair. "But dear, you must not say that! I don't want you to go. Not at all! We can work this out!"

He follows her out of the shop, a step behind her, wanting to stop her, address issues rationally. She absolutely cannot leave him! Her limo pulls up to the red zone in front.

"Thank you, my darling. But it will never work. Think about it! You can't continue to see me and suffer your mother's disapproval. I respect that. We had our fun. It was glorious, wasn't it? Now I must go. My plane departs in two hours."

But Reed won't hear of it. "This is unacceptable! I will only say *au revoir*," he says. "I expect to continue this conversation when you return." And there, in broad daylight, right in the middle of the busiest street in town, Reed kisses her goodbye. The kiss is delicious, soft and sensual. "Damn my mother," he mumbles, finally saying aloud the words that have been circling his mind for weeks. "It's you I love."

"Love you too, darling," she says quickly, giving him one final squeeze before stepping into the car. "Forgive me! I must go. Goodbye, my dear!"

He waves to her, although he cannot see her through the tinted glass. In the next heartbeat, he feels lost and alone. Why hadn't he gone with her? Oh, what a fool he is, not to have joined her! Why was he so afraid of taking time away from work and enjoying himself with this beauty? How many chances is a man like him going to get? Slowly he walks back to his car, despising his timidity, calculating how to spend the rest of his life with his beloved Skylar. She loves him – she said so. He loves her. What else matters?

Although his home is but two miles away from the coffee shop, he drives back to the courthouse. Quitting time is yet 90 minutes away, and though he has no specific work awaiting him in chambers, he prides himself on giving the taxpayers a full day of his time. There will be orders to sign and legal periodicals to peruse. Besides, he needs time to think, to plot out his future with Skylar. There's no better place for thinking than his chambers. He has lived the life his mother has imagined for him for sixty years. It is time for him to declare his independence. Nothing is insurmountable. *Amor vincent omnia*!

This is the very romantic thought that is in his head when he strides into his silent chambers. At once he is besieged by stacks of files towering over his ordinarily pristine desk. What in God's name has happened? Did the presiding judge send him some new horrible piece of litigation to manage? He steps closer to examine the wreckage. Why in the hell is a fat, pulsing divorce case on his desk, In Re Marriage of Irwin, Michael and Skylar? He doesn't do family law! Yet here's a second one, stacked next to it: In Re Marriage of Bonds, Ethan and Skylar. But this file was closed years ago – after lots of messy litigation apparently. What's it doing in his chambers? And here's yet a third one, quite an ancient case, In Re Marriage of Stone, Charles and Skylar.

On his credenza, next to the aromatic lilies, is the file he requested, Quinn v. Stone. Under that file are three more cases, all naming his beloved Skylar and her investment firm as defendants, all charging her with fraud.

He collapses in his leather chair. His hemorrhoids cause him to cry out in pain.

What a fool. What a stupid, stupid fool. The truth about Skylar had been right in front of him the whole time, but he never stopped to notice it.

And of course, his mother had to be right.

ANDY

28. ROSALITA

"My anger."

No! This time I won't! You've given me some bad assignments, but this is the worst. I have nothing to say on the subject because I'm not, absolutely NOT, ANGRY. Give me a break! Show some mercy! Besides, aren't you forever saying we must "guard against dark imaginings?" Redirect our "frown" to the "sunny side of town?" So you OF ALL PEOPLE should be thrilled to hear my news this week.

I'm happy.

Didja get that? I haven't said this since I was like 5.

I'm HAPPY! I am. I feel good! No cravings, urges, itches – not one. No sneaky, wistful thoughts of hidden stash or using. No night terrors or frightening dreams. I sleep well and practically leap out of bed in the morning. Like a triple espresso with a shot of sugar, I'm bursting with energy. And, oh – here's a sure sign of a successful probationer: my room is clean (except for, you know, the bed. And maybe some stuff in the closet. But nothing dead or gagifying).

So forget about "my anger!" Instead, let me reveal the exciting secret of my turnaround: Rosalita.

At a meeting last month, the speaker said exercise was her "magic bean" – got rid of her cravings, made her feel better, restored her health. She was such a convincing picture: cute, energetic, upbeat – plus, here's a girl who used to be exactly where I am today, slogging through Drug Court, squirreling herself in a room with a bong, and today she's smiling like a homecoming queen. Could that be the magic bean effect?

Me, I don't exercise at all. A parking meter gets more exercise than I do. I used to play team sports, but there's no team that would take me now, and pretty much no exercise opportunity anywhere. The School for Losers, Addicts, and Whiners doesn't have a sports program or even a PE requirement. (They're so relieved we show up for class instead of ducking in an alley for an illicit purpose that they don't dare put us out with forced exertion.) I'm not a member of any gym, and it's not like either of my parents has a pool or even a treadmill. But I keep thinking about what this AA speaker said, and finally decide: What have you got to lose? I feel crappy ALL the time, and even though I'm kind of used to it, I wouldn't mind an upgrade to semi-crappy.

This girl, JD, is a runner, and I asked her if she'll be my sponsor – for AA and for exercise. Since running doesn't require any special equipment, membership or opponent – I tell her I'll give it a go. She makes me commit to an hour a day for thirty days. Has me sign a lame-ass contract with myself and all. I dig out some sweats, find some old gym shoes – my feet have grown about two sizes since I wore them, but never mind. I venture out into the elements, ready to feel the runner's high, be the vibrant picture of health and happiness.

Fuuuuuuuuuuuuck! It's freezing cold out, everyone parks their cars over the sidewalk, and I'm forced to run in the street, which is pitted with potholes and pet poop. The wind is whipping in my face, and rain starts to fall. In July! When does it ever rain in the freakin' summer? My feet are slapping on the street, SPLAM! SPLAM! SPLAM! And people drive by looking at me like, Did she just burglarize my home? Ow ow ow! My knees are killing me, there's a stitch in my side, and I can barely breathe. I'm gasping for air, coughing up yuck. I check my watch. Five minutes – barely! I'm wheezing and choking and, wow, it's ugly. But I don't give up. I told JD I'd give it an hour, and an hour I'm going to give. I just can't run anymore.

So, like the gym class slackers on the track, I walk the rest of the way in the lousy weather – only now it's not cold; the sun is out and it's boiling. I check my watch about a hundred times, turn around at 30 minutes, and head back. Day one. One hour of exercise. No runner's high. Just achy knees and dog doo on my shoes.

Day two: 6 minute run, 54 minute walk. Almost hit by some jackass in a big-wheel pickup chatting on his cell and not doing his part to share the road. Fucker blew his horn at me after he swerved. How does exercise lower your stress level?

Day three: 7 minute run, 53 minute walk. More rain. It gets you WET and COLD, by the way. Legs in shock from overuse. The run is torture but the walk doesn't feel like exercise…until the next morning when my calves are screaming.

Day four: 7 ½ minute run, 52 ½ minute walk. At this rate, I'll be 40 before I can run two hours on JD's hill trails. Meantime, no runner's high, no walker's buzz, no toned muscle, no cute guys, not even a friendly dog, despite widespread evidence of them. The shoes are definitely too small. JD reminds me of my promise to live up to my 30-day contract, says if I'm not completely satisfied at the end, she'll give me a full refund of my misery.

Day five: Can barely drag my butt out of bed. Luckily for my exercise commitment, I'm staying at Mom's and that's incentive enough to bolt out of the house for an hour or several. 8 minute run, 52 minute walk. I say "run," but it's more like "plod," "lumber," "look like an ass."

Day six. 9 minute run, 51 minute walk. Wind blows my Giants hat off my head and into a muddy pothole. Ahh, the great outdoors. In spite of everything, I'm kind of pleased — tomorrow will be one week.

Day seven. 10 minute run, 20 minute walk. The turnaround point is a little shingle house with a garage sale in progress. Lawn mowers, ladders, power tools, cribs, kids' furniture, and assorted male garage clutter. There on the driveway practically in my walking path is the sweetest turquoise ten-speed ever. I stop and stare.

How did I forget about bike riding? What a dope! I used to love riding around on my pink Schwinn with the white basket and the "look how cute I am" tassels! I'd ride up and down our street, venturing ever farther. How much more fun would riding be than this sucky run-walk? I could go places on a bike! Take myself to meetings, school, even back and forth between my parents' houses.

"Got your eye on my old bike?" Mr. Garage has a major Spanish accent and looks about my dad's age. Grease around his fingernails, paint splatters on his jeans and DeWalt sweatshirt. Dark brown eyes, bushy black eyebrows, shy smile.

"It's gorgeous," I blurt, petting the frame like it's a dog. "I'm just thinking of all the places I could go on it."

"This is a bike for going places," he says. "Got me here from Texas." He pronounces it "tay-has."

"No way?" I am impressed. This guy is old! And, you know, not exactly your picture of the biker stud – more like the Ace Hardware guy. "You rode this bike across, what four or five states? I didn't know you could do that."

"I didn't know I could, either." He holds out his hand. "Santos." His hand is tough, calloused, and warm.

"Andy," I say. "Tell me about your ride from Texas. I can't even imagine!" Which is true. I've never been outside California. Well, technically I was in Nevada for a minute and a half, but since I was on a boat in the middle of Lake Tahoe, I didn't form a big impression of the Silver State. We were supposed to go to Cabo San Lucas once when I was little, but, as usual, things blew up between my parents and we ended up at home locked in separate rooms.

"Uno momento," he says, as a big-ass SUV pulls up to his driveway. "This nice lady bought the patio furniture and I want to load it up. Why not take her out for a spin? See how she fits?"

"Really? You'll let me ride it?" I can't believe he trusts me – I can't even pee in a cup without someone watching me. I know I should tell him I don't have the money, that I'm just stumbling by, but the handlebars are already in my hands.

"Sure," he smiles. "Only way to find out if she's right for you."

I jump on the saddle and zoom down the street. The sun is shining, and the plum trees are bursting with fat, juicy fruit. There's a light breeze, and it blows the sweet, summer fragrance in my face. I hear myself singing. I forgot what this feels like! Flying! I ride around the block and return in a flash to casa de Santos. I don't want him worrying about his bike.

He's loading the last chair in the SUV.

I am smiling ear to ear.

"What, you no like her?" he asks.

"Are you kidding?" I answer. "I love it! It's perfect! I haven't had this much fun in years!" Fortunately, I stop just short of blabbing out my entire life story.

"Let me move the seat. We need a half-inch or so." He gets to work adjusting, testing, fine-tuning, and I hop on and off the seat as he directs.

"That the Gitane you advertised on Craig's List?" A stranger's voice jolts us to attention. It comes from an ultra-fit athlete who has rolled up on a bike. He's wearing a space-age helmet, race jersey, spandex, and those dumbass wraparound sunglasses. I don't know anything about bike gear, but this guy looks like the cover of *Hot Shit Bike Magazine.* I instantly hate him.

"Yes sir," Santos answers, glancing at the intruder's ride. He whistles. "Beautiful Trek you have."

"Nah, it's not that nice," Hot Shit says dismissively. "It's last year's model. Picked it up for six grand. The pros are riding the Madone, and that's what I have my eye on now."

Of course, I don't know a Madone from a trombone, but I can tell this guy is bragging. Maybe the reason I hate him is he hasn't noticed me at all. It's like I'm invisible. He's practically drooling on Santos's bike, and since I have no idea what he's talking about I can't even make fun of him.

"Still have the original Reynolds 531 tubing?" Hot Shit asks, his face so close to the frame I could do his girlfriend a favor and kick him.

"Of course," Santos says, adjusting the handlebar so it's easier to reach.

"How quaint." He pulls a fat wallet from a pocket in the back of his jersey. "I need an old junker to cannibalize for parts, and yours will do. I'll take it. Here's your $150."

I drop my head and bite my lip. Fifteen minutes ago, I didn't even know I wanted a bike, and now I feel like I can't live without this one. And $150! Where would I get that kind of money? Don't cry, *you jerk! How could you be surprised? This guy, unlike you, has a stash of cash!*

Santos straightens up. "I'm sorry, señor, but you're too late. The young lady bought it and, you can see, I fit it for her."

My heart practically leaps out of my chest. I realize I've been white-knuckling the handlebars during this entire conversation. I nod my head vigorously to show my agreement with the imaginary deal. Shoot, if I had to guess, I bet I'm ten times the liar as old Santos.

Hot Shit scowls. I can't see his eyes through his reflective sunglasses, but an angry crease digs across his smooth forehead. He pulls out two more fifties and thrusts them in my face. "It's your lucky day, miss. You can make a hundred bucks without lifting a finger. Enough to buy yourself another garage sale clunker and a little herb too."

The bike discussion was over my head, but this kind of talk I understand.

"Fuck off," I say.

Santos doesn't laugh until Hot Shit finally rides off. "That was a bad thing to say."

"Sorry," I say. "But what kind of a jerk was he?"

"The kind to take apart my Rosalita, use the frame, and scrap the rest for parts."

"Rosalita? Your bike has a name?"

Things are heating up at the garage sale, so Santos doesn't have time to tell me now how Rosalita got her name, but says the bike is mine! Sells it to me for $125.27, payable in monthly installments of $20, due on the first weekend of every month. I give him an IOU along with the $5.27 from my pocket. I'm to ride over with my hard-earned cash — he says I have to use my own money, not my parents' — and he'll check the chain and the gears and tell me how Rosalita got her name. Before driving off, Santos instructs me to check the tire pressure and wear a helmet.

Since then, every day has been great. I love riding my Rosalita. Shifting is still awkward, so I've got my eye on the white line on the side of the road most of the time, which is how I learned that we have railroad tracks everywhere. This is funny to me because I've never seen a train. Every once in a while I look up from the limit line, and it's so weird! I always notice something new: a rock garden with a Snow White and the Seven Dwarves. A bocce ball court with a bunch of old guys in checked pants and brown hats shouting to each other in Italian. A brick factory (did you know people still made bricks? In Sequoia Valley?).

Dad lets me work in the downtown shop the day after I buy my bike. I make $30 washing coffee cups and promptly ride over to Santos' with my first payment and a box of lemon-coconut cupcakes. He *shows me how to check the tire pressure and how to oil the chain, and sends me home with my first-ever can of chain oil. Tells me I'll need it "if I want to keep Rosalita happy," which of course I do.*

The Killer is amused. She doesn't smile or anything but her mouth is twitching like she's tempted. Because school is closed for summer break, we're meeting at her office, a cramped room with metal furniture on the second floor of the Juvenile Services complex. Her window looks out on the exercise yard at Juvenile Hall. I recognize two of the kids playing basketball in their humiliating orange sweats: Miguel, from Drug Court – he's in for a week because he gave a dirty for cocaine and lied about it to his PO (so breathtakingly stupid) – and Syd, a guy who used to hang with me at Pixie Park. I happened to ride by the park the other day, and wow, it was not the happy place of my dreams. It was full of garbage – broken bottles, fast-food wrappers, a moldy sleeping bag – and smelled horrible.

"Aren't you glad you aren't spending your summer with those goofballs?" The Killer asks, as if reading my mind.

I nod. For all I know, Miguel is wearing the same sweatshirt I had on New Year's Eve. "Syd used to be so cute! I can't believe how bad he looks." I heard he was dealing meth, and from the pasty looks of him, it's probably true.

"Yeah," she says. "Not like you! I don't have to wait for the results of your UA to confirm that you've been clean this week. You look great! Your skin is clear, your eyes are sparkling, even your hair is shiny. It's just like you say in your essay – you're happy. It shows."

I'm embarrassed. And, I don't know, pleased. "Thanks," I manage to mumble. "So, can I show you my new bike? I rode it here today."

The Killer checks her GI-Jill watch. "I'd love to, but I'm running off to a staff meeting. How about this? Next week you'll have 150 days of sobriety. Let's celebrate by going for a ride. I'm training for a triathlon in September and should be riding 100 miles a week."

"That'd be fun!" I say. Weirdly, I mean it. What does it say about me, that going for a bike ride with my PO would be the most fun I've had, well, all year.

"This is perfect! I'll take you out on my favorite ride to the Redwood Grove Reservoir," she says, gathering up my papers and sliding them into a folder.

"You're going to kick my ass, aren't you?" I ask, picturing the long and hilly climb to the reservoir.

"You don't know the half of it," The Killer says. "And, FYI, just because you wormed out of your homework this week, doesn't mean you're done. I will expect to hear all about your anger next week."

I start to object, but she interrupts. "Remember when we first met?" She nods toward the Hall, as if that little detail might have slipped my mind. "Your anger was a twelve on a scale of ten. What's changed since then?"

"Oh, only everything!" I say. Hasn't she noticed? I tick the obvious changes off my fingers: "One, I stopped using. Two, I stopped hanging around with my old friends. Three, I started exercising. Four, I go to meetings and have a sponsor. Five, I show up to school."

"Right," she says. "All those address your *recovery*. They don't address why you used in the first place. A girl like you doesn't start smoking pot every day on account of she's so thrilled with her life. I'm sure you had your reasons. Let's start with anger."

Fuck me! Just when I'm starting to feel good about my PO, she pisses me off all over again.

BRYAN

29. ROCCO ROAD

Bryan is at work in the downtown shop early in the morning when the bakery delivery arrives. Before the pink boxes are opened, the scent of the rich goods fills the shop. Every few months, his bakers treat him to their killer coffee cake – a buttery, not-too-sweet, yellow cake topped with a cinnamon-pecan crunch. The stuff is like heroin – no one can resist it, and it flies out the door faster than fireworks on the Fourth of July. Over the years, Bryan has seen perfectly respectable grown-ups lick the wax wrapping to capture every last crumb. Maddeningly, the bakers only make it when the mood strikes them. They refuse to produce it on request. What with the eggs, butter, vanilla, nuts, and spices, the cake must cost them a fortune. Still, they could charge whatever they damn well please for the stuff. Never mind, they do it for love, not money. Obviously they're onto something with their strategy because when the coffee cake shows up, good things happen, at least for Bretano's.

"Jaya, snag me a hunk of that," he nods to the shop manager. "I need a peace offering for my lawyer this morning."

She rolls her eyes and slides a slice into a bag. "Yeah, right. 'It's for a friend.' Like I haven't heard that one before."

He doesn't have the starch to protest, because just thinking about today's visit to the Law Offices of R. Seamus Shields makes him wobbly in the knees. He hates everything about the place. At least when you get a root canal, you go to the office in horrible pain, but the pain goes away when the procedure is finished. With a divorce, you're never done and the horrible pain never goes away.

A few minutes before nine o'clock, Bryan makes a nonfat, no-whip mocha for Misty, the lawyer's receptionist/wife, stirring in an extra shot of syrup for good measure. She'll love the chocolate boost and what she doesn't know about the calorie content won't hurt her. He remembers to pick up her coffee cake. It's a good thing the manager set it aside, because there's not a slice available in the display case.

On his way out the door, Bryan shouts out an order to restock the pastries.

"Thanks for the help, Boss!" Jaya calls back. "Remind me again why you're paying me to manage the shop?"

Rocco's office is only a block away, so the coffee is still piping hot when he hands it to Misty. She looks in desperate need of a pick-me-up. Her hair – usually poufy and girlish – is pulled back in a matronly style, and though he's not the kind of guy who notices this kind of thing, he sees that it is in urgent need of re-blonding.

"Here's something special for you, dollface," he says, handing over the killer cake. "Figure I might as well make your day while your husband is ruining mine."

But neither the gift nor his wit has the intended effect. He can't swear for sure, but thinks she might have tears welling up in her eyes. It's hard to tell because her face is hidden behind an inch of pancake batter and she's wearing tinted glasses.

"You're a sweet man," she whispers. "But I can't."

"Oh, come on, live it up," he urges. "You're gonna love it. It's the best stuff we got."

She hangs her head. "Tell me the truth. Do I look fat?"

Warning, warning, warning! He might be a dumbshit, as evidenced by the fact that he's still having the same damn fight with his ex for a decade, but he has learned a thing or two from being married half his life. Having stepped in this messy one a few times too many, he knows you never, but never, answer this question. It's a trick question of the worst sort, because there is no right answer.

"You, my dear, are a goddess," he says. "Men should worship the ground you walk on."

She frowns. "Well, my husband doesn't worship it, or anything close. He told me my ass is as big as a double-wide."

"Well, he's a peckerhead, and you know it," Bryan says. "Just 'cause he charges $450 an hour doesn't mean he knows what he's talking about."

She frowns unhappily before taking her first sip of the mocha. "Mmm, yum. Maybe I better take a peek inside that little bag you brought me. I don't want to be rude."

Before long, she's nibbling on the cake, and perking up a bit as they chat about this and that. They have some time to kill because his lawyer was called into court for some last-minute emergency motion, the kind requiring twenty-four hours notice instead of the usual three weeks. Bryan pities the poor client, as he himself has been on the wrong side of those motions too damn many times. Misty chats away, and the longer Bryan looks at her, the more he worries that the dark circles around her eyes were not caused by a lack of sleep.

She's explaining how much she'd like to get away for a few days to visit her family, how much her sainted mother misses her, how she'd love to meet her sister's new baby, when Bryan jumps in. "Did that fucker hit you?"

"What?" She looks momentarily scared, the kind of wide-eyed alarm no amount of makeup can conceal. Then she pushes out her lower lip and shakes her head "no," just like Andy used to do when he'd ask if she'd been using drugs. "Oh, no. I'm so clumsy – I just ran into the wall. Didn't have my glasses on."

And, see, this is what he doesn't understand. Misty is a *nice* girl. All she wants is a nice little life. She's working for her husband for probably 8-10 bucks an hour, getting dolled up every day for him, acting like his crude jokes are funny and his hairy back is sexy. And what's she getting in return for her efforts? A knuckle sandwich to keep her in her place. He's about to tell her to drop the thug and find someone who deserves her when the prick himself busts in the front door looking angry as a bear.

"Fucking judges!" He fumes. "Who chooses these idiots? This fucking judge dumps a giant turd all over the courtroom, and I'm supposed to call her 'Your Honor?' What the fuck?"

Misty and Bryan look at each other with wide eyes and zipped mouths.

"Goddamn shit-for-brains, arrogant, sack of shit!" he screams, storming through the reception area and slamming the door to his private office.

Misty smiles sweetly. "Mr. Shields will be with you in a few minutes."

"Listen," Bryan whispers. "If that prick so much as lays a hand on you, you call the police. He is not worthy of you."

She pops the last bit of coffee cake in her mouth and blinks provocatively. "I don't know what you're talking about. But thanks."

She excuses herself to tend to her husband. After a few minutes, Rocco returns in shirtsleeves, gives his client a crushing man-hug, and ushers him into his office for the meeting Bryan has put off for as long as he could.

"Hey Bro, sorry to keep you waiting. You want the good news or the bad news?" he asks, plopping into his big lawyer chair.

Bryan shrugs. It's all bad, he knows that much.

"Okay, the good news is, we don't have to go to court next week after all. Connie dropped her demand for a DNA sample, thanks to my brilliant legal maneuvering, and she has also agreed to put off her motion for child custody for a few months. So that takes a little pressure off us."

He swivels his chair around and picks up a stack of papers from his showy credenza. "She has filed an amendment to her motion for sole custody, adding a request for vacation days and holidays. Yadda, yadda, yadda, we've been through this before," he says flipping through the legal papers. "Here's what she says. Ah, yes: 'I request that the vacation dates and holidays for the next twelve months be fixed in a court order so that there are no unpleasant calls to the police or to federal authorities.'"

Bryan snorts. The only time he has ever called the police is when Andy hasn't come home. Now the ex is making it sound like he's some international kidnapper. His face is starting to heat up, and his gut is tightening in that familiar knot.

"But that's not the bad news," Rocco continues. "This motion of hers for partnership accounting? What a ball-buster. Might as well grab your ankles now. Connie's gonna drive you all the way to Cleveland on this one, and it doesn't look like you'll even get a kiss when it's over."

In the many years Bryan has been locked in litigation with his ex, his lawyer has always found a way to put a happy face on everything. This is the first time he's given such a dire assessment. But, hell, Bryan thinks, why am I paying him all this money for him to tell me what I already know?

"She's asking you to cough up 50 grand in unpaid profits plus another 50 as a penalty for wrongfully withholding payment."

Rocco picks up another stack of papers and tosses it over. "Now for the really bad news. Here's the preliminary report from the accountant. It's grim." He fans through the pages and shows Bryan a summary chart. "According to his calculations – this is the bean counter who's on our side, remember – you substantially underpaid the partnership profits. Paid a bunch of personal bills from the business account, booked a couple unauthorized loans to yourself, took a larger draw than authorized by the partnership agreement. He says you owe her about $100,000. And that's before interest and penalties."

Holy crap! One hundred grand? Where is he supposed to get that kind of cash? "I don't have it! What's she going to do? Put me in prison?" Suddenly Bryan is so incensed he could punch his hand through a wall. He's just a working stiff! All he does is work his ass off to keep up with the bills.

Rocco tilts his chair back and hoists his short legs on his desk. "She can't put you in prison, you know that. But she could force a sale of the business. It could get ugly, especially if she got wind of the fact that your competitor is itching to buy you out. It would be preferable if we could crush the living daylights out of her, like we did on that DNA motion, or find a way to pay her."

"I'm not selling out to Starbucks." Bryan pounds his fist against his thigh. "My house is mortgaged to the hilt. I've got nothing in savings. It's all in the business. The economy sucks. Loans are impossible. I don't know what to tell you. She's the one with the dough."

Rocco sighs. "Yeah, I know. It's a raw deal. We can't let her get away with it. She doesn't deserve anymore money, that's for damn sure, and we're not about to give her the satisfaction. What the hell do these bean counters know about real life, anyway? I'll give Mr. Pocket Protector a call and explain how he's got it all wrong, that this is just a little overly technical bookkeeping boo-boo. Let me see what I can do. Our response isn't due for a couple weeks. I can put the bitch off for a while with my charm and my legal song-and-dance. There are some documents she wants that I haven't given her. Maybe we can reach a settlement. You never know."

But Rocco and Bryan both know. Connie is not the settling type. Especially when she finds out that her ex owes her even more than she thinks he does. She'll think she's hit the fucking jackpot. And maybe she has.

HON. STRATHMORE REED, JR.

30. FROM THE DESK OF MISS BETTINA

Her judge has not left his chambers in three weeks. He comes to work as usual every morning at eight o'clock, turns on his computer, closes his door, and that's the last anyone sees of him until he slips out at 5:15, after court staff is gone. He stays in his chambers all day long, doing God knows what. He won't come out for lunch dates, judges' meetings, or, most frighteningly, court proceedings. He won't accept telephone calls or visitors – not that he has many of either. Bailiffs wanting to share new jokes, lawyers wishing to gossip, police detectives needing a search warrant, even file clerks tracking down lost files, all are redirected to other departments. His Honor refuses to communicate with anyone except his trusted courtroom clerk, Miss Bettina.

So far, no one suspects anything, although court staff is starting to whisper. Is he sick? Did his rich old mother finally bite the dust? Will he retire? His clerk reveals nothing. If only he would sit in court, even for thirty minutes, that would shush the wagging tongues! But Miss Bettina cannot pry him from the safety of his chambers. He continues to sign orders, review correspondence, rule on motions, and conduct his morning calendar. Miss Bettina figured out that she could reroute the telephonic appearances into the judge's chambers. He has no problem presiding over matters from inside his office, but he cannot be persuaded to enter the courtroom. During the static-laden telephonic proceedings, Miss Bettina sits in a judgeless courtroom, takes minutes, records appearances, and directs any lawyers appearing in person to speak to the judge from her telephone. Out of habit, she occasionally glances up at the bench to check on her judge. Each time she is jolted by the sight of an empty chair. What will it take for him to resume his position?

This arrangement can't last much longer. Jury trials and Drug Court are the problem.

So far, Miss Bettina has been able to reset the trials herself without ruffling any feathers, but his calendar will be an unfixable disaster if he ignores it much longer. A trial judge has to keep cases moving along; one logjam is like a wreck on the highway, it messes up everything downstream. He has a five-year case coming up in two weeks, and Reed will have to try it or explain to the presiding judge why it must be reassigned to another department. Pigs will fly before he asks his PJ for help with a case assigned to him.

Miss Bettina tries to talk to him about taking a vacation. He cuts her off, tells her he won't hear of it.

She buys his favorite blend of fresh-ground coffee from Bretano's and makes him her best decaf cappuccino. He thanks her but doesn't touch it.

She is desperate. She is worried. So, even though she's six months pregnant and her figure is shot to hell and her husband would not be at all happy if he knew, she wriggles into the shortest skirt she can fit in, because her legs still look great. She borrows a low-cut blouse from her sister, because finally she has something to show off. And on this day she comes to understand how bad it is for him. Because he doesn't even notice. His eyes don't light up, the endearing blush does not spring to his cheek, he doesn't mumble a compliment, nothing.

It's Miss Stone, the Lily Lady, she knows. Anyone could see how happy he was. What a thrill it had been to see him loosen up a little! He was kind of handsome when he smiled – boyish and bashful. That surprised her. Oh, the day he skipped the judges' meeting to meet his girlfriend for lunch – it was so romantic! He may as well have been Romeo at the balcony! Made her heart skip to think that this so-serious man whom she so respects could have some fun in his life. When she told her husband, an electrician, he said, "Sounds like the old fucker got himself a new set of batteries!" And it was like that for a while – he was brighter, louder, surer. But the batteries died the day the Lily Lady was unmasked.

It was all in those fat court files. Such horrible details about Miss Stone! Miss Bettina hated to be the bearer of bad news, hated delivering the tell-tale files to his chambers. But her judge is an ethical, upright man. He would not want to be living a lie. And in any event, it wasn't her decision to make. He asked her to retrieve a file for him. True, he hadn't asked for all the other files, but they were listed there in the court's computer system, and she knew he would want to know about them, even if they would break his heart.

And that's what they did. They broke his heart. The pleadings were downright creepy. Three marriages, all to men of great wealth. It seemed as if Lily Lady had the same marriage three times in a row. In each case, the husband knew her less than a year when he married her – two of them were crazy enough to leave their then-spouses (and children) to marry Lily Lady. But around year seven, each husband despised her, and spared no detail in the lengthy descriptions of her lies and manipulations. With each divorce she acquired more homes, cars, luxury items, stocks and savings. She also received staggering sums of alimony. Each husband described her as a "fraud" and a "gold digger" – and those were among the kinder terms. Her most recent divorce was finalized only five months earlier. Each party had incurred attorney's fees of $250,000. Husband #3 was paying her $16,000 a month in alimony, which he would continue to pay for another three years, unless either of them died or she remarried. Fortunately, she only had children with her first husband. He raised them himself. They are adults now and don't speak to their mother. There's so much dirt in divorce files! Miss Bettina was shocked by the vicious things each spouse revealed. Cosmetic enhancements (his and hers), extra-marital affairs (ditto), prescription drugs (mostly hers), suicide attempts (only his) – all of it is right there in the public file for anyone to see. Daytime television has nothing over real life.

Lily Lady's civil cases told a similar story: wealthy clients were sweet-talked out of huge fortunes; Stone Financial placed the funds in high-risk investments; months of pleading, demands, promises, delays and lies, lies, lies; finally, the truth: after the deduction of large fees for managing the investments, nothing is left. In each case, there was a demand for punitive damages.

These files remained in her judge's chambers for six days. Miss Bettina was under strict instructions to refuse any entry into his chambers. Accordingly, she declined to accept four exceptionally large deliveries of lilies, three pieces of perfumed correspondence sent by messenger, and a dozen breathy phone calls. On day seven, all eight files were stacked in her judge's out-box. Miss Bettina had little doubt he'd read every word. No wonder he looked ill. He makes his living by judging, after all – and he'd misjudged the Lily Lady completely. Not only was his heart broken, but his confidence was shaken to the core. He had loved Miss Stone. She was nothing but a fake – using him for his connections, his status, and probably for his perceived ability to improve the outcomes of her legal cases. But how little she knew of him! Her judge would never permit his position to be used to gain an advantage in a lawsuit or to "advance the pecuniary interests" of someone. Those are the rules, and her judge follows them.

As is her custom, Miss Bettina brews her judge his morning cappuccino. Today she has the information he asked her to research. She knocks on his door and hears his dull permission to enter.

"I have your coffee, Your Honor," she says cheerfully.

"Thank you." He doesn't look at her, continues to stare at the document on his computer screen. If she's not mistaken, it's the same document he was working on yesterday and the day before, a ruling on a simple motion, something he could ordinarily knock out in 10 -15 minutes.

She sits down across from him and waits for him to acknowledge her. He gazes at his computer screen and clears his throat several times. Miss Bettina studies his computer screen. That's when she sees it – the solitaire icon. He's sitting in his chambers pretending to work and playing solitaire all day! No wonder the ruling isn't finished. Her husband does the same thing when business is slow and he's depressed, plays game after game of mindless solitaire while munching through cans of salted peanuts. It's better than going on a bender, she supposes, but not by much; it's just another way to check out of life. Now she worries that her news will make things even worse. "I asked Jury Services your question."

That gets his attention. He looks at her. Does he even notice she's pregnant? She's worked for him for seven years, has been a size two her whole life. She now looks like she's hiding a basketball under her shirt.

"There is no record of Miss Stone ever having served on a jury in our county. She was summoned twice and failed to show both times."

Reed nods. His face is lined and pale. "All the greater fool am I. Thank you, Miss Bettina. There will be no more such imprudent inquiries. That will be all."

He won't let her say anymore, so she has no choice but to leave. She was hoping today she could break the news to him – that she is going on maternity leave in a few weeks and he needs to find a replacement clerk. But she can't bring herself to tell him now, not after everything he has been through. Maybe she should make the selection for him. After all, he might not have the confidence right now to pick the right woman for the job.

Unfortunately, though, the one thing she cannot do is his job in court. He's going to have to do it himself. Drug Court is this afternoon, and she cannot persuade the commissioner to cover for him again. In desperation, she picks up the phone and calls the IT department.

"You have remote access to Judge Reed's computer through the mainframe, right? Yes, well, he would like to have the solitaire game removed from his computer forthwith. And he needs to have the email address of skylar@stonefinancial.com assigned to spam. All e-mail to and from that account should be deleted from the system. Thank you."

She'll smoke him out, that's what she'll do.

ANDY

31. P.O.'D AT MY PO

There's only one thing I'm angry about, and that's being forced to write this ridiculous paper. I'm NOT angry. Why won't you believe me? It's so frustrating! I'm finally starting to feel semi-okay. I don't see how it helps the world – or my recovery— to dwell on old resentments. I feel healthy and energetic. I love riding Rosalita. JD is an awesome sponsor. I see other kids screwing up in Drug Court, and it makes me feel proud of myself. Sobriety doesn't seem as hard as it used to be. I haven't had a dirty UA, unexcused absence, or curfew violation in months. At this rate, I'll graduate from Drug Court in <u>six weeks</u>. True, it would be nice to have a friend, and I vaguely remember that a social life was a plus, but I'm not angry. After watching every kid in court relapse because they hooked up with old using buds, I've grasped the risk factor of friends.

In meetings, they always say, "Act as if." The first couple times I heard this expression, I'm *all: WHAT? Why does everyone think that is so profound? It's not even a complete sentence! But after hearing it so many times, I see how it can be useful. If you're lost and don't know what to do, you should <u>act as if</u> you're already where you'd like to be. Say you have no idea how to stay clean. You act as if you already are: you go to meetings, stay away from slippery places, don't use. So I will "act as if" I'm angry.*

Question 1: If I were angry, who would I be mad at?

Might as well start with my mother! That's where it all begins, right? My mother is impossible. She's always pissed off at someone, usually my dad. She jumps all over him for every little thing. In her case, "jumps" means an endless ability to go to court and invent mean stuff about him. Where was her high school guidance counselor when she enrolled in culinary school instead of law school? Such a waste of her natural talent to argue, inflame, and disagree. And what's so weird about her is, I can do no wrong, no matter how much I mess up! You'd think from a kid's standpoint that would be a dream come true, but it's not. She never gets mad at me, not when I bring home horrible grades, get arrested, sneak out of the house, lie, cheat or eat the last piece of cake. She considers each of these to be my dad's fault. He was too permissive, treated me like a friend instead of his child, married a bitch, whatever — it's never my fault. I'm her daughter and all she wants is to share every tender moment with me.

But she's my mom! I love her — of course I love her. I just can't stand to be with her. I feel like she never sees me for who I am. Instead I'm this made-up model daughter. Like if she keeps saying how wonderful I am and how bad Dad is, then it will be that way. And even though she's always telling me how much she loves me, how beautiful and darling I am, how can I believe her? Because if I really were so adorable, wouldn't she love me for who I am instead of the girl she pretends I am?

But, then again, who could love me for who I am? Because, look! I am such a loser! I can hardly blame my mother for trying to cast me as a better version of myself. Anyone would want a daughter who is smart, creative, and talented. I'm just not her.

So forget my mother. Why blame her? Everyone blames their mother. It's unoriginal. The person I should be blaming is me.

How did my life become such a mess? I used to have such a good life! I mean, maybe it wasn't perfect, but how much would I LOVE LOVE LOVE to have that life back. Parents who trusted me. Friends. A real school where I'm challenged and on my way to college. Playing sports. Maybe even a boyfriend. That sounds pretty great.

But I threw that life away with using. Getting high was the most important thing for me, more important than friends or family…more important than my health, dignity, and reputation. Thinking about what I flushed away is enough to make me want to use again.

I hate myself for doing what I did. And it happened so fucking fast.

Question 2: Damn, where were my parents?

Parents are supposed to protect their children! That's their job. How come mine didn't notice when I was walking out of the house looking like a slut? When I stumbled home in the middle of the night blasted out of my mind? Why didn't they make me stay in my room, send me to bed without dinner, stop me from going out? Okay, maybe they couldn't have stopped me, but they could have maybe at least tripped me when I raced for the door.

But no, they bought my lies, lie after lie, they bought them all, and the lies came so easily to me. Why? Because I knew exactly how to get to them. I'm a genius when it comes to making them feel crappy about themselves. It's so simple. All I have to do is threaten to walk out and live with the other parent. And then they start scrambling. They don't want to lose me. Or, maybe, they don't want the other parent to win.

I exploited their trust and their fear, all so I could go out and mess up my own life big time.

Yeah, I sure knew how to hurt them – by ruining my life.

I did not think this through very well.

Question 3: Hey, anyone else you're mad at?

Well, yeah! I'm mad at my damn PO who was so sure that I was angry when I knew I wasn't and now it turns out she was right. I hate it when other people know more about me than I do. Nice way to put the icing on the dumbass cake.

The Killer is in her most murderous glory today. She really does try to kill me this time by taking me out on her favorite bike ride – out Panorama Road and up the mountain, bend after bend of uphill torture. She is in awesome shape, decked out in a snappy red-and-white race uniform from her college days. Annoyingly, Ironwoman barely breaks a sweat on the endless climb, makes it look ridiculously easy with her muscular legs. Meanwhile, I struggle far behind, panting and groaning, muttering vile curses which only Rosalita can hear. But when we finally coast into our turnaround point, a full hour after I swear I can't possibly push myself another inch, The Killer delivers big time. She has reserved a beautiful spot for us in the Redwood Grove Reservoir picnic area, a dreamy old wooden table in the shade of a giant redwood tree. There's a huge view of Sequoia Valley and the bay beyond. A little creek runs by our site. It's all so perfect, and I'm so done in by exertion, I want to weep.

"I hope you're hungry," The Killer says. She slips off her backpack and unpacks a feast: turkey sandwiches on whole wheat bread, trail mix, sliced vegetables, apples, and homemade oatmeal-raisin cookies. She carried all this food on her back up that long hill! I want to be in that kind of shape. The Killer is not one for small talk, and I'm too exhausted to do more than grunt, so we pass an agreeable 10 or 15 minutes sitting side by side on the picnic bench, eating every scrap of food, listening to the brook gurgle, and sighing at the amazing view. And just as I'm starting to relax and enjoy myself, I'm ordered to clean up our area, hydrate, and stretch while she strolls over to another table to read my anger essay.

As always, I'm nervous as she considers my innermost thoughts – these are confessions I don't tell a soul including, you know, me. At this point, I feel disloyal for saying mean stuff about my parents, shame over what I wrote, and embarrassment for resisting the assignment in the first place. I shouldn't have made such a big deal over it, should've just done what my damn PO asked me to do. It's not like she's ever led me astray. When finally I hear the crunch of rocks announcing her return, I'm too embarrassed to make eye contact.

"Congratulations," she says kindly. "You did it."

"Almost killed me," I mutter.

"See?" she elbows me in the side. "That's the point of the exercise! You *think* it's going to kill you to face up to your feelings, but feelings aren't fatal! In fact, it's a lot more work to avoid them than to just feel them and be done with it!"

I nod. "It's just so humiliating that I had no idea I was angry, and then once I started writing, it felt like I was angry about everything!"

The Killer snorts. "Get over it. Most people are completely out of touch with their feelings. Where do you think road rage comes from? All these drivers think they're perfectly happy people until someone cuts in front of them and suddenly they're honking their horns and screaming obscenities. These are angry people, Andy. But instead of doing the hard work of facing their anger, as you did, they take the easy way out by yelling at strangers."

She might be right. I've met some angry drivers on my bike, and they scare me. Next time one of them yells at me for riding over the white line, maybe I can suggest they spend thirty minutes taking their anger inventory.

The Killer takes a long drink of water from her bottle and refills it at the fountain. "Look, Andy, a girl like you could do that anger exercise every day for a month, and you still would have plenty to write about at the end of the month."

"You wouldn't do that to me, would you?"

"You keep whining like that and I will!" she jokes. "Anger is a very instructive teacher, but I see that terrified look in your eyes. I'll back off. Don't kid yourself, though – you'll have to face it sometime in your life, and the sooner you do it, the better."

I'm relieved. For now.

"There is something I want to talk to you about today. Something serious. I wouldn't bring it up if you weren't ready for it."

My stomach does a back flip. Why can't we talk about tire pressure, chain oil, or the best all-purpose bike tool?

"School," she says.

"I'm not doing anything wrong in school!" I protest. "Look at my grades! I've turned things around. All A's and B's. No tardies. No write-ups."

"Are you done?" she asks in her vaguely bored voice. "Or do I have to sit through more of the Andy defense case?"

"Is this why you brought me out to the middle of nowhere? So you could torture me and no one could hear me scream?"

She ignores my effort at hilarity. "You were put into County School because of your drug use, defiance, and truancy. You're now clean, attending classes, and only a little defiant."

I wrinkle my nose and give her the glare so she can see how unfunny I consider her observation.

"You know where I'm going with this," she says. "A smart girl like you belongs in a mainstream school. I propose that you start school next week at SVHS. You can catch up on your units over winter and summer breaks. If all goes well, and I think it will, you could get back on college track, and graduate with your class."

"No, no, no!" I'm shaking my head and trying to make her stop before her whole horrible proposal comes out. I can't think of a worse idea.

"Come on, Andy, stop acting like a child. You can do this."

"Please, you can't do this to me!" My heart is pounding like I'm on the bike climbing a hill. "Do you have any idea how humiliating this would be for me? To go back to the school where everyone knows all the embarrassing things I did? Are you trying to kill me?"

But The Killer is unmoved. "You keep saying that. It actually takes a lot more than that to kill a person. You thought this week's homework was going to kill you, and then you went and learned a few things about yourself. Could it be you're underestimating yourself? And perhaps being a little overly dramatic?"

"What about my sobriety?" I argue. "A bunch of my old using friends are at my old school, as are all the places and triggers where I used."

"You can't run away from them forever. Might as well do it while you're on probation with the support of Drug Court. You have to face up to them some day."

"No, I don't," I retort. "I'm not that same person anymore. I don't want to be reminded of who I was and the stupid things I did. Why are you doing this to me?"

"Because you can do it. You can't keep running from yourself. You hate your current school, you want to go to college, and graduation from a mainstream high school is the best way to get there. Because I'm smarter than you about your life at this point."

"I hate being on probation," I yell. "Just because you're my PO doesn't mean you get to live my life for me."

Her eyebrows shoot up but she doesn't respond. Instead, she hands me my helmet and mounts her bike. Before taking off, she gives me her parting shot.

"Look, you don't have to decide right now. I just want you to think about it. Now let's ride home. Remember, it's all downhill from here."

She's not kidding. "All downhill" is exactly how I feel about our relationship and her dumbass ideas for my life.

All downhill and over a fucking cliff.

BRYAN

32. COMING CLEAN

Bryan is in the doghouse. Damn it! And he was doing so well too.

Yesterday, he and the boys got to catch a Giants game. His lawyer scored four field-level seats from some unlucky son-of-a-bitch client of his who had to go to court-ordered anger management classes. Bryan couldn't help but think, if that poor guy was angry already, he must've *really* been pissed about forfeiting $400 of tickets to the best game of the season. It was San Francisco and Los Angeles in late-summer play. And what a great game it was, even if The Bums hammered the home boys mercilessly. 10-2 – ouch! The twins loved their first trip to the park – the crowd, the hot dogs, the cotton candy, the foul balls, the cheering, and, every so often, the actual game. Isn't every father's dream to spend a couple hours at the yard cheering on the home team with his kids?

It was a beautiful day at the yard! Full sun, blue skies. Somewhere around the third inning Rocco picked up a couple of beers and handed one to Bryan. Ball game, beer – Bryan didn't give it a damn thought until it was down the hatch, and then he remembered, Shit! I'm not supposed to be drinking! Monica's going to kill me! Did he ever feel guilty. But what's a guy to do at that point? Most of it was gone already, and there were still four innings to go. Well, it was a long-ass game, full of base hits, mound conferences, and pitching changes, so they threw down a few more brews. The kids were beat after three-and-a-half hours of baseball plus the two hours of driving. By the time they got home, the kids didn't look so hot, what with exhaustion combined with mustard and sugar souvenirs from the concession stands. Monica immediately took them into protective custody. Then she looked her husband up one side and down the other and told him in her iciest voice that he could spend the night on the couch. He wasn't shit-faced or anything, but he wasn't feeling any pain either. Before ushering the boys into a soapy bath, she gave her husband that look, that "we'll talk about this in the morning" glare. Crimeny, makes him shiver just to think about that look.

Back in the doghouse. Aaaa-oooooh! He's spent a lot of time in there over the years, and it's a cold and lonely place. With Monica, there's no charming your way out with bouquets of pretty flowers or high-end chocolates. You don't get out until she's good and ready to let you out. At least Andy was at her mother's, so she didn't witness her father's fall from grace.

Well, thank God for work, is all he can say. The following morning he gets a call from Jaya, his manager at the downtown shop. Her two baristas just called in sick with some highly suspicious flu – embarrassing really, because the talk of the shop for weeks has been that these two have the hots for one another; frankly, everyone has just been waiting for them to figure it out. He guesses they finally did last night, and as a result neither can come to work today. The manager is freaking out, asking if Bryan can spare a barista from the Redwood Park shop. Knowing what his wife has in store for him today, Bryan offers to cover the shift. Not only is he an old hand at the espresso machine, he enjoys the pressure of a busy Sunday morning, when the line is often backed up to the wall. Especially when his wife is giving him the sub-zero, arctic vibe. Brrr! No global warming at his house, that's for damn sure. Before leaving, he places Monica's morning cup of coffee on the bedside table and clears out of the house faster than the game-ending double play the Giants suffered late yesterday afternoon.

At the shop, the morning flies by in a noisy whirl of lattes, mochas and cappuccinos. Hardly anyone orders decaf on a Sunday morning. Sunday is all about extra shots and pastries. His bakers whipped up a heavenly batch of yeasted cinnamon rolls, and the sweet, spicy aroma is calming. Even the skinny tennis moms are finding it impossible to resist the pastries today. Bryan rarely works the front counter, so it's fun to see so many of his old customers. They haven't been bitten by the Starbucks bug, God bless 'em. He even sees the damn Drug Court judge, coming in after church most likely, looking grim and downhearted. Bryan is sweating bullets when he hands the judge his decaf cappuccino and nonfat bran muffin, but what a stiff! He doesn't even recognize Bryan, nor does he put any money in the tip jar, the stingy bastard. Why is it that rich people are always the tightest with a buck?

"Okay, boss, it's quittin' time," Manager Jaya, of black T-shirt and orange hair fame, says just as Bryan finishes a big order of iced mochas with extra whip for a team of middle-school lacrosse players.

"You sure?" he asks.

Jaya snorts. This gal has the strength of a wrestler, the tattoos of a sailor, and the skills of a goalie. Nothing, but nothing, gets by her. "Practicing avoidance again, are we, Boss?" she asks sweetly. She's been with the shop for years and knows him too damn well.

"All right, all right," he grins. "I'm busted. Guess I better go home to face the music."

"That's my boy," she says, even though she's a decade or two younger than he. In the next instant, she plucks the apron from his hands, swats him on the butt, and sweeps him away from the espresso machine. The afternoon shift starts seamlessly filling orders, and Bryan is no longer needed. There's no place to go but back to the lonely doghouse.

Well, what the heck, he might as well clean up the newspapers, coffee cups, and pastry dishes before checking out. The place takes a beating on weekends. He grabs a damp towel and wipes down the tables in the dining area. In a quiet corner table of the shop, he spies one of his most loyal and longtime customers typing away at her laptop.

"Helena," he says. "You're still here? I made that nonfat latte for you hours ago!"

She looks up from her computer and smiles. Helena has got to be his mother's age, and – how does she do it? – always looks absolutely terrific. Short white hair, beautiful skin, nice figure – in fact, she looks like a model for one of those new magazines for over-50 working women. No fake boobs, no Botox, just a great looking, ageless gal.

"Why hello again, Bryan," she says, removing her rimless reading glasses and smiling warmly. "You should charge me rent for as long as I've been here. Forgive me! I couldn't bear to spend another minute in my office. I hoped that a change of scenery would prompt me to finish my work."

He straightens chairs at neighboring tables and picks napkins from the floor. He thinks half the reason people like going out for coffee on a Sunday is so they can trash someone else's place. Or do people in their own homes really blow noses into napkins and leave the snotty rags right there on the kitchen tables? Monica would freak out if she saw this stuff. "Well, did you finish?"

"Why, yes," she answers, executing a few functions on her keyboard. "Here's the PowerPoint for a conference presentation tomorrow in the City."

He carefully balances used coffee mugs, dessert plates, and silverware on the tray. "Yeah? What's your topic?"

She turns her laptop around so he can read the title:

SUBSTANCE ABUSE
AMONG CHILDREN OF HIGH-CONFLICT DIVORCE
HELENA M. HARTE, Ph.D
SEQUOIA VALLEY, CA

Bryan doesn't drop the tray, fortunately, but he slams it down rather abruptly, and it makes a huge, embarrassing clatter. Swiveled heads, stray whistles, and lots of grief: "Nice goin', boss!" "Need some help, old man?" "Hey, was that an earthquake?"

"Maybe you should sit down," Helena says, calm but firm. She gestures to the seat across from her.

As if his feet are yanked out from beneath him, he drops into place and gazes at the words on her screen. "Really? There's a connection between divorce and a child's substance abuse?"

She nods her head slowly and rotates her laptop away from him. "Yes, Bryan. And not just drug and alcohol abuse, either. The high-conflict divorce is linked to depression, delinquency, and mental illness in kids. Children suffer deeply when their parents' divorce war rages year after year."

He shakes his head, suddenly feeling lost. Why can't he ever escape his divorce? Lots of people split up and, you know, it hurts, but it ends. His, though, his is like some horrible disease that you can never get rid of no matter how much time, money, or treatment you throw at it. Like an intestinal parasite, maybe, or genital warts.

"How are things with you, Bryan?" Helena asks, penetrating his eyes with a caring and profoundly uncomfortable stare.

He sighs. "Fucked!" Beyond fucked, actually, now that he hears that his never-ending divorce is ruining not just his life but his kid's life too.

She nods. "Yes. I can see that. Do you want to tell me about it?"

"Yes. No. I don't know," he says.

"Okay," she says. "I'm going to refill my coffee cup. Why don't you think about it for a few minutes. Here's a little water. Don't go away. I'll be right back."

This is humiliating! But suddenly it's as if he can't hold it all in another moment. As soon as Helena returns, it all comes spewing out, like a sink clogged up with coffee grounds: his daughter's drug problem, her run-ins with the law, his crazy ex, the ongoing court battles, and constant accusations. Financial pressures everywhere, huge legal bills, and then yesterday, the doghouse.

"Monica told me I have to stop drinking, says it sets a bad example for the boys. I hate being told what to do! I don't have a drinking problem. I've never missed a day of work in my life. Never been picked up for a DUI. Yeah, I enjoy a beer, but I am not a drunk. At least I don't think so."

"But you're worried anyway," Helena observes.

"Yeah, it's hard to stop!" He admits. "What's with that? It bugs me. I feel shitty all the time – excuse the technical term. And then I see this stuff you're talking about, and I wonder, What's my problem? I've been fighting for ten years to protect my daughter, and her mother has fought me every inch of the way. Now I'm starting to think, maybe that stuff my ex says about me is true! Maybe my daughter would be better off without me!"

"I doubt it," Helena says. "It's very clear how much you love Andy. I'm sure she knows and values that."

"Then, what the hell?" He asks, frustrated but slightly relieved to hear her say this. "Do you think I've got a problem with booze? Tell me the truth."

"Truthfully, Bryan, I have no way of knowing," she answers. "There are many possibilities. That's one of them. There are others."

"Well, like what?"

She takes a sip of her coffee. "Bryan, have you ever talked to anyone about your situation?"

He bangs his hand on the table, and the noise it makes is way louder than anticipated. Poor Helena, she jumps back. "Sorry, didn't mean to make so much noise," he says. "Who haven't I talked to? Lawyers. Mediators. Facilitators. Judges. Accountants. Monica. It's all I ever fucking talk about. My divorce is like those old-fashioned pop-up clowns. I punch it down and it pops right back, and always in my face, too! I don't want to talk about it anymore! I want to be free!"

She nods. "Yes, I can see that you've talked to a lot of people about the legal dispute. I'm wondering whether you've ever talked to anyone who just wants to understand and support you."

What's she getting at? Like a minister?

"Someone like a therapist," she says, evidently sensing his confusion.

This is too much for him. "My *ex* is the one who's *crazy*! Not me!" he argues, feeling completely indignant. "She's the one filing all the damn motions. Yeah, I filed for divorce 10 years ago, but beyond that, the only time I go to court is when my ex drags my sorry ass in there. She's the one who should be in treatment! Not me!"

"Sounds like you don't like the idea of therapy," she says.

"You got that right," he says. "All that me-me-me pointless crap. Besides, the shrinks I know are more messed up than I am. Present company excepted, of course. I can handle my own problems."

"I'm sure you can," she says. "But I wonder if it might be worthwhile to try something different. It just seems like you've been suffering."

"Suffering," he repeats. "Yes, that's it. That's the word."

"Have you heard this one? 'In life, pain is mandatory; suffering is optional.'"

He shakes his head. Everything is all jumbled up. His ex always tortured him with tricky word stuff, like the difference between hearing and listening or looking and seeing. "What's that supposed to mean?"

She laughs. "I'm sorry. To me, it means that pain is inevitable. Disease, death, disasters – they happen to everyone. But suffering – how that pain affects us – well, that's a choice. It doesn't always feel like we have a choice, but we do."

It's too much for him. He feels overwhelmed, off his game.

"That looks like enough talking for one day." She opens her purse, takes out a business card, and hands it to him. "Bryan, I've enjoyed our visit today. Thank you for opening up to me. I'm happy to continue the conversation when you feel ready. You've suffered enough. Call me. I can help you."

He takes the card, wishing he could say right now, I'm ready! I'm ready! But he can't say the words. He mumbles thanks, hangs his head, and retreats to the cold safety of the doghouse.

HON. STRATHMORE REED, JR.

33. IT'S A SAD, SAD, SAD, SAD WORLD

Reed has been staring at the same text on his computer screen for over an hour. He has an overdue decision that he must, absolutely must, issue today. It is a sticky and technical issue, dull and poorly briefed, but surely within his capabilities. He has put it off for as long as he possibly can. What is his problem here? Just decide, man! Grant it or deny it, one or the other, how hard can it be? Each lawyer has submitted a proposed order. He could just pick one, sign it, and move on! Why is he wasting a sunny Saturday afternoon agonizing about it? At this point, the parties would likely settle for *any* decision – one side would believe it's the right one even if the appellate court might not – and, really, the parties just need the ump to do his job and make the goddamn call.

Although the case has been hoarding valuable desk space for a month, Reed feels himself losing his battle against indifference to its thousand pages of briefs, declarations, and exhibits. The parties are waging a scorched-earth war over some negligible procedural advantage that won't make a whit of difference in six months. He shudders to think how much money each side has expended to put this tempest-in-a-teapot skirmish before him. Wander, wander, wander, his mind is wandering. He flips through pages and pages of turgid, tortured arguments without absorbing a word. He used to take great comfort in spending a weekend in chambers on a difficult submitted matter, studying the lawyers' briefs, puzzling over the facts and the law, sitting with the problem until he got it right, feeling a sense of satisfaction as the decision took shape. But these days, the quietude of his chambers offers no comfort at all – in fact, quite the contrary. He feels as if he's in a cage, stuck in a cage like a trapped and helpless animal, only not as wild or wily as one. An animal with any instinct would escape the moment the opportunity arose.

Reed, however, dutifully walks into his cage, day after day, and locks the door behind him. His cage is his home, and he hates himself for it. But he has nowhere else to go. How did his life get to be so small?

He thinks of her all the time. The excitement, the pleasure, the sheer newness she brought to his life. So what if he was being played! It was the thrill ride of a lifetime. Utterly unexpected and coming so late in his life. What are the chances of ever experiencing that again? He doesn't want to think about her, of course, but his thoughts are beyond his control – they're like his juvenile delinquents, running where they will run, stirring up trouble, frequenting dark and risky places, fighting, complaining constantly. And, much like his juvenile offenders, he frequently feels sad, self-pitying and bored. He finally gave up trying *not* to think of her, and that, at least, relieved him of one task he failed at a thousand times a day.

And what of the shocking news from his own daughter, Bitsy! The cold letter informing him in businesslike fashion that she is a lesbian. She had not felt comfortable, she said, telling him to his face, and he needed to accept it because she wouldn't hide it from him any longer. Never will he escort his daughter down the aisle on her wedding day, never will he have a grandchild to bounce on his knee. He knows he must call his daughter and acknowledge her letter, but he simply has not felt up to the task. He quite simply does not know what to say.

He has grown accustomed to the constant, dull ache in his heart. But it's not just the absence of her. It's everything. How had he never noticed how sad the world is? Black-and-white movies with their tragic endings. Sweet acoustic guitar arrangements. TV commercials – especially the ones with families going out to eat together after the little girl gets cut from the soccer team or the father can't close a business deal. Even his court cases make him sad. He never before noticed how poignant they all are, how each case is its own story of heartbreak: the loss of a family home, the death of a beloved parent, betrayals of every sort – between business partners, employees and employers, landlords and tenants, husbands and wives. Treachery abounds. Pain and disappointment are everywhere.

And then it hits him, why he feels so much worse today than usual. It was that awful story he heard at his last Drug Court team meeting. Good heavens! No wonder he can't shake off the sadness! The news involved that young woman with the striking hair – what was her name? Sahari! He had developed a mnemonic device for her when he presided over her Drug Court graduation: sa-HAIR-i. What a lovely moment that was, Reed remembers: proud family, promising future, one teenage girl's triumph of determination over adversity. But the future did not fulfill the promise of the moment. According to the probation officer, Sahari started smoking marijuana again soon after graduation, fell in with a group of low-lifes, found herself pregnant. Boyfriend high-tailed it out of town, Sahari dropped out of school and decided to keep the baby. The good news: she stopped using drugs. The bad news: she is doing exactly what her mother did, which is more or less why she started using in the first place. The cycle continues for another generation. It all seems so pointless.

Maybe he should retire. His work no longer interests him. He doesn't enjoy the company of his colleagues. It's not as though he needs the money. His lovely Miss Bettina has left him to start a family. He can't even play solitaire anymore – some virus got into his computer and ate the game, along with all his saved email messages to and from Skylar, and he can't bring himself to ask IT to fix it. But the biggest argument in favor of retirement is that he no longer trusts his judgment. How could he? His job, as he presides over one dispute after another, is to separate the truth-tellers from the liars. It doesn't say much for his ability to discern fact from fiction when he falls for a fraudfeasor's flattery – hook, line, and sinker.

What a fool he is, what a stupid old fool. His father had been right about him after all. He'd tried so hard to prove him wrong: worked long days, sacrificed leisure hours to the law, tried his damndest. Growing up, Reed's father let him know on countless occasions how weak and ineffectual he was, how the most he could achieve with his modest gifts was mediocrity. Despite his upbringing of silent and spoken disapproval, Reed followed his father's footsteps, hoping he might exhibit a scrap of his father's brilliant legal and political skills. He dutifully went to law school, took a position at Father's firm. How miserable he was, year after year, to be reminded of his shortcomings! How painful were the inevitable comparisons of him to his legendary parent! Remarkably, the old man lived long enough to witness his son's ascension to the bench, and Reed foolishly thought: Finally, he will be proud of me. "Brag to me when you're appointed to the federal bench or to the court of appeal," his father had responded when Reed was still puffed up with the great news of his career change. "State court judges are nothing but hacks."

Reed stands up from his computer and stretches. He paces across his small office, makes an effort to think other thoughts. Maybe he should find time to exercise, start taking morning walks, play a little tennis at the club. That would certainly please his cardiologist. Or maybe he could join one of those discreet singles dinner clubs for professionals, get out a little and meet new people. Maybe he should buy a new car. Or a dog. But he doesn't want a new car and he doesn't particularly like dogs. He knows he needs to do something. There's just nothing he cares about any longer.

There on the bookshelf in front of him is a framed portrait of Dory. He picks it up and studies it. She sat for it, at his insistence, on her 50th birthday. How adorable she looks! Gazing straight at the camera, looking intelligent, respectable, and amused. He can practically see her thinking, can we please get this over with so I can plant my petunias? Reed closes his eyes and hugs the picture to his heart. Dory! Why did you have to die! You were my partner for life. You weren't supposed to leave me. We had a deal! You left me holding the bag. Nothing makes sense anymore. I hate my job. Our daughter tells me she's a lesbian. I've gone off and made a fool of myself with another woman. "How weary, stale, flat, and unprofitable seem to me all the purposes of the world!"

The grief is unbearable. And it's true, it's all in his heart, and his heavy old heart is breaking! Tears fill his eyes and he begins to weep. Creaky old tears for the wife he no longer has. Tears of disgust for the mediocre judge he became in spite of his intentions. Tears of sorrow for the loss of his vitality, his wife, his passions, interests, and dreams. Yes, tears for Skylar too, damn it. For love lost as soon as won. "For the best laborer dead and all the sheaves to bind," as Yeats put it. Gone, all of it is gone.

After several minutes of sputtering and wailing, embarrassment brings him to his senses. He replaces his wife's picture on the shelf, washes up in his private bathroom. Takes stock of himself in the mirror. There must be something you care about!

Come on, man! What has meaning?

The law.

He cares about the law. He took an oath, ten years ago, that he would bear true faith and allegiance to the law, that he would support the Constitution of the United States and the Constitution of the state of California. His old friend Hank had sworn him in, back when he felt honored, overwhelmed, and awed by his new position. How's a judge supposed to know the answer to every problem that comes his way? What's a judge to do when he has no clue about the law? How is it possible for any human being to remain dignified, patient, fair, and interested in every little squabble that comes before him? Hank's answer had been elegant and memorable. "Simple," he said. "Just do the right thing."

He returns to his desk chair with a sense of purpose. He will not be a hack. If work is the only thing he has, he will give it his all, even if his all isn't much. He pours himself a cup of coffee, picks up a stack of briefs, and reads. He can already picture the logical way to rule on the issue before him.

ANDY

34. FAMILY COURT SERVICES

The mediator assigned to my parents' shock-and-awe child custody war works in the same building as Drug Court but on a different floor. The information kiosk directs me to the Office of Family Court Services, located on the top floor of the Family Court wing. Even though I'm not going to court, I still feel that same jumpiness I get when I talk to the Drug Court judge, maybe even worse today. I'm dizzy and pukey and clammy and gross, which is just so stupid because for once in my life, I have a plan, an actual exit strategy. If it works, and I'm pretty sure it will, I really hope it will, there will be an end to these endless axis-of-evil battles which have been tearing apart everyone in my family for as long as I can remember.

If this were a movie, there'd be heroic, upbeat music playing in the background and I'd be pulsing with purpose and enthusiasm. Instead, though, there's just the dinging of slow and crowded elevators and the cursing of couples on their way to court. Far from feeling energetic, I feel like shit – so full of dread. It's almost a joke – would The Killer see the humor in this? Her probationer is trying hard to do the right thing but hasn't felt this shitty since the morning after her last bender. This thought oddly makes me want to smoke right now...ah, the freedom of oblivion.

When I am spit out of the elevator, I join the mob of stressed-out people backed up behind the screening station, much like at an airport, in a long line that all but shouts THERE IS NO WAY IN HELL YOU WILL GET THERE ON TIME. Everyone has to take off belts and jackets and place them with their papers, files, briefcases, and assorted pocket crap on a conveyor belt for x-ray examination. Holy crap, these male lawyers are pulling all kinds of shit out of their coat pockets: wallets, phones, keys, Tums, coins, i-Pods, aspirin, nail clippers, receipts, breath mints – these guys are like walking drug stores. Someone needs to tell them about purses! There's a herd of gossiping lawyers in front of me. The stuff they're saying is so embarrassing! They're like people on cell phones, stuck in a private little world and somehow oblivious to the fact that everyone around them can hear – like it or not! – the dirt they're dishing about clients, other lawyers, judges. One loud-mouthed jerk with a big red face is trying to speed things up by pushing everyone forward, growling how he's going to be late, late, late for a very important date! Give me a break, pal. You think a pilot would really give a shit if a passenger shows up at the airport a minute before takeoff? We are not in your hurry.

Although there are plenty of babies in strollers and toddlers in hand, I'm the only teenager in line. I don't have a backpack, belt, or briefcase, and a skinny security guy pulls me and a few other non-lawyer types from the line and lets us walk through the screening station quickly while lawyers open briefcases. I want to send a neener-neener look to the pushy red-faced lawyer, but who knows, he might be my dad's lawyer, so I take off down the scuffed-up hallway before I abort my mission.

I'm going to end it today, and I finally figured out how. It's so simple.

I give up.

It's like what The Killer always says in Drug Court: When your way isn't working, try our way – it works.

The Office of Family Court Services is not hard to find. I check in with the receptionist, who sits behind a bullet-proof window. He finds my name on a computer list, tells me to check all keys, purses, briefcases, bags, jackets, and cell phones with him, then buzzes me into a small, windowless waiting room. He tells me to hold my hands in the air while he runs a hand-held metal detector up and down my body. When I pass inspection, he orders me to be seated on a metal folding chair.

I sit on my hands to stop them from shaking. If I have to wait long, I'll never make it to my interview – I'll bolt.

An interior door opens and a hugely pregnant woman emerges. She has beautiful black hair, red glasses, a maternity dress that might double for a tent in the off-season, and huge gold earrings. She looks up from her clipboard. "Andrea? Bretano?"

I nod.

She smiles politely. "I'm Dr. Montoya. Thanks for coming to see me. Follow me."

My heart is hammering insanely as I jump to my feet and follow her shiny black ponytail to an office door. "Sequoia Montoya, Ph.D, Court Mediator," reads the name plate. Is that supposed to be a joke or could that be a real name? She has a key card at her hip which she uses to open the door. Inside, there's a metal desk pushed against the wall with a computer on it. In front of the desk are three chairs, each with a box of Kleenex on the seat. I remove the Kleenex and sit down.

"A few things before we get started," she says, adjusting her chic red glasses and smoothing back some stray hairs. She smiles reassuringly, like a teacher on the first day of class. "One. I'm only going to take 15 minutes of your time."

She presses the start button on the timer and looks at me. I nod in agreement.

"Two. Your parents both love you, and they both want what's best for you. Unfortunately, as you well know, they are unable to agree on what that is. Although courts try to keep the children out of their parents' court cases, it does sometimes happen that if the child is old enough, as you are, the court will direct the mediator to find out the preferences of the child."

She pauses for me to take this in, and I nod. I'm glad I don't have to talk, because my throat has developed an obstruction the size of a cantaloupe.

"Three. Your preference is not binding on the judge, but the judge will carefully consider it in making a final determination in your parents' case. Four. Any questions before we get started?"

I shake my head. She picks up her clipboard.

"Let's get to it then," she says. "Did either parent talk to you about today's proceeding?"

"No," I say, shaking my head for emphasis. It's good to get that first lie out of the way.

"Either parent give you any suggestions or advice about what you should say in your interview with me today?"

"Absolutely not."

"Any coaching? Reminders? Promises?"

"No," I answer, wide-eyed and sincere. "Nothing."

"Nothing?" she looks at me, the shake of her dangly earrings distracting me a bit.

"Nothing," I repeat.

"How'd you know to come here today?" she asks, eyes narrowing slightly.

Because my mother has been talking about this non-stop for the last three months!

Because she has repeated again and again what I should say to you! Wait, I can't say that. Trick question! "You wrote me, remember? You wrote me a letter and gave me a time."

She flips through her clipboard, as if for confirmation. "Oh, indeed I did. Very good. So, before we go further, is there anything you would like to tell me?"

"Yes," I say. Do it, do it, do it! "I want this to end."

She writes that down.

"My parents have been fighting for ten years. I *hate* it. I hate hearing all the swearing and the arguing and the name-calling. I hate all the battles about school and homework and money. I hate the stress and the threats and the nastiness."

My heart is really pounding now. It doesn't seem like it's really me talking, more like I'm outside of myself and watching me talk. In a weird way, it reminds me of what it was like to try to talk seriously when you're stoned.

"I've been such a horrible daughter!" I cry. Am I yelling? I can't tell. "I haven't been good at all! It's not their fault! I'm not the person they think I am! They didn't do anything wrong. But no matter how good or how awful I am, they keep blaming the other one for how I am. If I do well at something, it's because one parent nurtured me. If I flunked something, it's because the other parent fucked up." I clap my hand over my mouth and squeeze my eyes shut in shame. "Sorry. What I mean is, everything I do makes them fight. I want it to stop."

Dr. Sequoia Montoya stops scribbling. Her clipboard is on her desk and she is looking at me solemnly, slowly rubbing her big swollen belly.

"It's just not working," I rattle on, out of control, way off script. "Before I started high school, I pitched a fit for this arrangement. I wanted to live with my dad, see my mom on alternate weekends. I thought it would work. But it hasn't. My school work is crap – I got kicked out of regular school and was placed in a dumbshit continuation school. I'm on probation. In Drug Court. My parents' fighting is worse than ever. Time to face the facts! I was wrong. We gotta try something else, or the fighting is going to go on and on and on and on."

I am not going to cry, but I yank out a few tissues just to do something.

"So we need to do something different. My dad, I love my dad. He loves me, he wants to protect me, he's my friend. But he's remarried. He has a nice wife. I love

Monica – she is such a good mother and such a caring person. They have adorable little twin boys. Shouldn't they be able to have a life, one that's not run by a fuck-up, defiant teenager? All I do is mess things up for them. And my mom, I'm her only child. I'm it for her. Sure, she's a little nutty, we know that! But no matter what, she's my mother. Shouldn't she be able to enjoy a little time with me without being in a huge uproar over every single detail of my life?"

Sequoia Montoya slips off her flats, wriggles her toes, sets her stockinged feet on the floor. Says nothing.

"Look, I know my mom. She should've been a lawyer. She's a genius with words! She has never lost a fight with my dad, and she never will. She's a fighter, and he's…oh come on, he's kind of a dope," I explain. "And the only reason she hasn't won this fight is because I put up a big stink two years ago, chose to live with Dad instead of her, and she went along. But you know what? It didn't work. Everyone is miserable."

I could really use some water. My ears are on fire.

"Okay. So. Please tell the judge we need to change custody once and for all. No more fighting. Give my mother sole legal and physical custody," I say. "That will end it. She'll be satisfied. My dad won't bring her back to court. He hates the fight. I know he won't file any motions. Let's end this war. Let me live with my mom until I'm old enough to, hopefully, go off to college. That way everyone is happy. Please."

Bee-beee-beep! We both jump a little as her timer goes off.

I'm on my feet.

"Okay, I'm done," I say. "That's what I want. Let the judge know. Thanks."

The mediator nods and I am out the door.

My dad will be so devastated when he hears what I just said. But my mom, God, she'll be thrilled. She'll want a transcript of every word, will eat it up like a box of See's dark chocolates. I'm not stupid enough to think it will make her actually happy, but I do think it will finally end the Battle of Bretano.

The stairway is sealed for security reasons, so I wait for the elevator which takes forever. When the doors open, I almost fall over from the overpowering aroma of pot.

"Hey," says the sole occupant, a shaggy, smiling boy about my age. Tall, pink cheeks, blue eyes, goofy smile. He's standing in the corner holding a big stack of library books.

I haven't read that much in three years, much less in the three weeks the library gives you.

"Hi," I say.

"Yeah," he laughs. "I sure am. Name's Kyle."

"Kyle," I repeat, feeling the awful knot in my stomach loosen a bit. "I'm Andy."

"Andy," he says. "Andy? Will you help me, darlin'? I can't find my way out of here. Somehow I got turned around when I left the library."

I laugh. He must really be stoned. But he is kind of cute and he's got a book of illustrated Rumi poetry at the top of his stack. That must be some kind of qualifier.

"Okay," I say. "Follow me."

BRYAN

35. HAVE YOU SEEN HER?

"Hi, Connie. It's Bryan. You know, the jerk you used to call husband. Uh, B-r-y-a-n. I'm sorry to call at home, but I'm worried about Andy. She's…I don't know. She doesn't seem like herself. I don't know if it's this new boyfriend or what. After school today she'll be at your house for her custodial week with you, and, well, I know you already do this, but keep an eye on her. See what you think. Something doesn't seem right to me. I know you'll do the best you can. Sorry to bug you at home on your voicemail. I know we're not supposed to talk. I wish we…uh…I'm sorry that…oh, hell, I don't know. Would you let me know if anything comes up? Thanks. Sorry. Sorry. Bye now."

HON. STRATHMORE REED, JR.

36. CONTINUING LEGAL EDUCATION

TO   : PRESIDING JUDGE
FROM: JUDGE REED
RE   : REQUEST FOR EDUCATION/
          PERSONAL LEAVE

MAY I PLEASE ATTEND THE UPCOMING STATEWIDE CONFERENCE ON DRUG COURTS IN MONTEREY? THE BROCHURE IS ATTACHED. I HAVE BEEN PRESIDING OVER JUVENILE DRUG COURT FOR ALMOST A YEAR AND THE TIME HAS COME FOR ME TO FIND OUT HOW I AM SUPPOSED TO BE DOING IT.

ADDITIONALLY, I REQUEST PERMISSION TO TAKE OFF THE LAST WEEK OF THE MONTH FOR

PERSONAL TIME. MY DAUGHTER WILL BE PRESENTING A PAPER ON A SCHOLARLY SUBJECT OF WHICH I KNOW APPROXIMATELY NOTHING. THE CONFERENCE IS IN NEW YORK CITY. FOLLOWING HER PRESENTATION, WE WILL EXPERIENCE SOME EAST COAST CULTURE AFTER WHICH, I AM CERTAIN, I WILL BE MOST ANXIOUS TO RETURN TO MY HUMBLE ROUTINE IN SEQUOIA VALLEY.

THE RUMORS OF MY IMMINENT RETIREMENT ARE ENTIRELY FALSE.

ANDY

37. FOUND & LOST

I hate myself.

I fucked up. Truly, badly, deeply.

Now I'm back in the Hall. I never thought I'd end up here again. You have to be a special kind of stupid to spend the night in a place like this more than once in your life. Yet here I am, locked up, hung over, "screwed, blued, and tattooed," as my dad says.

My dad. I'll never be able to face him. He was just starting to like me, starting to look at me again like his darling daughter, and not like some vicious, alien slutware messing up the hard drive of his life.

My PO. Oh, shit. I'll never be able to face her. She won't be "mad" at me – oh, no, I could handle mad. No, it will be so much worse. She'll be "disappointed" in me. Disappointed because she believed in me, trusted me, thought better of me. How wrong was she?

My sponsor, JD, warned me to take it easy with Kyle. Asked me to meet her for coffee. Knew I was lying when I told her I couldn't. How will I ever be able to face her again?

I'm so ashamed. Six months of sobriety, six months of perfect performance in Drug Court, thrown down like it was nothing. Now I'm in the goddamn juvenile lockup facility, feeling like absolute shit, like absolute shit warmed over, thrown back to my familiar, fucked-up life.

I deserve to be here.

I hate myself. With a passion.

They let me take a shower. It helps a little. You know the soap and hot water can't wash away the pukey feelings and the awful memories, but you feel like maybe it might, maybe you'll start to feel like your healthy, whole self again. You think of bubble baths and swimming pools, clean hair and wet skin, and you start feeling like maybe you could join the living again.

Toweling off, I catch a glimpse of myself in the metal reflective thing that passes for a mirror in this place. When my watery image appears, I almost scream. What happened to the healthy girl who followed the rules, the glowing girl who rode her bike across town, up hills, over bridges? She is nowhere to be found, not even in the soft, steamy mist. Instead, what appears is a haggard, horrible witch, a scarecrow, a ghost – or, actually, forget the folklore. What's in the mirror is a drug fiend.

That is what I am.

I lied, I lied, I lied.

I used, I used, I used.

Everything feels awful and unbearable. Things were going so well for me on the outs, and now...now I'm here in the cinderblock prison, all alone with my cruddy thoughts, my sickness, my shame. I hate being an addict.

I can't just have a little fun like the normies. No, I have to use and use and use until I puke or pass out, then wake up, feel like crap, and fiendishly chase the next buzz, jolt, oblivion.

It doesn't make any sense, no sense at all, to be a drug addict. You know the shit's going to kill you, but you don't care, you just want it anyway. And I guess you kind of want it to kill you. Because a part of you already feels like you are dead. You are so sick and tired of trying at life and constantly feeling horrible.

Then when you are feeling your absolute lowest, you hear it: The voice. The evil, cunning voice that always wins in the end.

"Over here! Hello?" Oh, she knows when to talk to you, when you are most vulnerable. You can try to not hear her, but it's no use. Her call comes in even louder, and you are always tuned in to her channel. "Deary, dear, I'm over here! You didn't forget about me, did you? I can help. Come here, little girl, I will make you feel better! I can fix it! I have my potions and my lotions. I can give your life commotion! Why do you resist? I'm here, here, here, little dear, you deserve some fun, little one. Here's some medicine, see? Isn't that better now? Ahhhhhh…"

If only it were a *little* medicine, but no! Not me. I use, use, use, and then…Oh, I do terrible things, things I would never do if I weren't out of my mind, crazy, blitzed out, faded. I'm not me anymore.

Now I do want to die. It would be a favor. I wouldn't have to face my parents, my PO, my sponsor, the judge. I wouldn't have to face myself or think about all I lost.

What I lost: my sobriety, obviously. Plus every shred of self-respect. But it wasn't just that I lost. My hopes for myself. My dreams of something better. My future. The good feeling I had of doing things right. Still, I might be able to get some of that back again. What I lost is bigger than all of that. Because this time – how could I? – this time I lost something I can never get back, never, ever, ever. What kind of careless scum could lose what I lost?

Rosalita!

I lost her. My beloved bike, my ticket to freedom, my trusted friend. She is gone. ROSALITA!

On my big, so-called fun bender, I left her at the park, locked up at the bike rack, and when I went back for her, she was gone. The lock was broken, and my beautiful, sweet Rosalita was missing.

It was the end of me. Even in my fucked-up state, I knew it was the end.

I sat down and cried and cried and cried. Then started calling out her name, as if she were a dog, calling and screaming and yelling until the police came and asked who was I calling for and when they found out it wasn't a friend or a little sister or even a stray cat, they asked very nicely would you please put your hands behind your back, uh-huh, that's our girl, and that's the last thing I remember until waking up in this cold bleak cinderblock cell.

Where I belong.

BRYAN

38. THE PARTY'S OVER

Back in the day, Bryan's friend Jake was the proverbial life of the party. He wasn't the studly football player, nerdy class president, or smooth ladies' man; he was just an easy-going, fun-loving guy with an outrageous sense of humor. He had this magical quality about him – somehow he made everyone around him feel lively and upbeat. You could tell when he walked into a room because right away there was a buzz. The air changed, somehow; the excitement level jumped a few notches along with the volume. He had a big, loud laugh, a ready joke, and an amazingly optimistic outlook on life – that life had to be lived in all its glory. When the high school crowd was old enough to move the party from the beach parking lot to the local watering hole, Jake could always be found right in the thick of things, with a knot of eager friends lined up to buy him a drink. When Bryan was single, he passed many a pleasant evening with Jake at the Fourth Street Tavern, watching whatever game might be on TV, throwing down the brewskis, and laughing like hell. Those were some fun times.

But Jake's party came to a screeching halt when he suffered a massive heart attack at the ripe old age of 36. Holy crapoli – Jake? Unthinkable! Mr. Eternal Youth himself? No! Hadn't he just been in the shop grabbing a tall coffee with an extra shot, joking about some late-night escapade involving snorts of tequila and the sexy ex-wife of a singer from a semi-famous rock band? Jake came *this* close to meeting his maker, but his luck held and, against all odds, he pulled through. Well, sort of. Because when he came out the other end, he wasn't the same Jake. According to his mother, a longtime chai tea and flax muffin fan, something snapped during the grueling months of rehab. The day he was sprung from treatment, Jake up and joined a Buddhist monastery in some far-flung pocket of New Zealand, trading his legendary life of nonstop parties and easy money for vows of chastity and poverty. What was *that* about? To Bryan it seemed like a major overreaction.

What could have happened to Jake during his hospital stay? Bryan was mystified by what would make a guy change his life so suddenly and completely. But now...now he might understand.

In movies, midlife wakeup calls come in the form of helpful, loveable spirits: *It's A Wonderful Life, Heart and Soul, Scrooged, Family Man* – Bryan has always loved these stories about guys who get some supernatural assistance in finding their right path. In real life, you hear about an occasional wakeup call, but they're not as painless or sweet as an encounter with a friendly ghost; no, they tend to involve hospitalizations, arrests, bankruptcies, loss of a loved one, or a near-death experience.

Bryan's came this morning in the form of a report from Family Court Services.

He had forgotten all about Jake, which is one of the hazards in his line of business. You see so many regulars day in and day out, you learn their drink orders and personality quirks, you share a quick greeting like you're old buds, but when they stop coming in, they drop off the fucking map. Years can pass and it's only if they reappear that you realize you used to talk to this person every damn day; when did that stop? How long has it been?

The pathetic thing is, five years can go by, and you still know his drink order. What a waste of valuable brain space, but that's what's in Bryan's.

Jake didn't reappear in the shop for a tall coffee with an extra shot – unfortunately. However, he did pop into Bryan's head and slap him around a bit when Bryan read that report from Family Court Services.

It seems that at some point in Bryan's life, don't ask him when, he settled in and stopped making an effort to see things from the other guy's point of view. He started believing that he had things figured out, that if there was a problem, it was the other dude needing to fix things. Here's a random snapshot of his brain: That asshole ran a red light! My ex is a cold-hearted bitch! My teenager doesn't talk to me! *They* need to change – why aren't they more like me! I'm a safe driver, loyal husband, good dad; what's everyone else got wrong with *them?*

So it takes some kind of huge whack on the head – or, possibly, a ghost if you're lucky – for a guy to realize: no, ya big jerk – *you* got it backwards! "They" don't need to change. They are fine. But you? Dude, wake up and live in the fucking world. You need a 180 degree reorientation.

Jake's heart attack must have served as such a wake-up call for him. Maybe from his hospital bed he got a perspective on his life and didn't like what he saw. While the rest of the world considered him a fun-loving party animal, maybe he saw himself as an introverted loner who wanted to offer up his life to Buddha. Maybe what his friends thought of as "fun" he thought "alcoholic." Who knows? The bottom line is, Jake suddenly was able to see things in a whole new way, and he engineered a bold plan to steer his life onto his true course.

Bryan guesses he should feel relieved that he didn't have to suffer a fucking heart attack or a criminal indictment to rock his world; still, what his daughter said to the mediator has turned his life upside down.

She doesn't want to live with him. It's right here on page one, plain as day. "Child's statement: 'I want to live with my mother. My previous preference for my father's home was a mistake.'"

A mistake! Christ, he's been fighting for his daughter's happiness for 16 long years, trying with all his might to protect her, raise her, love her. He thinks about her more than he thinks about himself. He has spent a fortune on her clothes, recreation, therapy, education – and she calls it a "mistake."

Truth is, he can't fault her for hating him. It's been hard on her: the divorce, of course; living in two homes; his long hours at work; the remarriage, stepmother and twins plus her adolescence – none of that stuff is easy. Still, when you see her truth written out on a piece of paper, it's tough.

Monica tried to calm him down, said she was sure there was more to this than meets the eye, urged her husband to sit on this for a day or two. But his lawyer called right away, said he had to get his ass in to see him ASAP, said not to panic, that there are lots of things they haven't tried, many arguments still to make, and several obvious errors in the report. The lawyer talked him into scheduling an appointment, so Bryan can drop another $500 into the bottomless pit of his divorce case and listen to his lawyer lecture for the thousandth time on how his ex is a whack job, how the system is failing him, and on and on and on.

As usual, Rocco is yakking on the phone when Bryan walks into his office. He can hear him through the wall, busting a gut over some hilarious lawyer humor. His sexy wife isn't around to greet him today. Either Rocco has given her the day off or she's as sick of him as Bryan is. Bryan is stuck looking at the crappy wall art: faded, metal-framed museum posters from decades-old exhibitions. Tall silk plants gathering dust. Stacks of magazines shout out promises of how to lose ten pounds of belly fat, redo your kitchen in a weekend, and kick-start your love life. Not a one can tell you how to get your precious daughter back.

Finally, Rocco gets off the goddamn phone and ambles out to the reception room to greet Bryan. He's wearing a silk Aloha shirt, a thick gold chain around his neck, khakis, and some soft Italian loafers that retail for $500 at Nordstrom. Bryan probably paid for the goddamn shoes himself.

"Yo, bro," Rocco claps his hairy arm around Bryan's shoulder. "Thanks for coming in right away. You want some coffee or something?"

Bryan shrugs out of his embrace. "Hey, asshole, I run a fucking chain of coffee shops. I don't want any of your goddamn, commercially roasted office coffee."

"All right, all right," he laughs good-naturedly. "Cool your tool, dude. How about a beer?"

"Can we just cut to the chase?" He snaps. "I've got a court hearing in a week and have just heard the worst possible news. My daughter wants out of my house. I don't want to drink a fucking beer with my lawyer."

"Jesus, Bryan, don't bite my head off," Rocco says. "We've been through this before. It's going to work out. It always does. Come in and sit down. Jesus, Mary, and Joseph!"

Like a dog on a choke chain, Bryan follows him to his inner sanctum, tail between his legs, ready to take his chewing-out.

"Let's review the basics," Rocco says, tapping his fingers together. "Connie is a ball-buster. She's never going to forgive you for leaving her. She's owns a piece of your business and is the mother of your child. And, let's not forget, she's a nut-job. So relax, bud, and take a deep breath. She will be on your ass for the rest of your life."

Why is it that when someone tells you to relax, your stress level shoots up so high you want to jump out of your goddamn skin? The words he's heard a thousand times hang in the air as the lawyer swivels around to his credenza and digs through his litigation box, pulling out papers with post-its, legal pads with scribbled notes, briefs with yellow highlights.

"She's going to be on my ass for the rest of my life," Bryan repeats.

"Yeah," he says cheerfully. "You should never have married the bitch."

Bryan opens his mouth and out come the words: "You're fired."

"Yeah, and you're an asshole. What's with you today anyway?"

Bryan rises from his chair. "What's with me? I don't have a clue. Maybe I'm out of my mind or maybe I finally get it. You're right, damn it! Don't you see? She's going to be on my ass for the rest of my life. We've been doing battle with her for ten years, and none of it has worked. I'm not going to fight her for another year, much less ten or twenty! All it's done is made me miserable, cost me an arm and a leg, and turned my daughter against me. There is no "W" at the end of this game. Enough already."

Rocco jumps out of his chair, pulls his arms in front of his chest as if he might take a swing at his client. "Listen, asshole, you can't fire me right before a big hearing. What are you going to do, represent yourself? You can't do that. She's better at this than you are!"

"Don't I know it? I was married to her," Bryan says. "But you know what? She's better at this than you are too."

"Fuck you," Rocco growls, giving his client the old "table for one" for emphasis. "Without me, you're toast."

"You're probably right," he says. "I'm fucked, that's for sure. But, listen. We sit around and talk about what a bitch Connie is, and let's face it: I owe her the money. So, in this case, who's the bitch? I shouldn't have short-changed her. I can't fucking fight this fight anymore. I give up. I surrender!"

"That's your litigation strategy? 'I surrender?' You're a moron, Bretano!" he says, bullying Bryan to come back to his way of thinking.

"Yes," Bryan says. "I'm going to tell the judge myself. It can't be any worse than this. Thank you for your services. Send me a final bill. I'm done."

"You will regret this, asshole," he says.

"You might be right," Bryan says. "If so, you can have the pleasure of watching me come back to you on my hands and knees and beg you to be my lawyer again."

He sprints out of the office before the lawyer has a chance to yell at him some more. He is not changing my mind, and if he sticks around any longer, he'll just have to pay to listen to him tell him what an asshole he is. Why pay for something you already know?

He can't believe he didn't think of this before. He surrenders! She represents herself – he can too. He's practically giddy. No more lawyers in his life – he could sing! Monica will be thrilled. She can't stand Rocco and hates paying his goddamn legal bills. He digs around his jacket pocket for his phone. He's going to call his wife and tell her the news.

But the moment he switches the phone on, it rings. "Yeah," he says. "Bryan here." It better not be his goddamn lawyer begging for a second chance.

"Mr. Bretano? This is Faro at Juvenile Services. Your daughter was arrested earlier today and is in our custody. She was pretty agitated when they brought her in, so the nurse evaluated her and gave her a mild sedative to help her calm down. The probation officer knows about the new charges for public intoxication, resisting arrest, and possession of marijuana and has issued a probation hold. She asks that you let Andrea sit in the Hall for a few days before visiting. Ms. Washington will visit and call you with the particulars. We just wanted you to know that your daughter is safe. I'm calling the mother now and relaying the same message."

Incarcerated? Not his daughter – she's with her mother! Intoxicated? Not his Andy – she's six months clean and sober! Monica says she's the absolute star performer in Drug Court. And if she's in the Hall agitated, how is she safe? She's not safe!

This can't go on.

Shit, Jake, wherever you are: pray for your old friend and his girl. Pray with all your broken, beautiful, Buddhist heart.

HON. STRATHMORE REED, JR.

39. START SPREADING THE NEWS

Strathmore takes a deep breath before picking up the phone to contact his mother. The view from the fifteenth floor of his room in the Mandarin Oriental Hotel is nothing short of spectacular, with thousands of sparkling lights and the hustle and bustle of big city life spread out below. Mother answers on the first ring, which means either that she is already in bed or is anticipating a call from one of her people at this precise instant.

"I certainly was not expecting you, Son!" she barks, as if he has crawled in through the bathroom window rather than telephoned at a perfectly reasonable hour. "Aren't you in New York with Bitsy?"

"Exactly right, Mother," Strathmore reassures her. "I've just returned from a rather extraordinary day."

"Well I'm expecting a call from Lyle Livingston in five minutes, so please make it brief!"

By nature, Strathmore is not a fast speaker, so when his mother asks that he pick up the pace or get to the point – as she has many times over the decades – he tends to stammer and sputter all the more. But his day with his daughter has been so full of new experiences and mind-boggling information, he launches into a babbling narrative. First about the commanding speech his daughter delivered to peers at her professional conference, how full of pride he'd been for her knowledge of the subject matter and her confidence in her delivery. Then about the superb show they'd seen on Broadway, how unexpectedly exhilarating it was to hear live music and view professional actors on the big stage; and finally about the late dinner they had shared at a packed and trendy restaurant with his daughter's close companion, Pat.

"She's in love, Mother," Reed says. "I have never seen such a thing. Her eyes were sparkling, her face was lit up, she was smiling,

Mother! It was, well, astonishing! You know our Bitsy is not much of a smiler."

"That is delightful news, and so surprising too!" Mother says. "And what about this Pat? Is he worthy of her?"

Reed gulps. "Worthy of her – yes, absolutely. Quite a remarkable, educated, erudite individual."

"Oh, out with it, Stratmore! Don't start stuttering now. We've no time for that! Tell me about him!"

"The thing is, Mother, her Pat? She's a w-woman. Our Bitsy is…well, she's gay."

Strathmore closes his eyes and waits. He dreads his mother's pronouncement, but has told his daughter and her girlfriend that he will defend their relationship to the death. It was truly a shock when his daughter broke the news of her longtime girlfriend to him; he gaped uncomprehendingly for many minutes before the announcement sank in. He hadn't really accepted or believed his daughter's earlier pronouncement about her sexual orientation. And yet, as the evening unfolded, it began to make perfect sense. All the years when he sensed his daughter was dating but never brought her dates home to meet the parents. All the years of tense, brief exchanges of personal information. All the years of pain and stand-offishness, because his daughter was afraid her father would not accept her. And, Reed must concede, she was right. He was a rigid, narrow thinker. When he said goodnight to Bitsy and Pat, he folded both in his arms and told them he loved them – in the most stammering and uncomfortable way possible – confessed to them how ashamed he was to have caused them pain. Bitsy squirmed out of his arms, thanked him, told him there was no need to go overboard; Pat said after so long, she would gladly take any hug he would offer; and the three shared an awkward laugh.

After a deadening silence, his mother answers. "Dear me, it does seem to be in favor these days. Well, I guess it can't be helped. How did we not see it, Strathmore? It seems rather obvious now. How's she doing?"

Reed smiles and begins to breathe again. "She's happy, Mother. I've never seen her happier. I think the only thing that could make her happier is knowing she has your blessing."

"You tell Bitsy I'm contacting the club tomorrow and reserving a place for Pat at our New Year's Eve party. Did Bitsy ever tell you what her resolution was last New Year's Eve? To bring her fiancé to the next year's gathering! I guess she must've said 'fiancée.' Your father would be proud of a granddaughter who met her goal. Now, Son, I really must say goodbye. Duty calls!"

"Goodbye, Mother," Strathmore says. "And thank you. Thank you for accepting my daughter for who she is. I will endeavor to do the same."

His mother hangs up and doesn't hear him say how very pleased he is that his daughter has at last found happiness. Isn't that what everyone wants? Happiness. Someone to love. Someone who will take you as you are.

If only there were someone in this big world with whom he could share the happiness he feels in his old beat-up heart.

ANDY

40. COMING TO

The guard, Tiny, unlocks my door and pokes his head in my cell. Tiny is the approximate size of a refrigerator and has skin the color of the night sky. He's the most talked-about guard here at the Hall; everyone has a story about him – not just kids but staff, too. All involve some version of his killing a man – some say while playing football in college, others say as a bouncer at a Hollywood club, but there's a ton of other theories featuring attack dogs, crack houses and fast getaways. The only version I'm inclined to believe is the one where he's a prison guard at San Quentin and shot some ax murderer before anyone else could get hurt. Tiny refuses to confirm or deny any of these rumors. In fact, I've never heard him say a word about himself. Most of his conversation has to do with Jesus and/or the need for the kid he's got in handcuffs to do a better job with the precious life the Lord has given her. But, true or not, the one thing we all take away from these creepy-cautionary stories is: Don't mess with Tiny.

"Hi, honey," he says in a soft, high voice, as if calling a stray kitten. How could that little voice come out of big him? "You have a visitor. Your PO is here to see you."

I've been dreading this moment. I knew The Killer would come to see me, I just didn't know when. It's my third day here and I haven't talked to anyone yet, not even my dad. Three days is a long time to be alone in a cell with your mean thoughts and your shame, but now that she's here for me, I wish I could wait a little longer, like maybe forever. She probably figures that by now my high has dissipated, my hangover has worn off, and I'm ripe for the killing. And, of course, she's right on target.

"I can't, Tiny," I simper, burying my head in the ragged orange sleeve of my ratty Hall sweatshirt.

"Ye-eess you can," he says slowly, giving his huge key ring a jingle.

It's pointless to argue with him, but my body won't move. I shake my head and squeeze my eyes and blabber just to stall the inevitable humiliation. You know what would be a really useful skill? To be able to conjure up this moment when the blunt is being passed. Because honestly, there's no amount of partying that could make a moment like this worth it. "Please don't make me."

I feel, rather than see, Tiny open the door and fill the frame with his massive body. The blare of a TV laugh track and the hoots of bored teenagers intrude into my cell.

"Now honey, you know the rules," he says, voice still soft but now unyielding. "I don't make them. But I do follow them."

Like I said, you don't mess with Tiny. I don't know what he'd do if I just stayed curled in my bed in a pathetic little heap, but I've no doubt he could pick me up like a potato chip and drop me anywhere he damn pleases, in the onion dip or back in the bag. So I surrender, struggle to my feet and glue my gaze to the floor.

"Sweet Baby Jesus, glory be," he says with a soft hum as I dutifully place hands behind back and step in front of him, head bowed and compliant. "Let's you and me take a ni-iice slow walk to the meeting room, uh-huh."

We shuffle past the boys watching sitcoms, and I feel them checking me out. But Tiny's got my back, and not a single one dares to taunt, tease, or even, you know, breathe. I keep my gaze on my shuffling step, stringy hair drawing a shabby curtain around my face, and retreat into the massive protection of Tiny.

The Killer is just finishing an interview with some unsuspecting new recruit. I hear her voice through the glass as she explains the rules of Drug Court, the importance of honesty, the weekly visits, blah, blah, blah. I can practically read the thoughts of the new kid: I'll breeze through this program, nail my probation in half the time, and slip right back into the pretty party life. Poor chump! This program will kick his ass. I haven't seen a single kid sail through it, but I have seen plenty of asses getting kicked – including mine.

The Killer sends an eye-signal to Tiny that she's ready to switch prisoners, and when the new recruit stands, I about faint dead away into my refrigerator escort. It's Kyle, the boy with the books – the very guy who helped me land where I am today. How did he end up in the Hall? I don't remember being with him when I was arrested, but then, I don't remember a lot. Which is another thing you don't want to think about too much. What kind of loser doesn't show up for her own life?

"Hey," he mumbles as we pass. He smiles sheepishly and shrugs. I duck into the meeting room without a word. It's against Hall rules anyway for girls and boys to talk.

The Killer is sitting tall in a swivel chair with her usual military posture: shoulders back, chest out. She's wearing a stiff khaki pantsuit and bad-ass boots. The cramped interview room is bleak and discouraging, with grayish-pink floor tiles and a lumpy sofa covered in an old-lady bedspread. A matted teddy bear is crushed in the cushions, so I pick it up, hug it close, and collapse into my sordid destiny.

"So, you and Kyle have met, I gather," she says, not cruelly.

I nod. It is so humiliating to be in the same room with her. Here's another key moment I wish I'd pictured before wandering off to Pixie Park to smoke with my fun-loving friends. How could I have been so careless? Doesn't my word mean anything? Am I no different from the other kids in court who say all the right things to the judge and then run out and break promises?

"You think we should let him into Drug Court?" she asks conversationally.

I shrug. Still haven't made eye contact. Can't. I might as well be standing before her completely naked for how exposed I feel.

"Yes, I see what you mean. I'm not sure about him either. It's pretty clear he's got a problem with drugs. His older brother has a medical marijuana card, for heaven's sake. Kyle says he doesn't want to grow up to be like him, tells me our program could do him some good. Still, I have one major reservation about admitting him."

I'm listening, not looking.

"Maybe I shouldn't tell you this, but my main reservation is whether admitting him would do a disservice to my star probationer."

Wait. Is she saying...? I look up questioningly.

"Yes, I'm talking about you." She pierces me with her sweet, forgiving brown eyes.

That does it. The teeny reserve that was keeping this all together falls apart in an instant.

"I'm so *not* a star student!" I cry. "I'm an idiot! And it was so stupid of me to run off and use! I had six months. Six months! I had my dad's trust! I felt semi-good about myself. You were treating me with respect. Thrown away on a boy I met in an elevator at the courthouse!"

Her chair squeaks with the shift of her weight. "What were you doing in court?"

Oh my God, I'd forgotten about that particular humiliation. My brilliant idea to solve my family's problem. That worked out even worse for me than every other solution my family has tried in the last decade. "Talking with my parents' mediator."

"About their divorce?"

I roll my eyes. "What else?"

"Huh," she says, staring off into space, or, in this case, speckled ceiling tiles. "I wonder what toll it's taken on you."

I guess I'm so relieved that she's not telling me what a disappointing kid I am, that I just start to blab.

"It's hard to know," I say with a huge, dog-like sigh. "It's always there. It's the air I breathe. The back-and-forth between them. The attack, defend, counterattack. One set of loyalties in one house, another set in the other. I'm so used to it, I hardly notice that it's a thing anymore. It's just the way it is."

Squeak, she crosses her leg. Squeak, uncrosses.

Why am I in here? Other teenagers are out having fun, going to school, working on college applications, flirting with members of the opposite sex. Having sex. I'm locked up in prison, talking to my probation officer.

What does this say about me? The teddy bear is snuggled so close to my chest I can feel my heart beating against it. I can't believe I'm holding a frigging teddy bear, but I'm not about to let it go.

"So here you are, back in the Hall," she says matter-of-factly. "How do you feel?"

"Horrible." It comes out like a croak, louder than intended. I am losing it, no control over my thoughts, feelings, voice. Definitely no control over my clothes, meals, activities.

"Horrible, hungover? Horrible, mad? Horrible, sad? Be specific. I'm trying to have a learning conversation with you."

"My hangover is gone, but it was a wicked one."

She taps her pencil against her clipboard.

"Well, okay, I deserved that hangover," I concede. "And yeah, I am mad at myself for being stupid. I mean, running off with a guy who couldn't find his way out of the library? That should have been a clue."

Tap-tap, next point. She knows there's more and she is going to pull it out of me. Won't let me get side-tracked by talking about a boy.

"I guess I'm sad too," I say. "Sad to let my parents down. Sad to behave so horribly when I was arrested. Sad to disappoint you. Worried about facing everyone."

Squeak, cross. Squeak, uncross.

"Yeah, I feel all kinds of horrible," I say. "That I have to start this all over, day one. It just kills me. That I have to rebuild everyone's trust. That I have to face the judge, when he was just starting to be kind of nice to me. Now he'll be all annoyed and cranky, like he is with the other kids."

Her eyes are burning into me as I stare at the cruddy industrial floor. Who designs this crap, pink streaks in a gray floor? Do they specially make this for lock-up facilities so people can feel worse than they already do?

"It's just so overwhelming," I hear myself say. "I want to give up." And I do. It would be so much easier to give up than to try.

After an excruciating wait, she speaks. "Help me understand. Where would that get you?"

I shrug. "I don't know. This is too hard for me."

"Do you suppose you're the only teenager in the history of the world who has felt overwhelmed by problems? Like, you know, you're a teenager and you turn up pregnant, total your father's car, get cut from the varsity team, dropped by your boyfriend, evicted from your home, kicked out of school? You think other teenagers have suffered setbacks?"

I can't tell if she's being sarcastic or trying to help me see straight, so I just answer. "Yeah. Teens suffer."

She nods. "So other kids have felt like you. I wonder how they've handled it. Let's say your best friend is kicked out of school and is so despondent she wants to give up. What would you tell her?"

If I even had a friend, she probably wouldn't care about getting kicked out of school. She'd be thrilled! She'd be sent to a loser school, where nothing would be expected of her. But what about a girl like Brittany? She used to be my friend. We used to talk every night, dream about being room-mates at Stanford. I can't imagine she'd ever be kicked out of school. What would I say to her? She would be devastated!

"I'd say something like, don't worry, Pookie, you're amazing, and it's going to work out. This isn't the end of the world. You might *like* your new school. It might not be so bad! If you work hard, I'm sure you'll be able to go back to your old school. You're only a teenager. This isn't going to ruin your life."

"Good advice," The Killer says.

"You think I can do that?" I ask, realizing I've been had. "You think I can just work hard, get back to where I was?"

"Of course," she says. "What's your option? Give up altogether, become a pothead who can't find her way out of the public library? That doesn't sound like a very attractive alternative."

"But I don't know how to do it! I thought I did. Look what happened. I'm back in the Hall."

"And I'm about to give you your Get Out of Jail Free card," she says. "Figure out the connection between your parents' divorce and your drug use. Write a letter. Make it good, because our judge is not going to like your new law violation."

I shake my head. No, no, no, I'm sick of thinking about this, wishing it were something else...

"Stop," she says. "You can. No one needs to see it except me. I'll be back tomorrow to talk. And Andy?"

I look up at her.

"Go easy on that teddy bear."

I look down. I've been so wrapped up with worry that I've crushed the poor guy in my arms, and I'm covered with little wisps of his stuffing.

❖ ❖ ❖

Dear Mom and Dad,

I wish I had the guts to give you this letter. But I write only because my probation officer is making me do it, and she swears "as an officer of the court" that no one but her will see it. And so, knowing I'll never say this to you, I give you here the rawest and truest words written on my very heart.

Here's what I hate more than anything else in the world, what I hate even more than myself (which is saying a lot at the moment): I hate it that you can't get along. You hate each other with a palpable, unrelenting intensity. You hate each other publicly and epically, hurling horrible hateful insults about <u>my</u> mother and <u>my</u> father, making cruel and cutting observations you wouldn't make about the most wretched human being on the planet, much less about the person you once considered the light of your life, the precious person who is the parent of your daughter. At this point in the game, you don't even need to say anything for me to feel the force of your nonstop vicious thoughts. I bet when you wake up in the middle of the night, your first thought it is, My ex is such a jerk.

Mine is: I wish they didn't hate each other.

You know how embarrassing it is when you're out at a restaurant and you hear a couple bicker, when you accidentally glimpse them swipe and hiss like mangy cats? It's so awkward, you just want to get as far away from them as you can, right? Imagine how much more horrible it is when that couple is your own parents, arguing in open court for all the world to see. And not just for a teensy, two-minute spat, either. You two have fought fiercely and ruthlessly, year after year, since that first heartbreaking announcement that we would not be a family anymore.

Hello? You are my parents! You are the heroes and stars of my childhood! You are the rulers of my country – and what a mean and war-ravaged country it is. I see parts of both of you in me, and when I feel your hatred for the other, I hate that part of me, too.

Confession: Your wild child is nothing but a corny cliché. Because what I want more than anything – so embarrassing to admit! – is for us to live together like a happy little family. (I'm sorry, Monica, because no one has been kinder to me during my rebellious adolescence than you. As weird as it sounds, this has nothing to do with you.) I have spent so much of my life longing for this dream and know each detail by heart. In this world, we appreciate Dad's hard work and Mom's weird genius. We laugh at our jokes and are extra generous during rough times. Dad goes to work with a smile on his face because Mom made him one of her award-winning waffles and kissed him at the door.

Mom says to herself as she cleans up the breakfast dishes, There goes my dearest husband, who works hard to provide for the family he loves. In my dream world, Mom can see how sweet my father is, and Dad appreciates how passionate my mother is.

I am so, so sorry to have been such a disappointment to you. Oh, I know you love me, worship me, would do anything for me. But I am a letdown – even to myself. I can almost hear your screams of denial about how precious I am, how much you love me no matter what. But let's face facts: Your daughter is a liar and a cheat, nothing more than a druggie. She's been booted out of two schools and arrested six times – six times! – for public intoxication, disturbing the peace, yelling at police officers, shoplifting. And these are just the times when she has been caught. You had to have hoped for more in a daughter.

So, why would a daughter who has been so loved, worshiped, and adored exchange her promising future, good friends, and even her health for cheap highs, street drugs, and disloyal dopers?

I'll tell you why. It wasn't to piss you off or to grab your attention. It wasn't peer pressure, curiosity, or a bad boy's urging.

It was to feel better.

It's that simple.

My early use was blissful, made me feel giddy and light, released from the burden of my worries.

So this is how happy people feel! Wow! I wanted more of that, who wouldn't? Instant friends and mega-popularity with boys, long nights of endless laughs, loud music and thrilling close calls. It wasn't completely innocent, of course. I'm not stupid – I knew it was cheating on happiness to use, but I figured I could handle it, that I could stop whenever I wanted, that I was in control. And, desperately, I couldn't stand the idea of going back to that old, awful feeling.

Somewhere along the way the drama of my party life became so big and unwieldy that it took all my effort to maintain it and manage it. New legal troubles! Meet a lawyer, go to court, tell a story, pay my debt. New troubles at school! Flunk the test, lose the credits, endure detention, plan my escape. New troubles at home! Slam doors, scream curses, run away, beg for another chance. I was busy running on every front, lying, using, planning and promising, and all of it kept me from feeling your hatred for each other.

Even at my worst, in my last crazy using binges, when I felt sick in my whole body, hung over, lost and wretched, it felt better than the horrible feeling of living between your fighting.

The big lie to myself: in my using days, I believed I was having fun, being wild and free. But when I think about how much I love you both, how I wanted nothing more than for us to be happy, I don't think

I was trying to have fun. I think was trying to be like you, to match my misery to yours. Mom lives in a prison of suffering where Dad's every move is criticized for its stupidity. Dad lives in a prison of financial doom, juggling the demands of running a business and supporting two households. I made a prison for myself out of trouble, guilt, and shame. All of us running around like crazy people, pissed off at the world, not noticing what we might be throwing away by living like this.

God, it's like we're related or something.

I'm starting to see more clearly now. We are never going to be the happy little family of my dreams, are we? There is nothing I can do to stop the two of you from hating each other, is there? No matter how rotten I am both of you will still want me anyway, won't you? And maybe you don't even want me — you just don't want the other parent to have me. I can wish all I want that we all get along, but I am powerless to change you.

BUT: I have choices about myself. I will not live like this anymore. I will not medicate myself, run away from myself, hate myself. I will heal. I don't know how yet but I will learn.

So I officially release my oldest and longest-running dream of living happily with my mom and my dad in our little home. It's funny, at this moment I'm scrunched up on this thin cruddy cot in a gray cinderblock cell, but I vividly picture myself standing on the top of a grassy hill — like the one above Redwood Grove Reservoir — holding a big bouquet of red, yellow, and green balloons — Mom, Dad, me, home, happy — and poof! I release them all and watch the cheery balloons drift off into the blue sky, each balloon floating off in its own breeze. Goodbye! Goodbye!

I'm not done with dreaming, not by a long shot. I have a new dream, bigger than the last. It is to graduate from high school in two years with straight A's. That's right, and why not? I've got no friends, nothing but free time and lots of units to make up, so I will use my time to improve my mind and formulate an exit plan. I plan to go as far away as I can from Sequoia Valley, and start college with a clean slate. Bowdoin would be great — it's in Maine — or maybe Brown — it's in Rhode Island. I'll have to nail the SAT and write a hell of a personal essay for either school to look at me, but I found a study guide here in the Hall, and it tells you how to do both of those. Maybe I can find a far-away college with a girl's bicycle team! Wouldn't that be something? To race in college? [Note to self: visit Santos as soon as you're out and tell him how you lost his Rosalita.]

That's the part of the dream I can control: grades, summer school, the SAT. The next part is trickier, because I need your help to make this happen.

When I graduate from high school, I'll be sitting on the stage with my class, searching the audience for my family. Where are they? Are they spread out all over the auditorium, sitting angry and apart? No! Look! There they are, my family finally got it together! They are sitting in a line with tears of joy in their eyes, pride puffing their chests. Mom, Dad, Monica, the twins, Granny – all of you sitting together and rooting for me. And I think, there they are! We made it to the finish line! This is my family. We went through a rough patch, but we figured it out. We figured out – before it was too late! – that we love each other, we can forgive each other, we can take care of each other. Sometimes we can make each other happy. Like a real family.

But before any of this can happen, I have to get out of the Hall. I have to find a place where I can be safe. But where?

I can't live with you anymore. I can't face your fighting. Can you send me away? Any distant cousins in Asia or Australia? Where will I be safe?

I don't care who wins anymore. I just want it to end.

I'm safe here in the Hall. Maybe I'll stay here. Like a prisoner of war.

Love, Your Andy

BRYAN

41. IN PRO PER

SUPERIOR COURT OF CALIFORNIA
COUNTY OF SEQUOIA

In re the marriage of
BRYAN BRETANO,
Petitioner   Case No. 03580
                    SUPPLEMENTAL
                    DECLARATION
                    OF BRYAN BRETANO
and
CONSTANCE BRETANO,
Respondent.

I, Bryan Bretano, declare:

1. I fired my lawyer and now represent
   myself.

2. I retract the earlier opposition to Connie's motion filed by my lawyer.

3. I agree that I owe Connie $100,000 in unpaid partnership profits. Unfortunately, I don't have the cash or the ability to borrow money. I am willing to make monthly payments of $5,000 to retire the debt. If that is not satisfactory, I will sell the business and pay her first from the proceeds.

4. I do not like the custody recommendation from Family Court Services but will live with it if that is what the court orders.

5. I believe that Connie has our daughter's best interests at heart, and I acknowledge her for being a devoted mother.

6. I am deeply sorry for the pain I have caused my daughter and my former wife. I ask them both for forgiveness and promise to do better by both of them in the future.

7. Under no circumstances will I fight with my family anymore.

8. I surrender.

I declare that the foregoing is true and correct to the best of my knowledge and that this declaration is executed under penalty of perjury pursuant to the laws of the State of California.

/s/ Bryan Bretano

_____

Bryan Bretano, Petitioner

❖ ❖ ❖

To   : Bryan@Bretanos.com,
         Monica@Bretanos.com
From: Helena@Hartetherapy.com
Re   : First meeting
Dear Bryan and Monica, It was such a delight to get the call from Monica and hear that you're ready to start family therapy with me. I have an immediate opening on Fridays at 11:00. Please read the attached office policy and notices of confidentiality. Also, complete the background information forms. I look forward to working with you and your family. Warmly, Helen.

❖ ❖ ❖

To   : "Bryan," "Connie," "Granny," "JD"
From: "Monica"
Re   : Andy's Court Today!
Dear Family and Friends of Andy: Just a reminder that Andy's Drug Court meets today

at 3:00 in Courtroom L. I met with Andy in the Hall, and she feels horrible about her relapse. She is saying she wants to go off to boarding school. I think it would be great for her to know that she has the love and support of her family and sponsor. I hope you will join me in court today to show Andy our love for her. If anyone needs a ride, call me and I'll pick you up.

HON. STRATHMORE REED, JR.

42. JUVENILE LAW

Drug Court is scheduled to start in 30 minutes, and Strathmore Reed, Jr. finds himself sorely lacking in the judicial temperament department. Damn it all! The ghastly news about his top-performing juvenile, the young lady whose family is connected with the popular coffee business – Bretano's, Andrea B., isn't it? – has him muttering curses and yanking dusty law books off his shelves. How could she do something so careless, so irresponsible? Here she was set on a smooth and steady course, six months sober, attending school and meeting expectations, making her UA's and court appearances, slowly but surely turning things around. Why, he could practically envision her heading off to college and making something of her life!

But no, she succumbed to the temptation of drugs and made a colossal mess of things. Whatever would possess a person to choose such a destructive and impulsive path?

Adding insult to injury, Ms. Washington – ordinarily a right-thinking, reliable probation officer – is pressuring him to release the lawless urchin from custody. As if ten days in the Hall is sufficient to penalize her for such transgressions! This girl has doubtlessly spent her Hall time doing little more than sleeping off the ill effects of her bender. No, he has something quite different in mind, something that will teach her a lesson or two about violating curfew, using drugs, lying to her parents, resisting arrest, possessing marijuana, and breaching her contract with Drug Court. The consequences must send an appropriate message of punishment to her and deterrence to the other participants. Why, he could terminate her from Drug Court for her new charges! Instead, he has a mind to lock her up for three, four weeks – or longer, if that's what it takes for her to learn that spitting at police officers will not be tolerated in a civilized society.

Still, he can scarcely reconcile the articulate and respectful young woman he knows from court with the brash and uncouth offender described in the incident report. Ten days, good Lord! Has Ms. Washington gone soft? What punishment for Andrea's brazen disregard for the confidence he foolishly reposed in her? Surely something more than a 10-day slap on the wrist is in order.

"May I come in?" He hears the upbeat and unwelcome call of his presiding judge, Marion Berkeley, as she simultaneously knocks on his door and steps into his chambers. He stifles a groan and glances up from his work, only to be met with a vision of swirling skirts and dangly earrings. Good Lord, has the woman never heard of a tailored suit? Her lack of sartorial professionalism has been a thorn in his side since the day they met.

"Marion," he manages. "How can I help you? I'm in a bit of a jam, about to go into court, just finishing up with a sensitive sentencing issue."

"Then I'll be quick," she chirps with a flourish of swishy skirt. "I just got a call from the Governor. She's filling the vacancy on our bench by appointing our very own commissioner, Elena Rodriguez-Medina."

Reed nods as a way of showing the approval he can't quite muster. He doesn't know the commissioner well. Their paths have rarely crossed in the year or two she has been on the bench. Still, she seems competent enough and has a charming, likeable personality. Reed had written the governor in support of another candidate, a dynamic young man from the district attorney's office who was a natural for the job of judging, and who would fit in nicely with the culture of the court. "Ah, excellent! Elena must be delighted! She will transition into her new position seamlessly." He tries not to think of the rant he will hear on Friday from his good friend, Hank Hellman, when Hank hears that a female former public defender twenty years his junior will be sitting in his old chair. Just as well Hank retired – he really couldn't take the changing face of the bench.

"Absolutely," Marion says. "In fact, I'm going to swear her in this afternoon, so she can start tomorrow as a judge. We are desperate for coverage in the Family Law Department."

"I'll stop by her chambers to congratulate her," Reed says, letting his eyes wander to the clock on the wall behind his intruder.

"Wonderful. I'll leave you to your work, then," she says, turning toward the door. Something on his desk apparently catches her eye, because she freezes mid-step. "You're working on a Bretano case too? The coffee people?"

"Yes, the daughter is in Drug Court," Reed answers. "She was doing quite well until this past week. Just got locked up again for a relapse."

His PJ shakes her head slowly. "I'm not surprised, the poor girl has had so much pressure on her. The parents are coming to see me next week, and I'd wring both of their necks if I could. I've been studying the divorce file, and it's been one bloodbath after another for 10 years, all over the daughter. But you say that she'd been doing well in Drug Court?"

"Very well," Reed answers. "She was our pride and joy until this slip. She's been in our program since January and was doing everything we asked of her. Our probation officer is exceedingly proud of the girl, fond of her actually. I suppose I had some vague notion that the parents were divorced, but not a clue that the girl's home life might be causing her any difficulty."

"Oh, her home life has to be a living hell," Berkeley says. "I can barely tolerate sitting in the same courtroom with these parents for a motion, much less living with them. In fact – odd coincidence – their case is the reason I'm anxious to move Elena into family law. I can't take it anymore. The cases are too sad."

Reed leans back in his swivel chair and studies his colleague. In the decade that they have served on the bench together, he has never once heard his colleague voice such a complaint. Ordinarily she is the tiresome chorus of how she but lives to serve – all that "happy hogwash," as his mother would say.

"Really?"

She nods and waves a dismissive hand in front of her face. "Oh, I won't bore you with my problems. You have enough of your own. But let's say I've had it with the harm done in the name of love. These parents who keep coming back to court proclaiming love? They're not helping their kids; they're hurting them. When you read a file like the Bretanos', you see why their daughter is in Drug Court. If they were my parents, I'd smoke pot too."

"Marion!" Reed sputters. The second most annoying thing about his colleague is the way she sprinkles outrageous asides into business conversation. It's almost as if she's trying to provoke him.

"Oh, I'm joking, Strathmore. But only a little. I for one go home and pour myself a stiff drink after spending a day in court with them. Go easy on the girl, if you can."

"I'll see," he responds noncommittally, thinking: It'll be a cold day in Hades before I follow your sentencing suggestions.

"Oh!" she exclaims. "Speaking of Drug Court – that was the very purpose of my visit here. I can assign it to Elena now if you'd like. You did the court a favor by taking it over at the beginning of the year. I'm happy to relieve you of the obligation now if you wish. Your call. Just let me know what you want to do." With a final rustle of gypsy ruche, the pushy PJ breezes out of his chambers.

His concentration now completely destroyed, Reed idly selects a law book from the stacks on his desk and scans the dry text:

The purpose of juvenile delinquency laws is twofold: (1) to serve the best interests of the delinquent ward by providing care, treatment, and guidance to *rehabilitate* and *protect* the ward; and (2) to provide for the protection and safety of the public.

Unlike adult criminal laws, juvenile delinquency laws are not *punitive* but *corrective.* The goals of Juvenile Law are to protect the welfare and safety of delinquent children and to help them grow into law-abiding, productive members of their families and communities. The central principal can be phrased thusly: what is in the best interests of the child? The juvenile judge may not take a "cookie cutter" approach to cases but must analyze each delinquent ward on an individual basis, matching the right care, treatment and guidance to the best interests of that ward. The juvenile's executive function is not fully developed, and the "folly of youth" is an accepted and well-known human experience.

Ah, yes, the folly of youth! Reed reflects. The law is so wise and reasonable – such a great composite of human learning and experience. Yes, of course, everyone makes mistakes growing up. That's what growing up means! For God's sake, a good judge should not be *surprised* when an adolescent makes a mistake! He should *expect* mistakes. Reed had been approaching the case entirely the wrong way.

The folly of youth, but of course. Reed certainly committed his share of adolescent antics back in the day, and he would not like to be judged today by his foolish escapades of yore. In fact, Reed muses, he would not want to be judged by some of the foolish things he did rather recently. Skylar comes to mind. He might demand of himself what possessed him to choose such a destructive and impulsive path?

Ah. The promise of pleasure.

Relief from the drudgery of everyday life.

In retrospect, the warning signs were all there – the way she played him, her intense and unlikely attraction to him, her coy and clever staging of their relationship – but in truth he did not want to see the risks. He made an unspoken choice to value pleasure over prudence, an option he had not selected since, quite possibly, the salad days of youth.

Perhaps this young lady, Andrea was motivated by something similar – the promise of pleasure, some relief from the everyday drudgery of her life.

Children are not adults and should not be judged by the same standards. Juvenile law is about second chances. So while a judge will not be surprised when a child makes a mistake, he may certainly require her to learn from it. Reed closes his law book and smiles, comfortable with his sentencing decision, effortlessly framed by the law. His job is not to chastise the young lady or express disapproval like a pompous, callous despot. His job is to help her learn from her relapse. If she can show him genuine remorse, identify where she went wrong, he feels comfortable with the probation officer's recommendation to release her. If, however, she shows him arrogance or disrespect, his role is not to feel indignant or reactive, but to help her learn a lesson so that she can become a law-abiding member of her family and society.

Reed slips an arm into his black robe. Sometimes he just loves the law. And another thing: there is no way in hell he's letting the presiding judge take the Drug Court assignment away from him.

ANDY

43. RELEASE

I'm so relieved to see Monica waiting for me in the run-down Juvenile Services reception room that I burst into tears like a baby, instead of the difficult and defiant delinquent that I am. After eleven long days in the Hall, I'm ready to go home.

I'm just not sure where home is anymore.

When Judge Reed told me yesterday that I'd be released from custody this morning, I almost fainted from shock and relief. The Killer had warned me that there was a chance that I'd get kicked out of Drug Court no matter how hard she fought. More likely, she said, I'd get some serious Hall time – 30-40 days is what she figured, but the judge could give me anything up to ninety. Ack! It was too horrible to imagine. The judge looked awfully annoyed when he called my name. He launched into a stern talking-to about how I was at a crossroads in my life, how I had to make a decision about which road I was going to take. Would I stay on Easy Street, run away from my problems, avoid responsibility, and leave a trail of lies, broken promises, and missed opportunities? Is that how I wanted to live my life? Or would I take the higher path, face my problems, live up to my potential, go to college and make something of myself? It was the most I'd ever heard my judge say at one time, and it was ultra-humiliating to have it directed my way. And yet, how could I disagree with him? The evidence was clear. I'd done so many stupid, shameful things. Was that the real me? Feeling about the size of a toad, I told him I was sorry to disappoint him; I was done running away from problems, had been researching colleges in the Hall and, if given the chance, would devote myself to becoming a college-eligible student. That felt good to say out loud – me, college, going some place, not stuck in Sequoia Valley and its Juvenile Hall forever. The court reporter wrote it all down, and that made it more real, somehow.

Then came the scary part. The judge didn't seem to know what to do. He hemmed and hawed, cleared his throat, started a few sentences, and finally asked the PO to approach the bench. She jumped up from the table and left me alone in the center of the courtroom. I was completely powerless. Not just because I was wearing baggy orange Hall sweats and wrist chains. But because my fate was in his hands. What's more important than your freedom? Why would you ever risk losing that? My heart was hammering, and I was praying, shivering, waiting, worrying. In that dizzy-sweaty moment, I made a promise to my innermost self, that I would never let myself land in this situation again. I am not that careless, and I am not that stupid! And yet there I was, acting like a careless, stupid girl – on probation, hanging out in the park where the troublemakers go, and smoking pot. Did I just let my brain go on vacation or what? The weird thing is, after you've been sober for six months, you can't even enjoy getting high anymore.

After a very long time, the huddle broke up and the judge leaned in closer to me. He cleared his throat and announced that my six months of sobriety and overall compliance with the Drug Court rules earned me one more chance to prove myself. He sentenced me to seventy-one days in custody – terrifying moment! – but eased the blow by staying sixty days of the sentence. He released me from the Hall on home restriction, ordered me to devote my best efforts to my schoolwork. He told me that I'm to transfer immediately to the mainstream high school to improve my chance of getting into college. He also ordered me to perform one hundred hours of community service work at the rate of ten hours per week. Oh, and to stay sober. My graduation from Drug Court was put off until December. He said that as long as I do these things, I won't have to serve the Hall sentence. But if I use or miss school or blow off community service work, it's back to the cinderblock cell and orange sweats for sixty days. Or, as I have come to think of Hall time, 420 dog days.

"Oh, honey," Monica coos, soothingly, wrapping me in her slender, yoga-cized embrace. She rocks me slowly side to side, and I smell her ginger-citrus shampoo, her lavender-scented laundry soap. Sweet. Clean. Not a thing like the chemical stench of the hall – ammonia on steroids.

"Monica!" I sob. "You came for me!"

Monica is unbelievable. I don't deserve her. She visited me by herself on Tuesday. Almost any visit in the Hall is a good one because you're lonely and bored, but our visit was stupendous. She said she'd come to ask my forgiveness. That was a mind-bender for me. Told me that those workshops she's been taking at the Healing Families Center had forced her to take a close look at herself, and that she didn't like what she saw.

"It all started with Drug Court," she explained. "Week after week, I'd watch the kids struggle to make the changes that were asked of them – Stop using, of course. But also change friends, get along with their parents, go to meetings and get to school on time. But what were the parents doing? Nothing! They weren't going to any self-help meetings. They weren't working on improving their relationship with their kids. They weren't sober. They believed their child was the 'problem.' Not one of them seemed like a very good parent." She shook her head. "And then it hit me. What made me think I was any better than them?"

She told me about her classes in meditation, listening, and forgiveness. Those brought her face to face with the ugly truth: that she'd been secretly hoping my mother would win the custody battle so I would be out of the home once and for all, and she could raise the boys without my unhealthy influence. She was ashamed of herself, she said, to see how selfish she was in her heart of hearts.

She started crying then and so did I. She asked again for my forgiveness, told me I was the only sister the twins would ever have and that they worshipped me. Said she loved me with all her heart. Pretty soon I was begging her for forgiveness too, telling her how sorry I was to have messed up her whole life, caused her so much grief and stress. I ended up reading her the letter I'd written to my parents. I told her I couldn't live with either of them anymore. I was homeless and scared, searching for a safe place to live. We cried some more. It was a real snot-fest. We forgave each other. It felt so sweet and so freeing. Both of us vowed to do better.

And now the time has come to start living those vows we made.

Monica smoothes my greasy hair and gazes into my eyes. I must be such a sorry sight: run-down, broken spirit, scared to start again in the world. "Andy. Of course I'm here. I'm here for you. We're family. That's what we do. We make mistakes and we try harder next time. Now let's go home."

I nod, not trusting myself to argue without sounding obnoxious or to speak without blubbering embarrassingly. I manage to wave goodbye to Faro, the nice receptionist who works at the metal desk behind bulletproof glass. She slides open her window and says what she always says: "Bye-bye, honey. Thanks for staying with us. Hope we don't see you again!"

She's not going to see me again. I'm done with the Hall. I'm not going to live my life on the installment plan.

Outside it's gray and drizzly, but the fresh air smells so sweet and pure I want to gulp it in by the bucketful. I tilt my face up to the sky and let the drizzle fall on me. "It's wonderful," I murmur. I'm free!

"I have lattes for us in the car," she says, opening the door of her Honda. "I guess we should talk before we start driving. I did the research you asked me to do."

At the end of our Hall visit on Tuesday, I asked her if she'd research places for me to live – Granny's house, maybe, or a live-in job somewhere; maybe even a boarding school.

I wrap my hands around the warm coffee cup. "What'd you find?"

She takes a sip of her coffee. "Good news. I talked to your granny. She has an extra room and would be pleased to have you move in with her right away. She has conditions, but they're fair enough. You have to come home every night, stay away from drugs, and do your part to keep the house clean."

My granny is a clean nut. So fussy she makes Monica look like a slob. I'd have to live in my mom's old bedroom, which is, you know, kind of creepy. I mean, look how she turned out.

"There are boarding schools all over the country. The best one is in Santa Barbara. It's a perfect place if you hate your parents. You can learn to ride a horse, throw a pot, speak Japanese. They have lots of rules about what classes to take, when you can leave the campus, how often you can see your family. They have an immediate opening. Your probation officer says she could transfer your probation to Santa Barbara County, and you could finish Drug Court there."

Maybe it's because we're sitting in the parking lot of Juvenile Services, but boarding school sounds a lot like the place I've just been, with more activities and better food, maybe, but same basic idea. Plus, how could I change PO's? I have to show The Killer that I'm no wuss.

Monica and I are staring out the front window, not looking at each other. The mist is gathering and droplets streak down the windshield, like fat tears.

"I loved what you said in court yesterday, about wanting to go to college," Monica says.

"Hopefully an East Coast school," I add. "I want to go as far away as possible!"

She nods. "That's great. It's important to get away. There are a lot of great schools on the East Coast. But going away means even more when you have a place to come home to."

She hands me a cranberry-almond scone with little chunks of sugar crusted on top. It is buttery and wonderful, maybe the best thing I've ever eaten.

"You told the judge yesterday that you were done running away. I can't help but feel that boarding school would be another form of running away. Maybe things would get better for you then, but I'd like to make things better now. After all, today is all we have. I want to be the family you want to come home to."

"Me too," I manage. "But I don't know how to do that. Do you?"

"Well, we all have work to do. The judge gave you some pretty tall orders, so you'll be busy with those. Your dad needs to do some rethinking, as do I. From what I've learned at Healing Families, we could all use some therapy. Family therapy, so we're all learning at the same time."

"Do you think Dad would do that?"

"I do," she says. "But you are not to worry about him. He's my responsibility. You don't have to take care of him anymore, Andy."

My heart lurches a bit.

"You're 16, Andy. Just two more years and you are out the door. I'd like to get it right before you leave."

I can't imagine my dad in family therapy. He hates to talk. But Monica says that's not my problem. I want my dad to love me, to feel proud of me. I can't see how therapy could make things worse. "Well, if he'll go, I'll go," I say.

"Wonderful," she says, putting her key in the ignition. "So can we go home now? The twins are so excited to see you. They're hoping you'll play *Giants & Dragons* with them."

As there is no place I would rather go and no game I would rather play, I say yes.

44. So Ordered

SUPERIOR COURT OF CALIFORNIA
COUNTY OF SEQUOIA

IN RE THE MARRIAGE OF:
BRYAN BRETANO,   CASE NO. 03580
    Petitioner,
    and
CONSTANCE BRETANO,
    Respondent.   /

HON. MARION BERKELEY, PRESIDING
FAMILY LAW JUDGE
OFFICIAL TRANSCRIPT OF
PROCEEDINGS
APPEARANCES:
BRYAN BRETANO, PETITIONER IN PRO PER
CONSTANCE BRETANO, RESPONDENT
IN PRO PER

THE COURT: Next case is Marriage of
Bretano. State your appearances, please.

MS. BRETANO: That matter is ready, Your Honor. I'm Respondent and moving party, Constance Bretano, appearing in propria persona. Please note I have made a written request, pursuant to Local Rule 3.01, for additional time for argument on my motions this morning.

THE COURT: Very well. Sir?

MR. BRETANO: Hi. Yeah, I'm Bryan. Bryan Bretano, Andy's father.

THE COURT: Thank you. Please be seated. I know you've been waiting for over an hour and a half for your case to be called, and I apologize. As you can see from sitting here today, this is a busy time of year in the Family Law Department. We try to put as many cases as we can handle on for hearing, but it makes for a long morning if you're placed at the end of the calendar. Now I must apologize again, but I need to take a short break. My staff and I have been at this since 8:30, and we have to catch our breath and replenish our supply of good humor and patience. We'll resume in 15 minutes. I promise I'll call your case first. Ms. Bretano, I see that you have something to say to me. I'll ask you to wait. Thank you.

(Whereupon proceedings were adjourned at 10:16 a.m.)

THE COURT: Back on the record. Good morning again, Mr. and Ms. Bretano. We're here on mother's motions to modify custody and for an accounting. I've read the papers submitted as well as the custody recommendation from Family Court Services. Because the issues raised in this motion have been before the court many times before, I took the opportunity to review the entire case file, or I should say files, in this matter. I've asked my clerk to put them on the bench here in court so you can see for yourself the reading I did to prepare for today's hearing. Impressive, isn't it? Your divorce papers fill some twenty-six file folders. These files occupy nine linear feet of shelf space in the clerk's office. Yes, I measured. It took me several days to read the thousands of pages of pleadings filed in your case. I feel well-informed to rule on today's matters. But before I do, I'd like to share a few observations.

When your case was first filed, oh, just about 10 years ago to the day, I was a brand new judge. My first assignment was in Family Law. Tough duty for a new judge because every case is so heartbreaking, every decision is so important, and perfect solutions are hard to find. Rarely does the Family Law judge get a simple legal issue to rule on. Instead, she is asked to decide such insoluble questions as: Where should these children go to school? What religion should this child be raised in? Should these boys use their after-school time to play football or piano? How many nights should this daughter spend with her mother and how many with her father? So often in those days, I would ask myself: How am I supposed to know? I'm just a judge, trained in contracts, civil procedures, and evidence. I've never met these children, never observed what makes one child tick and another miserable; how can I possibly know what is best for this family?

I got to meet the parents, the passionate, protective, well-meaning parents. What I observed about them without exception was their boundless and consuming love for their children, their absolute burning devotion to do their best for their child. These parents would drive hundreds of miles for a chance to visit, spend huge sums of money to provide for their child's education, change jobs to live closer to their child, and come to court at great financial and emotional expense to fight for what they thought was best for their beloved offspring.

For most parents, once in court is enough. No matter how skilled the lawyers or how favorable their ruling, most parents figure out pretty quickly that a courtroom is no place to raise a child. Sure, we judges do the best we can. We read the reports from the teachers, doctors, and psychologists; we listen to legal arguments; we try to figure out the best result for each family. But judges are not the experts on these children that their parents are. No one walks out of Family Court feeling triumphant; in fact, just the opposite. In most cases, each party emerges from court feeling battered and bruised, convinced that their ex got the better ruling. The great majority of parents come to realize sooner or later that they are stuck with their ex, and for the sake of their kids, they have to lay down their weapons, let go of their anger, and learn to live in peace.

But for a small percentage of families, once is not enough. These families come back to court for more, to correct a ruling they believe is wrong, to protect their child from perceived harm, to insist on certain benefits. Their declarations are full of suffering and sadness, accusations about how evil the other parent is, how poorly the child does in that parent's home. And always these accusations are accompanied by loving assurances: "I only want the best for my children." "I just want her to be safe." "I can't stand by and watch my child get hurt." "I will do everything I can do to protect my child." These parents will do everything, too. Everything, it seems, save one: forgive the other parent and learn to get along.

In some ways, it's the fault of our legal system. We have the same adversarial system for divorce cases that we have for criminal trials and civil disputes, where one side opposes the other in mortal combat, spy vs. spy, winner vs. loser. However, in child custody conflicts, there are no winners. Both parents are miserable, and the children feel even worse. Everyone loses.

Your case, Mr. and Mrs. Bretano, holds particular interest for me, because it started the same year I did. I had to see if I'd issued any questionable rulings when I was a brand new judge. Could I have made an order that launched 10 years of relentless litigation? Did I do something way back at the beginning that destroyed this family? Do you know what I found when I read your file?

You have been to court at least once a year every year for 10 years. Each motion, I note, was initiated by mother. We have had multiple trials, hearings, and motions to change custody, support, schools, holiday and vacation schedules; motions to appoint an evaluator, therapist, mediator, special master – to name a few. Goodness, if every divorce case had filings like this, our courts would shut down! Like the mythical Hydra, the monster that grows two heads every time one is chopped off, your case expanded every time an order was made.

But, Mr. Bretano, it seems like you finally get it. I read in your declaration that you withdraw your opposition to the motions filed by mother, you concede you owe arrearage on the partnership profits, that you will accept the ruling of the court on the custody issue. I note that after 10 years of having Mr. Shields represent you, you have elected to represent yourself. You tell me that you do not agree with the recommendations of Family Court Services, but that you refuse to fight any longer. I see that your wife, Monica, completed the Improving Families course at the Healing Families Center and that you have started family therapy. Hallelujah.

Mrs. Bretano, I'd like to help you drop your end of the rope too.

So let's see, we're here on mother's motion to modify custody. She requests sole custody of the parties' 16-year-old daughter. That motion is denied. There is no change of circumstances. Mrs. Bretano, here's what I'd like you to understand: Let your daughter have the dignity of her mistakes. She is doing very well in Juvenile Drug Court. According to my colleague, Judge Reed, she is one of the star participants. Drug Court is the best thing that could happen to her. Now, I know about her recent relapse. Slips happen. Let her learn from it. Don't bail her out. Don't blame it on her father. Don't excuse her. Let her own her slips as well as her successes.

The second motion is for an accounting. There is no disagreement on this motion. Mr. Bretano concedes that he underpaid partnership profits, that he owes respondent $100,000.

One more thing. Before Mr. Shields was substituted out of the case, he filed a request for attorney's fees. He alerted the court to mother's multiple litigation of these issues, and he submitted a declaration showing that his client, Mr. Bretano, has incurred some staggering sums in legal fees responding to the mother's motions over the years. The court has always deferred a ruling on this issue. In a remarkable coincidence, those fees total some $100,000. I will now rule on today's request for attorney's fees, as well as prior requests made over the life of this case.

Father's request for attorney's fees is granted. He is awarded the sum of $100,000 as and for attorney's fees.

Thus, Mr. Bretano is ordered to pay Ms. Bretano the sum of $100,000 for unpaid partnership profits. Ms. Bretano is ordered to pay Mr. Bretano the sum of $100,000 as and for accrued attorney's fees in this case.

Let's do better for Andrea, shall we? We're the grown-ups here. Let's work together to help her stay on track. We can do that by letting her focus her energy on herself, her school, and her recovery. She should not be expending an ounce of energy on her parents' conflict. I want to see both of you in the front row of your daughter's cheering section. She's almost grown up. You still have time to get it right. It's hard to tell a 16-year-old where she can live. I think she's proven to you time and again that you have very little control over where she chooses to stay. Your best shot at getting her to spend time in your house is to make your home a conflict-free zone. That will require you to stay out of court.

Those are my orders. Thank you.

MS. BRETANO: I ask for an immediate stay of this ruling so that I can file a writ in the Court of Appeal.

THE COURT: Denied.

MS. BRETANO: But – but – but! I object! I move to disqualify you from presiding over this matter. You are prejudiced against me and my case.

THE COURT: The motion to disqualify the court is denied as untimely.

MS. BRETANO: Then I will write out a declaration of bias and prejudice and ask your presiding judge to remove you from the case. I will contact the Commission on Judicial Performance and tell them how unfair and unethical you are.

THE COURT: You are free to do so. We will provide you with a copy of today's transcript. Your letter to the presiding judge may be addressed to me. Write the Commission, write your congressman, write your novel. But we are done here. Thank you.

Next case.

(Whereupon, the proceedings were terminated)

45. NEVER-ENDING STORY

SUPERIOR COURT OF CALIFORNIA
COUNTY OF SEQUOIA

In re the marriage of
BRYAN BRETANO,   Case No. 03580
Petitioner   NOTICE OF
                        APPEAL

and

CONSTANCE BRETANO,
Respondent.

Respondent CONSTANCE BRETANO hereby appeals from the ORDER DENYING RESPONDENT'S MOTION FOR CHANGE OF CUSTODY and the ORDER RE ATTORNEY'S FEES.

Respondent requests an interim award of attorney's fees to fight this miscarriage of justice in the Court of Appeal.

/s/ Constance Bretano

CONSTANCE BRETANO
RESPONDENT and APPELLANT

❖ ❖ ❖

TO : HONORABLE COURT OF APPEAL
FROM: Petitioner Bryan Bretano
RE : NOTICE OF NON-OPPOSITION

PLEASE TAKE NOTICE that petitioner Bryan Bretano will not participate in respondent's appeal. Petitioner cannot spend more time and money fighting with the mother of his child. Petitioner attaches for the court's consideration the Supplemental Declaration of Bryan Bretano, filed in the trial court before argument on the motion to change custody. Mr. Bretano states, "Under no circumstances will I fight with my family anymore. I surrender." Also attached is a transcript from the hearing in front of Judge Berkeley. Petitioner Bryan Bretano intends to devote himself to making amends with his family, being the best father he can be, and healing the wounds caused by his decade of divorce litigation.

/s/ Bryan Bretano

_____

BRYAN BRETANO
PETITIONER, Husband and Father

DECEMBER
HON. STRATHMORE
REED, JR.

46. GRADUATION

"Yes, Mother, I promise. We'll meet you tonight at six sharp," Reed says, unable to resist a habitual, nervous glance at his Rolex. The last Drug Court session of the year is scheduled to commence in little more than ten minutes, and Reed requires a few final moments to gather his thoughts and check his notes. Heavens, he must be as jumpy about today's ceremony as is his graduate.

"Tell me again the name of your new lady friend?" his mother asks for the tenth time since Reed first mentioned her existence at their Thanksgiving repast. Reed can't tell if his mother is becoming more forgetful or more obstinate.

"Mother, is your Limoges vase within reach?" he asks in his "good son" voice, knowing full well the precise location of the vase, as no furniture, furnishings, art, or accoutrement has moved in the twenty years Mother has occupied her condominium. Well, the apple didn't fall far from the tree, Reed muses, as the only change in his chambers over the last decade is the name on the case files stacked on his desk.

"My – why yes! It's next to the telephone, where it always is," she answers.

"Then please pick out a pen and write this down on your monogrammed note pad," he says. "Her name is Elena. E-L-E-N-A. She's a judge, Mother. She's brilliant, beautiful, and I am utterly unworthy of her affection, so I sincerely hope you don't scare her off tonight. Moreover, she's at least as nervous about meeting you as you are about meeting her," he says.

"I still don't understand why you and your lady friend won't join the family for New Year's Eve at the club!" His mother presses, even though Reed has explained their holiday plans firmly and frequently. Tonight's dinner and theater in the City is his peace offering, his way of honoring the holiday and introducing Elena to the family, especially to his daughter Elizabeth and her Pat. But Mother is nothing if not indefatigable – nor does she have much familiarity with rejection from her offspring – so he gives her credit for trying in spite of impossible odds.

"Her name is Elena. You're going to have to say it sooner or later," he says. "I suggest you start sooner, and let's hope you do a better job of it than I. The number of times I've called her Dory is positively unpardonable." He simultaneously smiles and shudders at the memory. A few nights ago, he twice addressed her by the name of his deceased wife – such an awful slip! Once could be forgiven, but twice? In the same evening? Elena, sweet-natured and unflappable, suggested he surrender altogether and henceforth refer to her simply as "*mi querida reina*" or, if that seemed a bit too over-the-top, "most beloved judicial goddess."

"Won't you and Ellen join me at the club New Year's Eve, then?" she sputters. "It's one of the few traditions we have left in the family."

And thank heavens for that, Reed jokes inwardly. He still has no idea whether his mother will give or withhold her annual gift, and though he can't honestly say he's past caring, he can say with an abiding certainty that he will no longer permit his mother's conditional largesse to dictate his comings and goings. "I'm sorry, Mother. You know how I hate to disappoint you. But my daughter will be there with Pat, and I will be in Paris with Elena. Paris, France, Mother. Doesn't that sound magnificent? Some say the City of Lights rivals the Sequoia Valley Golf & Tennis Club for food and festivities. Perhaps you would like to accompany us?"

"Such nonsense!" his mother scolds. "I've had reservations at the club for a year. And I do not appreciate being baited by you."

Reed chuckles. "Goodbye, Mother! Until tonight!"

Now, where are his notes? Reed is serving as the Master of Ceremonies for his afternoon session and wants to make sure he does justice to the occasion. The probation officer has been handling the graduations all year, but Reed recently learned at a seminar that in most Drug Courts, it's the judge who presides over said proceeding. When he returned from the seminar and discussed the matter with his team, Ms. Washington was only too happy to relinquish the task, so today is Reed's turn to step on to center stage and say a few hopefully uplifting words. He has been burning the midnight oil for the past week, preparing his thoughts, organizing his materials, and rehearsing the names of his Drug Court team and participants. It's a lot harder to remember names than it used to be, but he thinks he has them now. His shortcuts are the four Jordans (two girls, two boys), three Anthonys (one is Antonio, actually, but close enough), one Reid (a girl; same pronunciation as his name), and the lawyers, who can always be referred to as "counsel" in a pinch, leaving just ten names to remember. But in case butterflies get the better of him, he has written them down in his notes.

Showtime. He slips on his robe, gathers his notes, and steps out of his chambers. In the hall, he is met with a vision of beauty walking his way and smiling luminously. Elena! Slender, petite, and altogether lovely, his judicial goddess is graced with soulful brown eyes – he can gaze into them for hours on end! – and abundant, dark hair, cut short and featuring beguiling waves and a few dignified wisps of gray. She is wearing her robe – hers falls to the knee, so he can see

479

her lovely, stockinged legs and sexy (but still professional) black heels – and is carrying a large, festive platter.

How he would love to fold her in his arms right now, but he is ever aware of their positions with the court and the wagging tongues of court staff. So far they have managed to keep their relationship a secret from co-workers and counsel, but, Reed knows, there is no such thing as a secret in the back corridors of a courthouse. They have decided to make their relationship public in January by attending the annual bar dinner together. In the meantime, they agreed that Elena would inform their PJ of their liaison. He can picture Marion's eyeroll even now! He smiles in spite of himself, certain that any eyewitness could readily observe – without the benefit of an announcement – how smitten he is with his newest colleague.

"Judge Rodriguez-Medina," he says. "Whatever is the object of your asportation?"

She smiles angelically. "Behold, Judge Reed: cookies. I made them for you, for your Drug Court graduation today. Your clerk has agreed to take delivery of them."

"You made cookies for our graduation?" he asks, his heart swelling with admiration. "You're in the middle of a high-conflict, child custody moveaway trial, and you baked us cookies?"

"What better way to keep your sanity and celebrate the wonderful work we do in court? They're Mexican wedding cookies, a specialty of my family. I'm partial to the chocolate, but my mother insists that the powdered sugar cookies are the only genuine article. So, I made some of each. Enjoy!" She delivers the plate to Reed's waiting clerk and pokes her head in the courtroom. "*Dios mío*! It's standing room only in there! You'll be wonderful. Tell me all about it later!"

"Thank you," Reed says. Before entering court, he adds softly: "Judicial goddess."

Elena smiles with a backward glance and places a shushing finger over her lips. She is the kindest, most beautiful and generous woman he has ever met. And to think, he worked just down the hall from her for two years and never noticed her. How could he have been so blind? What a fool. And then two months ago, at a judges' meeting, no less, she sat next to him, noticed he had no lunch, and handed half of her tuna sandwich to him. Just: Here, eat. The way you'd feed a stray dog. Perhaps because her gesture was so natural, he took it from her without his usual social awkwardness, as if they'd been trading sandwiches for years. It didn't take long before he was eating out of her hand on a regular basis. In addition to her other talents, she is an accomplished home chef. Her way of managing stress is to cook elaborate meals while sipping wine, singing to herself, and filling the kitchen with the blissful aroma of sautéed onions, grilled meats and – what's that odd spice she stirs in every sauce? Cumin, that's what it is! The flavor takes some getting used to, but nonetheless offers a welcome change from decades of tired lemon-pepper and predictable Italian seasonings. He feels like the luckiest officer on the bench! What she sees in him remains a mystery which, fortunately, he need not solve.

Reed strides to the podium as his bailiff calls the proceedings to order. The place is packed, as Elena described, but what really strikes Reed is the room's absolute transformation from solemn to celebratory. Bouquets of flowers, bunches of balloons, trays of pastries and little cakes, a sea of smiling faces – never in his thirty-five years in the law did Reed imagine that a courtroom could look anything like his does today.

He clears his throat. "Welcome to the graduation ceremony of Andrea Bretano," Reed smiles to his graduate, who is seated at counsel table looking fresh-faced and jubilant. At her side is the probation officer, sitting straight and tall. The graduate's family is in the first row, holding balloons and looking proud and presentable: parents, stepmother, squirmy young brothers, grandmother. "I am Judge Reed, and it is my privilege to preside over the Sequoia County Juvenile Drug Court."

He introduces the members of his team as well as the teen participants in the program, and experiences a flush of relief as he makes it through all the names without stumbling. The audience is generous with smiles and applause, so his nervousness melts away. It's his courtroom, by God! And he wants everyone there to feel informed and welcome!

"It is fitting in so many ways that we should end this year's Drug Court with Andrea's graduation. The year started with her admission to our program. Andrea spent last New Year's Eve in Juvenile Hall and appeared in court the first Thursday of January. This was, I surmise, not the New Year's Eve celebration she planned."

Reed glances over to his graduate and is relieved that she is laughing at his little joke. The probation officer gives the graduate a knowing elbow in her side.

"I remember that day vividly, in part because it was my first experience with Drug Court, too. At the time, I knew nothing about it and had no idea of what to expect. In the usual course of things, a judge sees the parties once or twice during the life of their case – when they come to court for a hearing, or a settlement conference, or a trial: the judge rules on their case, and it's over – he never sees them again. But in Drug Court, it's a completely different experience. I see the participants week after week, month after month, and, it turns out that what I see is nothing less than miraculous. Because over time, what I see is transformation.

"Our graduate, Andrea, is living proof of that miracle. A year ago, she was a daily drug user. She was flunking out of school, fighting with her parents, in trouble with the law. She joined Drug Court and was put to work. Her probation officer, Ms. Washington, is quite a notorious taskmaster." Here, Reed's band of lawless hooligans moan in unison. Their PO hushes them in a stage whisper.

Reed continues with his prepared remarks, describing the essays, chores, exercises, and homework prescribed. He has come to believe that the magic of Drug Court is due to the intense personal relationship each participant forms with the energetic and devoted probation officer, supported by the accountability offered by weekly court appearances and the threat of Juvenile Hall. He pauses at the end of his description and gives Ms. Washington a respectful nod. "From my observation, Ms. Washington's workload would make an army boot camp sergeant blush.

"What was asked of our graduate was arduous. She experienced some slips and setbacks along the way. What always impressed me about Andrea is that she kept coming to court and trying, even if she didn't agree with what was asked of her. In the end, her hard work and her commitment paid off. Because today, Andrea is 93 days clean and sober. She has just completed the first semester of her junior year at Sequoia Valley High, and she has earned a near-perfect 3.75 grade point average. She is working 10 hours a week as a volunteer at the Healing Families Center, counseling children whose parents are divorcing. And she is about to graduate from Drug Court."

Reed joins the audience in thunderous applause. Andrea is smiling like an Olympic skater who has just nailed a difficult jump and can hardly believe she pulled it off. Reed finds himself wiping the moisture from the corner of his eye. Damn it, he will need to discuss this emerging ocular weakness with his ophthalmologist!

"Now some of you parents might be wondering what is the big deal, after all? Drugs are bad – so stop using them! And I say to you: When was the last time you were able to effect a major change in your life? For example, is there anyone here who has tried to lose ten pounds, exercise three times a week, drive in rush-hour traffic with a sweet temper, learn a word a day, be nicer to your mother? Easy to say, hard to do, that's my experience. What we ask of our teenagers is something far more daunting: to change their lives completely and permanently. I bet many of you, like me, wish you had that kind of fortitude."

Reed notices many heads nodding in agreement. It was Elena's idea to throw in the analogy to weight loss, and he sees he scored some points with experienced dieters who struggle to take off the extra ten pounds, only to gain it right back when their old friend Mr. Dark Chocolate demands an audience.

Checking his notes, Reed introduces the speakers, and one by one, each gives a heartfelt and moving speech. The father barely makes it to the end of his remarks before yielding to emotion; he thanks the Drug Court team for helping him and his family get through a tough time, and tells his daughter how proud of her he is – how, thanks to her, he is sober too and is determined to learn how to be the best father he can from this day forward. The probation officer, usually tough as nails, is today as soft as a campfire marshmallow. She relates the story of her probationer's transformation from an angry and defiant Hall hellion to a mature and responsible young adult. "You did it, Andy! I could not be prouder of you if were my own daughter," she says to her graduate while delivering a terrifyingly muscular hug. "I expect you to ride competitively when you're in college, and to give me a run for my money when you're home on break! Today I present to you as my parting gift the bike helmet I wore in October's Ironman." The PO produces a racy bike helmet, which the graduate hugs to her heart. Much to Reed's relief, the PO introduces the graduate, as the lump in his own throat might create a vocal obstruction.

The lovely young graduate is as poised and articulate as a lawyer when she thanks the Drug Court team for its help: "For your faith in me, and for not giving up – even when I wanted you to kick me out of this program because it was too hard!" She thanks her family for their love and support – "especially for my stepmother, Monica, who didn't have to love me, but she did anyway, and I totally didn't deserve it. Thank you, Monica, for your love and support. And for giving me a home." She finishes by saying a few words of encouragement to the other participants in Drug Court, mostly to the effect that nobody can make you change but yourself, and the program gets a lot easier if you do it their way. "It's hard to admit that your way isn't working," she says. "But let's face it: If our way was so great, none of us would be here now."

When she finishes, Judge Reed stands for the presentation of the diploma. "Andrea, it is now my privilege to present you with your diploma. Congratulations on your graduation from Drug Court. You are now officially off probation. The 60 days of stayed Hall time is discharged permanently. Remember that the legal drinking age is 21. Remember too there is no legal age for illegal drugs. Your juvenile record is sealed, and while all of us in the room will always remember this day, no future school, employer, acquaintance, private detective or prospective boyfriend can ever find out about your year in Drug

Court. We're so proud of you, Andrea. Now go live your life!"

When the vibrant young woman takes the diploma from his hand, her exuberance must get the better of her, because she gives Reed a quick hug. A hug! In court! Whatever happened to decorum?

"Thank you, Your Honor! I did it! Thanks for helping me make it to the finish line!"

"Oh! My dear!" Reed says, utterly swept away by the sweetness of her youthful embrace. "You are quite welcome!"

Decorum be damned! He hugs the young lady in return. For the law has been here for centuries of conflict and misery; it can certainly accommodate a few moments of bliss.

ACKNOWLEDGMENTS

So many kind, helpful, and smart people have contributed to the making of this book, and I am deeply indebted to them for their guidance, support, and inspiration.

Thank you to the brilliant and dedicated professionals on my Drug Court team. Ronald J. Ravani has helped countless kids by serving on the Marin County Juvenile Drug Court since its inception. Marta Osterloh has compassionately represented juveniles for much of her exemplary career in law. What a joy to work with Wardell Anderson, Donald Carmona, and Jay Shaw, probation officers extraordinaire; Meg Sherry and her superb team of mental health professionals; and all others who have worked with our Juvenile Drug Courts. Ron Johnny was instrumental in teaching me about Drug Courts and helping to implement ours, and I owe him a special thanks.

Thank you to the talented and generous members of my writers' group: Lawrence G.

Townsend and Peter B. Logan, dear friends and wonderful writers both.

Thank you to my dear friend Marcia Nelson, for reading early drafts of the novel and helping me understand the character of Monica; thanks too to Marcia and her darling husband Gary for letting me write in their beautiful Villa Daze, where much of this novel took shape.

Many early readers of the manuscript supported and encouraged me: Verna Adams, Eileen Barker, Carla Eisley, John and Sue Feder, Nan Haynes, Kenneth L. Kann, Mark B. Simons, Alexandra Socarides, Kim Turner, Matt White, and Beverly Wood. I thank them for their friendship and valuable critiques.

Thank you to my darling sister, Sue Duryee, who told me to write a book and stop making excuses; and to my famous mother-in-law, Freddy Moran, who gave me a copy of *The Artist's Way* and convinced me that I could be a writer.

Laura Merlo of Eagle Eye Editing has edited this book as well as my other two and has found thousands of diction, grammar, and punctuation errors in the process. I thank her for her eagle eye and for her willingness to continue being my friend despite my annoying habit of needless hyphenation.

Thank you to Anne Lamott, for writing my all-time favorite book about writing, *Bird by Bird*. Her "SFD" advice got me through many a paragraph in this book and others.

Thank you to my first writing teacher, Donna Levin, for her guidance and wisdom.

A heart-felt thank you to the many young people who have struggled through Drug Court, graduated, and come back to visit, to report that they're working or in college or helping others with sobriety. Special thanks and congratulations to my star student, Lindsay L., who not only excelled in Drug Court, but who has joyfully returned year after year to share her experience, strength, and hope with others in the program. I am so proud of them all!

Thank you to my colleagues on the bench, in Marin County and across the state, for the remarkable work they do, day in and day out, to improve lives and administer justice. Special thanks to my dear friend Hon. Richard H. Breiner (Ret.) for serving as my mentor judge and to Hon. William H. Stephens (Ret.) for launching my writing career.

And to my darling, devoted husband, Neil J. Moran: Thank you, dear, for believing in me, year after year, and for coming through with your carpentry skills every time I dream up a new project for my Drug Court kids.

Author photo: Michael Fahey

ABOUT THE AUTHOR

Lynn Duryee is a judge of the Marin County Superior Court, where she has served since 1993. A frequent teacher and writer, she has published two books of essays and has written a column for "The Bench" for many years. She is the proud mother of two funny, smart, and altogether wonderful daughters. She lives in Northern California with her husband and their rescue dogs. When not in court, she's preparing for her next class, taking long walks with the dogs, or writing her next novel, also about Drug Court.

Made in the USA
Charleston, SC
03 August 2010